TRUST NO ONE,
PROMISE NOTHING

TRUST NO ONE, PROMISE NOTHING

A Tale of Family,
Vengeance & Atonement

GINGER WAKEM

TRUST NO ONE, PROMISE NOTHING

A Tale of Family, Vengeance & Atonement

First Edition

Copyright © 2024 by Ginger Wakem

Published by

Munn Avenue Press
300 Main Street, Ste 21
Madison, NJ 07940
MunnAvenuePress.com

Paperback ISBN: 978-1-960299-51-2

Hardcover ISBN: 978-1-960299-52-9

Printed in the United States of America

DEDICATION

To my husband, Peter, who encouraged me, kept me fed, and left me alone to write. And to my children, Griffin, Peter Jr., and Kace, for their love and continual support.

CONTENTS

Part Four

PART ONE

CHAPTER ONE

Ray Lewis
The Vow of Omertà
February 12, 1938
Seaport, Florida

"Be prepared. Your life is about to change," they said. "Wear a black suit and tie. A limo will pick you up at 4:30. For the rest of the day, you will only be addressed by your formal Italian name, Raimondo Sabatini Martinelli Luigi. Get used to it."

The heavy scent of cigarettes and sounds from a bustling bar across the room greeted me as I entered Old Town Hotel's penthouse. Dressed in pinstripe suits with bulging holsters beneath their jackets, burly men shouted their congratulations. Several offered me a drink as if I was a movie star trapped in their spotlight.

I relaxed as soon as I caught sight of my closest friend and mentor, Franco, the Don's eldest son and his Consiglieri. Thin and wearing wire-rimmed glasses, he was easy to pick out among the heavier tough guys congregating around the room. He waved me over to the window, where he took a quick look through the Venetian blinds.

"Pop should be here any minute," Franco said and handed me a slip of paper. "Before he arrives, memorize this."

It contained a single sentence. I raised my eyebrows.

"After you rub the ashes together, recite those words." Franco pointed to the note and smiled. "You'll know when, don't worry, Raimondo."

"They're here," Angelo said. Muscular and in his late twenties, Franco's bodyguard towered over us as he pointed at the window's blinds.

We watched four men step out of a navy-blue Cadillac sedan five stories below and hurry under the hotel's black-and-white striped awning.

Angelo redirected my attention and murmured, "See those guys across the room having a tense conversation?"

I turned to see who he was talking about. "You mean Franco's three brothers?"

"Soon they'll be your family, but they'll never be your friends. Be careful around them."

"Angelo, that's enough," Franco said, frowning as a loud knock quieted the room. Guards standing by the door signaled a thumbs up.

Sporting a black silk suit with a black felt fedora, Don Marco Catanetti Sr. strolled into the crowded suite surrounded by his three bodyguards. The air thickened with respect as the Don greeted his sons and top men with a kiss on both cheeks and acknowledged his half dozen capos.

As he made his way around the room, he stopped to chat, shook hands, and gave words of praise and advice. My body was buzzing with anxiety when he finally invited me to join him at his table where his sons were gathered.

The Don's authority filled the room as he loudly addressed me. "Raimondo Sabatini Martinelli Luigi, you've met challenges with intelligence and bravery. Today, I invite you to seal our relationship. Doing so will grant you our protection for the rest of your life."

My heart raced as the Don recounted the story everyone in the room already knew.

"Hundreds of years ago, a corrupt Sicilian government denied our ancestors justice for crimes committed against them. Our people had to protect themselves in order to take their revenge. They swore an oath of silence called Omertà to guard the identities of those who punished criminals on behalf of the victims and their families."

The gravity of this ceremony carried the weight of tradition and history. I held on to every word, reminding myself to breathe.

"These are the words of Omertà, so pay close attention and save this vow in your heart." Don Marco pointed to my chest with passion and, narrowing his brows, stared so intensely it would have frightened the Pope himself.

I took a deep breath and watched Don Marco place a small picture of a saint and a silver-bladed knife on the table behind him.

"Only a fool or coward seeks help from the authorities. You must solve your own problems. It is shameful to betray even your worst enemies to the police. If you are wounded and live, seek your own revenge. But if you die, your assailant is forgiven. All feuds end."

Frozen, my eyes were fixed firmly on Don Marco.

"If you break your oath of silence, the punishment is death."

I nodded, a deer-in-the-headlights kind of nod.

"You must be a good, honorable, and respectful person at all hours—exhibit class, be independent, show courage, and heart. Do not whine or complain. Display bravery when faced with adversity."

More than prepared to meet these requirements, I muttered, "Yes, I understand."

I could taste the seriousness of this vow, the consequences of breaking it, and the honor of being invited into this powerful family. I straightened my stance and maintained eye contact with the most influential, dangerous, and highly respected Mafia Don in the world. He then asked me to explain the code of ethics in my own words.

Not expecting his request, my voice was a little wobbly at first.

"Do not steal... from members of this organization. Never... go to public clubs or... take drugs... of any kind. Do not socialize with police officers."

Franco had gone over these rules so many times, I knew them by heart. My confidence grew with each sentence.

"Always respect women and elders. Never harm the families of associates... look at or touch their wives, girlfriends, or daughters. Tell the truth, be available at a moment's notice, and keep every appointment."

Briefly closing my eyes, I swallowed hard and finished in a quiet voice.

"Never take a life without permission."

The room was deadly silent as the Don's dark brown eyes stared at me.

I froze. He knew I'd already killed three men, and I wasn't even twenty yet.

Don Marco's Sicilian accent rang out strong and clear, "Raimondo Sabatini Martinelli Luigi, do you swear to this oath, promise to live by our code of conduct, and know the penalty for breaking our sacred vow of Omertà?"

My chest tightened. Once said, there was no going back. My life would be forever intertwined with this powerful Mafia family who would kill me if I failed to meet their standards.

"I give you my word that I will live an honorable life, uphold my pledge, and understand the price for violating my oath is death."

Don Marco Catanetti Sr. picked up the silver knife and the saint's portrait from the table. After he pierced my thumb and squeezed my blood onto the portrait, he then handed it to me, struck a match, and set it on fire.

I carefully collected its ashes, rubbed them together between my hands, and recited the words I memorized from Franco's note that would seal my fate.

"May I burn in hell for all eternity if I betray this organization or my friends."

Don Marco Sr. announced loudly, "Raimondo Sabatini Martinelli Luigi— welcome to the Catanetti family."

A deafening cheer filled the room as he kissed both my cheeks, Italian style.

Franco and Angelo were smiling and applauding.

Family. Friends.

Franco's three brothers, however, were silent. Frowning.

Family. Not friends.

What the hell kind of family had I gotten myself into?

CHAPTER TWO

Ray
Forty-Two Years Later
April 9, 1980

It's been two shitty months since my son died. After his funeral, I locked myself in this boring-ass bedroom and got drunk. And stayed that way. I'm angry at myself and the world. And I'm especially angry with the Catanettis.

My son's death opened my eyes to the life I've sacrificed and the happiness I've lost. And for what? So I could give the Catanettis my blind allegiance for over forty years—follow their dangerous orders, honor their stupid rules, and make them billions of dollars.

I don't need them. Never did. They needed me—the Italian kid with a spotless reputation and balls of steel.

Since my son's funeral, I've avoided all contact with them, which is risky. But in my current state of mind, just shoot me now because I'm done—as in getting the hell out and as far away from them as I can, even if they try to kill me.

Which they will.

It'll be difficult to leave Franco and Angelo. They've stood by me through the worst times in my life. However, I won't miss Franco's brothers. Angelo warned me about those assholes long ago.

Rico, that murdering creep, enjoys killing as if it's an art form. He's always had a hard-on for me. When I leave, he'll be the first one to come after me. I might as well plan on taking that evil piece of shit out now.

His twin, Luca, is a different story. Luca's friendly face hides his sinister side, but I know he's silent and deadly. *Stay off my radar, Luca, or you'll die too.*

And then there's Junior, that is, Marco Jr., the Don of the Catanettis. I haven't crossed him yet out of respect for his late father. If we clash, one of us will die, and it sure ain't gonna be me. I'm leaving and Junior can't stop me. He can die trying, though.

Grace, my wife, taps on my bedroom door. "Ray, someone named Mr. Franco is on the phone."

She knows nothing about the Catanettis. I've worked hard as hell to shield Grace from them and now they're calling my house. *What the hell!* My heart races with anxiety. It's not like I haven't expected it, but shit, I really don't want to talk to Franco. He damned sure better be using a safe phone with all the wiretapping going on these days.

I snatch my bedroom door open, and glaring at Grace, grab the phone, steaming that its long cord is wound into crazy knots again. It won't reach across the hall from the kitchen into my bedroom, so how in the hell am I going to have a confidential discussion with my Mafia boss? This is not a good situation. It's dangerous for her to hear any of our conversations.

Trudging past her into the kitchen, trying to untwist the cord as much as possible, I clear my voice, check my shitty attitude, and greet my oldest friend.

"Mr. Franco." My voice lifts, then cracks. "How can I... help you?"

He responds a little louder than I expected, "Dammit, Ray! I've left a bunch of messages with your answering service, and you haven't returned any of my calls. Rico's running his mouth trying to get Junior pissed off at you. It's getting hard to keep Rico muzzled and on a leash."

Why am I not surprised?

"Thank you, Mr. Franco." I force myself to use a calm voice, hoping to take some of the vinegar out of his words.

"This can't wait, so listen up." Franco lowers his tone and speaks slower. "Our biggest shipment arrives in Juárez this weekend. Since Carmelita wouldn't answer her phone either, I sent one of my guys to her apartment."

Oh shit.

"She needs to do her damned job so you can do yours. Hai capito?"

Cupping the mouthpiece, I move deeper into the room. "I understand. How is she?"

"Uh, Ray, I'm sorry." He lights a cigarette, inhales, and blows out the smoke. "I'm told she looks terrible. We know your son's death has been tough for both of you."

I manage a quiet thank you and feel my shoulders slump when I hear how bad she looks. It kills me to know the woman I've loved my whole life is in such deep pain. What's even worse is knowing after our son died, I lost her too. Sucking in a deep breath, I try not to lose my cool.

Franco takes another drag and exhales. "It's Wednesday. Be in Denver by Friday. Junior wants that cargo out of Juárez fast. There's close to a million dollars in it for you. And don't worry, Carmelita will answer her phone now."

With Grace tuned in like a hawk, I'm short and discreet.

"Understood. I'll leave right away."

"Good luck with Carmelita and be careful."

After I hang up, I step over to the sink, pour a glass of water, and take my time drinking it. I need to think without Grace interrupting.

As I shift to the kitchen window, I stare out over Grace's front porch and its railings. Beyond is the yard I landscaped, and the cement driveway I paved, which leads to a garage I built onto the side of her house. I've lived here for nineteen years, but it will always be her home. The one she inherited from her deceased first husband. My ex-partner, Stephen—that jerk.

Moving on.

What's the worst that could happen if I quit the Mafia? Since the Vow of Omertà binds me until death, retirement means six feet under. But if my Mafia brothers care about Carmelita and me, maybe they'll let us go. The only way I can proceed with this next step is by believing Franco will make sure the Mafia's code of ethics protects Grace, our twin daughters, and our home from his shithead brothers.

The glass clinks when I turn it upside down and put it in the dish rack. Grace is staring a hole through my back.

"What did that man want, Ray?"

She doesn't fucking need to know, but I gotta tell her something.

As I hurry back to my bedroom, I mutter over my shoulder, "The contract I've worked hard to pull together will be canceled if I'm not in Denver by Friday. It's big money for our company."

I've got shit to do.

It's April and already in the mid-eighties. My South Florida clothes are useless. All I need to pack is my down jacket and some underclothes. My winter clothes are in Denver where Carmelita and my son live.

My son.

Those words stab me so deeply I choke back sobs. This bedroom looks like I feel: stripped to the core. I don't know why I stuffed my crap into garbage bags and disposed of them while Grace and the girls slept. Maybe it was intuition, or the haze of booze. But I had to start somewhere.

My antique trunk, and the two cashmere sweaters my son gave me the Christmas before his injury, are the only things I want to keep. As I fold the sweaters, my fingertips linger a moment over the soft wool before I place them on the trunk's top tray, then close and lock its curved lid. There're a lot of batshit crazy hitmen who're afraid to cross me and I'm choking up over some sweaters and a big old trunk I can't take with me. I slip the trunk's key into my usual place, under the padding of my right snow boot. I never bring those damned things. They never fit right, anyway.

After a quick shower, I throw some clean underclothes in my black leather duffel bag, noting there's still plenty of room for the cash I'll get for the Juárez job. What an enormous relief to know Carmelita answered Franco's phone call. Since our son died, she wouldn't pick up when I called. Maybe she will now. She needs to know I'm coming, no matter what she said after our son's funeral.

Grace is still in the kitchen, folding dish towels. Even though she doesn't know about my son or his mother, I no longer care what she hears. Everything is in motion now. I've made my decision. It's time. I dial Carmelita's number while frantically untangling the phone cord. She answers on the sixth ring. A lifetime.

"Hi," I mumble.

She breaks down sobbing, "I'm sorry, I'm so, so, sorry. I didn't mean it... it wasn't your fault he died."

The lump in my throat hurts so much I can't speak or swallow.

"His trophies... they're everywhere. I'm so... broken... I want to go home... Please, Ray... I need you."

It takes a few grunting sounds to unlock my voice.

"I'm on my way. I'll be there soon."

My knuckles are white from gripping the phone. "Wait for me."

"I love you," she whispers.

"I know. Me too" is all I can get out.

The moment we hang up, Grace goes detective on my ass.

"Who was that? What's going on?" she demands.

"The client. They've agreed to wait—only if I leave Seaport right now."

She distracts me with, "You can't drive straight through. It's too dangerous."

She doesn't know I'm flying or that my rig is already in Colorado.

Too much explaining. She can think whatever she wants too.

"All I need is lots of coffee," I lie, cross the hall, and close my bedroom door.

These are the last moments Grace and I will spend as husband and wife. She has always tried to please me, but I couldn't love her like a husband should. Our history makes intimacy, well, deficient on my part. She's a caring mother. Our daughters will be better off without me fucking up their lives. From now on, our connection will be our partnership in Hunter & Lewis Trucking. And who knows? If I get my ass killed, she'll be a widow for the second time.

I entered a risky game long ago, where the odds of survival are slim, and I'm about to learn just how slim they are. It's impossible to think past this point because every trip is dangerous, but if I live, I'll come back for my antique trunk and a notebook filled with incriminating information I've gathered over the years. The notebook is stored in a hidden safe at my office, as life insurance for Carmelita and me. Our ticket to freedom.

Junior better pray I never let my little notebook fall into the Committee's hands. If they learn he ordered some of their Mafia family members killed, and other people they did business with assassinated, they will whack him in a real shitty way. And I won't feel bad about it either.

After I gather my duffle bag and slip the padlock on my bedroom door's hasp, Grace's muted voice comes from behind, startling me.

"Ray?"

Unnerved, I turn, clutching my bag and down jacket, worried that I'm forgetting something important.

Grace, a beautiful, kind woman, tall and slender with lovely dove gray eyes, like my mother's, stares back at me, confused. She tucks her silver-streaked short blond hair behind her ear. It's her *tell*, a self-calming gesture I recognize.

"Promise you'll be careful," she whispers.

My life's unpredictable. I don't make promises. But this is the agonizing moment I've been subconsciously preparing for. When I leave today, I'm abandoning her and our twelve-year-old adopted daughters, Patty and Merry. I hope they forgive me for the shitty way I'm doing it, but each second counts on this hazardous journey, and I'm out of time.

What can I say that sums it all up? Even though I haven't held her for ages, I pull her close and say the words that will end our marriage.

"This is goodbye, Grace."

CHAPTER
THREE

The Locked Trunk
Grace
April 9, 1980

GRACE WONDERED WHAT IN THE HECK HAD JUST HAPPENED. First, Ray was angry at everyone for months, then he bolted out of there like his tail was on fire, saying a strange goodbye.

Grace needed advice. After straightening the tangled phone cord, she called Natalie and, disappointed, left a message on her best friend's answering machine.

As she hung up, she glanced across the hall and saw that the padlock on Ray's bedroom door was hanging open, which was strange. Grace knew Ray always locked that door to prevent the girls from finding the weapons he said he kept stored in his room in case he needed them for protection on particular runs. Ray had explained there had been a few hijacking attempts over the years. Grace reasoned he must have forgotten to lock it when she distracted him as he was leaving. But then, nothing about that entire scene was typical. The strange phone calls and the unusual hug goodbye—they hadn't hugged for at least ten years now and he never called or talked to his clients from home. All abnormal.

Without hesitation, Grace slipped the lock off and entered his darkened room. When she flipped the overhead lights on, she was startled to find the biggest antique trunk she'd ever seen positioned at the foot of Ray's bed. It was maybe four feet long and at least three feet high. Grace wondered how he dragged that thing into her house without her knowing about it. She was blazing with questions. *Where did it come from and how long had it been here?* And Grace was confused. Ray's words made her believe he had left them for good, but if there was anything valuable in this lovely antique trunk, she was pretty sure he was coming back.

With the closet doors closed, the bed made, and the furniture surfaces empty, Ray's room looked like a hotel suite—except for that trunk. Across the room, the top of Ray's waist-high oak dresser was empty. Above it, a double set of windows, covered by gray blackout curtains, were closed.

Grace crossed the space and pulled open the dresser drawers, finding shorts, T-shirts, and underclothes. The few clothes left hanging in Ray's closet were short-sleeved, lightweight shirts and pants, a black suit, and a black leather dress jacket. A few pairs of shoes lay on the closet floor, which included his snow boots. *Huh? If he was going to Denver, why didn't he take them?*

Okay, let's see what's in that big ole fancy trunk Ray snuck in here. And, of course, it was locked. *What is it with this guy and locks?* Grace reasoned if he took the key with him, *wouldn't he risk losing it?* If it were her, she'd hide it somewhere out of sight that was easy to get to. *But where?* Grace looked at the most obvious place—the closet.

Standing on tiptoe, she ran her hand across the top shelf. No key. She turned and surveyed the room. Since the trunk's edges sat flat against the floor, she knew it couldn't be under there. Grace pulled up the edge of his bedspread, felt around the rim of Ray's mattress, and came up empty-handed again. Nothing was taped or attached to the back of his headboard. Nothing was tucked tight against his windowsill. Grace then checked his bathroom medicine cabinet, rattled aspirin bottles, and anything that could hide a key. Zero. Grace even looked inside the toilet tank. Nope.

Dang it.

Defeated, she headed to the laundry room, put the girls' tennis clothes into the dryer, and started a load of towels when the phone rang. It was Natalie.

"Your message sounded stressed. What's going on?" she asked.

"I'm not sure, Nats, but something's wrong. I've got a bad feeling. Ray took a strange call around one, packed a bag, said a weird goodbye, and practically ran out the door. His bedroom is empty, but he left a locked trunk behind. I'm searching for its key now but haven't found it yet."

"Did he say where he was going?" Natalie asked.

"He said to Denver for a job he doesn't want to lose."

"I bet he'll be back, Grace, so don't worry. Sleep on it and let's talk tomorrow, okay?"

"Good idea, but something's not right, Natalie. I can feel it in my bones." Grace glanced at the kitchen wall clock. "Oops, gotta pick up the girls at school. I'll call you in the morning."

Later that afternoon, after the girls' tennis lesson, their coach encouraged Grace to let them join the twelve-year-old county division team in the fall. "With their strong two-handed backhands, they're ready for competition." Grace promised she'd talk to the girls about it and get back to him. It delighted her to know how well Patty and Merry were progressing.

The rest of the day flew by. Homework, showers, dinner, and off to bed. Those two were asleep in minutes.

After the kitchen was clean, Grace checked the dryer. The towels had a few more minutes left. *Like me,* she thought, feeling worn out by the day's events.

When she adopted babies at forty, she was sure she'd be okay, but at fifty-two, keeping up with all their activities, wiped her out. No matter how tired she was, Grace was determined to keep looking until she found that trunk key.

She had checked out most of the places earlier, so all that was left to search were the clothes and shoes in Ray's closet. Again, she thought it made little sense for Ray to leave the snow boots behind. *Wouldn't he need them in Colorado?* They looked like they'd keep his feet nice and warm in the snow.

Curious about what they'd feel like on bare feet, Grace slipped her foot into the left snow boot. It felt furry, like a slipper. The right one felt the same, but boy, were they big.

The dryer buzzed, so she clomped off to the laundry room, still wearing the boots, and folded the clothes. As she headed back to Ray's room, her toes slid to the front of the boots.

Yikes! She yelled, realizing something lumpy was under the padding in the right boot.

Alarmed, she yanked her foot out and furiously shook it, praying a scorpion didn't drop out. They loved dark places like closets and shoes. She'd be in a world of hurt if one stung her with its poisonous tail.

When nothing fell out, she pulled the padding out. That's when an old key slid down into the heel section.

What a great place for Ray to hide it, but did the key fit the trunk's keyhole?

It did.

If Ray was telling the truth, Grace then expected to find some guns in his trunk and lifted the lid, surprised at how light it was. A deep wooden tray with handles on each side laid across the entire opening. Nestled on top of the tray were two folded pullover sweaters, light gray and navy blue. They covered a dark-colored wool jacket of some sort. Grace moved the sweaters and saw it was an old military jacket, with bullet holes in the chest area and brown stains—she assumed were from blood. *Why would Ray keep that gross old thing?*

A frayed Have-A-Tampa cardboard cigar box with a flip-up lid was snuggled beside it. Inside were two bone-handled knives and two sets of metal things with round openings, along with an Army tag inscribed with numbers and the name Henry Lee.

Grace glanced back at the bloody Army jacket and saw the name Lee on it as well.

Who is Henry Lee?

It was no surprise to find a long gun with two barrels and a box of big bullets tucked under it all. Alongside the gun were a couple of oily rags wrapped around two small handguns, with more boxes of bullets near them. They would have to be moved for her to see what was beneath the big tray, but there was no way she was going to touch them. Grace knew nothing about guns, but she knew who did. Someone she trusted who had stayed in touch with her over the years—her deceased husband's high school friend, Detective John Myers.

Grace then locked the trunk, turned out the lights, and closed Ray's door, wondering if it was too late to call John. If he wasn't in, she could leave a message with Seaport's Sheriff's Office for John to call her tomorrow.

She hoped she wasn't overreacting, but after Ray's tense phone calls, his strange goodbye, and the way he bolted out of there—weird stuff was happening. Stuff she couldn't ignore.

Grace called the sheriff's office and left a message for John.

CHAPTER FOUR

Reconciliation and New Plans
Ray
April 9, 1980

I LEFT MY TRUCK AT THE SEAPORT AIRPORT TO DEAL WITH LATER. Luckily, a few seats were still available on the Denver flight, which started boarding soon after I purchased my ticket. With a layover in Dallas, I'll be in Denver by the end of the day.

My window seat in the back of the plane has no one next to me. It's the quiet space I need to think—about Carmelita and about my Mafia brothers. For now, I'm cramming Junior and the whole damned bunch of them into a handle-later box, and slamming it closed.

Carmelita's the one I'm concerned about. I never should have left her after our son's funeral. From what Franco said about her state of mind and what she sounded like when we talked on the phone, I'm worried.

The accident Rayban had two and a half years ago was hard enough, but his recent passing broke us. Much as I want to think about so many other things, I blame myself for his accident—my bad karma for all the terrible things I've done in my lifetime.

The truth is, when I lost this boy, this child of my heart, it left me half a man. This must be what hell feels like.

It's almost sunset when I arrive in Denver. It's so damned cold, I quickly pull on my down jacket, hurry through the airport, and hail a taxi.

After the nerve-wracking conversation with Franco and then walking out on Grace, I'm still feeling apprehensive and a little shaky when the cab driver pulls into the parking lot of Carmelita's high-rise condominium. I hope it's not too late for us.

My throat tightens as I take the elevator to her penthouse apartment and let myself in.

Her balcony overlooks the city of Denver, whose twinkling lights are turning on as the golden hour of sunset highlights the snowy mountain peaks rising out of the west. Packing boxes are stacked all over the living room floor.

She's barefoot and cross-legged on the floor, crushing newspapers, stuffing them in a box, and doesn't hear me right away. Her favorite navy-blue velour sweatsuit can't hide her lovely curves. A blue checkered scarf is tied over her dark hair to keep it off her face, a single braid falling to her waist. Her warm-toned skin is smooth, her lips full and soft, but she looks so sad and tired. It's unusual to see her without makeup, her eyes red and swollen. Only ten years younger than me, she's still so damned beautiful it makes my heart race seeing her. God, I've missed her.

When she leans back to stretch, she catches sight of me and shrieks. Before I can put my bag down, she's in my arms, hugging me, and telling me about Franco's stern phone call.

Holding her tight, I don't want to let her go but confirm he called me too.

"I have to give you this before it gets lost in all these boxes." She retrieves a package and hands it to me. We both know it's filled with cash and a list of names.

"They dropped this off earlier." She points to the list. "I've already verified them. Tomorrow they'll deliver the bonus money along with the keys you'll need."

I drop the cash and the list into my black bag to sort out later. It can wait.

She lays her head on my chest, and my arms tighten around her.

"Please forgive me for all the terrible things I said, Ray. It kills me now that I used Stephen's death date in Rayban's obituary to hurt you. I wanted to punish you for not choosing us. Please forgive me. I can't bear to lose you, too."

I'm a miserable bastard, it's true. But with her, I'm a tender fool. My soul is bare, and I choke up, knowing I almost lost the only woman I've ever loved.

"It's me who should ask your forgiveness, Carmie. I hate myself for leaving you, for not fighting harder to stay. You've done nothing wrong. This is my last job. When it's over, I'm telling the Catanettis we're finished... we're both retiring. Together."

Carmelita pulls away and looks up, her eyes full of questions. "You left her?" Carmelita's narrowed brows betray her uncertainty.

"Yes, I did. I'm yours for the rest of our lives."

Holding this woman in my arms, I know I've done the right thing.

Damn the consequences and damn the fucking Mafia.

Up before six, we head out to Mile High Storage. It's an hour-and-a-half drive south to Colorado Springs where I keep my semi. We leave her car there and drive back to her apartment in my truck.

Since she sold her condo furnished, the move is much easier. By the afternoon, with all the food from the refrigerator emptied in the condo's dumpster, we drove back to Colorado Springs and unloaded her boxes and packed suitcases into the unit I rented.

Exhausted beyond belief, we checked into the Broadmoor Resort Hotel, a few miles south of the storage unit. After dinner, we firmed up our plans before Carmelita went to bed. I'm surprised she made it through her meal.

Tomorrow I'm going to Mexico and she's driving home to Lewisville—with most of the cash, including what I pick up at the Brown Palace tomorrow. All I need now is enough money to bribe the border guards and to cover my travel expenses. With a shipment this big, I gotta stay on guard every second. Especially if word leaks out about the value of this cargo. Who knows how hijackers learn this shit? They're dangerous psychopaths and I've faced more than a few.

It's time to make the phone calls that will ensure our plans go smoothly from this point forward. After reciting the number to the hotel operator, within three rings, José Jr.'s sleepy voice answers and accepts my collect call.

"Sorry for the late call, José. I'll keep this short. Carmelita and I are moving back to the farm. She'll arrive in a few days. Could you get the house and cabin ready for us? There's plenty of money in the farm's expense account for whatever you need."

"Sí, Señor Ray. We're happy you're coming home. Tomorrow, we will stock the kitchen, and put clean sheets on the beds and towels in the bathrooms. It's still pretty cold here, so I'll stack fresh logs by the fireplaces in the house and cabin."

"Carmie and I appreciate everything you're able to do, José."

There's silence.

"Is there anything else?"

He lowers his voice. "I'll make sure there's hot chocolate in both kitchens."

He knows my son loved hot chocolate. It's José's way of saying he misses him, too.

"Thank you. That'll be nice. Take care of Miss Carmie until I get there."

"Sí. Buenas noches."

After we hung up, I sat for a moment filled with memories of how much everyone on the farm adored our son. José Jr. was there when he was born. So many of them watched him grow up. They were heartbroken when... If there's a heaven, then my son's with all the people I love. I've always believed heaven doesn't exist, but now, I hope it does.

It won't be possible to make a collect call to the night manager of Hotel del Sol in Juárez, Mexico. I'll be charged an arm and a leg by this resort, but no problem, I'll just add it to my tab, along with a spa day for Carmelita tomorrow while I'm in Denver.

Despite the Mexican night manager's broken English, we're still able to communicate.

"Tú room es ready for when you come, Señor. Ugh, locks es okay. I protect for you. No one es near tú room. I tell el day-hombre mañana."

"Gracias, a diós."

It doesn't matter about the locks. I'll install new ones when I arrive.

All I have to do is get through this last job, retrieve my trunk and notebook, and deal with one last problem. Tell a dangerous, egotistical Mafia Don I quit. I haven't quite figured out how to do that yet.

CHAPTER
FIVE

Who is Henry Lee?
Grace
April 10, 1980

GRACE YELLED DOWN THE HALL. "GIRLS! GET UP, WE'RE GONNA BE LATE! The alarm clock didn't go off. Put your hair in banana clips today."

With no time to prepare their lunches, Grace handed them money when she dropped them off at school and headed home. Ready to dive back into Ray's room, Grace planned to search his clothes more thoroughly than she did the night before.

But first, she called Natalie. "I've got coffee if you want to see all the crazy stuff I found in Ray's trunk last night."

"Miss Nosy will be right over," Natalie said.

As soon as she walked through the door, she sniffed the air. "Coffee ready?" she asked and hung her purse over the back of the dining room chair. Then she pointed to Ray's room. "May I?"

"Sure, go check it out. The trunk's already open. You'll see some guns in it. There's other stuff laying on the bed. Would you please bring the cigar box back with you?"

Natalie was back in a minute with the cigar box and sat down at the table on Grace's left. "Yup, there are definitely guns in that trunk," she said as Grace pushed the filled coffee cup, cream, and sugar toward her.

"Did you tell Mark I think Ray left us?" Grace asked, taking a sip of her own coffee.

"Yes. Mark said he's finished writing Sunday's sermon. Call him if you need him."

After Grace spread the box's contents in front of them, she asked Natalie if she knew what they were.

Natalie selected one knife. "These switchblades sure have some beautiful antler handles on them. See these little silver things sticking out? They keep your fingers from slipping on the blade when you flick it open. My daddy always carried one, but not as nice as these."

Natalie pointed the knife away from them and pressed a button on the handle. A long thin blade flew out with a swish sound.

Grace yelped and jumped back in her chair.

"Oops, sorry, I'd forgotten how quickly it does that." Natalie pointed to the other knife. "Now you try. It's not scary once you're prepared."

Unsure, Grace picked up the second knife, turned it around, and held it away from her. Natalie then showed Grace where to push the small button near the top of the handle. When it flew open, Graced somehow managed not to drop it or cut herself.

"Natalie, this one has brownish stains on the blade. Blood?" Grace asked.

Natalie inspected hers. "There's a stain on this one too. But it's at the hilt. I don't want to think about what that means."

When Grace asked how to close it, Natalie showed her. "Like this. Protect your fingers while you use the thumb of your other hand to push the blade in. Now you do it," she said.

After Grace used the switchblade successfully, she switched her attention to another item.

"What are these?" Grace held up one of the metal things with round holes.

"Brass knuckles," Natalie said and continued, "Daddy had these too. Said he learned how to use them in the Navy. Put your fingers in the holes and slip them up to your proximal interphalangeal joints—which are your second knuckles. Don't push them down to the knuckles next to your hand."

"Oh, Nurse Natalie, I love it when you use those sexy medical words."

Natalie winked. "Mark likes it, too."

Grace tried to get the image of Pastor Mark liking Natalie's sexy medical words out of her head as Natalie inserted her fingers through the holes and showed Grace how to grip the brass knuckles the proper way.

"When you close your fist, it gives punching power in a fight. If you hit someone hard enough, it'll crack their skull. Working as an emergency room nurse taught me that."

Natalie leaned in. "This elderly widow lady, who barely weighed a hundred pounds, lived alone. When a burglar, who must've weighed two hundred and eighty pounds, broke into her home, she climbed up on a chair, jumped on his back, locked her legs around him, and pounded the top of his head with those things."

"Ouch, that must've hurt," Grace exclaimed.

"That man was a whimpering puppy when they brought him into the examination room. The cops told me the old lady's husband taught her how to use them when they were first married. She'd waited a long time for that opportunity."

"Oh, my," Grace said, pushing back from the table. "Come on, let's go see what else is in Ray's trunk."

A minute later, they were staring down at the guns. "I know we've gotta move these first to see what's under the tray," Grace said, "but how do we do that?"

"No problem," Natalie said. "My daddy taught me to always face a gun away from people, unless you mean to kill them. I'll pick up the twelve-gauge shotgun and its bullets. Daddy used to turkey hunt with one like this. Protect your clothes before you pick up the small guns wrapped in those oily rags. Do you have any hand towels you can use?"

While Natalie moved the bigger weapon, Grace grabbed a small towel from Ray's bathroom and wrapped the oily rags and guns around them.

When they finished putting the guns on the far side of the bed, Grace was ready to remove the wooden tray, but Natalie, busy studying the inside of the trunk's arched lid asked, "When's the last time you saw gorgeous red velvet upholstery like this? I bet this trunk is at least a hundred years old."

Natalie ran her hand over the soft fabric of its lining, then looked at Grace and pointed to a section. "Feel this. There's something flat behind here."

They tugged at the seams, searching for a way in, when Grace unsnapped a corner and said, "Here we go." She then snaked her hand in, dragged out a manila file, and opened it.

"There's a bunch of old, yellowed Seaport newspaper clippings." Grace looked up at Natalie. "Also, there's a Denver newspaper report from two years ago and a recent Denver obituary."

"What do they say?" Natalie asked.

Grace squinted. "I can hardly read them. Let's go back to the dining room where the light's better."

With the file spread open on the table, Grace inventoried the contents of what appeared to be newspaper articles about unsolved murders and read them out loud. "Tito Zayas, 1938. Stanley Hunter, 1943. Hey, that's Stephen's grandfather!" Grace moved to the next one. "Barry O'Hara, 1949."

Natalie gasped. "That's my ex-husband. But... the police solved his murder!"

"That's crazy. Why is he in Ray's file?!" Grace exclaimed.

Natalie looked away. She never talked about her ex, so Grace didn't ask.

"Victor Hellman, 1955, and Stephen Hunter, 1959." Grace sat up straight and looked at Natalie. "Dear God, both our deceased husbands are in this file, along with Stephen's grandfather! Stephen wasn't murdered, he died from the flu. What in the heck is this file about?"

They exchanged confused looks before Grace proceeded. "Are you familiar with the other two guys, Victor Hellman, and Tito Zayas?"

"Not at all," Natalie said.

"Okay, then. After you read the Denver accident report and I read the Denver obit, let's switch."

The Rocky Mountain Post

August 14, 1977

Bicyclist in Critical Condition

Ramón López,18, of Denver, was severely injured Saturday during Bikefest, an annual bicycle race from Boulder to Denver.

Mr. López was airlifted by helicopter to the Denver Trauma Center, where he's listed in critical condition. His parents are unavailable for comment.

Police are asking anyone who may have witnessed the accident to contact them.

The Rocky Mountain Post

Tuesday, February 12, 1980

Ramón Lewis Lopez, 21, born July 5, 1959, died Monday, February 11, 1980, after being in a coma from injuries sustained while riding his mountain bike in a Bikefest race event on August 13, 1977. His mother, Carmelita Lewis Lopez of Seaport, FL., and Denver, CO., survives him. He is predeceased by XXXXXXXXXXXXX.

Survived by hundreds of friends who fondly called him "Rayban." Ramón graduated from Cherry Creek High School, where he excelled at football, tennis, basketball, baseball, swimming, and hockey. He was an Eagle Scout and a triathlete. Ramón loved barbecue ribs, Yoo-Hoos, crazy hats, and sports games.

Ramón was accepted at the University of Notre Dame on a full sports scholarship and was scheduled to start classes in the fall.

Visitation is 4-7 p.m., Thursday, Feb. 14, at the Denver Chapel, 2092 S. Colorado Blvd. Santa Maria Catholic Church funeral services are at 1 p.m., Saturday, Feb.16, at 3689 East Colfax, Denver.

He will be interred in a family plot in Lewisville, W. VA.

They sat for a moment, taking in the gravity of what they had just learned.

"Natalie—wow. I'm absolutely floored. This is horrible. Ray must know this boy. Could this be the reason he's been in a funky mood for at least two years now? That boy's been in a coma since 1977. His death a couple of months ago was around the time Ray came home and locked himself in his room. All he would tell me was that a friend died, nothing more. I had no idea it could be something as terrible as this."

She nodded and asked. "Could this lady, Carmelita, be an ex-wife you don't know about, and it's their son who died in February? Remember how upset you were when Ray missed the girls' Valentine's birthday party?"

Natalie leaned in and pointed to the newspaper article lying between them. "Patty and Merry's birthday party was the same day as this young man's funeral."

Perplexed, Grace pushed her hair behind her ears and waved at the article. "It says his mother survived the boy, but it doesn't mention Ray as his father." Grace tapped the article. "In fact, it says, *'He is predeceased by,'* and someone scribbled over the words that follow. Why?"

"You're right," Natalie said. "Why would anyone do that? Unless—maybe the information was incorrect, or they were angry?"

Grace looked at her. "You know what's getting crazier by the minute? The boy's ashes are being taken to Lewisville, a town in West Virginia with Ray's last name. What the heck?"

One minute Grace was sad about the boy's accident and death and the next she was angry with Ray for never telling her about the boy and his mother. Grace couldn't sit still any longer and stood up. "Come on, I'm ready to see what else's in that trunk."

Natalie then mumbled something about hoping there were no dead bodies in it to go along with the newspaper articles.

They positioned themselves at each end of the open trunk, grabbed its handles, yanked them upward, and shrieked in surprise at what was below.

"Oh my God! How much money is in there?" Grace yelled, staring at Natalie across the top of the trunk. Bundles of cash lay neatly banded together in row after row. They filled the trunk—front to back and side to side.

"I've got to sit down." Grace swiped the sweaters and Army jacket aside.

Natalie plopped down next to her and muttered, "Wow, that's a lot of money."

"What if Ray robbed a bank? What'll I do now? Should I call the police?" Grace asked.

"Grace, tell me—how can I help you?"

"I don't know. I'm confused," Grace blurted out. "Ray says a strange goodbye, leaves after some stressful phone calls, and then we find all this money." She looked at her watch. "School's over at 3:30; it's Thursday, so the girls have karate lessons after that, then baths, dinner, and homework. Once I digest everything, I'll call you."

Natalie covered Grace's hand with her own. "Grace... Mark and I deal with family trauma all the time. I'm going to call him. He'll know what to do once you explain everything to him. Show him the trunk. You guys can figure out what needs to happen next. But just in case you decide to call law enforcement, the girls need to be safe someplace else."

Natalie put her arm around Grace's shoulder for a quick hug. "Let me pick my goddaughters up from school, take them to karate, and bring them home with me. They can stay overnight. I'll take them to school in the morning."

Grace stared straight ahead. "Are you sure?" she whispered.

"Absolutely. If everything's good—they can come home tomorrow. But throw in their play clothes and Sunday dresses in case they need to stay the weekend. Remember your Girl Scout motto—be prepared." Natalie smiled and looked at her watch. "I still have time to grab some extra things from the grocery store before I pick them up. There's gonna be a chocolate cake in their future because I plan to spoil them rotten."

Grace nodded. "I'll let the school know you're picking Patty and Merry up."

Within a half hour, Mark was sitting on Grace's sofa. "Natalie told me Ray deserted you and left some strange belongings behind. Tell me what's going on."

Grace found it hard to tell Mark everything without breaking down. Not just because he was her pastor, but because he had been a dear friend most of her life. Mark helped her bury her first husband, Stephen, and now he was there when it looked like Grace's second husband had abandoned her and her daughters. At least Grace was thankful the money in Ray's trunk meant she wasn't penniless like Stephen had left her.

"He said a friend died?" Mark's question showed his concern.

Grace handed him the obituary about the young man. "I didn't know about this boy or his mother. Ray has never uttered a word to me about them... ever."

Mark finished reading the newspaper clippings and shook his head, commenting that, from Ray's recent behavior, he believed the boy was Ray's son, regardless of the crossed-out portion of the article.

Then he asked Grace, "What did Ray take with him?"

"Only a small black duffle bag and his down jacket. No enormous suitcases, like you'd expect if someone were moving out forever," she replied.

He nodded, then asked to see what she and Natalie found so disturbing. When he followed Grace into Ray's room, his eyes went wide, seeing what was in the trunk.

"Mark, something weird is going on. Last night, I called a friend, Detective John Myers, and left a message. He hasn't returned my call yet. Maybe Ray's in some kind of trouble."

"I know Detective Myers. I'll call the sheriff's office again. Then I'll clear my calendar for the afternoon."

An hour later, Detective Myers arrived in plain clothes, but with a significant bulge under his jacket. His short, once-dark hair was salt and pepper now.

At fifty-six, John was still trim, in excellent shape, and always tanned thanks to his Mediterranean heritage. A few crow's feet lined his dark brown eyes as he smiled and pulled Grace into a hug with his muscled arms.

"Grace, you just don't age. You're more beautiful than ever," John crooned.

Yup, he's still charming, Grace thought.

"Come in, John. Mark's here too. I'm embarrassed to ask for your help with my personal life, but I need to make sense of what happened after my husband abruptly left town yesterday."

As Grace closed the door behind him, John greeted Pastor Mark with a handshake and then joined her on the sofa.

John started out right away, making Grace feel comfortable. "Grace, we've been friends for a very long time. You don't have to worry about asking me for anything. I returned your call early this morning, but I missed you. What's going on?"

Grace was uncertain if she'd forgotten anything, but when she finished, John stood, offered his hand, and pulled her right up to his chest. She was not used to being this close to a man. Her heart pounded as he stood over her with eyebrows knitted and his eyes gazing into hers. She was mesmerized, unable to break away from his intense stare until one side of his mouth lifted into that small, wry smile that flowed up to crinkle his eyes and relax his forehead. In his deep, mellow, slow, and steady voice Grace could drown in, he asked, "May I search Ray's room?"

It took a moment for Grace to realize John was waiting for her answer. "Sure ... yes, of course." She cleared her throat and took a step back as if to break his spell or whatever that was.

"Uh, his room ... is across from the kitchen. The door is... open," she stammered.

John stood at the entrance of Ray's room and scanned it.

Mark and Grace followed, staying in the doorway after John stepped in and began his inspection of the closest bedside table drawers. He took extra care to examine the bloodstained, bullet-riddled Army jacket as he made his way down that side of the bed. Then, moving past the closed trunk, he pointed to it and raised his eyebrows. "That's where the guns were stored?" he asked.

Grace nodded.

John continued around the bed and examined the guns, then opened the other bedside table drawers. Finally, he turned to the front of the dresser under the windows. Kneeling, he pulled out each drawer and flipped them over before putting them back. But as he held the last one upside down, he looked at Grace. "Do you have a safe anywhere in the house?" he asked.

"No. Why?" she responded.

"These numbers are written like a combination for a safe. Does three R seventy-one, two L nineteen, and one R fifty-nine mean anything to you?"

Seven, one, nineteen fifty-nine felt like a punch in her face. Feeling lightheaded, Grace sat down and hugged her knees.

"I'm okay, just a little dizzy." She glanced up, then down. "That's the day Stephen died."

"Grace, do you need a break?" John's voice was full of concern.

She shook her head no and asked, "Why would he write Stephen's death date that way?"

John sat next to Grace and gently put his hand on her back.

"We've found that people often record their safe combinations in weird places. This is a perfect example. Be aware that Ray might have a hidden safe somewhere. Who knows why he did that?"

As John headed back to the closet, Grace mentioned she found the trunk key in Ray's snow boots.

"Good, I'll start with the shoes," he said.

Mark and Grace watched John run his fingers into the toe of every shoe and then tap their heels on the floor as if he were dumping sand.

Nothing. *Not even a scorpion. Thank goodness.*

John then moved to the hanging clothes, patted down each short-sleeved shirt, and all the trousers. Again, there was nothing in them.

That left a black leather dress jacket and a black suit. John reached toward the leather jacket's pockets as he looked over his shoulder at Grace.

"You, okay?" he asked.

"I'm better, thank you. Keep going."

"Right pocket has a ripped receipt. Let's see." John smoothed out the tiny piece of paper, squinting as he tried to read it.

"It's from a Hotel del something, Avenue something, that starts with part of a word... Ben, then Méx. The last half is gone. My guess is Mexico. It's dated February 18, 1980, though."

He looked at Grace. "Why would Ray be in Mexico on February 18th?"

"No idea, but it explains where he was two days after he missed our daughters' birthday party."

Even though Grace sounded like Miss Pissy, she remembered the boy's obituary and felt bad for her tone of voice.

"I have no explanation for why Ray went to Mexico and not straight home. He knew he was in charge of cooking the hot dogs and hamburgers for the girls' party," she said.

John smoothed out the torn receipt pieces on top of the dresser and returned to the leather dress jacket. He then dug into the left pocket and retrieved wadded-up receipts that might've gotten wet and tried to read them.

"This one's from the Ship's Ta..., something or other. I can't read the rest of the word, it's so faded. There's a date that starts with F and a fifteen. The year's gone."

He unfolded the second receipt and held it up to the overhead light, straining to read it.

"This one's for a cigar and two shots of whiskey. The faded twenty is where the other receipt's date is. These receipts resemble each other in size and layout, which means nothing. It's a common cash register form."

He placed the fragments of receipts on the dresser with the ripped one.

"Does February 20th mean anything to you?" John asked.

"All I know is Ray wasn't here on Saturday, February 16th," Grace replied.

"The sixteenth was the date of your daughters' birthday party?"

"Yes, and I'm still hurt that he missed it," she said.

John then hung the black leather dress jacket back in the closet, pulled out the black suit, and hung it on the closet door. Diving his hand into the jacket's hip pockets, he moved his fingers all around, checking for rips in the lining, and shook his head. There was nothing in either of them or the breast pocket. But inside the suit's right inner pocket, he pulled out a folded white handkerchief, laid it on the dresser, and unfolded it. It was clean.

John then checked the jacket's left inside pocket. "Bingo! A drink receipt from The Kentucky Club, 640 Avenue Benito, Juárez, Mexico, dated June 9, 1979. Six margaritas for a party of three." He turned to Grace and smiled. "This proves Ray's connection to Mexico. To Juárez, in particular."

Encouraged, John removed the suit pants from the hanger and spread it across the top of the antique trunk. He reached into the right pocket and pulled out a pair of red lace bikini panties. Eyebrows raised, he glanced at Grace's surprised reaction and, without a word, laid that on the dresser.

In the left pocket was another handkerchief, wadded up and drenched with dried brown stains. The troubled look on John's face showed he understood the horror on Grace's. He placed them on the dresser with the receipts, then turned to Grace.

"Even though the red panties and the stained handkerchief are shocking, they're only incriminating evidence. It doesn't mean he committed a crime. The stains could be from something as simple as a nosebleed."

John rehung the suit pants under its jacket, returned them to the closet, and then looked back and forth between Mark and Grace.

"All these clothes are replaceable. The guns are old and usable, but of little value. Perhaps he kept the old Army jacket and other things for sentimental reasons. Honestly, Grace, I think Ray isn't coming back."

"Oh, he's coming back all right. Open the trunk," Grace snapped.

John lifted the lid and stared at the neat rows of bundled cash filling the entire space.

"I wonder how much is in here," he muttered, stony-faced and unfazed.

John turned to Mark and asked if he would mind counting the rows and stacks while John counted a single bundle of cash.

Grace's mouth dropped open when John finished and announced, "$50,000."

Mark chimed in, "There are approximately four hundred stacks in this trunk."

Grace did the math.

"That's $20 million," Grace said, trying to appear calm. But inside, she was screaming.

Who in the hell is Ray Lewis?

CHAPTER
SIX

Confusion and Clues
Grace
April 10, 1980

Grace took a moment to prepare iced tea for John and herself after Mark declined. John sat at the dining room table skimming through the newspaper clippings she and Natalie had found earlier. Grace hoped John could make sense of why Ray kept those particular articles. It confused her to see the one on Stephen's death. Everyone knew Stephen died from the flu, so why did Ray keep it? She thought maybe because they were partners, but still found it creepy.

John read the names of the murdered guys out loud, sorted them chronologically, and separated them into people they knew: Stanley Hunter, 1943, and Stephen Hunter, 1959.

Then the ones they didn't know: Tito Zayas, 1938; Barry O'Hara, 1949; and Victor Hellman, 1955.

Mark spoke up, "Uh, John, Barry O'Hara was Natalie's former husband. He died in a hunting incident when his drunken teenage companion accidentally shot him."

"Huh, I wonder what his connection was to Ray," John mused and turned to Grace. "Did you know Barry O'Hara?"

"Not really," Grace answered. "I didn't know Natalie when she was married to him. But earlier today, she mentioned he was her ex-husband, whose death was solved. I remember Stephen talking about a young man Ray fired for stealing who was killed in a hunting accident, just as Mark said. Maybe that's why Ray kept the article. Still, it's weird that he saved that one."

Mark checked his watch. "I've gotta go. You and John have a lot to talk about. Call if you need me. I'll see myself out."

They said their goodbyes with a hug from Grace and a handshake from John.

Grace returned to the table with the iced teas. "Cheers," she said, then tapped John's iced tea glass. John must have been thirsty because he drank half his tea in one gulp, then moved Barry O'Hara's article into the people-they-knew stack.

While Grace grabbed a few fresh ice cubes and plunked them into what was left of their tea, John read the Tito Zayas article.

The Gulf Coast Independent

St Petersburg, Florida   *Wednesday, March 9, 1938*

El Cuero Club Owner is Shot

Seaport, March 9 - Sheriff Robert Bell today said Evaristo Zayas, also known as "Tito," an underworld figure of Seaport, was murdered in the early morning hours today by two blasts from a twelve-gauge shotgun. He was 36.

As he arrived home, two gunmen hiding behind his porch shot him and fled, according to his driver, who drove him home from his nightclub, the El Cuero, in Old Town. Discarded shotgun shells are the only clues to the weapon used in his murder. Mr. Zayas died on the scene. There are no suspects. Anyone with knowledge of this incident, please contact the sheriff's office.

John then asked if Grace had read the Tito article yet.

"Yes," she replied. "It was a gruesome, cold-blooded murder. So was Victor Hellman's."

She pointed to Victor's article. "They were both assassinated—like there was a personal agenda. Whoever killed Victor was furious about something, whereas Tito's murder seemed like he was put down—like a bad dog."

John studied the Victor Hellman article.

The Gulf Coast Independent

St Petersburg, Florida   *Wednesday, April 20, 1955*

Underworld Gangster Murdered

Seaport, April 20 - Sheriff Ed Black said the body of 75-year-old Victor Hellman, of Old Town, Seaport, was found in his home today, the apparent victim of homicide. He was discovered by his wife, who had just returned from a trip. The retired gangster suffered multiple stab wounds, his throat was slit, and his head flattened by a bloody baseball bat found nearby.

Hellman, the son of a former mayor of Seaport, began a life of crime selling drugs in the 1920s. He became known for operating a majority of Seaport's illegal Bolita lottery games. Over the years, the authorities suspected him of bribery, theft, murder, kidnapping, extortion, and prostitution, but witnesses never testified against him.

The sheriff's office suggested Mr. Hellman may have known his assassins, as he often entertained friends late at night with alcohol and cigars. There was no sign of forced entry.

Unsolved Murders

An investigation is underway. The police say they have no clues to his killers. The deaths of two of Mr. Hellman's closest friends remain unsolved. Tito Zayas was murdered outside his home in 1938, and Stanley Hunter was murdered in his parked car outside a hardware store in 1943.

Sheriff Black asks that anyone with information contact his office. Mrs. Hellman offered a $10,000 reward for information leading to the arrest and conviction of those responsible.

"Hmm. Victor Hellman was best friends with Tito, yet they were murdered seventeen years apart. It's hard to connect murders committed that far away from each other," John speculated and continued reading. "Seems Victor Hellman was also a close childhood friend of Stephen's grandfather, Stanley Hunter."

John then drank the last of his tea and pushed away from the table. "Let's come back to these in a little bit. Meanwhile, I want to search Ray's bathroom. Be right back."

Grace picked up their empty iced tea glasses and took them to the kitchen, thinking about who would have known those people all those years ago.

Seconds later, John slid into his chair. "Got any fresh ideas?" he asked.

"There might be some old timers at church that would remember that far back in Seaport's history. I'll talk to Natalie about it tomorrow," Grace suggested.

"Good idea. Let me know what you learn. Now... I'm puzzled. Why are there no trash cans in Ray's bedroom or bathroom?"

"It's one of his eccentricities. He saves his stuff in a paper bag, and when he's home, he takes all the household trash to the outside cans every night. When I asked him why, he said, *'It's my thing, it's what I do.'* I accepted it as normal behavior after that."

John glanced away, then back at Grace. "Can I ask you a delicate question? And please don't answer if it makes you feel uncomfortable."

Graze froze. Her mind went in all directions. "I... I... suppose."

"How long have you and Ray slept separately?"

A deep sigh escaped as she gathered the right words. "When Patty and Merry were eighteen months old and into everything, I had no time to pay attention to Ray. He was hardly around anyway. For all intents and purposes, I was a single wife and mother. One day he just moved into the guest bedroom, which truthfully, was an enormous relief to me."

"Let me guess. The padlock was to prevent the girls from finding his guns?" John asked.

Grace nodded. "That's what he told me. Now I feel stupid for not asking more questions. I should have demanded a key to that padlock. I should have known about that trunk. I'm still stunned that there's $20 million in it."

John offered his hand. "Speaking of which, I think we should secure the trunk in case your daughters return before you decide what to do with the guns and money."

After they packed everything back into the trunk, locked it, and closed the door to the room, John put the trunk's key in the palm of Grace's hand and closed her fingers around it, telling her to keep it safe.

John's eyes always seemed to sparkle when he smiled. "Let's take a break from all this tough stuff. I'd love to hear more about your daughters."

John's request was so sweet, Grace's face lit up. "Wait until you meet Patty and Merry—fiery red hair and crazy curls I'm always trying to tame. Give me a second."

When she handed him a picture of them, arm in arm, their freckled faces filled with joy, he studied it longer than most people would. "They're twelve? When were they born again?"

"Valentine's Day, February 14, 1968. I adopted them when they were only a few days old. Ray was out of town and boy, was he miffed when he returned looking like death warmed over and found two infants he didn't expect in his house. Plus, a bunch of church ladies carrying all kinds of baby paraphernalia in and out."

He handed the photo back. "Sounds like Ray had an unusual homecoming."

Grace chuckled. "That wasn't the only unusual thing. The babies came with an odd gift from their birth mother, as well."

"Go on." John encouraged her.

"I never met her, but she gifted each baby with their own Barbie doll, complete with a custom-made, full-length Lilly dress. My girls love that fabric so much they asked for Lilly bathing suits for their birthday this year. Put your sunglasses on and come see their bedroom."

John followed Grace past Ray's room, and the laundry room, to the end of the hall. She stood back as he took in the girls' room with its neon hues of yellow, pink, green, and orange. "It's all their doing, "Grace said, "except for my grandmother Martin's quilts at the end of their beds."

"I see what you mean about the sunglasses," John said, laughing, but stopped when he spotted the brightly dressed dolls lying on Patty and Merry's pillows.

"You're right." He turned to Grace. "These dolls are very personal to their birth mother. She's influenced them without ever meeting them."

Then he shook his head and changed the subject. "When did you eat last?" he asked.

Grace blushed. "Early this morning? I hope my stomach hasn't been rumbling loudly."

"Come on," he said, "I'll poke around your kitchen and fix us a little something. Okay?"

And just like that, John headed to Grace's kitchen while she trailed behind him.

"There's sandwich meat and salad stuff in the fridge. Help yourself. I'm going to freshen up," she announced and headed to her room.

John asked over his shoulder. "Are you a mayo, ketchup, or mustard kind of gal?"

"Mayo," she replied, shutting her bedroom door.

By the time she returned, John had two plates stacked with turkey sandwiches, chips, and a couple of Cokes on the table. Grace was so famished, she wolfed hers down in minutes, pushed her plate aside, and thanked him, but she was grateful for more than the sandwich.

The reality of the situation hit her full force. Her friends were caring for her daughters, so this man could help her unravel what was going on in her very bewildering life, married to a man she obviously didn't know.

With a slight tilt of his head, John leaned in closer; his eyes locked onto hers.

"It's been a stressful day for you, with so many unanswered questions. I'm here as your friend, so whatever we learn, for now, it's off the record unless Ray's involved in something illegal. Then it may have to be reported. I think we should discuss what to do next."

The seriousness of John's words hit her, unleashing tears that had been building all day.

Twenty-four hours ago, her husband had walked out with a cryptic goodbye. She then found all kinds of baffling things in his bedroom, along with some disgusting things, not to mention all that money. Her life was uncomplicated and normal two days ago. Now she didn't know what the hell was going on or who she was married to. It was unnerving not to know what to do next. She felt so damn foolish, so stupid—head-in-the-sand kind of stupid. Everything was confusing. She was grateful John was there to help her figure things out.

John sighed and reached across the table for her hand. "I'm sorry, Grace. Take a minute and breathe, honey."

Grace couldn't look at him. Crying was something she rarely let herself do. When the tears came, they were ugly. She didn't want him to see her like that. Grace just needed a few minutes to wash away the day's stress. "I'm going to grab a hot shower. Will you excuse me?"

When she returned, wearing comfortable pajamas and a light robe, John had cleared the table and was relaxing on the sofa. He patted the seat next to him, his eyes filled with kindness.

"You smell nice," he whispered as she sat down. Sensing she was still stressed, he pulled her close and held her until she relaxed.

"Thank you," Grace whispered and moved away, grateful for his reassuring embrace.

"Believe me, it's my pleasure," John said, his voice warm and steady.

Grace felt safe with John there and realized she didn't want to be alone, so she dared ask him if he would mind staying for the night and sleeping on the sofa.

"Don't you worry. I've no intention of leaving you by yourself tonight. I'm fine sleeping on the sofa. I'll make a phone call and ask for some of the vacation days my boss has been begging me to take. We're going to figure this out together," he reassured her.

Grace's throat tightened. "You know, I want answers, but I'm struggling. Honestly, I hope Ray has left us for good."

John's warm hand held hers. "Don't beat yourself up. It's understandable for you to feel that way." He tipped her chin up so he could see her eyes and said, "One thing I've learned in my career is that everyone has secrets. Some secrets are kept to protect others, while some protect the person."

John meant well, but Grace stiffened. "Keeping secrets from me seems to be the theme of my life," she replied. "First, my mother wouldn't talk about my father's death or why we moved out of our lovely home into a tiny apartment. Then, before Stephen died, he was moody and withdrawn. Now it turns out Ray has a ton of secrets too. I'm so sick of it."

Her eyes were stinging as she held back another round of tears. Scooting to the edge of the couch, Grace took a deep breath and lowered her voice. "Before we finish up for the night, I'd like a cup of herbal tea. How about you?"

"Yes, I would love one," he said, as she headed to the kitchen.

When she returned with two hot mugs of chamomile, John was at the dining room table, studying Stanley Hunter's unsolved murder newspaper article. Thanking her, he blew on the tea, took a sip, and put it down. "Did you ever meet Stephen's grandfather?" he asked.

"Yes, long ago. I was around fifteen."

Grace's tea was still too hot, so she put hers down too and explained, "About a dozen of us were on St. Peter's Church's Cemetery Beautification Committee. It was made up of the elder and youth groups; we met on Saturday mornings to pull weeds and plant flowers near the headstones. Mr. Hunter and I often ended up working together."

Adjusting his position, John moved his chair, crossed his legs, and concentrated on her memory of that time long ago.

"Mr. Hunter had lots of stories about Seaport in the old days. According to him, our town was like the Wild West. He told me it was a tough time with some rough people and he grew up with them all. When one of his friends turned to crime, he had to break off their friendship."

"Old Seaport had an interesting history," John said as he took a sip of his tea.

"This one time... Stephen's grandfather and I were tending his wife's grave. He told me about building this house before they got married. She rode her father's horse over one day and suggested adding a covered front porch to provide an outdoor room in the winter when the weather's wonderful."

After a sip of tea, Grace paused and leaned back, remembering some other things Mr. Hunter had told her. "He explained earlier in the century, most houses were left unpainted, but his wife insisted he paint it white, saying, 'If you honor a home by making it beautiful, it will honor the people who live there.' Mr. Hunter and Stephen always repainted this house white until Ray changed it to mocha brown after we married. I figured—new husband, new paint job."

John didn't interrupt as memories came flooding back. "Mr. Hunter was a nice, white-haired old grandfather with a friendly smile, proud of his grandson, Stephen, and shared pictures of him dressed in his Navy whites."

John nodded and recrossed his legs.

"When I was around sixteen, Mr. Hunter and I had a picnic lunch in the church's memorial garden. It's in the rear where the enormous oak trees shade the benches."

"Yes, I've been there before," John said.

"The benches have plaques with people's names inscribed on them. Mr. Hunter pointed out that our bench plaque was engraved with his son and daughter-in-law's names."

John nodded again.

"Mr. Hunter knew my dad died when I was younger and told me his son and daughter-in-law were killed in an automobile accident years earlier. To cheer us up, he asked if I'd like to go to the picture show with him sometime, his treat. We set a date, but he wasn't there that night. The next day, I found out someone had killed him."

John uncrossed his legs and sat up straight, a bit surprised. "Does an old man inviting a young girl to the movies seem normal to you?"

It was Grace's turn to be taken aback. "I liked Mr. Hunter and trusted him, so why not?"

John's voice changed to investigator mode. "Was your mother aware of your plans to meet Mr. Hunter?"

"That I remember. She never told me anything or took part in anything I did, which made me angry. I didn't tell her on purpose. Even when Mr. Hunter was murdered and everyone was talking about it, she didn't mention it."

Grace's tea was perfect, so she took a moment to enjoy it before she continued. "When I met Stephen, he was on leave from the Navy to attend his grandfather's funeral. I haven't read Mr. Hunter's article in years."

John slid it over.

The Gulf Coast Independent

Seaport, Florida   *Friday, November 12, 1943*

Murder of Local Business Owner Sparks Questions

November 12 - Seaport Sheriff Cal Pepper today said the body of 68-year-old Stanley Hunter was found dead in his car in the parking lot of the Calusa Heights Hardware Store early in the morning of Wednesday, Nov. 10. Police believe he died the previous evening from a puncture wound to the head. No weapon was located. According to the police, there were no signs of a struggle. The hardware store employees found Mr. Hunter slumped over his steering wheel when they arrived for work. An investigation is underway. Police have no suspects.

Hunter was the owner of Hunter Trucking. His wife, son, and daughter-in-law predeceased him. His grandson, Stephen Hunter, who is currently serving in the U.S. Navy, survives him and has been notified.

A longtime resident, Stanley Hunter, born in Seaport in 1875, was instrumental in the area's growth. He was often seen with Mayor Hellman, and his son, Victor Hellman, a childhood friend.

The Pastor of St. Peter's Community Church reported the funeral services will be announced at a later date.

When Grace finished, John asked her what she thought about the article.

"It's another unsolved murder that falls into the assassination category, much like Tito and Victor. However, unlike Tito and Victor, it seems to me this murder probably involved one killer who had a job to do. The police told Stephen an ice pick would make that kind of puncture wound. We never understood why someone would kill his nice old grandpa."

"Didn't Stanley Hunter tell you when he was a boy he knew all the tough people in Seaport's criminal world? Maybe he had secrets that got him murdered."

John had a point. It was something that hadn't occurred to Grace or her deceased husband, Stephen. Everyone in the community had liked Mr. Hunter.

John went on. "Despite Mr. Hunter's upbringing, he built a successful trucking business that's still going strong under your care."

John was being nice, but Grace had to set him straight. "I own sixty percent of the company, but I don't manage it. Ray does. There's an answering service for the phone calls and independent contractors for our local jobs. He drives all the cross-country contracts because he doesn't trust anyone with his precious Peterbilt semi. He even had it custom-painted hunter green."

John placed Stanley Hunter's article next to Barry O'Hara's.

"We don't need to review Stephen's article." He pushed it away, hesitated, then pulled it back, and looked at Grace with sadness in his dark eyes. "I'm sorry I couldn't be here for you after Stephen died. It must've been difficult."

Until now, Grace had never thought about it. "Where were you, John?" she asked.

He looked down at the table and took a deep breath. "I was undercover for the Palm Beach Sheriff's Office, working on a drug sting that lasted two years."

John's eyes met hers. "When the case was over and I could finally contact you without jeopardizing both our lives, it was too late. I learned you'd married Ray." There was that sad look again.

"I'm just glad you transferred back to our coast," Grace murmured.

"Unfortunately, it was under terrible circumstances. A Seaport detective friend of mine was murdered, so I filled his position, hoping to discover who did it. I have an idea, but can't prove it, which is very frustrating."

"I'm sorry about your friend, but glad you're here," Grace said.

"Thank you," John said, pushing Stephen's article to the side. He then hauled out another one and pivoted it so Grace could see it.

"Let's look at the young man, Ramón's, obituary. Refresh your memory and tell me what you learned from it."

Grace took a second to scan it.

"The blackened-out date grabbed my attention right away. Who did it, and why was it scribbled out? Natalie suggested maybe it was done in anger. This is when I first learned about the boy and his mother, plus a town in West Virginia with Ray's last name. And the boy's funeral was the same day as my girls' birthday party. I'm still trying to digest this new information."

Grace turned the obituary around. "And you? What did you notice?"

John took a moment, choosing his words. "This young man's mother lived here in Seaport before she moved to Denver. She's wealthy or has financial support. A boy who is this active in sports needs a great deal of athletic equipment to practice and compete, especially if he excels. Someone with money paid for it and took him to those events."

Sitting back, he crossed his arms and focused on Grace.

What John said conjured up memories for Grace of taking her daughters to their practices and the happy day she bought them their tennis racquets. Her stomach flipped, thinking about how she'd feel if something happened to them.

"That's true. I hadn't considered it that way," she said.

He leaned forward and searched her eyes before he continued. "Plus, you don't receive a full scholarship to a blue blood school like Notre Dame without also being brilliant, along with being talented." John took a breath and tapped Ramon's obituary and the newspaper report of his accident. "I see a well-loved and nurtured young man who was critically injured doing one of his favorite things. It must have been horrible for his parents."

He picked up his cup, drained it, and put it down with a small thud. He covered Grace's hands with his own, his voice now almost a whisper.

"That gifted boy," John paused, his eyes dark with meaning, darted back and forth with her own, "had a fabulous future and left two grieving parents behind."

Tears welled up. Grace's chest tightened. "I am so lucky that it wasn't me."

She swiped her tears away and cleared her throat a few times. "You're right, of course. He must've been... a wonderful young man."

Grace stared off into space, thinking of Ray's self-imposed imprisonment and how horrible the boy's mother must be feeling. Then she remembered something.

"John," she gripped his hand, "even though Ray had turned away and was whispering, I think his last call was to a woman. Her voice was loud at first and broke up a few times. After that, I couldn't hear anything. If it was the boy's mother, it makes perfect sense for Ray to say he was coming, especially if he's Ramón's father."

John squeezed Grace's hand and leaned back a little. "Ramón is Spanish for Raymond. Why do you think he had the nickname Rayban?" he asked.

"Probably because Ray only wears aviator sunglasses. One year he offered to buy the girls a pair, but they said they'd rather have pink rhinestones on theirs instead of those ugly boy sunglasses. I bet his son wore them, too."

John nodded. "Makes sense."

"Oh, no!" Grace said loudly, "I've lost track of time and didn't say goodnight to the girls." She excused herself and dashed to the bedroom to call Natalie, who picked up on the first ring and assured Grace she'd put them to bed a half hour ago with a kiss from her.

"God bless you, you're a saint," Grace said.

When Grace returned, John was studying the fragmented receipts. "I can't make out anything new from these. I can only speculate that Ray was in Denver for the boy's funeral and may have traveled to Mexico as well."

"It's been a long day," Grace said, yawning as she pulled out her chair, plopped down, and apologized. "Sorry, I'm not bored. Just tired. Please keep going."

"The Ship's Ta might be a seafood restaurant like the Ship's Table or even a tavern. Once we find that, I hope there's another establishment nearby that sells booze and cigars. Otherwise, I've got the entire country to investigate." John shook his head, knowing it was a slim clue.

"Should you start with Denver?" Grace offered. "You can call 411 and ask about a Ship's Ta something. But why am I telling you this? You're the detective."

John looked up and smiled. "Thanks, but I have a cop friend in Denver. He'll know more than the information operator."

Grace pointed to the kitchen. "The phone cord stretches to the table but it tends to curl, which can be very annoying."

John cleared his voice and took a deep breath, then leaned in. He wasn't smiling.

"All the cash in that trunk points to illegal activities. Just so you know, if your husband's getting paid to transport narcotics, and he's caught, your company and you are on the line too."

Grace's throat tightened and her stomach churned just thinking about what could happen to her and the girls. *Dear God, let this not be true!*

John stopped and looked as if he wasn't sure he should say more.

But Grace wanted to hear it all, no matter how painful it was. Sitting up straight, shoulders back, she demanded, "Tell me the honest to God's truth."

John took a deep breath and calmed his voice. "Trucking companies with excellent reputations are the best method of transporting narcotics into the U.S."

He paused, then slowly told Grace, "I'm suspicious because the interstate that runs south from Denver goes directly to El Paso, Texas. Juárez, a well-known drug crossing, is over its border."

John then tapped the receipts. "These point to Mexico. Every single day, cocaine and heroin are trucked out of Juarez into this country."

Grace nodded, maintaining eye contact, but the thought of her company trucks making that border crossing loaded with drugs took her breath away. Her nerves were ramping up. She wanted to know what the possibilities could be, but this was all the negative data she could take for one day. Grace refused to believe this terrible information.

Her chair screeched against the wooden floor as she shoved away from the table, stood, and asked harshly, "Are you connecting Ray and our trucking company to transporting drugs based on a couple of ruined receipts?" Her voice rose another octave. "That's what you think he might be doing?"

She silently prayed. *Please, God, if I'm married to a dangerous drug runner, my daughters' lives are at risk. Give me the strength to know what to do and where to start.*

John wasn't through, though. He tapped the receipts again. "These put Ray in one of the largest known drug cartel cities, and there's a ton of money in Ray's trunk. If he's getting paid for moving drugs," John scratched his jaw where the stubble of his five o'clock shadow was visible, "it'll be in cash. Better to hide it than draw attention by making large deposits. Especially if he can't prove where the money came from. We need to know what he's up to as soon as possible."

Holy hell. John might be right! There's $20 million pointing to Ray being involved in only God knows what.

Grace's voice was snappy. "While I agree that it's strange to have all that money hidden in a trunk, I'm still not convinced he's using our trucks to haul drugs into the States. Nor can I go running after him to prove it, either. However, there are some things I can do."

John eased his chair back and rose to face her. "Go on."

"I can snoop around my office, check out the financial records, and look for a safe. I'll tell you if I find anything suspicious."

John pointed to the newspaper articles. "You had a good idea to ask Natalie about any elderly people in Mark's church who might recall these crimes from long ago."

"I'll do that too, but John, it's late and I'm exhausted. Let's get you settled on the sofa."

A warm smile spread across his face. "Just show me where you keep an extra blanket and a pillow."

She pointed to the hall closet. "Help yourself."

Tired lines were etched around his eyes and his heavy beard shadow was sprinkled throughout with gray. Grace had no idea when John started his day, but she knew he had to be as tired as she was.

Neither of them said goodnight, but John's gentle expression made her think he wanted to hug her.

She'd been a little rude, so a hug would have been a pleasant way to end their tense day. Instead, he looked down, muttered goodnight, gathered their mugs, and headed to the kitchen.

Alright then, she thought. *He's a cop. I'm married. We're just friends.*

Grace closed the door to her bedroom and was asleep before her head hit the pillow.

She woke up screaming. In her nightmare, Ray was stomping toward her wearing the blood-spattered Army jacket, threatening her with an open switchblade in one hand and an icepick in the other, shrieking, "It's all your fault my son is dead!"

Her heart was hammering as she tried to get away from him, yelling, "No! No! No!"

In real life, John was there in an instant, flipping on her bedside lamp, calmly saying, "You're okay. Grace... Honey, I'm here. Open your eyes."

Slowly, she adjusted to the sudden burst of light, then her surroundings, and finally to him. He was so close. "John," Grace whispered and saw the concerned look in his eyes.

"It's just a nightmare. You're safe," he whispered and lifted his hand toward the side of her face, but stopped and sat on the edge of the bed with only his profile visible to her. "Are you okay now?" he asked, his voice husky, almost cracking.

"Yes. I'm sorry I scared you," Grace said, struggling to pull the blanket up that hung half off the bed.

John realized he was sitting on it, stood up to free the covers, and mumbled, "Call me if you need anything."

Grace thought John was going to leave without another word, but he turned, letting his eyes sweep over her. He reached down, grabbed the quilt, and pulled it over her breasts. His hands were so close to her body, Grace's breath quickened.

"You're so damned beautiful," he murmured and descended further, pausing inches from her lips. John's eyes were dark and flickering in the lamp's light as he hovered. Then, closing them, he kissed her forehead.

"Goodnight, Grace." John clicked off the lamp, left the door open a bit, and returned to the sofa.

Grace's chest was pounding. She wasn't sure, but asked herself what she would have done if he had kissed her. Her brain warned her it was too soon. She made that mistake when she married Ray. But Grace's heart begged to differ. Thirty-four years of friendship was not too soon.

Unless... he thought it was.

CHAPTER SEVEN

Putting Plans Into Action
Grace
April 11, 1980

THE RICH AROMA OF COFFEE WOKE GRACE AND LURED HER OUT OF BED. She ran her fingers through her hair, slipped into jeans and a pink T-shirt, and followed the delicious scent.

John was sitting at the kitchen table with a pen and a legal pad, studying a list. An empty coffee cup with 'World's Best Mommy' blazed in pink letters sat in front of him. He had drawn through a few things on his list already.

"Good morning. How'd you sleep?" John asked with no morning gravel in his voice and continued to write stuff down.

Grace couldn't believe John was still there after how rude she had been to him the night before. She asked herself if he was sick of her drama yet. But then he looked up and smiled.

John was clean-shaven and had changed into a thick black wool turtleneck sweater over jeans and hiking boots. *Handsome. No other word for it.*

A long, dark gray down parka hung over the back of his chair, with a knitted scarf thrown over one shoulder.

"Coffee," she croaked and headed to the kitchen. With her mission accomplished, she returned with another 'World's Best Mommy' cup, but this one blared it in blue. "No more nightmares, thanks to you. When did you go home?" she asked.

"Earlier this morning. I swung by my apartment for a shower and some things I might need in Denver."

"Well, that explains your sweater and that winter coat. It's probably freezing in Denver."

John pushed his yellow legal pad over so Grace could see the names of airlines and their Friday morning flight information. He pointed to one that was circled.

"This one leaves shortly. Do you mind taking me to the airport?" His eyebrows were raised, his dark eyes hooking her again. "It's faster to leave my truck here than drive home and take a cab. Don't know how long I'll be gone, so I'm not keen on leaving it at the airport."

John smelled wonderful. Fresh and clean.

Lord, please let this caffeine kick in soon.

"I'd be happy to," Grace replied with her elbows on the table, hands surrounding her warm cup. Then she looked straight at him. "But you don't have to do this, you know."

"We'll both rest better if we know what Ray's up to." John's determined voice told Grace not to argue. Then he lightened up, grinned, and added, "Besides, all good detectives are basically nosy."

"Okay, Mr. Nosy. Other than a ride to the airport, how else can I help you?"

"I need a photograph of Ray if you have one."

His smile is as delicious as my coffee.

"I do, I'll get it for you. But what about your job?"

"I spoke to my supervisor last night. He gave me the week off. And I called my detective friend in Denver, who has a few ideas we can check out."

John looked at his watch, then checked his wallet, flipping through his credit cards.

Oh my gosh—he's also planning to pay for his expenses! Not gonna happen.

"I insist you take two of those bundles to cover your expenses. I know it's a lot of cash, but you don't know what you might come up against. Since this is *my* house, it's my money."

Grace tried to seem lighthearted, but her voice sounded a little bossy, at least to her.

"I've never accepted $100,000 from a lady before breakfast," John teased, his grin priceless. "But, for you, I'll make an exception this one time. Thank you. I'll be careful with *your* money."

He stood, offered his hand, and pulled her up to his chest, just like he did the day before. Holding her hand next to his heart, she felt the scruff of his wool sweater as they stared at each other. A moment of silence reminded her of last night's sweet confusion.

John then mumbled, "Let's go."

Go?

His wry smile and twinkling eyes returned.

"Open Ray's trunk again."

As Grace merged onto the interstate toward the airport, John unexpectedly asked, "Why did you marry Ray?"

She was taken aback and thought of how to answer his question, which he interpreted as having offended her.

"I'm sorry, Grace, that's none of my business. Please forget I asked."

"It's okay, John. I've asked myself that many times, but I don't regret it. I have Patty and Merry to show for that decision."

Since they had another twenty to thirty minutes of travel time, depending on traffic, this was as good a time as any to talk about it.

"After Stephen died, I was scared and alone. Then one day Ray showed up. From that moment on, he took care of me and spoiled me. For the first time in my life, I didn't have to worry about money. Even though there was no fire between us, I felt safe and chose security over passion."

Grace checked her watch. Two more exits to the airport. They were making good time.

"After a while, security wasn't enough for me. Volunteering wasn't enough, nor was reading every recent novel that hit the library. I asked Ray if I could help him at the office. He had everything under control and didn't need me. He told me to find something I'd like to do and make it happen."

"Is that when you started adoption proceedings?"

"My motherhood clock was ticking away. I was running out of time. So yes."

I'm sure not going to tell John I forged Ray's signature on the adoption forms and got Pastor Mark's secretary to notarize them.

"What happened after that?"

"Ray stayed away on his so-called business trips for longer periods of time, never sharing information or even checking in with me. When I questioned him, his answers were always, 'I've got this. You don't need to worry about it.' He was secretive even then. I'm ashamed of being so naïve. I should've pressed him for answers."

John checked his watch. "If you don't mind me asking, why didn't you change your last name when you married Ray?"

"Ray said it would be easier if our legal names reflected the name of our company when we borrowed money to purchase new trucks. Also, I admit, I just didn't want to go through all that trouble."

Grace took the airport exit and minutes later, pulled over at the departure area. John squeezed her hand and promised to call her after he knew something. He smiled reassuringly, stepped out of the car, and pushed through the airport doors with his bag and coat thrown over his shoulder.

As Grace pulled back onto the interstate, a flood of questions hit her. Discussing her acceptance of Ray's secrecy opened a door into her past. One she'd not explored for a long time. She asked herself why it seemed natural to accept Ray's evasive answers.

A little voice inside her whispered, *Your mother conditioned you not to ask questions because you'll never get answers.*

Well, Grace was asking now. Where did the $20 million come from? If Ray was involved in something illegal, did he hide the cash in his bedroom under the guise that being a family man would keep it protected?

Someone gave him that cash. If they wanted it back, maybe they'd check the company's office first, but her home would be next. What if they broke in while her girls were there?

Oh my God! I need to get that money out of my house as soon as possible.

As Grace pulled into her driveway and turned off the ignition, her mocha brown home, a color she didn't select, stared back at her. Grace's head was clear. She knew what she wanted to do and how she would do it.

God, if You help those who help themselves, today I'm taking back my power.

Grace tossed her purse on the table, headed straight to her bedroom closet, and pulled down an old jewelry box stored on the top shelf. Stephen's keys were lying under some shell necklaces she should've thrown out long ago. Along with her house key and a larger key she hoped would still open the front door of the Hunter & Lewis Trucking building, there was also an antique key with long, funny teeth that Grace didn't recognize. She dropped the keys into her purse and headed to the phone to make her first call.

CHAPTER EIGHT

Following the Clues
John
April 11, 1980

FLYING ALONE GAVE JOHN TIME TO EITHER THINK OR CATCH UP on some sleep, provided the person next to him wasn't chatty. Thank goodness his seatmate had his nose stuck in a Robert Ludlum paperback as the flight attendant instructed everyone to raise their tray tables.

John's direct flight was just short of four hours, which put him in Denver around lunchtime. It would be three hours earlier when he landed, making it breakfast time, again. Fingers crossed, the extra time he gained would help make it a very productive day.

He got little sleep after Grace's blood-curdling scream last night. His libido shot straight into overdrive after seeing her thin pajamas pulled tight across her breasts, her blond hair all topsy-turvy, and her gray eyes wide and vulnerable. He almost blew it. Thank God his training kicked in.

Also, Grace didn't know it, but that Hellman dude was part of Seaport's history. Victor Hellman was one scary guy who pitted his gang against the Mafia time after time. If Ray took part in Hellman's murder, then he associated with some disturbing people. Ray was no one to dick around with; meaning, being too friendly with Ray's wife could get John killed.

John had been an undercover detective for many years and had to admit Ray had skills. He traveled; had a lucrative and legitimate trucking company he controlled alone; had a churchgoing, attractive wife; some charming kids; and lived in a modest home in a middle-class neighborhood. Either Ray was perfect or he had been perfectly hiding something for a long time.

So yeah, John had to be careful. Especially around Grace.

As John exited the plane with his carry-on, he slipped on his down parka and headed outside Stapleton's Airport. A freezing wind slapped him in the face and wrapped itself around his balls. He was shivering his ass off, waiting for his friend, Detective Tom Fisher, to arrive.

Tom was a fascinating character. Raised on a Colorado ranch, Tom was long, lean, and strong as a bull. John looked forward to Tom's wicked sense of humor, which made his eyes crinkle up in laughter. Those same eyes could shoot daggers when crossed.

John and Tom shared a common belief in street justice: let the criminals kill each other so they didn't have to. If it meant breaking a few rules, neither of them opposed that idea either.

Tom was one of the few men John trusted with his life.

Speaking of the devil, Tom's silver Jeep Cherokee pulled up just as John had lost all feeling in his feet and legs. Tossing his bag into the back seat, John jumped in the front, thankful the heater was on full blast. On cue, Tom handed John a steaming cup of coffee he instantly wrapped his frozen hands around.

Tom's white-blond hair was pulled back into a ponytail, which made him look like a surfer dude from California. "Hey, man, welcome to Denver," he said with a cheeky smile. "It's great to see you."

"You too, and thanks for helping me track my friend's mysterious husband, Ray Lewis."

"So, who's this gal you're going out on a limb for, you old dinosaur?" Tom grinned as he pulled away from the busy pickup area.

"Hey, fifty-six ain't that old," John grinned. "What're you—forty-five? You young whippersnapper."

"How long have you and this lady been friends?" Tom asked.

"Probably about thirty-four years. I met her the day she married a high school buddy of mine named Stephen Hunter."

"Wait a minute. Didn't you tell me she's married to this mystery dude, Ray? What happened to your friend?" Tom asked.

"He died from a severe case of the flu. I almost missed his funeral because I was undercover. She was such a mess. I'm not sure she knows I was there. Then, within two years, she married Stephen's business partner. That's the guy we're tracking."

Tom took an exit onto a busy downtown Denver street. "Our first stop is at the Ship's Table Bar and Grill. Did you bring that receipt?"

"Sure did," John said, digging it out of his coat pocket. "It's pretty mangled though."

Tom pulled into a strip mall and parked in front of a restaurant whose front windows were decorated in all kinds of tacky sailing stuff. Their closed sign was on and their inside lights were off.

"Let's check the kitchen entrance, and see if the staff has arrived," Tom muttered as he headed around the corner of the building to the rear of the restaurant.

Lucky for them, a half dozen workers were already prepping food. Tom flashed his badge to the manager and explained the situation. John showed him the receipt in question.

"Nope, we use a small green and white order pad. The one you have is from a cash register, like the ones used in bars and fancy hotels."

They thanked him, hurried back to the Jeep, and waited for the heater to warm up.

"There's a hotel downtown we're gonna check out, but before we head into that godawful downtown traffic, let's drop by the church mentioned in the obituary."

Tom eased back onto the street, passing strip malls lining both sides. John thought they looked the same everywhere. Goods and services, lives spent inside one building doing the same thing every single day. It wasn't for him.

"That's it." Tom pointed to a tall cross off in the distance.

"Speaking of holy institutions, how's your divorce coming along?" John asked.

"Almost final."

When Tom's shoulders slumped a little, John thought Tom wasn't over his wife yet. John knew the feeling. He'd never gotten over losing his chance with Grace after Stephen died.

They pulled into the church parking lot and followed the sign to the rector's office. His secretary, an older gray-haired lady, was helpful and made a copy of Ramón's obituary for them while she chatted about how well-attended the boy's funeral had been.

"Some were college students and one young girl had already started her family. Cute little fella never made a peep during the whole service."

She handed John the copied obituary, which he scanned for the missing date. John's hands shook as he read, "...his father predeceased him on July 1, 1959."

What the fuck? Not expecting that disturbing information, John backed up and leaned against the office door, digesting the implications. All he could come up with was more questions.

Tom asked the secretary a few more questions about the deceased boy's parents, but John was too anxious to stand there any longer and headed out the door. Taking John's cue, Tom expressed his gratitude for the secretary's help and followed John back to the Jeep.

Sitting behind the wheel, shooting questioning looks, Tom waited as John stared off at the distant snowcapped mountains. Tom couldn't know how one little smudged-out area on an obituary would affect Grace. John handed him the obit.

"Now I'm confused. Spell it out for me," Tom rubbed his hands together, while warm air poured out of the vents.

"It means the boy, Ramón Lewis Lopez, is the son of Grace's first husband, Stephen, who died on July 1, 1959."

"Your old high school buddy, right?"

"Correct. Telling Grace that Ramón was Stephen's child would devastate her. She had three miscarriages while she was married to him. They couldn't have children."

"Holy shit. Bummer." Tom shook his head and put the Jeep into gear.

"Yeah," John said, "especially since she's just getting used to thinking Ray is the boy's father. She didn't know about the young man or his mother. Now this."

Tom changed lanes and passed John a slip of paper.

"That is Miz Carmelita Lopez's address. It's close by. Let's go check it out."

The view of the mountains from the parking lot of Carmelita's five-story condominium knocked their socks off. When there was no answer at her penthouse apartment, they tapped on the neighbor's door and learned she moved out—frickin' yesterday.

"Sorry officers, the lady told me she sold the apartment and she won't be back."

Damn. This keeps on getting stranger. Where would Carmelita go and why?

Shot down, they returned to the Jeep.

"At least we know Ray didn't drive his semi across the country. Not in that short of time. He's gotta be storing that big rig around here, somewhere," John said, sliding into his cold seat.

Tom agreed. "Yeah, you don't park those things in any old place."

"Let's rethink this. Grace told me about the upsetting call Ray took from a Mr. Franco that prompted him to leave Seaport immediately. Who has that much power over him? And why Denver? Does he meet someone here who gives him instructions or is it because the boy and his mom live here? Besides moving out of a pricey condo with a stunning view, what else do we know about this woman?"

"All damned good questions," Tom said.

As they chatted, they held their hands in front of the blasting hot air. As soon as John's hands warmed up, he put them over his frozen ears. Tom reached behind John's seat and flipped him a beanie.

"Pink? Really? It's not your color, Tom." John laughed out loud.

"It's my soon-to-be ex-wife's, smart ass. It's reversible, gray inside."

Tom smirked when John plopped the soft, thick cap on with the pink side showing and, trying to keep a straight face, asked, "Does this color make my butt look big?"

"No, but it sure makes your cheeks look rosy."

They laughed as Tom started driving again.

"I forgot to tell you I spoke to my flight attendant this morning about Denver. For cigars and whiskey shots, she mentioned a historic hotel downtown and a ritzy resort in Colorado Springs. Do you know either of those places?"

Tom pulled into traffic. "Yup. The Brown Palace is where we're headed now. It just so happens there's a Ship's Tavern in its lobby. If we're lucky, it'll take us about twenty minutes to get there."

As the traffic thickened, slowing them down, John yanked the pink beanie further down over his still-frozen ears.

As luck would have it, there was a parking space behind a red Mercedes across the street from the Brown Palace Hotel's entrance.

Dashing between the heavy traffic crawling past them, John took in its majesty and commented, "What an unusual building."

"Here's your history lesson for the day: Mr. Brown built this in the late 1800s using red granite and sandstone. Hold on to your britches. Wait until you see the inside." Tom signaled for him to follow.

John's jaw dropped the second they stepped into its elegant interior. The lobby rose eight stories above the ground floor, displaying a magnificent stained glass ceiling skylight. Six stories of balconies overlooking the lobby were crafted from intricately woven wrought iron. Humongous marble columns were frickin' everywhere.

John was fantasizing about spending a few days there with someone special but had to shut that shit down when Tom interrupted his wayward thoughts.

"There's the sign for the Ship's Tavern," Tom pointed left, then right, "and Churchill's Cigar Bar is across the lobby."

"I think we've found our place," John said.

"How about we go undercover? We might get more answers, plus it should be fun," Tom remarked as they made their way through the hotel's regal lobby to the reception desk.

"Welcome to the Brown Palace, Denver's historic five-star hotel," the clerk spouted the hotel's spiel, but John interrupted him and placed a black-and-white photograph of Ray on the counter.

"Hi, I'm John, this is my brother, Tom. We don't have reservations, but we're here for a family reunion and want to surprise our cousin a day early. Has he checked in yet?" John shot him a friendly smile and waited for his answer.

He raised his eyebrows. "Sorry, I'm not allowed to divulge information about our hotel guests."

When John pulled out a thick wad of hundreds, the clerk's eyes widened as John peeled off a few. The clerk's hungry look said he might change his mind... for a price.

John slid three of them across the counter. The clerk's bony hand snatched them and shoved them into his pants pocket. Grinning like a hyena revealed major crooked teeth.

This guy's an orthodontist's dream come true.

"Henry Lee checked in at noon. I suspect he's close by. Let me see something." The clerk scanned his records, then looked up and gave John a knowing smile.

"We have a room with two beds available next to Mr. Lee's room with adjoining doors. Mr. Lee might not know that. It's not his usual room."

Tom's voice came from behind John. "Hey, bro, it sounds like we're checking in."

John shelled out two hundred for the room and told the desk clerk, "If you see Cousin Henry, remember, mum's the word."

Then he pulled off an extra hundred, grinned, and pushed it across to the clerk. "Call my room when you know where he is, so we can... you know... surprise him."

The clerk nodded and slipped their keys over the counter. "Seventh floor, near the elevator. Don't forget to leave the keys at the desk when you check out."

Then he winked and made a click-click cheek sound.

John hated it when people did that. *If they think it's cute, it's not.*

"I'll get our bags from the Jeep and meet you upstairs," Tom said as he scooped up one key and hustled out. John took the nearby elevator up to their room and crossed his fingers, praying he wouldn't run into Ray.

He wanted to talk to Grace before Tom got back, but first, he had to see the view and shoved the curtains aside. Breathtaking snowy mountains off in the distance looked like the famous Albert Bierstadt landscape paintings from the late 1800s he'd once seen in a museum.

John had to admit, the room wasn't shabby with its marble countertops, silver showerheads in the bathroom, and satin bedspread. It was a swanky joint, for sure.

Since the telephone was on the nightstand next to the bed, John sank into the soft bedding and waited for his collect call to go through to Grace. He wondered why he was chasing a guy he'd never met but had envied for almost twenty years.

Other than possibly leaving Grace, which benefited John, the most questionable thing Ray Lewis had done was store $20 million in an antique trunk and stick some red panties and a bloody handkerchief in his trousers' pockets. That was not a crime. Tax evasion was, though, if Ray got that money illegally.

After John hung up from his brief conversation with Grace, Tom walked in with their bags and dropped them on the bed.

"Sorry, the desk clerk flagged me down. Your bribes are paying off. Ray's in the cigar bar with some Mexican-looking dude. I checked. They're still in there."

Tom opened his bag, pulled out a small black gadget, and, with a big grin, announced, "I brought a tracking device with me." He then showed John its controls. "This little four-inch square box is a prototype for a locator called the Predator. The six-inch one is its receiver. My contact in Air Force Intelligence loaned it to me and hopes I return it, but if I can't, they can track it."

He pulled out a small tool from his jeans pocket and headed to the adjoining door. "Let's see what's in Ray's room."

John was close on Tom's heels as he unlocked it.

While John searched the bed and side tables, Tom took the bathroom and closet.

"Well, well," Tom said, hefting a black leather bag from the closet's top shelf. He plopped it on the bed and removed twenty bundles of cash, banded just like the money John found in Ray's trunk.

"All hundreds." Tom grinned as he fanned one bundle.

"At least a million dollars, give or take a few pennies," John confirmed.

Tom commented as he continued his inspection, "I bet Ray is being paid big money to do something that ain't exactly legal."

"What else is in the bag?" John asked.

Tom fished out two brand-new unopened boxes of padlocks and three alternating sets of folded men's underpants and undershirts from the bottom of the duffle.

More locks? John wondered as he ran his hand around the bag's interior, felt a small zipper on the lining's edge, and removed a printed list of Spanish names with puzzling numbers. "This makes no sense to me," he said and handed it to Tom, who studied it.

"Nope, me either," Tom slipped a small notebook from his back pocket. Using the hotel's complimentary pen, he recorded all the information.

Suddenly, the phone rang next door. They left everything on the bed and dashed through to their room.

"Mr. Myers? This is the front desk. Your cousin just left the cigar bar and is walking his friend to the hotel's entrance. I'm watching him now. I'll let you know if he heads upstairs."

"Thanks, man... I owe you!"

Tom quickly turned the Predator on and headed back to Ray's room. As John watched from the doorway, Tom slipped the small tracking device inside the bottom folded T-shirt, replaced everything in Ray's bag, zipped it up, and put it back on the closet's top shelf.

They then locked the adjoining door, gathered their belongings, and waited for whatever happened next. The clerk called two minutes later.

"Mr. Lee has checked out and is headed upstairs to pick up his bag. I didn't want you to miss him, so I told him his cousins arrived earlier, and I gave you connecting rooms."

"You told him we're here?"

Some people can't keep their stupid traps shut.

"Yeah, I did, and he's pissed about something. He just shoved his way through a bunch of guests blocking the elevator."

"Thanks." John slammed the phone down and looked at Tom.

"Grab your shit and let's go."

Bolting out of the room, they flew down the open carpeted stairs to the sixth floor and threw themselves against the wall, just as the elevator dinged one floor above them. A minute later, Ray stomped down the hallway, cursing loudly, and reentered the elevator.

By the time they made it down the six flights of stairs, reached the lobby, and pushed past a ton of people checking in with luggage stacked everywhere, Ray was gone. The desk clerk caught their room keys as they dashed past him and out into the icy afternoon air.

Tom sprinted across the street and had already started the Jeep by the time John jumped in, tossed his bag into the backseat, and crammed the beanie, gray side down over his ears.

"Damn, it's freaking cold," John complained, fumbling with the zipper on his parka.

"Welcome to Colorado in April, my friend," Tom smirked and handed John the Predator's receiver, showing him where to lower its obnoxious beeping sound.

Within a few minutes, they located the source of the signal. It was coming from the red Mercedes they had parked behind.

For well over an hour, they tracked Ray through the heavy traffic moving south on I-25. It was almost sunset when they saw the Colorado Springs city limits sign.

John then noticed the red car had its right blinker on. "He's exiting onto Lake Avenue."

"Got it." Tom then stayed a couple of car lengths behind Ray until Ray's left blinker flashed. "It looks like he's going to the Broadmoor Hotel. That's the fancy resort you asked me about earlier."

Tom followed the red Mercedes up the long driveway to the resort's grand covered entrance, where it stopped. As Tom's Jeep snaked past Ray, they watched Ray step out, grab his bag and hand the keys to the valet, who drove the Mercedes away.

Tom slowly steered toward the exiting blacktop while John watched Ray disappear inside the hotel. They waited with the Jeep Cherokee pulled tight against the curb, engine running.

Fifteen minutes later, Ray appeared, accompanied by a striking dark-haired woman wrapped in a full-length deep brown mink coat, just as the red Mercedes drove up. Ray tossed their bags into the back seat as the valet opened the driver's door for the woman whose long, dark hair draped down the back of her fur.

"Your guy stays in extravagant hotels, drives a fancy Mercedes, and his lady's decked out in a frickin' mink coat. Who are these fucking people?"

"That, my friend, is Ray Lewis, Grace's husband. I'm guessing the lady is Carmelita, Ray's ex-wife, the deceased young man's mother."

Staying four cars behind, they followed the Mercedes north on the interstate back toward Denver.

The sedan exited right onto Fillmore Street, continued for a short distance, then turned left onto a smaller road. Strip centers filled with mom-and-pop businesses lined both sides of the street. Concerned, because no cars were between them, Tom turned right into a tattoo shop's parking lot and pulled into a space with an unobstructed view of the road.

The red sedan turned left into the Mile-High Storage Unit's property and parked on the far-left side of the building. A hunter-green Peterbilt semi with a very shiny grill, extended hood, and sleeper cab was backed along the right side of the building.

"Whoa! That monster's hood's gotta be twelve-to-thirteen feet long!" Tom exclaimed.

Ray stepped out of the Mercedes, popped the trunk, and hurried down the alley into the storage area, out of their view. Within minutes, he returned, dragging two sizable suitcases, and heaved them into the car's trunk. After slamming it shut, he opened the driver's door and helped the woman out.

They had a relaxed, warm conversation, held hands and pointed at the car. Ray caressed the side of her face as he tucked a long strand of hair back under her fur coat. After they talked for a few more seconds, she unwrapped her coat and put her arms around his neck, snuggling her breasts close to his chest. With one arm circling her waist, he drew her in tighter and kissed her deep and long.

That confirmed Ray and Grace were definitely over. Part of John was cheering. Another part still heard warning bells. *Too soon, John. You don't know how deadly he is... yet.*

Ray and the woman looked at each other for a long moment. He unzipped his jacket, drew out a folded shiny red cloth object, and gave it to her before helping her back into the car.

"Damn! If my soon-to-be ex-wife kissed me like that, we'd still be together. That was one helluva kiss." Tom said wistfully as he stared across the street.

"No shit, Sherlock. It's obvious they care for each other."

Ray stood alone, his eyes fastened on the retreating car as if he was searing the image into his memory. Then he strolled over to his big rig and was out of sight as he climbed up into its cab. The diesel engine growled and roared to life, grumbling as it warmed up.

Black exhaust fumes, now turned gray, floated in the air and drifted across the empty field beside the storage facility. After idling for a couple of minutes, Ray put the massive truck into gear, crept onto the pavement, and rumbled past Tom and John, who watched intently.

Tom eased his Jeep to the edge of the parking lot and looked upward through his windshield at the sky. "Twilight's almost gone."

John nodded. "Yeah, it's gonna be pitch dark for the next few nights. It's a new moon."

The semi was at the end of the street, turning right. "Follow him?" Tom asked. "Cause I've got a few days off, and I have my passport with me in case he's going to Mexico."

"How's your Spanish?" John inquired.

Tom grinned. "Hablo un poco de Español."

"Yeah, I speak a little too. Hopefully, enough to get us safely out of Mexico."

CHAPTER NINE

Taking Control
Grace
April 11, 1980

AFTER GRACE DROPPED JOHN OFF AT THE AIRPORT, it was noon by the time she finished moving everything from Ray's trunk into Uncle Robert's storage facility, a ten-minute drive from her house. Once the money and guns were out of her home, she felt safer.

But for some unknown reason, Grace dropped a bundle of cash and the antler-handled knives and brass knuckles into the bottom of her purse before she left her storage unit and headed out to the Hunter & Lewis office building twenty minutes away.

Mr. Williams, the local locksmith Grace had called earlier, was waiting by the front door when she arrived. Grace wanted him there in case Ray had changed the locks, but since Stephen's key worked, Mr. Williams could change the building's locks for her and help look for a hidden safe. If there was one, Grace would wager it was somewhere in that building.

After the locksmith checked Grace's driver's license to make sure she was who she said she was, they stepped inside the building, only to be hit with the strong musty smell of mildew. Near the front door, a receptionist's desk, covered in dust, sat empty except for a two-line telephone. A faded landscape painting hung crooked on the wall behind it. Grace couldn't help herself and straightened it.

Mr. Williams followed her down the hall to Ray's and Stephen's offices. Stephen's office was unlocked and hadn't changed a bit. An empty desk, a chair, and a wall unit housing manuals and books were arranged against the far wall, also covered in a fine layer of dust. His grandfather's rust, blue, and gold Oriental rug spread across the center of the room. Grace had forgotten how beautiful it was.

Mr. Williams headed next door to Ray's office. "Mrs. Hunter," he called, "want me to open this one? It's locked."

"Absolutely," Grace called back and joined him.

Mr. Williams did his magic, stood back, and held the door open.

Facing them was an eight-foot-tall bookcase filled with transportation manuals, maps, and boxes labeled with dates from previous years. Against the left wall was a three-drawer metal filing cabinet. Ray's desk was on the opposite side of the room, with two baskets lining its front edge for mail and paid bills. The unopened mail contained utility bills from two months ago. The other one was empty.

"Shall I change the locks now, Mrs. Hunter?"

"Not yet, Mr. Williams. Help me find a hidden safe that might be somewhere in this building—most likely in this room or the one next door. Check the other office first. See what you can find."

While Mr. Williams did his thing, Grace rifled through Ray's desk drawers, the boxes sitting in the bookcase, and then his file cabinet. Four business-sized, three-ring binder checkbooks joined manila folders filled with bank statements, tax returns, old personnel files, and payables. Grace gathered them and took them out to her car.

When Grace returned, Mr. Williams, a tall, thin man, was on his knees inspecting the bottom edge of Ray's bookcase. He commented over his shoulder, "I couldn't find anything next door, but this bookcase is on rollers, which is unusual. If I can find a latch, it might move away from the wall."

They heard a click as his fingers released something on the backside of the bookcase just above its bottom roller.

"Here we go." He stood and rolled the bookcase forward. Their attention was instantly drawn to a small safe installed into the wall midway up. Mr. Williams pulled the bookcase further away and asked, "If you know the combination, I'll open it for you."

Grace couldn't remember exactly how the numbers on the bottom of Ray's dresser drawer went, but she knew it was Stephen's death date.

"Try seven, then one, then fifty-nine," Grace suggested.

He spun the dial back and forth and shook his head—no.

"Try seven, nineteen, then fifty-nine," Grace said.

He spun the dials again and frowned. "What numbers are you shooting for?"

"I'm trying for July 1, 1959."

"Here, let me try this. Seventy-one, nineteen, then fifty-nine." He smiled and stepped away as the small door swung open.

There wasn't much inside besides a brown, five-by-seven, address looking book, and a small key the locksmith identified as a post office box key, most likely the extra one.

After Grace slipped it on Stephen's key chain, she asked Mr. Williams if he could identify the funny-looking old key she had found earlier.

"It's a very old safe deposit box key from a bank established around the turn of the century. Just that key alone is worth something in antique stores."

"Thanks for your help, Mr. Williams, but I have to leave now. I'd like you to stay and change all the building's locks. I'd appreciate it if you'd bring the new keys to my house. Those locks need changing, too. However, leave this room exactly like it is—open and unlocked."

Grace handed him her address along with $1,000 in cash because she was feeling especially generous.

A quick trip to the post office revealed another two months of unpaid utility bills and bank statements in the box. Grace drove home and added them to everything she took from Ray's office. After she dumped it all on her dining room table, she prepared to make sense of it.

The first thing she paid was the utility bills from her personal checkbook and put them in her handbag, wondering why the lights and water hadn't already been shut off.

Then she tackled the correspondence. Everything was normal except for an annual statement from a bank in Seaport addressed to Mr. Stephen Hunter for the rental of a safe deposit box she didn't know about before now. Most likely that long, funny key would open it.

Hmm, Stephen's been gone for twenty-one years. Someone's been paying this bill the whole time. That someone can only be Ray.

Grace then called the phone number on the annual statement and spoke to a very polite employee in the safe deposit department. The box could be accessed if she had identification that proved she was Stephen's next of kin. Grace's driver's license and Stephen's death certificate were proof enough. She said a silent thank you for never changing her name.

With that established, she found the relevant document in Stephen's death file, tucked it into her purse, and returned to the checkbooks and bank statements. Ray had three accounts at the same bank in Seaport, one of which was their joint account. His fourth account was in Denver. Grace would save that one for last.

Since she used her little pocket checkbook to pay all the household bills, she started with their joint bank account statement, which she never saw. Ray said he deposited $3,000 in her account each month for their household expenses and balanced that account because she was too busy with the girls. Grace expected there to be around $5,000 in her account, give or take a hundred, but was astounded when she saw the last balance.

What! How can there be $100,000 in there? God, I feel so stupid for never checking before now.

Ding, dong... ding, ding, ding... knock, knock, knock.

It was Mr. Williams. He handed her the new office keys, along with several copies of her new house key. Grace set one aside for Natalie as Mr. Williams changed the house locks.

Five minutes after the locksmith left, Mr. Morris, a painting contractor she had made an appointment with that morning, arrived to discuss restoring her house to the beautiful, pristine white it once was. One caveat though, he must start first thing in the morning and finish by Sunday afternoon. Mr. Morris accepted her substantial offer on a handshake.

"My men and their families will be grateful for your generosity. Expect us bright and early tomorrow morning."

Since it was only three-thirty when Mr. Morris left, Grace grabbed her car keys and hustled over to the church, pretty sure Mark would let her use the church's copy machine once she showed him Ray's address book.

When Grace recounted where she found it, Mark agreed to safeguard the original for her and provided the padded envelopes needed to mail out some copies. One copy went to John at the sheriff's office and another to John's home address, which Grace discovered from the telephone book, was only a few blocks away from her home. That explained how John showered, packed his things, and got back to her house before she woke up that morning.

Grace made it to the post office seven minutes before they closed—but in time for a local delivery the next day.

Just as soon as Grace started to second guess herself for running around like a madwoman, she reminded herself about all the stuff boxed up in her newly rented storage unit. Grace knew she wasn't making this up. Ray was not who he pretended to be. The red panties, guns and $20 million proved that.

It was just after five when she pulled into her driveway. Grace was used to busy days, but this one had been a doozy. Her feet were throbbing, her back hurt, and she couldn't wait to kick her darn shoes off.

When she opened the front door, the phone was ringing. Trotting to her bedroom, she plopped down on the bed and grabbed the bedside phone. John was calling collect saying he and his detective friend had checked into the most incredible hotel John had ever seen and confirmed Ray was staying there.

First, Grace recounted her day's adventure of searching the office, finding the safe, and what she did with the address book and its copies. Then she kicked off her shoes and laid back against the pillows, wiggling and stretching her toes.

John approved of how she handled everything. However, Grace bet he wouldn't approve of the third copy she kept for herself or that she had moved the stuff in Ray's trunk into storage.

Not that it was a secret, she would tell John—just not yet. Grace wanted to read Ray's book without John's input, no matter how much she liked him.

John took a deep breath. "Can I ask you something important?"

Grace's dread skyrocketed. "Go on."

"Last night when you said you hoped Ray wouldn't be back. Does that mean you're going to divorce him?"

Grace breathed a sigh of relief. "Absolutely."

"Is there space in your life... for me?" John asked hesitantly.

Whoa, I need to think about this. Grace swung her foot up and took a moment to massage her aching arch.

"Grace? Are you still there?" John sounded worried.

"Yes, I'm here. I've been racing around all day. I'm so exhausted, I can hardly think."

John lowered his voice. "I understand, and I'm sorry if I've pushed you."

Grace didn't want to hurt John because she liked him. And he was doing all this for her. But she knew John deserved an answer.

"It's just that I'm a package deal. It's going to be hard enough when my girls learn I'm divorcing their father. If we... ugh, you and me, see each other socially and... it doesn't work out... I don't want them hurt again. Whatever we're feeling, it needs to go slowly. I hope you understand."

"Yes, I do," he assured her, "and I can wait. It's for the best that I find out what your husband is up to first."

"Could you please refer to him as Ray? I can't bear to think of him as my husband for another second. Thank you for everything you're doing, John. I appreciate it and hope you ask me that question again when all of this is over. Please stay safe and come home soon."

After they said goodbye and hung up, Grace closed her eyes and thought about what she was feeling. *John wants me. I've been fantasizing about this man forever, but now that I know he wants me too, it means being intimate again. It's been so long since I felt desired.*

Grace remembered making love with Stephen when they were trying to start a family and how wonderful it was then. But something had happened and Stephen changed—he came home late, drunk, and nasty-tempered. Grace never knew why Stephen stopped caring for her. Many a night, she wondered if it was her fault that she didn't want to be his lover and lose another baby. Grace had prayed it would get better between them, but it only got worse.

No more fooling myself. Before he died, Stephen was mean and horrible.

The painters arrived at the crack of dawn. Ladders and paint buckets were all over her front lawn as they started their job shouting orders and laughing at each other's jokes.

Around eight, Grace called the girls and learned they were coming over to pick up their bicycles, excited that Mark and Natalie were taking them on a trail ride down to the beach later that morning.

A confusing mess waited for Grace on the dining room table. Once she took a big breath and looked it over, she remembered where she'd left off last night. After pouring a cup of coffee, she was ready to tackle the tax returns, focusing on whether their taxes were filed on time.

All was in order. Hunter & Lewis made a profit each year, but Grace didn't know their attorney and accountant were in West Virginia. It seemed there was a lot she didn't know.

Either Ray worked hard to keep it that way or I'm stupid, which I'm not.

Getting back to the checkbooks, it made sense to match each checkbook with its bank statement. No need to dive into hers. *Already did that. Still not over it.*

The checkbook for the Lewis farm was a good place to start. Five years of check stubs showed payments for farm supplies, taxes, a small payroll for a few employees in the winter, and a bigger payroll in the summer. It aggravated her that Ray had never mentioned owning a farm in Lewisville, West Virginia.

There were a couple of interesting check stubs from the farm account for $10,000 each. One was dated early in 1978 for Jose Sr.'s funeral. The other was dated a couple of months later for Rosa's funeral. *Who were they, and why did Ray pay for their funerals?*

Grace saw that the farm's balance was double the amount in hers. Even though she felt pissy about all the money she didn't know he had and the farm Ray owned, at least the farm was profitable and not going bankrupt.

Okay, so good for you, Ray. Did you buy this farm or inherit it? What does it look like?

When Grace thought about it, she realized people lived there and worked for Ray. People he talked to. Probably often. Jose Sr. and Rosa must have been part of that history.

Where is Lewisville, anyway?

Grace dug through a drawer where she kept the state maps Ray brought back from his trips and left for the girls. Once she found the West Virginia map, she needed a magnifying glass to locate Lewisville. It was due west of Washington, D.C., on the eastern side of the Appalachian Mountains.

As she tried to picture his farm perched at a higher altitude, a memory flashed of roosters crowing and cows mooing. Grace sat back in her chair, closed her eyes, and sensed cool air mixed with the smell of barnyard odors while the flickering image of giant yellow flowers swayed in the distance.

Someone said, "She has your eyes," and then it was gone.

Where did that come from?

After Grace put the map away and freshened her coffee, she continued snooping.

Next was Ray's Denver checkbook and bank statements that showed a balance of $350,000.

What in the ever-living hell? How much money does this man have?

Flipping to the start of the checkbook to see what Ray paid for in Denver, Grace discovered a condominium's utilities and car maintenance bills.

Wait, what? A Mercedes dealership oil change? Ray owns a Mercedes in Denver? He drives a doggoned pickup truck in Seaport!

Grace took a deep breath and reminded Miss Pissy to move on. There were more checks she needed to focus on. Like the one for $2,000 whose memo recorded: "Cash for Rayban's Notre Dame trip." Most likely, they went to Indiana to see the school. A happy moment for them. But Grace couldn't touch that right now, especially with the tremendous amount of betrayal she was feeling, and prodded herself to move on.

Another cash stub for $1,000 recorded the purchase of Rayban's mountain bike, evidence that Ray bought the special bicycle for the boy. As much as she didn't want to, she could relate. The girls were giggling with joy and twirling the brand-new tennis rackets they took hours to pick out when Grace wrote the check. The feeling of losing one of her daughters in an accident punched her right in the chest.

What would I do? Retreat to my bedroom? Growl at anyone who bothered me? Drink like a fish to numb the pain?

One minute Grace was angry at Ray and wanted to strangle him with her bare hands and the next minute she felt sorry for him. Thank goodness, her moment of anxiety was broken by the happy twirlers who rushed through the front door, creating a flurry of activity.

"Mom, we love it!" they shouted together.

"Paint the porch rocking chairs hot pink!" Merry yelled, running through the house.

"No! Bright orange." Patty shouted in hot pursuit.

"Slow down, girls, they're going to paint them dark green."

"Cool." The girls reappeared, swinging their Lilly bathing suits above their heads.

"We might go swimming, too!" Patty yelled, running out the front door.

"We're riding our bikes back to Pastor Mark's house now. See ya." Merry let the door slam behind her as she chased after her sister.

What a whirlwind! Poor Natalie and Mark. Grace chuckled, knowing their household was under siege by her two wild and crazy girls.

Grace took a quick potty break and forced herself back into the books, determined to get through it—today, if possible. She needed her life to get back to normal as soon as possible.

The Hunter & Lewis checkbook had over three years of check stubs in it. The entries were what she would expect: utilities, truck repairs, taxes, and insurance on the house and the office building, plus Ray's salary.

According to Ray's canceled checks, sometimes he deposited his paycheck in the farm's account and other times in his Denver bank. And there was a check stub for that safe deposit box she just learned about. *Well, that answered that question.*

A check stub recorded "CLL" with a big three next to it. Once again, the canceled checks showed Ray paid Carmelita L. Lopez $3,000 on the first of each month. The check memo said: Rayban. When Grace flipped the canceled check over, the back of the check showed it was deposited in the same Denver bank, but to a different account number.

Grace didn't need to look through the past years' bank statements to prove what her gut knew. Based on the boy's age, Ray had given CLL money for over twenty years. Two years before they got married and right after Stephen died. That was close to three-quarters of $1 million he had paid for his other family, using their company funds.

Mister, you played your hand well when you married me and gained control of my business, along with its income. Two can play that game. I've hidden your $20 million and only I know where. Chew on that, you thief!

Grace's emotions were all over the place. She needed a break before she dove into Ray's address book. Figuring the rest of that mess could wait, she shoved the paperwork into a sloppy pile. A few files containing old employee records slid off the table and spilled all over the floor, making an aggravating mess for her to clean up.

One file caught Grace's attention right away. Boldly marked in red on the outside, it read, "Permanently retired January 1, 1949." It was Barry O'Hara's.

The newspaper clippings were nearby, so Grace pulled Barry O'Hara's over.

The Gulf Coast Independent

Seaport, Florida   *Monday, January 3, 1949*

Man Killed in New Year's Hunting Accident

Seaport, January 3 - Sheriff Cal Pepper's office says Barry O'Hara, age 28, of Seaport died in a hunting accident on Saturday, Jan. 1.

An under-aged companion was charged with homicide, illegal possession of firearms, grand theft of firearms, and auto theft.

The police report discloses the minor stole his parents' vehicle and his father's loaded shotgun, which was used to kill Mr. O'Hara. The minor claims he was unconscious stating Mr. O'Hara purchased alcohol for them earlier in the evening and claims he did not know about the shooting. The minor was released into his parents' custody shortly after his arrest.

Mr. O'Hara's parents predeceased him. He leaves behind his wife, Mrs. Natalie O'Hara, age 25. A memorial service will be held at 2 p.m. on Saturday at St. Peter's Memorial Church in Calusa Heights, with Pastor Mark Pruitt officiating.

What kind of man would leave a beautiful young wife at home to hang out in the woods and get drunk with an underage kid who had stolen his parent's car and a loaded shotgun? A terrible guy, that's for sure.

It made sense that Barry O'Hara could be the one Ray fired for stealing. Thank goodness, there was nothing in that news article that connected O'Hara to Hunter & Lewis Trucking.

Grace resolved to talk to Natalie after church the next day if they could find a private place to talk, and wondered if Natalie had any idea her deceased husband had worked for Stephen and Ray thirty-one years ago.

In the late afternoon, Mr. Morris came to the door. "We'll touch up the outside in the morning, then move inside to give all the rooms a fresh coat of paint. Plan on us finishing somewhere around four o'clock tomorrow."

Grace handed him $10,000 in cash, half their agreed amount. "I hope this makes your men happy. See you bright and early?"

After he left, Grace stood outside and admired her white house, thrilled at how well the hunter-green shutters and the matching green porch chairs turned out. *A few potted palms and some hanging ferns will dress it up nicely.*

Grace was sure Stephen's grandfather would be proud. This project might seem like a minor thing to others, but it was immensely symbolic to her. She was restoring order to her life, eliminating Ray's footprint, and spending as much money as she wanted on whatever she wanted.

Screw you, Ray Lewis. Stay in Denver for all I care or go back to that West Virginia farm where I bet your lying, shitty life began.

PART TWO

CHAPTER TEN

How It All Began
Sebastian and Marlene Lewis
Lewisville, West Virginia
1918

GOSSIP AT THE LEWIS FARM WAS ALL ABOUT BERNADETTE, the pretty Irish housemaid with long black hair. She was pregnant, unmarried, and seventeen years old. Everyone thought the baby might be Jack Lee's, a local Appalachian mountain man twenty years older, who called on her a few times.

When she refused to reveal the father, the kitchen staff bet Missus Marlene would dismiss the young girl, but they were mistaken.

Mrs. Marlene Lewis, who was pregnant herself, worried about what would become of the sweet-natured girl if they threw her out into the world in that condition. She'd be homeless with only the gift of finding the elusive ginseng as her sole means of income. Besides, it was comforting to have her nearby so they could share their aches and pains as their pregnancies progressed.

Clara, the Lewis family's elderly semi-retired cook, and the local midwife, converted a section of the basement used for injured farm workers into a birthing area and made similar changes in the master suite. Clara was prepared for the two births. Just not at the same time.

The mid-September morning was chilly, dark, and rainy when Missus Marlene's labor began. Clara tended to her at once, insisting she stay in bed and keep warm.

When Bernadette's water broke later that afternoon, the entire household was thrown into turmoil. Within hours Clara rushed to the basement to help Bernadette give birth to a healthy baby boy she named Henry.

As soon as she swaddled Bernadette's newborn in a yellow cotton blanket and placed him at the girl's breast, she lugged her old bones back up two flights of stairs to the master suite where Sebastian Lewis, Missus Marlene's husband, paced outside the master bedroom's door.

"Mr. Lewis, you are adding to everyone's stress. As soon as I'm sure your wife is ready to deliver, I promise to send for you. Now, please find something else to do. You might go see Bernadette's fine new baby boy, Henry."

Clara hurried back into the bedroom, closing the door as another hard contraction hit Marlene.

Taking Clara's suggestion, Sebastian bounded down the stairs to the ground floor and took the next set of steps that led to the dimly lit basement. Quietly, he moved a small cane chair near the slumbering girl's bed. He stared into the cradle nearby where his innocent and precious newborn son, Henry, lay sleeping, warm, and swaddled in his yellow blanket.

How many sleepless nights had he spent thinking and planning how to ensure Bernadette and her baby have a good life and how to explain it to her? He prayed she would be gone by the time Marlene delivered their child. Or if Bernadette didn't survive childbirth, he wouldn't have to worry about it at all.

"Bernadette." He lightly shook her. "Wake up. I've made plans for you and your son's future."

Struggling to see who woke her, she groggily replied, "Mr. Lewis?"

"Are you listening?"

"Yes, sir." She focused on the ceiling, willing her eyes to stay open.

"I own a cabin on five acres on the opposite side of this mountain. From my farm, it's two miles down the mountain to Main Street. When you get to Main, you'll see Buster's General Store across the highway. Turn left on Main Street, then left again onto the gravel road that runs back up the mountain. It's on the left, about a mile up."

"I know where it is," she mumbled.

"I'm deeding it to you and Henry with the right to gather ginseng on all of my land."

She nodded and closed her eyes.

He shook her again. "The cabin's clean and has some furniture. I stocked the pens with chickens and there's also a dairy cow. You'll find harvested vegetables stored inside the cabin waiting for you. I've given you work tools, feed for the animals, and enough provisions to get you through winter into next year's planting. Do you understand?"

"Hmm, yes, thank you," Bernadette murmured.

"The thing is, you must marry Jack Lee today before I complete Henry's birth certificate. This child cannot grow up as a bastard. Jack likes you and has agreed to marry you, even though he doesn't know who Henry's real father is. Promise me you'll tell no one it's me."

"I promise, Mr. Lewis," she said, and she continued to bat her eyes, trying to focus.

"Bernadette, please assure me this boy will go to school." Sebastian's forehead furrowed as he stared grimly at her to make his point.

She nodded. "I promise he'll learn to read and write."

Sebastian Lewis knew he was in a difficult position and must tread carefully. "I beg your forgiveness for taking advantage of your kindness when my wife was feeling unwell. I hope giving you the cabin and land will reduce your burden."

"Can I... still work here?" Her eyes flew open, staring at him.

He glanced away, knowing it was best that they left. After all, as the boy grew, he might look too much like him.

"After you leave with Henry, I'm sorry, but no. However, if he's injured or in trouble, contact me privately right away."

He scrutinized her young, worried face.

"Mr. Lewis, please don't send us away," she cried, the tears seeping from the corners of her eyes rolled into her hair. "I care for Missus Marlene. Please let me stay and work for her. Henry and I will be no problem. I promise."

Sebastian shook his head no. "My dear, I'm trying to give you a fresh start with a home of your own. I urge you to marry Jack and move into the cabin with your child. Have a new family. Would you do that? For your son?"

Bernadette turned away from him.

Sebastian stood up. "I'll ask the Reverend to be here as soon as possible. Rest until the marriage ceremony. Jack and the Reverend will come down to the basement. You must be quiet and quick."

Without another glance toward Henry, he left.

Believing Bernadette agreed to cover up his deception, Sebastian returned upstairs to the sounds of his wife screaming in pain.

As soon as it stopped, he tapped on the door. Clara, weary with fatigue, shuffled into the hall. "Sir, your wife's labor is severe. I tried to turn the baby, but I'm not sure it worked. We'll be lucky if one of them survives. You must prepare for the worst and pray for the best."

"Can I come in?"

"I'll send for you the minute I think you should come. Go rest while you can." Turning, she hurried back inside as the screaming began again.

Filled with horror that he might lose her and the child, he fled to the guest room and threw himself on his knees, praying for Marlene's life, for their child's life, and for their future together. He prayed Bernadette and Henry would find a life away from him. And he prayed for forgiveness for every damn thing he'd ever done wrong. He wept and turned everything over to his creator.

Exhausted, he slumped to the floor and fell into a deep sleep, dreaming of his wedding day when he married the woman he'd worked so hard to win.

The voice of her stepfather warned him. "Love her, protect her, and never, ever break her heart, no matter what you have to do."

Hours later, Clara tapped on his door. His son had arrived, hungry and wailing at the top of his lungs. Marlene was alive but unconscious.

Clara swaddled the tiny infant in a white cotton blanket and handed him the baby. "Mr. Lewis, take your son to Bernadette to nurse. I will stay by Missus Marlene's side in case she wakes up. But I must sit down before I fall down."

Bernadette, still angry over her earlier conversation with Mr. Lewis, couldn't believe he was discarding her and his own child. How dare Mr. Lewis forget how well she cared for Missus Marlene after Missus lost her third child and fell into a deep depression!

It had broken Bernadette's heart to hear Missus Marlene reject Mr. Lewis from their bedroom so many times that Bernadette couldn't resist wanting to comfort him herself.

Didn't he remember the night he was tipsy, almost drunk, and stumbled up the stairs to the guest bedroom, insisting she must not be there? How she had helped him undress and loved him when he needed it so much? Now he wanted her and Henry, *their boy,* gone from his life?

If she stayed, Henry would have a wonderful place to grow up. He would have a friend, a half-brother, or a sister his age. She wouldn't tell. Sobs tore through Bernadette, and the pounding ache in her heart took her breath away. She didn't want to leave this lovely place. The only place she'd ever felt cared for.

She also disliked Jack Lee. The thought of bedding him disgusted her and it angered her that Mr. Lewis had forced her to marry that stinking old man.

Bernadette was sitting in the cane chair, dressed in the simple white dress she had gotten married in, rocking Henry's cradle, when Mr. Lewis appeared in the basement with a shrieking infant clutched in his arms, swaddled in a white blanket.

"Mr. Lewis, is Missus Marlene alright?"

"She's exhausted, and we can't wake her. Could you feed this little fellow for us? He won't stop crying."

Bernadette sat up straight and stared at him as the baby continued screaming.

"You know I'd do anything for you and Missus Marlene, but Mr. Lewis, you're sending us away. I'm going to need a little more help if me and Henry are going to make it, especially since you made me marry Jack Lee a few hours ago."

"What do you mean? You want money?"

The young girl smiled shyly, "Well, yes sir, that'll help a lot."

"How much money?"

"Five hundred dollars?" She shrugged her shoulders and gave him a questioning look.

Sebastian frowned and handed her the ravenous baby. "I'll bring you the money before you leave."

The baby latched onto her full breast, bringing blessed quiet to the room.

"Thank you, Mr. Lewis."

Holding the baby close, Bernadette cooed to the wee infant and smoothed his dark hair. She pointed to a tiny blue birthmark on the back of his head with a questioning look.

"Yes, it's just like mine," Sebastian Lewis said.

"Two fine sons, Mr. Lewis. Leave him here. I'll tend to him until Missus Marlene can."

"Thank you, Bernadette. Clara or I will be back to get him when my wife wakes up."

When Mr. Lewis was gone, Bernadette thought again about being forced to marry that stinking, dumb Jack Lee. She hated the idea of that lazy idiot raising her son. She didn't feel the least bit bad about asking Mr. Lewis for money. Unfortunately, it might not be enough to give her son all the things she wanted for him. She should have asked for more. Mr. Lewis took her offer way too quickly.

As Missus Marlene's infant suckled at her breast, it occurred to her that if she couldn't save herself from living with Jack Lee, at least she could spare her son from that fate.

That's when she knew exactly what she needed to do.

Clara sobbed when Missus Marlene and her infant survived. It was a miracle. She praised God over and over. Having not rested for two days, Clara's arthritic seventy-five-year-old body hurt all over from the tremendous ordeal. Now that Missus Marlene was fast asleep, and the bedroom darkened, Clara snored, slumped down in a big, overstuffed chair with her feet propped on a soft footstool.

It startled Clara when Missus Marlene woke before dawn, crying out.

"Where's my baby?"

Not thinking clearly, Clara wobbled as she stood up, painfully stretched, and turned on the small dim bedside lamp.

"I'll get him, Missus Marlene. Don't you worry none."

"Is my baby dead? Did my baby die? Why isn't my baby here? I need my baby!" Missus Marlene sobbed.

Clara grabbed the side of the bed to steady herself as she pushed her puffy feet into her worn slippers. "Bernadette has him."

"I want my baby now!" Marlene beseeched her, struggling to sit up.

Bone-weary, Clara, clinging to the stair railing, she hauled her heavy body to the basement, where Bernadette dozed, with an infant at her breast. Another newborn swaddled in a white blanket slept in the cradle beside her bed. Clara picked up the infant from the cradle, lumbered back upstairs, panting and puffing, and placed the bundle in Missus Marlene's arms.

Pure joy filled the exhausted young mother's tear-streaked face as she gazed at the tiny miracle she held. She wiped away the wetness and asked, "Can you find my husband for me?"

The old midwife then shuffled down the hall and tapped on the guest bedroom door to wake Mr. Lewis.

Marlene's bright smile greeted Sebastian when he entered their bedroom. "Darling, meet your perfect new son. See, he has your hands and feet."

She had already inspected every inch of her infant's sweet little body and opened the white blanket for Sebastian to see his naked newborn son. Sebastian took the baby from her and agreed that the baby did indeed have his long second toe and long ring finger. He snuggled the baby in the blanket again, breathing in the fresh newborn scent, and looked for their matching birthmarks on the back of the baby's head. It wasn't there. He was sure the infant he took to the basement screaming at the top of his lungs was swaddled in a white blanket.

Stunned, his heart rate went out of control as he focused on the child he held.

How could he tell his wife that this child, who bore his features, was Bernadette's baby?

If he confessed, it would kill her. He couldn't jeopardize their marriage. No matter what, he promised never to hurt her. He'd do anything. Even the unthinkable.

This day would haunt him for the rest of his life. With no other choice, he laid the babe in Marlene's arms and kissed her forehead.

"Darling, relax for now. I'll be back."

Bernadette woke when Mr. Lewis sat down next to her again. Tears streaming, he glanced at Henry's empty cradle, then stared at his own sweet baby still sleeping beside her, now wrapped in a yellow blanket.

"I'm so, so sorry... Clara mistakenly brought your little Henry to my wife."

She adjusted the baby at her side and leaned up on one elbow, staring over the edge of her bed into the empty cradle and back at him.

"What?"

"My wife believes Henry's our son because he has some of my distinct features. I cannot tell her about you and me—it will break her heart if she learns I betrayed her, even if it was only once. I cannot lose her. She is my whole world."

He broke down, sobbing. Finally, he wiped his eyes, leaned closer, and whispered, "I beg you, Bernadette, safeguard our secret. If I keep your son Henry, yours and mine, and support him, will you take my baby and raise him as Henry?"

Bernadette looked at him in disbelief.

"I recorded this baby's birthmark to prove his lineage and pledge that I will acknowledge him before his eighteenth birthday. You must swear you'll guard him with your life."

Bernadette stared at him wide-eyed in response. She need only play this last part and it would guarantee her son a lifetime of success.

"Oh, God! My baby, my Henry." She covered her mouth as if suppressing a loud, shocking reaction.

"I have tripled the money we agreed to." He handed her an envelope.

She tucked it inside the baby's blanket. "Thank you, Mr. Lewis. Please don't tell Jack about the money."

His eyes cast downward and nodded. "Bernadette, promise me you'll tell no one about any of this."

"I won't tell a soul. You have my word."

He stood and looked at both of them. A young girl with his rightful heir sleeping next to her. He would never forget this moment.

"My driver will bring my car around to the front of the house to take you, my baby, and Jack to your cabin. You must leave as soon as he arrives. I beg you to keep my child safe."

She watched in silence as he lifted his sleeping child, kissed him, wiped his tears, and left his baby to become her own Henry.

She laid back and breathed a sigh of relief. Mr. Lewis was such a good man. It never occurred to him what she'd done. From now on, Mr. Lewis was raising her child to be someone powerful and respected. Her boy would be a leader. She felt it in her bones.

Sebastian spent a few minutes in his study, sitting at his desk, staring into space after Bernadette and her new family departed. Ashamed, it was too late to undo it now. He pulled himself together and returned upstairs.

Marlene, still holding the baby, looked up as he entered the room. He glanced at her, and sat on the edge of the bed with his back to her, fighting hard to keep from breaking.

"Did you name our son?" she asked sweetly.

"Montford Sebastian Lewis. Montford is in honor of your late stepfather."

"He would've loved that."

Lightly tapping his shoulder, she asked, "Shall we call him Monty?"

When he turned, she offered him the baby.

"That will be fine," he mumbled, hating himself.

He took the wrong son into his arms. To do anything else would destroy his marriage.

CHAPTER ELEVEN

Abuse and Wounds
Henry Lee
1922

BERNADETTE ROCKED BACK ON HER HEELS, her apron lap full of fresh eggs, and called four-year-old Henry to bring the wire basket so she could unload them into it.

Together they picked wild fruit to make jellies and jams and threw grain around the perimeter of the cabin to encourage the wildlife to come closer, which allowed them easier access to meat in the winter.

She often experienced tears watching the child she'd stolen grow up in her own child's place, but Bernadette knew her son was safer with the Lewis family than he would ever be with her and Jack. She pledged to teach the boy everything she could to make up for her wrongdoing.

As soon as Henry was old enough, she let him tag along with her into the woods dragging her long-handled sang hoe behind him, while she pulled a small wagon with two baby girls tightly tucked in.

The sang hoe had a pick on one end and a sharp digging tool on the other. Together they dug up the treasured three-pronged ginseng roots and planted their berries nearby, so a fresh supply would always be available. Ginseng was Bernadette's biggest cash crop, other than some herbs she sold to the community for aches and pains, cuts, bruises, and unwanted pregnancies. The hoe also served as a weapon to kill rattlesnakes, which Henry watched her do many times.

1931

Henry watched from the edge of the woods as Pappy, his crazed old man, stinking of moonshine and foul body odor, stumbled onto the broken-down mountain cabin's front steps, hollering, *"git on 'n heah."*

Now that Henry was almost thirteen, he was closer to leaving his godforsaken life. Already tense knowing how shitty Pappy was going to be when he returned empty-handed from checking his possum traps, Henry braced himself for the beating he would most likely get. Unless Pappy was drunk and passed out first.

Pappy gave him a black look, then steadied himself in the doorway before he staggered back inside. The boy hurried up the steps and followed him into the dark cabin, anxious to avoid Pappy's leather belt. Even Maw suffered the old man's buckle when she tried to protect Henry.

Pappy stopped at Henry's two little sisters' room—a single bed pushed against the wall of a closet. The torn length of cloth that stretched across the room's opening hung sideways, exposing the terrified girls huddled and quivering in their stained nighties.

Pants hanging open, Pappy sneered, "Do whatcha told, boy. Hold this 'un down."

Startled, Henry stepped back. His eyes darted to the far edge of the bed where his sisters clung to each other, whimpering as they buried their faces against the wall.

"Now! Ya dumb bastard!" Pappy shouted, fiddling with his pants, and dropped them lower.

Shocked by Pappy's intentions, Henry exploded in a blind rage. Pappy's fist caught him square in the forehead, slamming him back onto the bed. Head spinning, his sight dim, Pappy jerked him up by the arm and hammered him against the log cabin's rough wall until blackness pulled the boy under.

Henry clawed his way back to consciousness through the sounds of his sisters screaming and squinted against the low light. Ma's crumpled body lay on the floor nearby. Henry was lying on his belly, naked from the waist down, bleeding. Pappy was gone.

After that, Henry protected Maw and his sisters by carrying out Pappy's hateful demands. Destroy crops, set fires, arrange accidents, and steal from anyone who offended the old man. His little sisters and Maw's safety depended on him. No matter how hard he tried, Pappy's list of grievances was never-ending. And always dangerous.

The summer before Henry turned thirteen, all the money Mr. Lewis had given Bernadette ran out. She and Jack fell behind on the mounting store debt needed to care for their family. Jack, fired from every job for drunkenness, fighting, and stealing, forced Henry to work part-time at Buster's General Store to pay their debt.

When Henry came to work one day with a busted nose and swollen black eyes, Buster, a kind, older man, asked how it happened.

Henry swallowed and looked away. "Pappy was drunk and... got into a fight with... that pig farmer," he stammered, hesitant to continue.

"Your neighbor? The one who lives across the road and up the mountain from you?" Buster stared questioningly at him.

"Yes, sir, that's him." Henry squirmed in his seat. He hoped to avoid getting into more trouble with Pappy or the farmer for telling on them.

"That man's unpredictable. His fists are like sledgehammers. He outweighs your Pappy by at least a hundred pounds, maybe more. What'd he do to Jack?"

"He broke Pappy's ribs, all his fingers, knocked out some teeth, and bit off half his ear at the top," Henry mumbled fast, pointing to his left ear, watching Buster's reaction.

"God, boy! It's a wonder he didn't kill Jack," Buster exclaimed. "Your poor maw. She must be going through hell taking care of him."

Buster then focused back on the boy. "But how'd you get your nose broken?"

Henry told Buster that Pappy had sent him to the hog farmer's place in the middle of the night to stick the mama sow in the throat with an ice pick, so all her baby piglets would die without their mama. "Then he gave me a real sharp ice pick."

Henry lowered his eyes in shame. He couldn't tell Buster that Pappy would hurt Maw and his little sisters if he didn't do what Pappy ordered him to do. Pappy being laid up wouldn't prevent him from punishing Henry or hurting maw and sisters when he recovered.

Buster shifted a little closer to Henry. "What'd you do, Henry?"

"I couldn't do it, sir. I was so scared, but I knocked on that farmer's door, then ran and hid in the trees so I wouldn't git shot. When that farmer come out, he had this here big ole shotgun ready to blast me away. But he couldn't see me 'cause it was pitch black last night."

Henry trembled, remembering his fear, thinking the farmer would shoot him.

"Go on, son," Buster said kindly.

"Sir, I would've rather dug a hole for that farmer to step in and break his leg or set fire to that farmer's tool shed than kill the mama of them baby piglets." Henry turned red from embarrassment. "I gotta better myself so I can get Maw and my little sisters away from Pappy."

"Does your Pappy make you do those things to folks?" Buster sighed.

Henry closed his eyes. "Yes, sir. But you can't tell no one."

"And your nose?" Buster asked.

"I hollered at the farmer that I jest wanted to tell him why I was there. He grunted. At least he didn't shoot me. So, I yelled out, 'Pappy's a devil. He deserves the beatin' you gave him.' When he pointed his shotgun at the ground, I walked closer and told him what Pappy wanted me to do."

Henry gulped, not sure how to continue.

Buster pointed to Henry's nose to keep him on track.

"I threw the ice pick on the ground and said, 'I need Pappy to think you caught me afore I kilt your sow,' and that's when," Henry's eyes widened, his face white, he finished, "he punched me in the face." When his eyes watered, he looked away and wiped his tears.

"Come on, boy, let's see if I can patch you up." Under his breath, Buster muttered, "And figure out how to get you better protected."

Henry was proud that Buster trusted him to make some of their deliveries, especially when they were the busiest. He longed to explore the world that lay beyond the mountains. Henry hoped one day he'd drive a big truck like the ones that passed through town headed to parts unknown.

This was his first time delivering bulky bags of seed and fertilizer to the Lewis Farm. He'd never met them before but knew they also owned the winery and vineyards that were a ways outside town, which gave jobs to a lot of the local families. Henry was told when he got to the farm to ask for the farm's manager, José Sr., who would unload the wagon.

The heavy smell of manure and fresh-cut hay filled the air as soon as the mare trudged through the farm's opening at the mountain's top.

By clicking his tongue, he guided the horse and wagon off to the left, onto the dirt driveway of the Lewis Farm. Straight ahead lay large fields filled with corn and vegetables. As the horse headed toward a two-story wooden barn built in front of the fields, a two-story white farmhouse on Henry's right took his breath away. He pulled back on the reins, shouted, 'Whoa!' and came to a full stop, staring at the most beautiful house he'd ever seen.

Steps led up to a covered porch. A screened door on the front of the house provided fresh air and kept out bugs. Two white rocking chairs with a small table between them were on each side of the porch. For a second, Henry daydreamed of sitting out there, sipping lemonade or iced tea, with a family he loved, one he was proud of. But it was only a flash of longing for something he knew he'd never have.

The house's grassy front yard faced a thick forest of maple, birch, and beech trees on its south. The property sloped down the mountain's east side, offering Henry a view of the valley below. To its west, beyond the barn, vegetables, and corn, stood the tall green stalks of giant yellow sunflowers with deep brown seed-filled centers. The far-off snowy Appalachian Mountain ridges lay in the background.

Henry's heart sped up seeing where the sunflowers grew. Something stirred deep inside him the first time the flowers were delivered to Buster's. It was something he couldn't put his finger on, but sitting there, watching the gentle golden giants sway back and forth, filled him with joy.

Beyond the fields, on the horizon, more than a dozen brightly painted cabins spread out in neat rows like colorful doll houses. He'd seen nothing painted in bright neon colors of green, yellow, or a blazing red-orange before. It would be a pleasure to live in one of them instead of the cabin waiting for Pappy to arrive drunk and violent. It felt happier here. The Lewis's Farm looked like a magical place.

As the mare eased forward, one trudging step at a time, Henry spied a long gravel driveway running down the east side of the farmhouse, leading to a two-story garage. He shook the reins, encouraging the older horse toward the two-story barn, with doors so tall they could drive large tractors and equipment into it. Buster's horse then quickened her pace and headed straight to the barn and stopped next to a truck parked in front of it. A boy about his age sat on its fender, watching him. Surprised, Henry waved.

The boy, with dark brown hair, jumped down and gave Henry a lopsided grin. His right-side tooth overlapped his front tooth, which gave him a friendly, fun look.

"Hi, I'm Monty Lewis. I live here." Monty's grin prompted Henry to smile.

"I'm Henry Lee. I work for Buster at the General Store. This here's your feed and fertilizer. Is José Sr. around? He's supposed to unload it."

"José's out in the fields. We can visit until he gets back."

"I reckon that'd be all right." Henry jumped down from the wagon, pleased to spend a few minutes with someone his own age.

"All my school friends are vacationing in Europe this year, so it's great to meet you," Monty said. "I'm bored outta my ever-loving mind. I've already read so many books this summer from my dad's library. Adventures are what I want. Not stories about them."

"The woods around here's got lots of things to see. I live on the other side of this here mountain, so I know." Henry nodded to the north, which was behind the farmhouse.

"Ah, here comes José Sr. now." Monty pointed to a short Mexican man who was approaching and quickly asked Henry, "Can we go exploring when you have time?"

"Soon's there's another delivery up this way, I'll tell you about some places we can go if'n you want me to."

CHAPTER
TWELVE

A Friendship Begins
Henry and Monty
1932

HENRY AND MONTY BECAME FAST FRIENDS and were thrilled to learn their birthdays were only one day apart. Monty begged Henry to take him exploring on his family's 500-acre estate and pushed for an easier way for them to meet.

"There's a deer trail that starts at the rear of our garage. Maybe it's a shortcut across the mountain ridge to your place," Monty suggested.

Troubled, Henry shuffled his feet. He knew about it because Maw had forbidden him from using it. Faced with the prospect of Monty wandering down that trail and running into Pappy drunk out of his mind, Henry feared Pappy would hurt Monty.

Henry's heart raced. "No good, Monty. Pappy is mean and drunk all the time. He will hurt you if'n you show up. It's too dangerous. I'll try to hack a bigger path with my machete, but you must never come to me. Understand?" Henry frowned, humiliated that he had to reveal his personal circumstances to his new friend.

"Sure Henry, I don't want to cause any problems."

"Give me a few days. I'll meet you Sunday afternoon out behind your garage."

It took Henry a week, working in his spare time to slash the thick underbrush and brambles away and carve out the safest areas to tread.

After that, Henry and Monty were together as much as possible, sitting on the old log, discussing their dreams and plans for the future.

"What would you like to do with your life?" Monty asked.

Henry was shy at first, but confessed. "First, I'd like to talk like you do, learn manners, and travel to excitin' places. Anywhere, as long as it's away from these here mountains."

Monty smiled. "No problem. I can teach you proper pronunciation and show you how to make introductions. The leaving part you'll have to do yourself. Maybe you could join the service. You'd travel to faraway places then. Let's hope this country isn't in a major war by then, though."

"How about you? What would you like to do, Monty?"

"I want to go on adventures, attend university, marry a movie star, and be a lawyer or a senator someday," Monty added with a cheeky grin.

Henry laughed a single hoot. "I can help you with only one of them things. I'll take you hunting on your dad's land, teach you about the critters in these here parts, and show you where the ginseng grows. Is that adventure enough for you? How about we meet here next Sunday?"

The following Sunday, they headed a few hundred yards back down the trail, then threaded their way into the deep forest that lay west beyond the farm's fields.

"Today we're hunting for ginseng with this here sang hoe, but watch out for rattlesnakes. They like to nest near them plants."

As the afternoon grew warm, the boys trudged through the shady coolness provided by thick trees, stopped to drink from a stream, and relieved themselves in the bushes. Henry identified raccoons, possums, and an occasional deer that scurried through the woods and away from their crunching boots.

"Hold up!" Henry pointed with his sang hoe's sharp cutting end. "See that plant over there plum full of berries? That's ginseng. They're under that big old tree, where a bunch of other plants are almost hiding it. If'n we pick the ginseng, we'll have to plant them berries nearby so they'll grow in the future."

Monty corrected him, "If we pick the ginseng, we'll have to plant their berries nearby to make sure more will grow in the future."

Henry nodded and pushed the crowded bushes away from the ginseng plant with his sang hoe when a furious rattle signaled an imminent strike from the deadly timber rattlesnake.

"Monty, stop!" he ordered and swung his sang hoe high over his head. In a single swift blow, he chopped off the rattlesnake's head with the hoe's sharp end. Then, swinging it again, he cut off its rattles, and, grinning, handed them to Monty. "That evil son of a bitch deserved it."

"Man, Henry, all I knew about ginseng was how much money I'll make when I sell the plants I'm given each year. I didn't know how risky it was to find them. You and that sang hoe thing are very impressive."

Henry just smiled; proud he'd given Monty a true adventure with a trophy to prove it.

Eager for more adventures before he returned to school, Monty begged to see different parts of his father's estate he'd never seen before. That's when Henry took him to a hidden glen where the deer rested near a small waterfall that spilled over moss-covered stones.

Later that day, hot from their long hike, Henry showed him one of his favorite places where a large, flat-topped boulder lay in the middle of a deeper stream.

After they swam in the icy mountain water, they climbed onto it and dried off in the afternoon sunlight.

As the sun lowered in the sky and the temperature dropped, it was time to head back. Along the way, Monty stopped near some spiky red flowers in full bloom and called out, "Wait up, Henry! I want to bring some of these to my mom."

"No!" Henry shoved him away from the poisonous castor bean plant. "Never touch or go near them flowers. They're deadly."

"Damn, is there anything in these woods that won't hurt or kill me?" Monty asked.

Henry shook his head. "You gotta be careful every second you're out here."

Not long after that, Monty introduced Henry to his father, whose face lit up as he shook Henry's hand and peppered him with dozens of questions.

Henry expected to meet a gray-headed, stern old rich guy. Instead, he met a tall, younger man who shared Monty's dark hair and eyes.

"Did you know your mother used to work here before you were born? Everyone liked her very much. But she got married and moved across the mountain. We were sorry to see her go," Mr. Lewis confided.

"I wish I'd known, sir." Henry couldn't wait to ask Maw why she'd never mentioned it.

"Say, I have an idea. We need some help around the farm. José Sr., my farm manager, could use an assistant. Do you think it will offend Buster if I steal you from him? I'd pay you a good wage." Mr. Lewis smiled warmly at Henry.

Henry eagerly jumped at the chance. "I'd love to work for you, but I've gotta talk to Maw and Buster before I accept."

Buster happily congratulated Henry, but Maw's face wrinkled in horror. "Oh, God! What've you done?" she shouted.

"Why, Maw?" Henry was confused. "Mr. Lewis said you worked there a long time ago. Aren't you happy for me?"

"Pappy hates them people with a passion. He hates everybody, especially rich folk like the Lewis family. If he finds out you're working there, he'll beat us both, so keep your mouth shut about them. We don't need no trouble. Pappy's vicious as a rabid dog these days."

"Why's Pappy so mean?"

Maw sighed. "Rotgut corn liquor. It fried his brains. That's why he steals my ginseng money, gets drunk, and fights everybody. Don't go saying anything about the Lewis family around him. God only knows what he might do."

"Maw, Mr. Lewis is so nice. I'm sure he'd give you your job back if you asked him. Why don't you?"

Maw looked stricken, closed her eyes, and sighed. "I did something I ain't proud of, Henry. I took something I shouldn't have. Mr. Lewis knows it's gone, but he doesn't know I'm the one who stole it. I can't face him after what I did."

Bernadette turned to walk away, but Henry grabbed her arm.

"What? Maw, what did you steal?"

She just shook her head. "One day Henry, you'll know. But not now. Not now."

CHAPTER THIRTEEN

Discoveries and Life Changes
Henry
1934

MONTY AND HENRY MET AT THE FALLEN TREE LOG behind the Lewis's garage and were in an animated conversation about Bonnie and Clyde when Bernadette stepped out from the trail. Her hair was tied back with a gingham scarf and her large canvas bag was slung across her worn, thin dress.

"Hello," she whispered.

Henry and Monty leaped to their feet.

"Maw, this is Monty." Henry's cheeks burned as he made a quick hand gesture the way Monty had taught him.

"I know." She stared at Monty.

"Mrs. Lee, it's very nice to meet you." Monty grinned, his lip sliding over the protruding tooth, as he offered his hand.

"It's a pleasure to see you again," said Bernadette as she returned his matching lopsided smile and gently shook his hand.

Henry's head spun back and forth as he realized Maw and Monty knew about each other.

"Thank you for the rare specimen of ginseng you leave for my birthday each year," Monty said. "It always brings a nice profit when I sell it."

"I'm so glad, Montford. It's easy to remember your birthday. You boys were born a day apart. After your mother had a hard time at childbirth, I nursed her infant until she was able."

"Then you aided in saving my life. Thank you for that."

"I didn't think of it quite that way," she winced.

"Maw, what are you doing here?" Henry blurted out.

"Just gathering some castor beans. We might need them soon." Bernadette kept her eyes fixed on Monty.

"Well, Montford," she sighed, "I'll go now. Always be kind... like your parents." She stepped closer, hesitated, then hugged him, kissed his forehead, and left.

Henry stared open-mouthed as Maw retreated down the mountain trail. Perplexed, he turned to Monty, "What the heck was that about?"

Monty smiled. "Every year a mystery person put a special bouquet of rare ginseng roots on the kitchen pie window with a simple note that said, 'Happy Birthday, Montford.' Each year, I asked everyone if they knew who sent the gift, but no one knew. But on my tenth birthday, I got up before dawn, and waited by my upstairs bedroom window, which overlooks that window below, and discovered who left the ginseng. I didn't know who she was then, but now that I've met her, it was your maw."

"Wow, okay." Henry backed away, then added, "Look, I'm glad you're home, but I need to check on Maw. Something's up. I'll see you later."

Henry ran down the mountain trail, watching Bernadette's stooped posture and slow gait. She braced herself with a branch she used for a walking stick. She didn't look well. Pappy made her life a living hell. He couldn't wait to get his maw and sisters away from that devil.

When he caught up, he asked, "Maw, are you feeling poorly?"

"It's nothing, Henry."

He stared at her for a moment, hesitant, "I gotta know why you give Monty your valuable ginseng on his birthday."

"Henry, one day you'll understand everything, just not now. I'm glad you're here. You need to learn how to extract the castor bean poison without killing yourself." She began walking toward the poisonous red flowers.

Henry followed her. "Why now, Maw?"

She turned to him. "Pappy's been acting real crazy. He told his brother to kill you, me, and your sisters if anything happened to him. We gotta prepare and be extra careful now. I think he's up to something."

Henry shivered. "Okay, Maw. Show me what I need to know."

1935

In September, the boys were one week shy of their seventeenth birthdays. The days were growing shorter and the air cooler when Henry and Monty met at the log behind the garage to say their goodbyes. Monty was leaving for his senior year in high school.

"This time next year I'll be on my way to Harvard University. I can't wait." Monty's crooked grin and crinkled-up eyes were filled with delight.

"Yeah, and you'll be closer to becoming a senator and marrying a real-life movie star." They both laughed, and then Henry grew serious. "See you at Thanksgiving?"

"No, not until Christmas. My friend and his family invited me to their hunting lodge in Canada for turkey shooting during my Thanksgiving vacation. But we'll have two weeks together at Christmas."

"I'm counting the days." Henry gave him a wry smile. Christmas was so far away.

When Monty stuck out his hand to shake, Henry grabbed him and hugged him goodbye.

"Early Happy Birthday," Henry said, slapping his back.

"You, too." Monty grinned and said goodbye just as his father's driver's horn signaled from the front yard that it was time to leave. They waved, turning in opposite directions. Monty climbed into his dad's car and Henry began his trek down the mountain trail to the cabin.

Daylight was fading as Henry followed the well-worn path, and imagined what it would be like attending a fancy university. He didn't even know where Boston was.

As he rounded one of the last curves a quarter mile from the cabin, screams of, "Die, you fucking bastard!" came from behind him before something horribly painful crashed into the back of his skull, sending him face down into the hard-packed ground.

When Henry regained awareness, his entire body screamed in agony. The night was pitch black, so he lay still and gradually adjusted to the darkness. He was stretched out on the ground and could feel the rich undergrowth of vines and scrubby bushes near his forehead. His nose was broken again, and choking for air, he was forced to breathe through his mouth. His head throbbed in sync with the pulsing blood flowing down his neck, soaking his shirt. Even the slightest movement caused red-hot pain in his legs and cracked ribs. Unable to stand or even get on his knees, he realized he could use his toes to push and his arms to pull himself forward.

As his thoughts cleared, he blamed himself for not expecting this attack. Pappy had gone berserk when he went to work for the Lewis family, but when Henry refused to steal farm equipment two days before, it had escalated into a screaming match. Henry fled the cabin and avoided Pappy after that. This was his punishment. Pappy intended to kill him.

Determined to live, he mustered bits of energy and dragged himself back up the mountain trail, bound for the Lewis farm. He passed out many times along the way. As he struggled through the night, the roosters crowed as he approached the log. Encouraged someone would find him as soon as the morning light came up, he crawled inch by painful inch through the dirt and past the garage. As he slithered down the gravel driveway, the rocks scratched every open wound on his legs and belly. He pushed and pulled himself into the soft grassy front yard, giving into blackness as the sun rose.

Henry woke up crying out in unbearable agony. An angel with the kindest dove gray eyes murmured words of compassion he strained to hear through the ringing in his ears. Sure he was dead, Henry labored to see the heavenly spirit with light brown curls falling around her divine face.

Mr. Lewis kneeled next to the beautiful angel. "Who did this to you, son?"

"Pappy," Henry mumbled, slipping into darkness again.

"Sleep, the doctor is coming."

Henry spent the next several days in and out of consciousness as the doctor shaved and wrapped his head, packed his nose with gauze, bound his cracked ribs, and splinted both of his legs. Multiple-colored bruises soon surfaced over his entire body. He was spoon-fed broth and water, and when the laudanum ran out, they used whiskey to dull his pain. Throughout this time, someone sat with him around the clock, never leaving his side.

Late one evening, Henry came to as a soft hand felt his forehead, and whispered, "the boy is sleeping." As Henry squinted through swollen eyes, Mrs. Lewis tiptoed across the room and joined her husband. They sat in front of the fireplace, in high-back chairs, facing each other with their knees touching. Although straining, he could just make out their conversation and gestures.

"What will happen to the monster who did this, Sebastian?" Mrs. Lewis whispered.

"After Henry recovers, I'll help him take his revenge. Meanwhile, it's all I can do to stop from killing Jack Lee myself."

"Monty's friend is Bernadette's child?" she asked as she gripped his hands tighter.

"Yes," his voice faltered.

Before he could say more, Marlene stopped him. "No, wait, Sebastian. I've thought about what happened the night I gave birth to our child. As I slipped in and out of consciousness, Clara continued praying we would live. After the baby came, she was sobbing as I fell unconscious again. When I woke and the baby wasn't there, I was sure Clara wept because our baby died."

Her voice broke as she recounted that heartbreaking memory. "I remember screaming for my baby, not knowing if we had a son or a daughter."

Her voice dropped as she focused on their clasped hands. "When Clara said he was with Bernadette, I was sure you persuaded her to allow us to raise her illegitimate child, but when Clara brought me the baby and he had your features, I was relieved to know our son had lived."

Her shoulders slumped as she turned to gaze into the fireplace. "Until..."

"Darling... don't," he began.

Marlene lifted her hand to stop Sebastian from saying more.

"Even though Monty had your hands and feet as he grew, well, he also had Bernadette's crooked smile. Part of me knew the truth then... that Bernadette's child is also your son, but I pushed it away. I was happy to have Monty, despite knowing you had deceived me."

Sebastian sat with his eyes tightly closed and a pained look on his face.

Marlene continued with a lowered voice and pointed across the room to where Henry lay, not knowing he was listening. "This boy's birthmark matches yours. He's the same age as Monty. He's our son, isn't he? Clara accidentally switched the babies, yet you said nothing."

Crestfallen, Sebastian stammered his excuse, "Darling, I wanted to tell you, but... but I didn't know what else to do." He stared into the crackling fireplace as a piece of wood settled, spewing its fiery ashes.

"Tell me now, my darling," Marlene whispered.

"I never meant it to happen." He lifted his head to meet her bewildered eyes. "Darling, you were severely depressed over miscarrying for the third time, and I was out of my mind worrying I would lose you. I longed to hold you, but you were so grief stricken you wouldn't let me touch you." He paused, searching her face.

"Bernadette, who adored you too, gave me her compassion. Once, my darling... only once, and I'm so ashamed. I sacrificed our child to hide my betrayal. All of this is my fault. My cowardice has jeopardized our marriage and almost cost our son's life. That cruelly beaten boy has paid for my weakness."

Sebastian held Marlene's hands and leaned forward. "I have only ever loved you, Marlene. I'm so, so sorry. Please say you'll... forgive me. Oh, God... please, don't leave me. I will die without you. Help me, my darling. I'm so afraid that when this poor broken boy learns the truth of what I did, he may never forgive me either." Sebastian crumbled forward.

Marlene lifted his chin. "Shh," she soothed him and used the hem of her long muslin dress to wipe his tears, then her own.

Henry strained to hear as she spoke in a hushed tone.

"Sebastian darling, you've proven to me you're an honorable man countless times. You're also human and made a terrible mistake, but you have my love and forgiveness, until death do us part. Remember? I will always be yours."

"Marlene, you are my heart and soul. I am yours, forever."

In awe, Henry witnessed intimate tenderness for the first time. Mesmerized, he watched as Mr. Lewis stroked his wife's face, tilted her head back, and tenderly kissed her. He pulled her into his lap and cradled her in his arms, his voice breaking as he repeated, "I love you. I love you," over and over again.

The couple sat in silence for a time before Mrs. Lewis softly asked her husband, "How are we going to help our son? You must repair this situation to ensure his future. And we have to protect Monty. I think it's best we wait until Christmas to tell him anything about this."

Clearing his voice, "I promised Bernadette I would acknowledge Henry before he turned eighteen, hoping by that time you'd forgive me. With your permission, I will honor my vow and fix this situation with Henry. As for Monty, I agree. We should wait. It's too much to explain in a letter. I must do it in person."

"Sebastian, restore our son's rights, no matter how society may judge us. I want this boy here, with us, and nowhere else."

Henry lay in stillness, listening to a man he respected confess a dark secret that would have ruined his marriage and destroyed his family. He witnessed forgiveness and their vow to return him to his rightful place as their son. He fought back sobs, but the tears came as he rolled away from them and breathed deeply to calm his beating heart. Finally, he knew the truth Maw had withheld.

Mr. and Mrs. Lewis were his mother and father.

This house is where his story began.

He was home.

CHAPTER FOURTEEN

The Truth is Revealed
Henry
December 1935

THE DAY AFTER CHRISTMAS, THE LEWIS HOUSE WAS QUIET. The servants had returned to their homes to celebrate their own holiday. During lunch, Sebastian asked Henry and Monty to join him in his study at four that afternoon.

Despite needing both canes to navigate, Henry arrived early and sat on his father's leather sofa across from his desk, waiting for Monty and Sebastian to join him. He was allowed to walk unaccompanied inside the house because his balance was much better, but outside, where the ground was uneven, someone was always with him. Henry knew a fall could set his recovery back, or even worse, he could be crippled for life, so he was mindful of each step he took.

Henry found it awkward to call his father Mr. Lewis knowing what he secretly knew, so he opted to address him as "Sir" and his mother as "Ma'am." But deep down, they were Father and Mother.

While he waited for Monty and Father, he thought about yesterday, Christmas Day. He had experienced nothing like it in his life. He had never celebrated Christmas before, so he didn't know it could be so wondrous.

Henry wished he could share these delights with his sisters in the future, especially now that Maw knew he was alive and healing. His sisters would be amazed to see the festive tree, its beautiful star touching the ceiling of Mother's drawing room, surrounded by bright gift boxes stacked high around it.

Between the scents of pine and the delicious meal being prepared, the aroma overwhelmed him with joy. The sounds of laughter filled the room as Monty tried to outdo his father with silly jokes.

The gifts Henry treasured most were the matching custom-made antler-handled switchblade knives and shiny brass knuckles Father gave him and Monty. "For protection," he said. He then showed them how to open and close the knives without cutting themselves and correctly anchor the brass knuckles.

By four, Monty and Father still hadn't arrived.

Waiting for them became almost painful. Henry hoped this would be the day Monty learned they were brothers and teared up, hoping that Monty would be over-the-moon happy about it. Henry sniffed through his stuffed-up nose, wiped the tears away with his shirt cuff, then ran his hand through his porcupine-like hair that itched as it grew out. His whole life he'd worn his hair long, tied back with a leather queue, but the doctor had shaved it off to treat his head injury. Now he was left with spiky sprouts, which he found easier to care for.

The study door swung open and Monty peeked in, laughing. "There you are."

Henry patted the leather cushion next to him and smiled as Monty joined him.

As soon as Monty sat, Sebastian hurried in, with a concerned look on his face, and headed straight to his desk. Henry clutched his canes tighter when he caught sight of Sebastian's narrowed eyebrows and downward lips.

After slipping into his desk chair, Sebastian closed his eyes and breathed before meeting their gaze. "Boys, what I'm about to tell you will be shocking, but I swear to God, it's the truth."

His voice quivered. "I'm sorry it took me this long to face my cowardice," he met Henry's gaze, "which almost cost Henry his life."

Monty stared at his father with concern. Henry simply nodded to his father.

"This is hard for me to confess, so please let me speak before you ask questions."

Tears welled up as Sebastian revealed the shameful truth and explained Henry and Monty's true relationship.

Monty's eyes widened in disbelief, with pain written all over his face as he pointed at Henry and then at himself. "You're saying he's your natural son? And I'm your bastard son?"

"Monty, both of you are my sons." Sebastian's voice trembled. "Please believe me when I tell you Bernadette Lee gave birth to you. Henry's mother is the woman you call Mom."

To prove his words, Sebastian pushed their birth certificates across his desk. "I prepared your birth certificates myself. The child born to Marlene Martin Lewis had a blue birthmark on the back of his head. Just like mine."

Monty turned toward Henry, searching for the blue birthmark. Memories of teasing him about it came rushing back. But now, it held a new meaning.

His anger rising, Monty jumped to his feet and pointed at his father. "You knew! From the moment I introduced you to Henry, you knew he was your son, and yet you kept it a secret. You, Sir... are a lying, cheating, fraudster!"

Sebastian tried to calm Monty down, but Monty's anger boiled over as he lashed out. "After all you've done to groom me for a political future, now you tell me I'm a bastard! That scandal alone will ruin any chance I ever had."

"Monty, we can handle this." Sebastian's words were soft, his eyes pleading for Monty's understanding.

But Monty was beyond reason. He clenched his fists, his voice shaking with rage. "Do you know... how disgusting it is... to hear you fucked Mrs. Lee? How dare you! You asshole. You and Harvard can go straight to hell. I want nothing to do with you."

Monty snatched up his birth certificate, proving he was born as Henry Lee, and stomped out of the study, leaving his father and brother shocked and devastated.

Heartbroken, Sebastian called after Monty, but Monty was gone.

After clearing his voice several times, Sebastian turned to face Henry, who was struggling to his feet. Step by step, Henry balanced on two canes and made his way to Sebastian's desk. "Thank you for telling us the truth, Sir. I know that was hard to do."

Within the hour, Monty dragged his suitcases down the stairs and pushed past his parents, who stood arm in arm next to the front door, pleading for him not to leave.

Henry held out one cane to stop him. "Monty, don't go. We can fix this. Please. . . Brother..." his voice cracked.

But Monty just looked at him and growled, "They're all yours, Henry. Enjoy my life." Turning to his parents, "I'll finish high school. I'm not stupid. But don't expect me to follow any more of your plans. This is goodbye."

Monty stormed out the front door just as their driver pulled up. Throwing his suitcases into the trunk, he barked, "Take me back to school immediately!"

After Monty left, Henry carefully made his way up the stairs to Monty's room, where he sat on the bed and freed his tears.

Sebastian soon tapped on the open door and asked, "Are you okay, Henry?"

Henry wanted to say he was fine, but he wouldn't lie to his father. He shook his head no.

Sebastian crossed the room, sat next to Henry on the bed, and waited patiently.

"I'm disappointed and hurt that Monty didn't want me for his brother. Monty is my best friend. Actually, my only friend. I've looked up to him for a long time."

He couldn't meet Sebastian's eyes and stared straight ahead. "This feels like a betrayal, not just to me, but to you and... Monty's mom. He abandoned all of us."

"I know, son." Sebastian patted Henry's knee. "Monty's a good person. He's going to work it out. I have total faith in him. Let's give him some time."

Henry turned to Sebastian. "This room holds too many painful memories for me. If you don't mind, Sir, I'd like to move across the hall into the guest room. I never want to step foot in this room again."

Sebastian nodded and tapped Henry's leg twice. "I will make it so," he said, stood for a moment, looking down at Henry, and asked, "Do you need any help?"

Henry reached for his canes propped against the bed. "No, Sir. I've got this." He stood, gained his balance, and without a backward glance, left Monty's room.

Despite Monty's silence, life went on. Henry's legs became stronger with daily exercise, at first walking, then trotting and finally running. He no longer needed the canes.

When a letter arrived from Monty postmarked May 15, 1936, Henry and his parents gathered to read the brief message. It contained only three sentences that struck their hearts like a dagger: "Don't any of you come to my graduation. Fuck Harvard. Any correspondence from now on will be through our family attorney, Mr. Goldman."

Monty didn't even sign the letter.

CHAPTER FIFTEEN

The Death of Jack Lee
Henry
July 1936

JACK LEE STUMBLED INTO THE LEWIS'S FRONT YARD, shouting for Henry at the top of his lungs.

Sebastian and Marlene rushed to the porch with Henry between them.

"Gi'me my boy, Lewis," Jack hollered.

"We both know he's not your son, Jack," Sebastian shouted back.

"Well, he's Bernadette's kid, an' dat makes'm mine!" he yelled.

"Monty is Bernadette's child. This boy is our son, the one you almost killed. You can't have him."

Understanding he was getting nowhere fast, Jack lowered his voice. "Bernadette's a dyin,' Lewis. Bof'r girls are beggin' to see him. If'n my wife can see Henry, she kin say her goodbyes and pass on'n peace."

Troubled by this disturbing news, Henry faced his parents. "Maw did her best to care for me. I've gotta see her. I won't be long, I promise."

Sebastian whispered, "I don't trust him. Walk slowly and keep a significant distance between you. I'll load my pistol and be right behind you. Stay on guard every moment, son."

Henry nodded and patted his pants pocket. "My weapons are right here."

As Henry left, walking several yards behind Jack, Sebastian shouted, "Touch my son and I'll kill you, Jack." Then he bolted into his study to load his firearm.

When Henry and Jack Lee stopped outside the cabin, Henry said he'd go in alone. As soon as his eyes adjusted to the cabin's dark interior, he could make out Maw's bed shoved against the corner wall on his right. Her small body, folded up, was lying on her right side. Henry eased down next to her, shocked at the skeleton of a woman he'd grown up thinking was his mother.

"Maw." Henry leaned over and touched her arm. "I know Monty's your real son. I'm sorry you didn't get to know him."

Bernadette's eyes darted open and narrowed as she stared at him.

"Why wouldn't you tell me or Mr. and Mrs. Lewis when you knew it all along?" Henry asked.

Even though her breath was shallow, Bernadette managed, "You shouldn't... be here, Jack killed sisters... kill you... they are... over..." Her eyes flickered to the curtain that separated his sisters' closet bedroom from the main room.

Henry's head swiveled in the same direction. "What! Oh my God, Maw, why did he kill my sisters? Why would he do that?" Henry cried out, sitting back, suddenly aware Jack planned to kill him too. His heart thumped out of control, realizing Maw hadn't asked for him. Jack Lee had tricked him.

"We die... he gets land... His pistol... pocket," she now gasped for air, but managed a few more words. "Get poison..." she nodded and closed her eyes.

Henry rooted around under her bed for the special place she hid her castor bean poison and pulled out a full vial. That amount would kill a herd of horses less alone, a single man.

"Put... in... whiskey..." she whispered, willing her last bits of energy to finish, "two glasses... put back... Tell... Mr. Lewis... I'm... sorry... I stole... you."

His eyes widened at her damning confession. Maw took him on purpose. She had stolen him! Shocked to the core, he understood the magnitude of her words.

Everything he'd been through was her fault. It was all her fault. But there was no time to judge Maw.

Henry had to move fast and poured the entire vial into the whiskey bottle sitting on the nearby table. Finished, he flung the empty vial under Maw's bed as Jack Lee stomped inside and locked the door.

Henry faced him. "Maw and I made our peace. She said the day she dies is the day she'll drink with you." Henry pointed to the two shot glasses on the table. He filled each one to the top and handed the first one to Jack.

Jack Lee gulped down the first glass and slammed it back on the table. "I ain't gonna waste no liquor on a dyin' bitch," and slugged the second glass. As he wavered back and forth, he dropped the glass and fumbled through his overalls, pulling out a small handgun.

That's when Sebastian pounded on the door. "Open this fucking door, Jack, or I'm going to kick it in!"

Everything flowed into slow motion as Jack lifted the gun with one hand, held on to the table with the other to steady himself and, aiming at Maw, fired.

Henry yelled, "Noooooo!" as the bullet hit Maw between her eyes and spattered the rough cabin wall behind her.

Jack then struggled for balance as the powerful poison struck him. He wobbled back and forth, trying to aim at Henry as the gun waved up and down. Henry sidestepped and, switchblade in hand, plunged its long, thin, sharp blade deep into Jack Lee's throat, slicing it open.

Sebastian crashed through the door just as Jack's bright red blood from severed arteries spurted out in a powerful gush covering Henry's hair, face, and clothes.

Horrified by the grisly death filling the miserable shelter he'd once called home, Henry cried out to Sebastian, "He murdered them—all of them! I couldn't save my sisters!"

Sebastian stepped over Jack's sprawled body and removed the bloody knife from Henry's hand, wiped it on his pants, and closed it. Gently wrapping his arm around his son's shoulder, he guided Henry out of the cabin into the late afternoon sun and urged him to listen.

"Let the animals out of their pens and close the gates behind them so they can't reenter. Wait for me on the trail. Go now," he said.

After Henry freed the animals, he stood mute and frozen at the trail entrance, waiting for his father. Dried blood clung in clumps in his hair and stained his clothes. Red streaks smeared his face where he'd attempted to wipe the dripping blood away.

He'd killed a monster who forced him to do terrible things to others and did unspeakable things to him, Maw, and his sisters.

"*Yes,*" a voice deep inside whispered, "*and that evil old son of a bitch deserved to die.*"

Twenty minutes later, plumes of gray smoke and fiery flames soared over the treetops just as Sebastian appeared and guided him up the trail.

"Let's go home, son."

A month later, a Circuit Court Judge appointed Mr. and Mrs. Sebastian Lewis as Henry's guardians before their petition to adopt him was granted. Sebastian and Marlene had agreed it was the quickest way to attain their goal with the least amount of scandal.

When the judge asked Henry what name he would prefer, he replied, "Raymond, it means protector. I would like to be called Ray. And I would like to add Sebastian, my father's first name, and Martin, my mother's maiden name."

The judge pounded his gavel, finalizing his order.

"The last thing on the docket today is your request to have the five-acre property titled in the name of Bernadette Lee and Henry Lee, a minor, transferred to this young man. I hereby grant your petition since Bernadette Lee is deceased. When this young man turns eighteen, you can transfer the property into the name of Raymond Sebastian Martin Lewis."

Again, the judge pounded his gavel, making it so.

Turning to his son, Sebastian asked him to make one more decision.

"What would you like to call us, Ray?"

PART THREE

CHAPTER SIXTEEN

A New Name and A New Life
Raymond Sebastian Martin Lewis
September 1936

THE SUNFLOWERS BLOOMED AND FADED BY THE END OF THE SUMMER. Still no word from Monty. The empty chair at the dinner table served as a constant reminder of his absence. Our hearts were heavy, hoping he would find his way home.

In September, Mother, Father, and I celebrated my eighteenth birthday. The following day, Father's attorney, Mr. Goldman, called. Monty had enlisted in the Army using his Henry Lee birth certificate.

We were heartbroken.

As the days turned into weeks, and the weeks into months, Mother and Father concentrated on improving my education. Mornings were spent with a private tutor who corrected my speech and diction, as well as increased my knowledge of literature and math while making me sit straight up and balance a book on my head. I appreciated becoming the new me, but I felt like a jackass with the book balancing thing.

Afternoons, I learned mechanics by helping José Sr. work on the farm equipment or I studied accounting and learned how to manage the farm and the winery from Father. He loved sharing advice about life and business.

"Cash is king, so always have some on hand in case there's an urgent situation or an opportunity. And be wary of letting anyone invest your money for you. Trust no one. And promise nothing you can't deliver."

Grateful for his guidance and eager to learn more, I asked Father what it meant to be *in the black*, a term I'd often heard him use.

He smiled. "It means a product or venture is profitable. If it loses money, then it's *in the red*. Don't waste your precious time or money on anything that doesn't give you a satisfactory return. That applies to people too."

Mother and I spent our time in deep discussions about life. She introduced me to Eastern philosophy, explaining that karma was getting what one deserves. Monty sure messed up his karma when he deserted us, but I kept that to myself. Pappy made me do so many terrible things. I figured my karma had to stink, too.

Mother and I also discussed stories from the Bible, ranging from creation to resurrection. She knew I understood resurrection. After all, not that long ago, they'd found me almost dead on their lawn.

To lighten the moment, I asked, "Tell me about your people."

She laughed and revealed that the Martin surname wasn't always their family name.

"My Italian parents arrived in the United States before the turn of the century. Their name was Martinelli. However, my mother, who was pregnant, was concerned about the stories of prejudice against Italians. When they got off the ship on Ellis Island, she told the officials her husband's first name was Eli. That's how Martinelli changed to Martin."

"What about Father?"

"Also from Italy," she said, with a twinkle in her eyes.

"Your grandfather's name was Luigi Sabatini Sr. When he brought his family to America, he changed Luigi to Lewis and made it his last name. Thus he became Sebastian Lewis Sr., and your father, Sebastian Lewis Jr."

"I'm pure Italian?"

"Yes, dear, you are Raimondo Sabatini Martinelli Luigi," she replied in a delightful sing-song Italian accent, rolling her r's.

"Oh gee, that's just what I need, another name," which made us both laugh.

On rainy days, Father and I relaxed in his study, chatting about how classic novels, like *Lorna Doone*, reflected real-life situations. I connected to the story of a young girl raised by criminals who tried to kill her, just like Jack Lee tried to kill me. I stopped referring to him as Pappy. He was Jack Lee. The man I murdered.

However, our favorite book was *Alexandre Dumas's* novel, *The Count of Monte Cristo*. We spent hours discussing the passage Father loved to quote: *"Life is a storm, my young friend. You will bask in the sunlight one moment, be shattered on the rocks the next. What makes you a man is what you do when that storm comes."*

In a rare moment of vulnerability, I shared with Father why I identified with the main character, Edmond Dantès, likening my time with Jack Lee to being trapped in the same prison cell as Dantès. He blinked away tears when I told him some of the terrible things Jack forced me to do to protect my sisters and Maw.

I never told him everything, though. Some secrets I would take to my grave.

Those quiet moments with Father carried me through the darkest storms of my life.

1937

Completely healed, I had also gained a healthy amount of weight and stood at six-two, an inch taller than Father. I wanted to see more of our country and learn about our business from the street side so, when the wine delivery driver for our Florida route quit, I asked for his job.

Mother wasn't too sure about me leaving yet, but Father said, "he has to meet people and see more of the world." The position was mine.

Within a week, I was delivering wine to the El Floridita restaurant, our biggest customer in Seaport, a quaint south Florida town on the Gulf of Mexico. Its manager was a chatty Cuban guy and, while joking around, I told him about my crazy new Italian name.

"Lots of people in this area have Italian names. I'd be happy to introduce you to a few of them if you're interested."

Father said I should meet new people. So why not?

In the weeks leading up to Thanksgiving, I accepted a dinner invitation at the El Floridita as a guest of Marco Catanetti Sr. and Marco Jr., referred to simply as Junior. When I joined them in their private dining room, I noted that they both dressed in white suits and cream-colored Panama fedoras. That was a style I'd never seen before.

After we finished an excellent meal, Marco Sr. showed an interest in our family's Italian heritage and asked where our farm and vineyard were located.

"My family lives on a mountaintop farm in Lewisville, West Virginia. It's due west of the capital. My father is also a partner in a coal mine in the southern part of the state."

"He sounds like a true entrepreneur." He smiled and signaled the server to top off our wine glasses. "I bet you are too, so I've got a proposition for you."

They wanted to hire my empty truck on its return trip to deliver some of their goods to various locations along the East Coast. They assured me the job was simple. I would receive a cash payment when the product was loaded into my truck in Seaport and a generous tip after I completed each delivery.

Father talked about seizing opportunities. Here was an interesting way to earn extra income on my own. "Tell me more about the job."

Junior leaned forward. "You drive to a specified warehouse at a particular time and wait in the truck. We don't want you to help or interact with anyone unloading the merchandise. As soon as they slip a cash bonus envelope through your driver's side window, you head home. It's as simple as that. Money in your pocket for the deal you make with us." He leaned back and looked at his father, who nodded in agreement.

Their proposition sounded good. Since the truck was empty on the return trip, anyway, why not? With enough money, I could start a transportation business I had been thinking about and make Father proud of me.

Within a few months, I had accumulated so much cash, I needed to store it somewhere safe. There was an unused antique trunk, complete with a lock, in the vacant apartment above my family's garage, so I used it.

However, after many successful deliveries, I learned how much danger was also involved.

One night, I drove into a dimly lit, fenced, seedy New Jersey warehouse with only one way in—a gate I'd just inched through. When the hackles rose on the back of my neck, I turned my truck around to face the open gate, and left my engine running while the product was unloaded.

When my truck's back doors slammed shut but the tip money wasn't pushed through my side window within the normal time frame, I got a creepy feeling and flipped open my switchblade, angling my body toward the door.

Not even ten seconds later, my driver's door was snatched open and a dark figure lunged toward me, only to be greeted by my knife slicing his throat open. He dropped to the ground, making choking sounds as I slammed on the gas and, with all four tires screeching, sped through the gate.

Had he been successful at pulling me out of my truck, I might have been a goner.

Alarmed that my personal protection skills were lacking, I hired our field hands to teach me how to fight with a knife. I was truly impressed watching their footwork when they fought—usually over a woman. At the end of the day when their work was done, using sticks as knives, they taught me to shuffle around my opponent, lunge, duck, and strike at the first opportunity. Jose Sr. interpreted their advice. "If you are the first to draw blood, the fight may end quicker."

Even with my newly gained abilities, I considered quitting delivering for the Catanettis. When they got wind of it, they increased their already generous cash bonuses and promised a swift and harsh punishment to anyone who attempted to attack me or my truck again.

Franco, who had become my best friend, advised me to move my tip box to the rear end of the truck. His brother, Junior, frowned and added harshly, "Get a gun and learn to use it."

Months later, on my first trip to Philadelphia, I found myself in another tense situation. I missed the exit road to the warehouse district and was far behind schedule when I pulled into the warehouse's drop-off zone. The dark, seedy surroundings were alarming.

First, I scanned the area with my headlights on high beam, then I circled around and pointed my truck's nose toward the exit, leaving my high beams on. With my motor running and the cab doors locked, my loaded pistol sat next to me.

When my truck's back doors slammed shut and the warehouse's door rolled down, I put my truck in gear and inched forward. That's when a large man stepped in front of my truck with a shotgun pointed at my windshield and shouted at me to get out. Gunning it hard, I slammed into him, knocking him under the truck. I then felt the sickening bump as my tires rolled over the imbecile, squashing his skull like a ripe melon.

I stepped up my fighting lessons.

When Father asked why, I mentioned the hijacking attempts, but left out that I killed both men. Concerned, he installed a punching bag in the garage and started my boxing lessons.

When I revealed I had purchased a handgun for protection and admitted I needed practice, Father then set up a target area and taught me to be deadly accurate, sharing a brilliant piece of advice.

"Never point a gun at someone to threaten them. Use it to kill them."

CHAPTER
SEVENTEEN

Save a Life and Take a Life
Ray
March 8, 1938

WHETHER FREEZING COLD OR SNOW, the winter dragged on in the mountains. It seemed like a great idea to spend a few extra days in Seaport enjoying the South Florida sunshine, its beaches, and playing Bolita. What's all the fuss about putting a hundred small, numbered balls in a bag, shaking it, and taking bets on which number was drawn? Whatever it was, the Catanettis made a fortune from it.

On my last night in town, Franco, and his younger brother Rico, insisted I meet them for drinks at The Cat House, their saloon in Old Town. Booze wasn't my thing, but the whiskey Franco ordered went down smooth. Maybe I could learn to like the stuff. After all, Father had similar bottles in his study.

Around midnight, Angelo, Franco's bodyguard, hurried over and whispered something in Franco's ear. That's the way it was with these guys. Everything's always hush-hush. Rico, with his bad boy grin, nodded towards the upstairs brothel—his style of invitation. We weren't friends, but at least he was trying. Curious, I followed him up the stairs and past a brashly painted older woman. He waved. The madam nodded.

At the end of the hall, we entered a dimly lit, large, padded room. Not sure what was happening, I remained by the door. Rico selected a small whip from a rack hanging on the wall nearby. A slumped naked woman, moaning in pain, was tied spread eagle to an x-like contraption in the corner.

He nodded toward the two men in the opposite corner. "Give her some more coke and she'll be fine." Then, with a leer on his face, he offered me the whip.

Rico was into some sick shit.

"No thanks, I'll look for something normal."

He just grinned and waved me away.

I returned to the madam who introduced me to a bunch of older gals with painted faces and sickening perfume. None were appealing.

"Someone much younger."

"You're sure?" she smirked and guided me to a small room at the opposite end of the hall. After she pulled out a bundle of keys and unlocked the door, she sneered, "Will this do?" and left me to enter alone.

I stepped inside and took in the meager surroundings. A single lightbulb on the ceiling exposed a slight Latina girl with waist-length, dark hair standing barefoot and motionless in front of an iron bed with filthy sheets I could smell from the doorway. Her frightened dark eyes were alert, staring.

A flimsy shift slid off her left shoulder, exposing her thin neck, slender brown arms, and long slim legs. The threadbare cloth fell to her ankles. Like a punch to the stomach, I understood this was a child they'd slapped bright red lipstick on to make her look older.

I said I wanted someone younger, but God, not this young.

She trembled when I stepped closer. Her eyelashes fluttered and her brows knitted. I'd seen that look on my little sisters' faces far too often: fear.

I came no closer, pointed to myself, and calmly said, "Ray."

Then I motioned to her.

"Carmelita." Her low voice was sweet and whispery.

Her English was nonexistent and my Spanish was limited, but I tried, "Edad niña?"

"Diez." She looked down at her toes, stifling a yawn.

Godammit! She's ten years old.

Jesus, I wished my Spanish were better.

"Da miedo aquí?"

"Si."

Of course, it's fucking scary here. How do I tell her I'll help her escape as soon as possible?

"Te ayudaré... uh, escape, uh, pronto."

Her eyes grew enormous.

"Gracias, Señor Ray," she whispered.

"Buenas noches, Carmelita." I left, easing the door closed.

Grabbing the madam by the arm, wiped the stupid smirk off her face. "If you value your life, do not send anyone into that child's room again. Ever! Do you understand me?"

Her head bobbed up and down as she stared wide eyed.

I threw down a fifty. "Feed the girl, clean her up, give her some new clothes and put some decent sheets and blankets on that filthy bed." Then I glared at her and said I'd be back.

It was already two in the morning when I returned downstairs. Franco frantically waved me over and signaled the server to send whiskey shots to his table.

"Franco, do you know..."

"Save it, Ray! We got shit going on!" he barked, as Angelo rushed over with an anxious look on his face and whispered to him.

Franco stood so quickly his chair screeched against the wooden floor and almost toppled. He asked a few questions in Italian. Angelo nodded. Franco responded sharply. Angelo hustled out the door.

Franco then pulled his chair over, sat, and leaned toward me.

"We've discovered the scumbags behind your two delivery attacks."

"What?" I sat back, stunned.

He slugged his drink and waved at the bartender for refills all around, just as Rico slid in next to me.

"A man named Tito Zayas is the devil who sent both those guys to hijack you. He's the top henchman and a close friend of our enemy, Victor Hellman, a local gangster. That bastard, Victor, grew up here in Seaport. Privileged asshole who thinks he's in charge because his dad was the mayor at one point."

Fresh rounds of whiskey arrived. Franco pushed the glasses toward us and indicated bottoms up. It took my breath away. I'm not used to their kind of drinking.

"Victor's angry about our success in the Bolita games and jealous of the East Coast deliveries you make for us. He's always trying to pick fights with us, so he ordered Tito to have you assaulted at the delivery sites. Now he wants revenge for both deaths."

Rico grinned. "Betcha didn't know there's a price on your head for killing them."

Franco continued, "Ray, this is when we decide what to do next. Hai capito?"

"Which means?"

"Do you understand?"

Rico raised his brows and snickered.

I nodded, feeling a little sick to my stomach.

Angelo returned, spoke to Franco, and left again.

Franco leaned in and lowered his voice. "We try to keep a low profile, Ray, but we just got permission to move on this tonight. Tito's gathering some guys to come after you as soon as he or Victor learns where you live."

"Jesus, Franco! What the hell? My parents are in danger."

"Tito's at his nightclub, the El Cuero on the other side of Old Town. When it closes, his bodyguard will drive him home. Tito lives nearby. Since he's already ordered two attempts on your life, is there something you'd like to do before he and his thugs leave Southwest Florida and show up on your West Virginia doorstep?"

Franco waited for me to process the information. If Tito Zayas thought he could hit me on my home ground, he was wrong.

The decision was mine. I had to protect my parents and stop him first.

I met Franco's gaze and nodded.

"Do you need backup?" Franco asked, studying me, then looking at Rico.

Rico grinned and signaled I should follow him.

Rico and I crouched in the shadowed area beside the back porch deck of Tito Zayas's two-story home. A few minutes after four, it was still dark as hell when his driver pulled into the yard, headlights blaring, and stopped. Tito stepped out laughing as he gave instructions.

"Pick me up at noon tomorrow. Tell the guys to bring firepower. We're heading north to burn down that little prick's winery in West Virginia. We leave at one."

As soon as Tito closed the car door and walked toward the porch, his driver slowly began backing down the gravel driveway, illuminating him in the headlights.

Medium height, wide shoulders, and stocky, with thick, curly black hair, Tito fiddled with his keys as he approached the first step leading up to his back door.

Rico nudged me, warning that Tito might make it inside before his driver left if we didn't act quickly. Despite the car's headlights, Rico and I stepped out of the shadows and shot him twice, at close range. Once in the chest and once in the gut. Definitely kill shots.

His driver roared back into the yard, punching his headlights on high beam.

Rico and I fled on foot to the next street over, where we left the car, and drove straight to the Catanetti compound. Franco was waiting for us, adamant that I leave Seaport immediately and to get rid of the shotgun I used somewhere along the way home.

"Be prepared in case Victor Hellman sends his hitmen after you. We have ears everywhere, so trust me. I'll keep you informed."

He handed me a slip of paper. "Call this number when you get home. If you hear, 'It's cold in the mountains,' all is well, hang up. If it's 'hot in the mountains,' leave your number and someone will call you back with instructions. Hai capito?"

At daybreak, I began the twenty-hour drive to Lewisville, hoping like hell the madam followed my orders to clean Carmelita up and let no one near her. I was going to address that problem as soon as possible.

I arrived at two in the morning. Even though I was exhausted beyond belief, I still called the number Franco gave me. All they said before they hung up was, "Nothing yet, call tomorrow."

Since I'd forgotten to dump the shotgun on my way home, after I woke and showered, I headed to the garage apartment to store it in my antique trunk in case Father saw it.

With everything that happened the day before running through my mind, I expected to feel shame after Rico and I killed Tito Zayas. Instead, I was relieved. I'd protected my family and solved that problem.

The problem I didn't solve, though, was getting help for that little girl with the frightened eyes locked up in that disgusting room. I hoped Franco would know what to do, because I sure didn't.

As I left the garage thinking about how to handle the Carmelita dilemma, I headed to the log, a peaceful place to think. As soon as I figured out what to do about the little girl, I'd call Franco.

All thoughts of saving Carmelita vanished when I stepped into view of the log. Monty, dressed in his olive drab uniform, sat in our spot, staring off into space while his duffel bag lay on the ground beside him.

My shuffling through the carpet of leaves and twigs alerted him. He leapt to his feet, with surprise and disbelief written all over his face. I was no longer the skinny, broken kid he'd left behind. Alarmed, his eyes darted over me, searching for any sign of negative intentions.

My emotions betrayed me. I couldn't stop the smile that lit my face.

"Monty, we've missed you, brother."

He returned his lopsided grin. Within seconds, we were hugging and slapping each other's backs, cheering and whooping at the top of our lungs.

"How'd you get here?" I waved toward the log for us to sit.

"I took my two-week leave and hitchhiked home to apologize to Mom and Dad. Especially Dad for what I said to him. Also, apologize to you. I was such an immature fool. The Army and the men I serve with changed me, hopefully for the better."

"You're home now. That's all that matters."

"I'm so sorry you went through the hell you did, being abused by that crazy drunk. Please forgive my thoughtless selfishness." He looked away, breathed deeply, then looked back at me. His eyes misted up. "I'm thankful for the wonderful childhood I had and the opportunities our parents gave me, but you paid the price. I'm so sorry about that."

"We're both innocent, Monty. Maw switched us on purpose. I think she knew she could never give you what our parents could. Before she died, she wanted Father to know how sorry she was for swapping us."

He tilted his head, just like Father did. "I was shocked to find your cabin burned to the ground and their graves nearby. I wish I could have met my sisters and talked to... Maw. I have so many questions."

"I'd like to tell you about them sometime."

"Yes, please. I'd like that." He paused. "Henry, what happened down there?"

"It's Ray now. When Mother and Father adopted me, we changed it. As for what happened, Jack Lee murdered our sisters and Maw. I killed him, and Father burned the cabin to the ground."

"Oh my God. They were murdered?" Monty's eyes widened.

"It still torments me every day knowing I wasn't there to protect them," I mumbled, looking down at my feet.

"I'm so sorry."

He patted my shoulder, then pulled his duffel bag to him. "Ray's a good name... I think it means protector, which fits you."

"Mother and Father prayed every day for your safe return, and here you are. Come on, let's go surprise them."

Monty threw his duffle bag over his shoulder and grinned. "Lead the way, brother."

Mother couldn't stop smiling as she marked Monty's homecoming on the kitchen calendar with a big circle around March 10, 1938.

During dinner, Monty delighted us with stories of his experiences in the Army and, of course, his opinion of what was happening in Europe.

"Things are getting boiling hot there. If the United States wants to protect its allies, it must give up being neutral, even if we have to break our treaty."

"Speaking of hot, that reminds me," Mother said, turning to me. "Your friend Franco called several times today while you were asleep. He said to tell you, 'It will get hot in the mountains soon.' Franco was adamant that you call him. His number is next to the telephone in Father's office."

I sprinted across the hall, my hand shaking so hard I had trouble dialing the phone.

"What's happening?" I yelled when Franco answered on the second ring.

"Tito's bodyguard recognized Rico and told Victor Hellman a young man was with him. After nosing around, they learned you were with Rico and me at The Cat House earlier in the evening. Victor can't risk a war if he comes after Rico. Pop will squash him if he tries. Instead, old yellow-belly Victor sent his tough guys after you."

My heart was thumping so fast I could've dropped dead on Father's wool rug. I dreaded telling Father about the nightmare that was coming and that I caused it.

"Goddammit, Franco! You couldn't stop them?"

"They were already gone when we learned what they were up to. Eight guys in two cars, armed with twelve-gauge shotguns, left here about six yesterday evening. Their leader is a goon named Top Dog. Tall, heavy guy, with thick red hair. Mean as shit. Expect them tonight."

"Good God! Anything else?" My head was spinning.

"Most likely, they'll split up. They plan to set fire to your vineyards and your farm, killing you and anyone near you. Angelo and my brothers, Rico, and Luca, are on their way in their fastest cars, with their own bodyguards and our two best drivers. They departed as soon as we learned the Hellman gang left Seaport. Take your family to a safe place immediately."

"The vineyards are ten miles east of town. Our farmhouse is a safe place for my family. There's only one way into our compound, a winding road up the mountain. Plus, we have extra men to help us. Do your guys know where Lewisville is located?"

"One of our new drivers, a guy named Bill, said he knows it's west of Washington, D.C. Hang tight. Eight of our men are on their way with plenty of weapons to help protect your winery and family. They left an hour after Victor Hellman's crew. Hai Capito?"

Franco was speaking fast, but I understood. Help was on the way. Before I hung up, I told him about the little girl being held prisoner in the Cat House's upstairs brothel. "Get Carmelita outta there as soon as possible."

"Consider it done. Pop's house has guards around the clock. I have two older sisters. Mama will know what to do. The girl will be safe with them."

"Thanks, Franco. When this nightmare's over, I'll call you."

I dreaded this moment. When I returned to the dining room, Monty was talking about the men in his unit. The moment he saw my face, he stopped.

"Ray, what's the matter?"

In as few words as possible, I described the two hijacking incidents. "Both guys are dead and their boss knows I killed them. He's mad as hell at me and sent two carloads of his hoodlums to attack us. Friends of mine are on their way to help and should arrive soon. But we can't waste a minute. Those goons are going to hit the winery and the farm tonight."

The stern look on Father's face as he stood up convinced me this was not the right time to tell him a Mafia friend, Rico Catanetti, and I also killed Tito Rubio to protect them from just this very thing. The less he knew about my involvement with the Mafia, the better.

"If it's a fight they want, it's a war they're gonna get," Father said, his voice decisive and confident as he strode to his study and unlocked his gun case. After pulling out a half dozen shotguns, along with a few handguns, he stacked them on his desk with boxes and boxes of ammunition.

"Monty," I said, "protect the house and our parents. I'll defend the vineyards."

Father was already on the phone explaining the situation to Pierre, the vineyard's manager. "Tell our men to bring any guns they own and get back to the vineyard right away. Ray's on his way with more weapons. It'll take him about twenty minutes to get off this mountain and drive out to you."

He hung up and called José Sr., his farm manager, with instructions to come up to the house and pick up a few shotguns. "Tell our workers to dress warmly, bring their machetes, and spread out around the property's edges. Stay out of sight, but prepare to kill without question."

"Father, send two men to the driveway entrance to warn everyone when they see headlights coming up the mountain."

He nodded and repeated my suggestion to José Sr.

"Mother, lock all the house doors and turn off the lights. Go up to Monty's bedroom and sit next to his window. Take the dinner bell with you to warn Father and Monty if you see any movement from the garage driveway."

"Stay safe, my son. I love you." She hugged me, then darted away, turning off the lights.

"Ray," Monty said, "the best view of the driveway and front yard is from your bedroom window. I'll set up at that position with Dad's twelve-gauge. Don't worry. I'm an excellent shot. I won't miss." Monty saluted me and we hugged.

"Don't worry about me, son," Father said, shaking my hand, then pulling me in for a hug. "I'll cover the same area from my bedroom window, plus I can still signal José Sr., down at the barn, from my west-facing window. We're going to be fine. You've got a twenty-minute drive ahead of you. Be careful driving down the mountain, but haul ass as soon as you get through town. Go now! Save the vineyards."

I grabbed two of Father's weapons and a couple of boxes of shells. With a last look around, I jumped into my truck and headed down the winding driveway, intent on making the ten-mile stretch to the vineyards in record-breaking time.

CHAPTER EIGHTEEN

A Visit from Victor Hellman's Thugs
Angelo
March 10, 1938

JUST AFTER SUNSET, TWO BLACK SEDANS, NEARLY OUT OF FUEL, drove north past a welcome sign that read:

Lewisville, West Virginia, Established 1915, Population 565

Its Main Street, a two-lane highway, runs between the Appalachian Mountains rising from the west and a scenic valley that stretches out to the east. Passengers on the right side of the cars spied Grandma's Diner's large plate-glass windows advertising hot, home-cooked meals. Meanwhile, the men on the drivers' sides were captivated by the vibrant blue neon sign for Crazy Phil's Saloon that offered alcohol. But what they needed more than anything was gas.

Up ahead, just past the diner's parking lot and a wooden phone booth standing near the highway, were two tall white Esso gas pumps in front of Dennis's Gas Station. Coca Cola on ice was displayed in the window.

While his drivers filled their tanks, Top Dog walked over to the phone booth and placed a collect call to his boss, Victor Hellman. Whatever Victor wanted done, Top Dog was happy to do. He got paid in women, drugs, booze, and cash, each of which was his favorite thing.

When he returned, his guys were drinking frosty bottles of Coca-Cola and clamoring for the hot, home-cooked meals advertised at Grandma's Diner.

Top Dog made nice with the waitress, Becky, a chubby, chatty teenager, while his men filled several of the restaurant's back booths.

After ordering half the menu for his men, he asked Becky a few questions about the area, and soon learned that the Lewis Winery provided most of the town folks with jobs.

When his men were finished eating, Top Dog pulled out a wad of cash to pay the tab, and commented to Becky, "Some snooty rich folks own that fancy wine-making place, huh?"

"Oh, no, sir. The Lewis's are the nicest folks you'll ever meet. They live in a big farmhouse at the top of the mountain."

"Oh, yeah? Close to here?" Top Dog baited the naive girl for information.

"The next business after the gas station is Buster's General Store." She pointed toward the gas station they'd just come from. "Across Main Street from Buster's is a gravel driveway that winds up the mountain to the Lewis Farm."

"They live so close, it's easy for us to get our vegetables, milk, and eggs from them. And in the summer, the Missus grows the most beautiful sunflowers. They aren't snobby at all."

"Well, that's wonderful. Thanks for the great food and friendly chat. Keep the change."

"Hey, thanks for the generous tip, mister."

The waning crescent moon produced a speckle of light as the Catanetti men slowly drove down Main Street. The lights from the restaurant and bar exposed two black sedans with Florida plates parked in front of Grandma's Diner. Since the Catanetti cars were almost empty, they pulled into the Esso gas station to top off their tanks, then parked their cars by the telephone booth next to the highway.

Angelo was in a foul mood. His driver swore he knew how to get to Lewisville ahead of the gang. "Dammit, Bill! If you hadn't taken that wrong turn, we could've beaten them."

"Sorry, boss. It won't happen again."

"Be sure it doesn't, or you won't be driving for me."

"Hey, Angelo, look!" Rico reached across from the backseat and poked Angelo's shoulder. "That redheaded asshole and his goons are heading to Crazy Phil's Saloon."

"Our men can stay here and keep an eye on them. We're going to Ray's vineyards first."

Angelo rolled his window down and spoke to the four men in the second car.

As Angelo rolled his window up, Bill asked, "Boss, do you know where Ray lives?"

"Yeah, right up there." Angelo pointed at an angle across the street and up the mountain.

Bill started the car and waited for Angelo's directions to the vineyards.

"Head north on Main Street, after the general store and a schoolhouse, bear right around a big curve. It's about ten miles east of town."

Bill parked Angelo's car next to Ray's delivery truck at nine-thirty. Luca and Rico Catanetti jumped out, with Angelo and Bill behind them. Ray vaulted out of the winery's front door with anxiety written all over his face as he shook hands with them.

"Hellman's thugs are hanging out at Crazy Phil's Bar," Angelo reported.

"Probably getting a snoot full of booze to bolster their courage," Ray said, inviting them inside the winery.

"And that's okay. The drunker they get, the more mistakes they'll make," Angelo reassured him as they followed Ray inside. "I'm leaving Rico, Luca, and my driver, Bill, here. Hellman's goons are notorious for late attacks, so stay alert." Angelo warned.

"As soon as I learn what's happening in town, I'll call you from the phone booth next to the gas station. I'm heading back now."

Top Dog and his men grabbed a couple of large booths at the back of Crazy Phil's Bar. His ears perked up when the guy from the gas station ordered a beer and mentioned all the cars from Florida that rolled into town that day.

"How many?" the bartender asked.

"I counted four cars with sixteen different people over the afternoon. There's still one car full of guys parked over by the phone booth. Don't know what they're waiting for."

Top Dog lowered his voice and pointed to one of his drivers, "Pull the car with our guns into the alley behind the bar, and open the trunk. We'll meet you there. Six of us are going to take a little stroll." He spoke to both his drivers, "You guys, be ready to pick us up the second you hear things get nasty. Chug your drinks and let's get going."

Fifteen minutes later, six shadowy figures, armed with shotguns, stepped out of the dark alley across the highway and headed toward the Catanetti car. The drowsy Catanetti men sat smoking and yawning and never saw them coming.

The Hellman gang lined up along the passenger side of the Catanetti sedan and, firing their twelve-gauge shotguns, shattered the windows and killed all the men inside. Crimson blood gushed over their bullet-ridden wool suits and flowed down the spattered seats, pooling onto the floorboards.

Top Dog shouted, "Let's roll!" as his cars roared up, pausing long enough for the six killers to jump in. They sped toward Buster's General Store and turned left, spitting gravel in all directions as they hauled ass up the mountain, slowing only for the hairpin turns.

Top Dog's new orders from Victor Hellman were to skip the vineyards and attack Ray's home. Kill as many people as possible. Since they'd just eliminated half the Catanetti's soldiers, Top Dog was confident it wouldn't take long to kill the rest of them.

As Angelo neared Buster's General Store, he spotted two sets of headlights snaking up the mountain toward Ray's farmhouse. He roared into the Esso gas station and slammed on his brakes in front of the phone booth where the Catanetti's ravaged sedan was parked, only to find it filled with bloody corpses.

Patrons from the bar and diner cautiously headed toward the bullet-ridden car as Angelo leaped into the phone booth, frantically dialing the vineyard's number.

"Ray, both of Hellman's cars are heading to your farmhouse now. Go! Go! Go!" he screamed, dropping the phone.

Angelo's first instinct was to speed after Hellman's thugs, but the anxious town folks continuing in his direction forced him to make a different decision. The less the public knew about them, the better. He grabbed his shotgun and pumped round after round into the mutilated car's full gas tank until it exploded into a flaming hot fireball.

The shocked crowd screamed and retreated in panic as Angelo burned rubber out of the parking lot, praying he'd make it in time. He swerved left up the gravel road and raced after the tiny red dots of the Hellman gang's taillights nearing the top of the Lewis family's mountain farm.

CHAPTER NINETEEN

The Battle
Ray
March 10, 1938

My stomach churned when Angelo slammed the phone down in my ear. Of course. Why waste time killing anyone at the vineyards when you can attack the farm and murder the whole family? Sounds like a lesson right out of Jack Lee's playbook.

I shouted orders at everyone, "Pierre, load up your cars and take Bill and your guys up to the farmhouse now! Rico, Luca, get in my truck!"

The three of us packed into the front seat with our shotguns propped between their legs. I slammed my gas pedal to the floor and raced back into town. As I made the sharp turn up my gravel road, the truck almost tipped over. We screamed as our bodies collided, but I kept a white-knuckled grip on the steering wheel and continued tearing up the mountain.

"Goddammit!" I shouted at no one.

Crazy thoughts darted through my mind as I prepared for the oncoming madness. I pleaded with God not to punish me for the terrible things I'd done. I begged Him to protect the people I love, promising to be a better person.

As I roared onto the property, I spied Angelo's car backed into the woods facing the farmhouse. He'd barely made it past the entrance. His headlights prevented the attackers from using the trunks of their cars as cover. Bullets pinged off the side of my truck as I zipped past them, down the side of the house, and screeched to a stop in front of the garage.

Gunfire was exchanged between the upper windows of the house and Hellman's men, who were hunkered down between their cars, closely parked side by side.

All the tractors and farm equipment faced the front lawn from the barn, their headlights blazing toward the gang to blind them.

Following my directions, Rico and Luca grabbed their guns and ammo, jumped into the rear of my truck, and clung to the cargo restraint straps. The thugs weren't expecting I'd use my truck as a weapon. But that's exactly what it was; a big powerful box capable of doing damage to anything in its path.

As soon as my truck's rear doors banged shut, I ground its gears into reverse, pushed the accelerator to the floor, and flew backward, crashing into the back end of the closest car. The truck shuddered as it forced the sedan to slide sideways into the opposite one, forming a V shape. Men dashed toward the front of the cars to escape being crushed while shots rang out from the farmhouse.

I pulled forward just enough so the Catanetti brothers could shove the back doors wide open. Armed and elevated, they could shoot anyone who popped into their view.

Scooting across the front seat, I exited through the passenger door with my shotgun in hand and crouched by its large tires, figuring out how to get as close to the gang's cars as I could. With Angelo's headlights illuminating their sedan's trunks, no one could hide there without Angelo shooting them. Confident that he would recognize me, I darted behind the Hellman cars and stopped at the rear of the furthest one.

Angelo's whistle came from my left where he'd backed into the wood's edge, but I wasn't sure where he was hiding. A brief wave from the passenger's side of his front hood caught my attention.

Abruptly, a shot rang out from upstairs, chipping off a hunk of his fender. My brother and father didn't know if Angelo was a friend or foe. They might not be aware I was at the rear of the Hellman gang's car either and think I was part of the gang.

A jiggling movement from inside the back seat of the car I squatted behind caught my attention. Curious, I waited. On the driver's side, the backseat rear door opened for a split second and closed. Someone was hiding in there.

Two of our farm workers screamed when the Hellman gang shot them. Luca and Rico then blasted two of their men and shot at whoever moved between the gang's cars.

I figured the gang must only have a few members left. They'd have to know they're trapped between my family upstairs with a primo view of their cars and the Catanetti brothers elevated in the back of my truck, picking them off one at a time. Not that they deserved it, but I could give them a chance.

I ripped off my jacket and shirt, removed my white undershirt, and redressed. After tying it around my shotgun's barrel, I waved it high, knowing it would show up in the illumination of Angelo's headlights behind me and the farm equipment in front of me. I hoped like hell my family wouldn't shoot me.

"Stand up slowly," my father roared from upstairs.

"Everyone hold your fire," I shouted, rising so my family would recognize me.

"Hellman gang, give up and we'll let you live. Put your weapons down and step out with your hands up."

The gang's hands shot into the air. Three men, illuminated by the tractor's headlights, walked away from the front end of the cars. No one had red hair.

"How many are dead?" I shouted.

One guy yelled back, "Four!"

"Any injured?"

"No."

One man was still unaccounted for.

I banged on the car's trunk. "You inside the car! Come out with your hands up."

The driver's side back door opened; long thick legs swung out, followed by a shock of red hair. Still seated, Top Dog held his left arm high for me to see.

"Get out and walk toward the front of the car," I ordered, my shotgun aimed at him.

He bent forward and stood up straight, angling his body away from me. Without warning, he swung around with a gun in his right hand and opened fire. Prepared the second that red hair emerged from the back seat, I put two shots in the broad expanse of his chest, causing his bullets to go wild.

That set off a chain reaction. Yelling and screaming, his men pulled the guns they'd hidden beneath their shirts and began shooting at the house and the Catanetti brothers.

Stupid move.

The Catanettis killed two of them. The last guy trying to escape was shot from the upstairs window.

Angelo appeared next to me, nodded, and left to join Rico and Luca.

My chest tightened as my heart hammered away. I wanted to check on my family, but I needed a moment to collect myself. This horrible nightmare was my fault. All because I killed Tito Zayas. How could I explain any of this to Father without mentioning the Mafia?

Moments later, a few cars pulled onto our property, their headlights sweeping over the bodies of Top Dog and all his dead men, lying where they fell.

The vineyard manager, Pierre, Angelo's driver, Bill, and the vineyard workers piled out of their vehicles. They lost no time helping carry the two fatally wounded farm workers to the porch, laying them on its wooden floor. Then they rushed to assist the three wounded men down to the basement, where there was an area designed years before to care for injured farm workers.

Father stepped onto the porch and shouted, "If anyone needs medical attention, come to the house! The doctor is on his way."

Mother covered the deceased bodies lying on the porch in white sheets. She then comforted the families of the dead and injured who were arriving from the safety of their migrant cabins beyond the field.

Rosa, our cook, returned. She exchanged a few words with Mother, who nodded and patted her shoulder before Rosa went inside.

My heart was still pounding when Monty joined Mother and Father on the brightly lit porch. The three of them, pointing at every part of the bloody scene, were searching for me.

I didn't want to worry them further, so I waved and fought back tears. Everything receded into slow motion, and only they existed, safe and alive. I thanked God they were unharmed. My soul took a snapshot of them and promised to produce it if I ever needed to remember their love.

As the time returned to normal, I hurried over, reassuring everyone that I wasn't hurt.

Luca and Rico shouted in glee, holding up a bag of cash they found in Top Dog's car.

Then two of the vineyard workers discovered, other than a few flat tires, both cars could still be driven.

After the guys from the vineyards changed the tires, they stacked the dead bodies in the car trunks. Father thanked them and before they left, promised a reward for their help.

The doctor arrived after driving from Romney, forty minutes away, and headed to the basement with his medical bag to care for the three wounded farm workers.

Father spoke to José Sr., handed him a bottle of something, probably tequila, and shook his hand. José Sr. called out to his workers, held it up, and strolled to the barn.

Exhausted, the rest of us followed Father into his study to celebrate our successful battle with shots of his finest whiskey.

It was midnight when we gathered in the dining room where hot roast beef, steaming vegetables, and buttered biscuits filled the center of the table.

Mother thanked my friends for coming such a long way to help us. Neither she nor Father knew any of them were Mafia—only that they were tough young men who fought bravely for us. She asked them about growing up in South Florida, frowning when they described what living with mosquitos, alligators, and hurricanes was like.

It came as a surprise to me when Mother told them her brother, Matthew, lived in Seaport but died about five years ago when his vehicle collided with a car and killed a young couple.

"Even though my sister-in-law has never responded to my letters, I think she and her young daughter still live there."

Monty inquired, "Mom, are they the ones whose little girl has gray eyes like yours?"

"Yes, dear. Do you recall giving her piggyback rides around the farm and showing her how to gather eggs without breaking them? She was four, I think. She must be eleven now."

"Mother, I wish I'd known. When I go back to Seaport, I'll check on them," I said.

"That's fine, son, but I hope it's not too soon. This was quite a frightful evening."

"I'm sorry, Mother. Don't worry, I'm sticking around for a while."

She smiled and turned to the guys. "We've got dessert and coffee coming up next."

Angelo slipped his chair back and put his napkin on the table. "Mr. and Mrs. Lewis, thank you for the delicious meal, but if you'll please excuse us for a few minutes, Rico, Luca, and I need to make a quick phone call. Mr. Lewis, may we use your telephone?"

"Sure, it's on my desk in the study."

"I'll come with you," I said. "I want to thank your brother for sending you guys. Your help was invaluable."

"Give him our gratitude as well, Ray," Father said, as I followed Angelo, Luca, and Rico across the hall.

CHAPTER TWENTY

The Witness
Rosa
March 10, 1938

AFTER THE HORRENDOUS EVENTS OF THE EVENING, Rosa smiled as she took the empty plates and serving bowls from the table back to the kitchen, thinking how nice it was to have Mr. Monty home with his family again. She was glad she'd prepared the next day's dinner in advance. All she had to do was pop it in the oven as soon as she arrived. The pies were ready, so she set them aside to cool.

Rosa didn't know who these dinner guests were. She only knew they'd arrived in time to help Mr. Ray save the family and farm. It made her happy they'd enjoyed every bite of the food she'd prepared. After hearing their stories about growing up in South Florida with its biting bugs, monster alligators, and huge killer storms, she vowed she would never go there.

When Rosa returned to finish cleaning the table, the driver, Bill, was concentrating on the conversation between Monty and his parents, who sat across from Bill. Missus Marlene, who always sat with the kitchen on her right so she could communicate with Rosa through the doorway, smiled at her and nodded. It was their code for everything is going well, to carry on.

As Rosa gathered the last few items, the driver, Bill, excused himself to use the bathroom. When he returned, he closed the dining-room door and took his seat with his back to it.

Rosa wiped the table while Mr. Monty, who sat at the head of the table with his back to the kitchen door, explained his plans after the Army.

"I'm going to study law at whatever university accepts me, then maybe run for office. I don't care about Ivy League schools anymore. The Army taught me to value real people. The everyday working man and his family."

"You'll be successful at whatever you do. I'm proud of you, son," his father said.

Rosa knew Monty would make a wonderful lawyer. *That boy could argue... oh my, he wouldn't stop until you gave up, especially when sweets were involved.*

She finished wiping the table and headed to the kitchen, thinking about how many coffee cups and dessert plates were needed. As Rosa passed her, Missus Marlene told the driver, who'd been quiet throughout dinner, that warm beds were being prepared for them in the empty cabins beyond the barn and fields.

"Young man, as soon as Ray and his friends return, we'll serve dessert. After that, our farm manager will drive you out there."

In a harsh voice, the driver snapped, "It's Bill."

"Excuse me?" Missus Marlene's voice climbed. Rosa was already in the kitchen gathering the dessert plates and thought the Missus's voice sounded clipped.

"My name. It's Bill Hellman—those dumbass Catanetti guys don't know that, though."

Rosa's ears perked up when Mr. Sebastian barked, "Now why in the hell not?"

Bill replied snidely, "Because, Victor, the man who rescued me when I was a little guy, stranded and living on the streets, gave me a special job to do. That's why I'm here."

When Bill's chair scraped across the floor, Rosa hurried to the kitchen door to see what in the world was going on. She had the entire dining room in her view.

In a loud, snotty voice, Bill sneered, "Compliments from Victor Hellman," and within seconds, Rosa witnessed the most horrifying event of her entire life.

Bill shot Mr. Sebastian in the heart. Swinging the gun towards Missus Marlene, he shot her in the head. Then he shot Mr. Monty once before Mr. Monty dove under the dining room table.

Terrified he would shoot her too, Rosa crouched down next to the doorway as Mr. and Mrs. Lewis's chairs skidded away, dumping their bodies onto the polished oak floor. Bill continued shooting through the tabletop at Monty, whose blood poured out of several bullet holes in his military jacket.

After flipping to his stomach, with his switchblade open, Monty wriggled toward Bill's legs and cut through the back of his ankle with a quick slicing motion. Yelling in pain, Bill collapsed to the floor, his gun banging into the dining room wall, sliding away from him.

Rosa began screaming for Mr. Ray as Bill snaked across the floor, reaching for his gun.

CHAPTER TWENTY-ONE

The Unthinkable
Ray
March 10, 1938

WE WERE ON THE PHONE WITH FRANCO WHEN THE GUNSHOTS started and Rosa began screaming, "Mr. Ray! Mr. Ray!" I hung up mid-sentence and bolted out of the study, almost tripping over Angelo, who was in front of me with his gun drawn.

He burst through the dining-room door and shot their fucking asshole driver in the back of the head. Bill's brains blew out all over the floor and spattered the wall.

I circled the table where Mother and Father lay together, staring at nothing, their blood mingling as it trickled across the floor.

Monty was struggling to breathe, trying to call me from beneath the table. Angelo and Luca hastened to move it out of the way so I could kneel and cradle him in my arms.

Blood pumped from the bullet holes in his Army jacket flowed across my pants and dripped onto the surrounding floor, painting it bright red.

"Don't die, Monty!" I cried, tears streaming. "I need to tell you about Maw and your little sisters. Please don't die, brother... I love you."

I had to lower my head to hear Monty's soft voice, "I... love..." and then as his breath faded away, I watched the light in his eyes—disappear.

Rosa sped past me, running toward the basement shrieking for the doctor who was still tending to the three farm workers, shot earlier in the evening. Just as the doctor dashed into the dining room, José Sr. rushed through the front door, only to witness a bloodbath.

A primal wail started deep in my belly as my ear-piercing screams roared from my soul. My anguish echoed beyond the old log, down the mountain trail, and swirled around Maw's grave, sorrowfully proclaiming her son was dead. When my screams became howls and then moans, I continued hugging my brother's limp body close, rocking back and forth.

Angelo and José Sr. took Monty from me and laid him beside my parents as I crouched near them and sobbed in despair over their lifeless bodies. My father, who taught me about life and business to ensure I'd be successful at whatever I did, and my sweet, beautiful mother, always so patient and encouraging, was dead.

How could I go on without them or Monty, my funny brother, my best friend? I had just gotten him back and now the one who taught me to laugh, wanted to marry a movie star, and become a senator was ripped away from me forever.

The doctor pronounced their deaths on Friday, March 11, 1938, at 1:30 a.m.

I was alone.

CHAPTER
TWENTY-TWO

Grief and Gratitude
Ray
March 1938

I LOCKED MYSELF IN MY ROOM THAT FIRST WEEK and refused to bathe or eat. I drank a lot of whiskey to ease my pain, but it didn't work.

Every day Angelo stood outside my bedroom door with updates from Franco trying to entice me out of bed, but nothing worked, except I was relieved to hear Carmelita was doing well in Mama Catanetti's care.

By the end of that week, Angelo yelled through my door that the front page of the Seaport newspaper was buzzing with the story of dead bodies discovered in two shot-up cars parked in the middle of the street in front of Victor Hellman's home.

The next time I returned from the bathroom, laughter rang out from downstairs, so I expected Angelo to bang on my bedroom door with the latest news. Sure enough, minutes later he yelled, "Hey Ray, they found an unidentified decapitated head on Victor Hellman's front porch, a couple of dismembered hands in his mailbox, holding his mail, and a leg rotting on his roof!"

I'm sure the bits and pieces belonged to Bill. No doubt Rico's doing.

After ten days, Angelo banged on my door and shouted, "Downstairs—fifteen minutes!"

"Fuck you, Angelo."

"Or I'll drag you out of there and throw your ass in the shower myself."

When I emerged showered, shaven, and dressed, I followed him into the study, where he pointed to the chair behind Father's desk.

"Sit," he said and pushed a page of notes in front of me. "I've got a lot of information to get through, so let's start with this list of people you need to contact."

First on the list was the funeral home.

"Headstones need to be selected. Rosa has already delivered your parents' burial clothes to them."

I made a note to thank her.

"Your father's attorney, Mr. Goldman, called. He's prepared the paperwork to transfer your father's bank accounts into your name so you can sign the payroll checks for the farm and winery employees. Their families depend on it."

I nodded and put a checkmark next to Mr. Goldman's name.

"Pierre, from the winery, calls every day, complaining about bottling difficulties, and that you need a new delivery driver. I told him to stop bitching, fix the damn machine, and hire a driver unless he needs his mommy to do it for him."

That made me smile, but his next words were blunt and hurtful.

"This is your house now, Ray. Your parent's possessions are boxed and stored in the basement until you can deal with them. Rosa and the staff are moving your things into the master bedroom right now. Get used to it."

I wasn't ready to make that decision. Maybe I never would be. But it's a good thing I didn't have to think about it. My eyes welled up.

Angelo didn't skip a beat and began talking about my brother.

"I told Mr. Goldman to send a copy of Monty's death certificate to his commanding officer before he's classified as AWOL. Rosa found a clean uniform in his duffle bag. Maybe you'd like to bury him in it?"

Angelo laid Father's key ring on the desk. The house key brought memories of my first visit here by horse and wagon to find the most beautiful home I'd ever seen. Now it was mine.

Father's car keys. His cherry-red Packard was only a few months old. God, he was so proud of that car. Now—mine, too.

The gun case key took me back to the night of the attack.

Angelo saw me studying it. "José Sr. cleaned and oiled your guns before locking them in your gun case."

"Father's gun case," I corrected him.

"It's yours now." He quietly stared at me until I nodded.

"Moving on," he said. "Your father's coal mine partners called. They want you to sell your father's shares to them as soon as possible. Those arrogant pricks think you're in a weak position. That's called a fire sale. Watch out. They'll try to fuck you."

"Thanks for the advice. I'll let Mr. Goldman know."

Angelo then pushed over a decorative box filled with cards and letters. "Besides these, some people sent flowers. You were in no shape to enjoy them. Here's a list of who sent what."

Last, he told me that Franco would arrive this weekend with a gift, and they'd drive back to Florida together in Franco's car. Angelo gave his car to José Sr. in gratitude for his help.

José Sr.—oh God, I'd forgotten how close he was to Father. And Rosa too. My throat tightened, knowing they were traumatized and mourning as well. I needed to do something special for them.

"You can take it from here," Angelo mumbled. "The Catanettis are your family, Ray. Let us know whatever you need."

I stood. "I know what I need. Whenever Don Marco is ready to put that worthless piece-of-shit murderer, Victor Hellman, out of his misery, it'll give me great pleasure to do it."

"I'll tell him your wishes. Don Marco believes sometimes an extensive period between hits can conceal motive and weaken an investigation. It's important that nothing points to you or us, so be patient and wait. Victor Hellman is a dead man. He just doesn't know it yet. But you must wait until you hear from Don Marco before doing anything."

"Deal. Now, if you'll excuse me, Angelo, I have a few phone calls to make."

After the driver Bill murdered my family, I journeyed through grief, wallowing in shock, denial, and depression. I also begged God not to punish me for my sins. He did anyway.

Late at night, I shook my fist at the ceiling and shouted, "Screw you, God! *You* allowed this to happen. I don't believe in *You* anymore. *You* don't exist."

Ten days were all my friends gave me to grieve before I began my journey alone. It was time to solve my problems without complaint, as I had vowed to Don Marco. But Father's favorite quote provided me with the strength to carry on:

"Life is a storm, my young friend. You will bask in the sunlight one moment, be shattered on the rocks the next. What makes you a man is what you do when that storm comes."

Forced to cast off the boy I was and allow a nineteen-year-old man to emerge, I had to fill the mighty big shoes of my father, Sebastian Lewis. The question was, could I do it?

CHAPTER
TWENTY-THREE

Franco's Gift
Ray and Carmelita
March 26, 1938

FRANCO WAS SITTING ON THE PORCH ADMIRING THE WESTERN VIEW of the Appalachian Mountains, still white with snow, when Angelo and I returned from my family's funeral. Off to the east, the magnificent sprawling valley, whose smoky gray color comes late in the day, filled the chilly air with a fresh, clean smell.

Everyone was ready for a stiff drink, especially me, so we settled in my study for a few glasses of Father's fine whiskey. It might be my study now, but it will always be Father's whiskey.

"Rico and Luca told me about your farm, but my brothers were only here at night. This place is paradise, my friend." Franco pointed in a circle, indicating all of it.

I looked at him for a second. "Before you leave, we'll hike down the mountain so you can see the paradise I grew up in."

Rosa popped in and reported dinner would be ready in about an hour.

Franco mentioned he left a gift in my bedroom, but needed a nap first after the long drive.

"That sounds perfect to me," I said.

I was exhausted as well. After excusing myself, I dragged my weary body up the stairs, forgetting about Franco's gift until I reached my room. A little angel was curled up in the middle of my bed, asleep under a brilliant crimson silk shawl, her head resting on my pillow. When I sat on the edge of the bed and lifted her silky hair away from her face, her sleepy eyes opened.

"Welcome to my home, Carmelita. Mi casa es tu casa."

"Gracias, Ray," she whispered as she began sitting up.

It broke my heart to bury my family today. But knowing I'd helped protect this damaged orphan when I wasn't able to save my little sisters pushed me over the edge. I couldn't stop my tears.

After dinner, I tucked Carmelita back into bed and joined Angelo and Franco, who relaxed on the sofa in the study. I poured us drinks and sat down in the overstuffed chair across from them.

"Franco, first, thank you for saving Carmelita. Second, I don't have an inkling how to raise her. Third, spill the beans, man. What happened? Oh, and don't leave out how she got that red silk thing, either."

Franco laughed. "It's funny now, but it wasn't then."

Then meaning when he left with his driver and two of his toughest guys to rescue Carmelita. He was furious that a child was being prostituted in one of their establishments. But knowing the madam never said a word about it angered him even more. Angelo enjoyed telling the story of Carmelita's rescue sixteen days before, the same day my family was taken from me. While I didn't want to think about that night, I was interested in how Franco rescued her.

He said after we hung up that night, he and his men drove to The Cat House Saloon and confronted the madam. Carmelita was still locked in that tiny space, wearing that same filthy top I described on the phone. That bitch didn't give the little girl anything clean to wear. Franco asked the madam to interpret for him since the girl didn't speak English. But what she said to the little girl was so distressful, Carmelita's eyes grew enormous, and she screamed. One of Franco's bodyguards dragged the madam out of the room and slammed her against the wall in the hallway.

"My remaining bodyguard recommended I speak slowly to her in Italian, since Spanish and Italian are close languages," recounted Franco. "It worked. When I explained you had sent me to take her to a safe place, where no one would ever hurt her again, she wept."

I realized that underneath our tough exteriors, we were all softies at heart. That last part made us all teary. I proposed a distraction to save face. Angelo glanced away as I offered to freshen everyone's drinks.

"Ray, she had nothing," Franco said, with sadness in his eyes. Frowning, he handed me his empty glass.

"No shoes, no hairbrush, no clothes," Franco continued. "Since I couldn't take her out of there in that disgusting thing she wore, I tore the madam's room apart and found a long black ribbon and that red silk shawl. I draped it around her shoulders and used the ribbon to tie it at the waist, making it into a dress."

I finished refilling our glasses and passed them back. Franco sipped his before setting it on the side table.

"After I gathered Carmelita up in my arms, I warned the madam if she said a single word about this little girl to anyone, I would... cut out... her wagging tongue."

That's the sinister side of Franco I hadn't seen until now.

"I advised the madam she was lucky to be alive after she disrespected me, and promised if she ever took another child as a prostitute or mistreated any of the girls, she wouldn't live to enjoy her job." Franco's voice cracked with tension as he took another sip of whiskey.

"One of my guys stayed to find out who dropped the girl off at our establishment while we waited in the car. Within minutes, he joined us and reported that a man, at least sixty years old, someone the madam had never met before, showed up one night and left the girl there. Then the madam pissed herself, swearing that was all she remembered."

"How'd it go when you brought an orphan home to your mother?" I asked.

"Mama took over and soon had the little girl bathed, shampooed, and dressed in the extra clothes she keeps on hand for my sisters' kids. She said Carmelita kept that red shawl with her at all times, like it was a freedom cloth or something. Mama taught her a bit of English, so the girl can at least fumble through telling you what she needs now."

I nodded and swirled my glass of whiskey.

"After a few days, though, Mama called me and said, 'Carmelita keeps asking for your friend, Ray.' I explained you were ill, but as soon as you recovered, I would bring the little girl to you for protection. I checked back later, and she assured me the answer satisfied Carmelita. Yesterday, when I picked Carmelita up, Mama told me every night before bed that little girl kneeled and prayed that you would get better soon."

I looked away and swallowed, trying to relax the lump in my throat, and changed the subject. "Why only give me ten days?"

"The police found the bodies of a couple of our prostitutes who disappeared the night after Tito died. The madam is missing too. No one knows where she is. We're positive it was Victor Hellman's men who killed them."

"That's terrible, Franco! And your dad? What did he say?"

"When Pop found out, he tripled the guards around his house," Franco replied. "But he also wanted Carmelita to leave Seaport as soon as possible, in case there was an attack at our compound. You needed to function for that to happen."

Now I understood the rush.

Franco continued, "Victor Hellman is a ruthless murdering prick with a giant, vengeful streak. He will kill anyone associated with whoever is on his shit list. But Pop decides when and where a war will happen, not Victor."

"I get it, Franco. I'm grateful to you and your family for protecting her." I looked down and yawned. "It's been a long, hard day. Let's say goodnight."

As I lay in bed, my mind was filled with all the changes in my life. I'd lost my parents and brother, but I gained an unconventional family with new brothers and powerful friends. And a young girl to protect, nurture, and educate. I just wasn't sure how.

It didn't matter. My supportive farm staff would guide me.

I took a vow. No whining or complaining—it was time to show courage in the face of adversity. I'm sure it's what Mother and Father would want me to do.

The day before Angelo and Frank left, I kept my promise to take them to the cabin where I grew up. Carmelita stayed behind gathering eggs and jabbering away in Spanish with José Sr.'s six-year-old son, José Jr. When we left, they were running around the farm, and playing with the animals under the watchful eyes of Rosa.

Our hike started behind the garage. Beyond it lay the dense foliage Monty fought through a few weeks earlier.

I hacked a better trail with my machete, pointing out the valuable ginseng plants just off the path, and avoiding the wide-leafed poisonous castor beans that popped up here and there.

It intrigued them to learn that four castor beans could kill a horse and one could kill a man. Before they got any ideas about taking any home with them, I made sure they knew extracting the poison was a delicate procedure that could kill the person preparing it. That's all it took to switch that light bulb off.

A mile later, stepping into the clearing, I led them past the graves of Maw and my little sisters, off to the side of my cabin's burned-out shell, and explained their murders.

"This is where I killed a man for the first time."

Nothing more needed to be said about my motives when we paused at the gravestones before heading back up the trail to the farmhouse. I then told them the story of my birth—the infant mix-up and growing up as Monty's friend—neither of us knowing we were half-brothers. I finished by explaining our special meeting place just as we arrived at the log.

When we began our trek earlier, they walked past the old log with no idea of its importance. But now it held a fresh perspective as the sun's mystical shafts of light spilled through the trees, creating a spiritual place where silence was its only language. The thick log, with delicate ferns and fragile mushrooms sprouting from its sides, waited patiently for the young boys, who once took solace in sharing their dreams, to return one day.

The next day, as they prepared to leave for Seaport, I asked Franco if his mama might want to drive Mother's brand-new lemon-yellow Nash Ambassador Cabriolet sitting in my garage, breaking my heart each time I walked past it. After one quick look, he was sure his mama would love it.

Our farewell was tough. Their friendship and brotherhood put me back on my feet. Franco rescued a little girl from a hellish future, and Angelo kept my farm and winery operating by sharing his leadership and management skills. Now I would be the one leading and managing.

With their suitcases tucked into their trunks prepared to leave, Carmelita timidly stepped forward and offered Franco her red silk shawl and said, "Gracias a tú madre."

Franco kneeled and told her in English that one day, when madre no longer needed it, the beautiful shawl would be returned to her.

Carmelita understood every word.

CHAPTER TWENTY-FOUR

Advice, Confidence, and a Third Father
Ray and Don Marco Catanetti Sr.
1938

THE WEEK BEFORE THANKSGIVING, I FACED A BUSINESS DILEMMA. Since Franco's strong suit was in finance, I asked him about the offer I'd received from Father's coal mine partners and their insistent pressure for me to sell. Franco said he would get back to me.

Sure enough, Marco Sr. called the next night. "Raimondo, I'm so sorry Bill Hellman slipped past all our security measures. It doesn't bring your family back, but know that the person who vouched for Bill paid a deadly price. Since then, every man who works for me has been thoroughly scrutinized."

"Thank you."

"Angelo filled me in on the conversation he had with your father's coal mine partners. I agree with him. They'll try to fuck you," Don Marco Sr. warned in a grave voice.

"I got that feeling as well."

"Let me ask you a few questions before we discuss how to handle your partners. Does coal make you so much money that it's worth all this aggravation? Or would you rather do something else with your time other than fill your father's shoes?"

That's a question I'd been struggling with. "The coal mine makes money, but I don't love it. I'll sell it at the right price."

"Understood, go on," Don Marco urged.

"As for doing something else, before Father died, I was working on a plan to set up a transportation business. If Father hired my company to deliver his fresh produce and wine to market, it would have eliminated the cost of the trucks and drivers from his expenses. I never got to pitch it to him."

After he lit a cigar, I waited, listening to Don Marco puffing away.

"Good to know, Ray. I'll keep that in mind. Meanwhile, regarding selling the coal mine, here are a few suggestions on how to handle your father's associates."

He cleared his voice while I pulled a few pieces of notepaper over and dipped my fountain pen into the inkwell, ready for his advice.

"Insist on meeting the partners without their lawyers in your attorney's boardroom early on a Monday morning. Arrive at least fifteen minutes late. That's your first sign of disrespect. Those guys knew your father's strengths, but they don't know yours. They're expecting a rich kid with no backbone. You're going to show them how wrong they are."

I jotted down: *Monday a.m., Atty's office, late.*

"Wear your best black suit. No tie. That's your second sign of disrespect. Also, wear a shoulder holster and make sure they get a glimpse. If they know you're armed, they'll understand why they shouldn't piss you off."

Suit, no tie, gun.

"Stroll in tough and look mean, like you'll punch them in the face if they give you any lip. Then slam some bogus files on the table and, in an outraged voice, tell them they've insulted you with their puny-bone-to-a-starving-dog offer."

The picture he painted was so enjoyable, I grinned from ear to ear, then snickered. It might have been my first chuckle since my family died.

Look mean, fake files, dog.

I couldn't wait to see their faces when I used that starving dog line.

"Go on, sir. I'm writing this down."

Don Marco continued, "Tell them Mr. Charles Luciano is a close friend of the family. He thinks energy is the ideal investment and offered you five times their amount. If you accept Lucky's offer, his top men will arrive within twenty-four hours to inspect their financial records and the coal mine. Warn them, they'd better be there to greet Lucky's men or it ain't gonna be pretty if they have to come looking for them."

"Isn't Lucky in prison, sir?" I asked, and added, *Lucky, 5x$$, 24 hrs,* to my list.

"Yes, he is. But your partners probably don't know that. If they do, assure them Lucky Luciano has an active organization. Even jail can't stop him from investing."

I could hear his chair squeak as he sat back, relit his cigar, and puffed away for a few seconds. After a slight cough, he cleared his throat and continued.

"Ray, here's where you intimidate them with your threatening attitude. Ask if they'd like to meet Lucky Luciano's top men because you can arrange it within minutes. Then snap your fingers—like this."

I heard the loud snap and laughed out loud, imagining their faces when a bunch of wise guys, dressed in pin-striped suits with holsters bulging under their armpits, showed up for a tour of the coal mine. Seeing that would make any hardship worth it.

"Finish by saying they have until five Thursday evening to submit their final bid. If it's less than Mr. Luciano's, you will accept his offer at nine Friday morning."

"Got it." I breathed a sigh of relief. It made sense to set a timeline, so I'd know what my next step would be if they didn't cooperate.

Last bid 5p Thursday, 9a Friday accept Lucky's, I wrote.

"After that, scoop up your files, turn your back on them, and stomp out. Expect a juicy deal before Thursday. If not, let me know and I'll send some of my wise guys along with my tight-ass accountant down there to scare the crap out of them. When he gets through with them, they won't know which end is up."

My list was done.

"Sir, that's a fantastic strategy. Thank you so much."

He chuckled. He was enjoying this scenario just as much as I was.

"Good. Now, to change the subject. My wife loves your mother's yellow Nash, which I must admit, is a beauty. I'd like to buy it for my wife's birthday. Are you interested in selling?"

I didn't see that one coming.

"Mr. Catanetti, it's my pleasure to give the car to your wife. Mama Catanetti helped my little friend, Carmelita, who adores her. I'm in your debt for protecting Carmie."

"Ray, call me Pop or Papa Marco. Angelo and my boys speak highly of you, and they care for you like a brother. I respect their judgment and it will be my honor to treat you as another son. I appreciate your offer, but the car is my gift to my wife. When you get my check, please send me the title."

"Yes, sir, I will, and thank you for the business lesson."

"Raimondo, call me if you need more advice. And give that sweet Carmelita a hug from me. Mama and I enjoyed spoiling her. Tell her Mama plans to wear the red shawl at Christmas and is proud of her for making it into the fifth grade. Goodnight, Ray."

After laying my pen down, I sighed in relief, relaxed my shoulders, and sat back in my chair, staring at nothing. I had a damned good plan.

By the end of the following week, the coal mine partners offered six times their original bid, and the sale closed soon afterward without a single problem. Papa Marco's advice worked. With that completed, I was extremely wealthy. The weight of people's lives and jobs was lifted from my shoulders. The farm and winery would be solvent no matter what happened.

But I learned something else. My greatest feelings of reward came from helping people.

In memory of my family, the widows of the two deceased farm employees received a substantial amount of cash to keep them comfortable throughout life. I also generously contributed to the injured men and the farm workers who protected us that night. The men from the winery received an extra month's pay to honor Father's pledge.

Then I turned my attention to José Sr. Together, we designed a large cottage for him and his family on a piece of property near my orchards. The moment we finished building it, they moved in, grateful to leave their small migrant cabin.

Rosa needed a car. When I told her she could have whichever one she wanted, as long as it was brand new, she started fanning her face and had to sit down.

Papa Marco received a dozen cases of his favorite wine in appreciation for his advice.

And I? Besides being a very affluent young man, the guardian of a charming little girl, and the caretaker of many employees, I was honored that Marco Catanetti Sr., one of the most respected and powerful Mafia Dons in America, considered himself to be my third father.

CHAPTER
TWENTY-FIVE

Trust No One, Promise Nothing
Ray and Carmelita
Summer 1939

I WAS AT MY DESK POURING OVER THE LEDGERS WHEN ROSA ENTERED my study asking to discuss *"our little lady of the house,"* her term of endearment for Carmie. We'd gone through so much together; we had an unspoken bond. I listened to her advice and said I would make it so.

———————◆———————

Most nights after dinner, Carmelita and I read in the study. She tucked one foot underneath her while I propped my big feet on a leather footstool. But that night, when I folded her book into her lap, she looked up in confusion.

"Carmie, if it's okay, may I ask you some questions about your family? Like, what are their names? And do you have any brothers and sisters?"

She jerked and stared back with sad brown eyes. I'd hit a sore spot. A subject we'd never discussed before.

"Mama and papa are Isabella and Manuel Lopez. I have a little sister and a brother younger than me. I miss them very much." She looked down, gripping her book.

"I'm so sorry." I patted her hand and raised her chin. "Let me ask you a different question. We need to track your age. When is your birthday?"

"Primero de Abril," she quickly replied. "Oh, I mean, April first. At my birthday parties, a paper donkey was filled with candy." The memory made her smile. "We took turns hitting it with a stick to break it open. Everyone grabbed the candy when it dumped all over the floor."

I smiled at her description. "That sounds wonderful. We'll celebrate on April first, then."

Her eyes filled with tears. "No, please Ray. Not without my family."

"Carmie, what birthdate do you want? You can pick a holiday like Christmas or Easter if you wish." I hoped that might cheer her up.

"Can I choose your birthday, Ray? Then I won't be alone."

It's a request I didn't expect. Monty and I celebrated our birthdays pretty much together, so why not?

"Well, sure. Even though you turned eleven in April, we will celebrate it in September, when I turn twenty-one. Is that okay with you?"

With that resolved, I moved to the next touchy subject that was way out of my element.

"Tomorrow, Rosa wants to explain some things to you that happen to girls when they become young ladies. Will you speak to her, please?" I'm sure my face displayed my discomfort.

Carmie stared at me and nodded yes.

With that lady stuff taken care of, I took a deep breath and prepared to talk about the really tough stuff. The day someone kidnapped her. I took her small hand in mine and lightly squeezed it.

"Carmie, what happened to you before I found you in that terrible room?"

A look of horror filled her face. She snatched her hand back, looked away, and fingered the edges of her book.

"It's okay, Carmie, take a breath. Whenever you're ready, just start with the first thing you remember."

She inhaled several times, stuttered a little at first, and began, "I walked home from school. An old man with blanco... ugh, white hair, and dirty clothes, grabbed me, and threw me in the back of his big... ugh..."

The truck she described using her hands was like my wine delivery truck. The kind that moves things. I curled her hand in mine, encouraging her to continue.

"I fell asleep on a stinky rug. The old man carried me over his shoulder into a house and put me on a bed. The room was dark." She halted, watching my eyes.

"Take your time."

"Only one light... across the room... a gray-haired old man gave money to the man who left me there."

Her words slowed. This was the hard part we both hated.

"The other man... hurt me. I don't know how I got to the place where you found me."

Carmelita hit her limit. Sobbing, she slumped into my lap. I mumbled some endearments, but knew we'd both had had enough.

"Time for bed," I said and helped her upstairs to my old bedroom. Rosa had decorated it in pink and white and added one of Grandmother Martin's bright quilts to spread across her bed. I tucked her in and said goodnight.

Without knowing why, I crossed the hall to the doorway of Monty's room. Memories of the night my family died came flooding back, making me nauseous. Even though Victor Hellman ordered the hit on my family, the men I trusted allowed their driver, Bill, to get close enough to pull the trigger and murder them.

Trust no one.

Didn't Father warn me about that?

Standing not quite in or out of Monty's room, I recalled the painful days and nights I spent healing from Jack Lee's vicious beating. When I fumed with anger at Monty for deserting us, I moved out of his room and vowed to never set foot in it again. What good were those words? The entire house was mine now. Shit happens and things change. But what have I learned?

That the risky unknown can alter life? That promises don't come with guarantees? An oath uttered in anger is only an empty sound spat into the air.

The Vow of Omertà was my last pledge. I would make no other.

Promise nothing.

As I entered Monty's room, his folded bloody, bullet-ridden army jacket was still lying on his bed. His dog tags, switchblade, and brass knuckles lay next to it. They fit into an empty cigar box resting on his dresser. Tomorrow the jacket and box would go into my antique trunk.

Needing to put the demons of my past to rest, I climbed into my old bed across from Monty's, burrowed under Grandmother Martin's warm patchwork quilt, and drifted into a deep, peaceful sleep.

CHAPTER
TWENTY-SIX

Don Marco Sr. Makes an Offer
Ray
Summer 1942

FRANCO CALLED THE FIRST WEEK OF AUGUST. His pop was heading to New York City for an important meeting with The Commission. Would it be convenient for him, two bodyguards, and their driver to stay the night with Carmelita and me?

Flattered, of course, I said yes. He would see the farm at its best. The corn was being harvested and Mother's sunflowers were in full bloom.

When they arrived, Carmie, now fourteen, greeted Papa Marco with a big hug, and I got a hearty handshake along with his old-world Italian kiss on both cheeks.

After dinner, Carmelita retired to her room to read the book Mama Catanetti sent her. *Gone with the Wind* was on the top of her list, but the public library in Romney, a forty-minute drive away, couldn't keep it on their shelves.

Papa Marco's men sat on the front porch enjoying their smokes while we retired to my study for a generous crystal snifter of Father's whiskey and a cigar for the Don.

"Raimondo." He got straight to the point in his gravelly voice. "As you asked, I've continuously made inquiries about the person who kidnapped Carmelita.

Recently, I learned it was a man named Stanley Hunter, who owns a trucking company in Seaport. He's Victor Hellman's oldest friend and often does favors for him. That little girl, Carmelita, was payment to Victor for her father's gambling debts. After Hellman raped her, his friend Stanley left her at my establishment. I hate that scumbag bastard." He frowned in disgust and took a sip of his whiskey.

"I hope whoever kills Victor Hellman makes it bloody, brutal, and shocking." That statement hung in the air as he shot me a knowing stare.

"There's nothing I'd like more," I said quietly, validating him.

He nodded, took a puff of his cigar, and continued. "At the right time, my boy... the right time. Now, as for why I'm here. Angelo told me about the dinner conversation when your mother shared that her brother, your uncle Matthew Martin, used to live in Seaport, back in 1933." He swirled his whiskey. Its amber color caught the light and my attention. Half empty. I'd make sure it stayed filled.

"There was an older couple who died in a fire that also destroyed their clothing store. Their hot-headed son-in-law ran around town, accusing us of setting the fire because the old couple wouldn't let us put our Bolita games in their stores. That was both true and untrue. We asked them, they refused, so we moved on. Why burn them down? My men liked their suits and plenty of other stores wanted our games. To stop their loud-mouthed son-in-law from drawing attention to us, we sent your Uncle Matthew..."

"What! Uncle Matthew worked for you?"

Don Marco lowered his eyebrows and stared at me.

I shouldn't have interrupted and mumbled, "Sorry, sir, please go on."

"I sent your Uncle Matthew to run their hot-headed son-in-law off the road in what's called a mock execution, which means to shut him up by scaring him. Sadly, the hot head wasn't alone. His young wife was with him. When their vehicles collided, it killed your Uncle Matthew and the young husband and wife in the other car."

"So that's how my uncle died," I muttered.

Did Mother know her brother worked for the Mafia? How long had Papa Marco known that I was Uncle Matthew's nephew? I didn't have the balls to ask him.

"The young couple who died was Stanley Hunter's son and his daughter-in-law." Papa Marco didn't take his eyes off me.

"What... the old guy who kidnapped Carmelita? My uncle killed his family?"

"There's a saying, Ray, 'When you least expect it, expect it.' It was true that day."

Papa Marco excused himself while I refilled both our glasses.

"When you least expect it" was a phrase that summed up my life and another valuable piece of wisdom from the Don I wouldn't forget.

He didn't miss a beat when he returned. He picked up his drink and resumed his story.

"Stanley Hunter blamed us for his kids' deaths, but he couldn't strike back at us—we could smash him like a fly. Plus, he and his wife had a ten-year-old grandson, Stephen, to raise."

Boy, I knew what raising a young kid felt like.

"We take care of our own, Ray. I keep tabs on your aunt and cousin to make sure they have a roof over their heads and food to eat. Last year, your aunt shared her concern that Stanley Hunter or Victor Hellman might retaliate against her and her daughter, especially since her daughter was growing into such a beautiful young lady.

"Victor Hellman is a ruthless bastard who would help his friend, Stanley Hunter, seek revenge whenever Hunter is ready. So, I had one of my men infiltrate Hellman's crew. After that, I learned everything Victor and Stanley discussed."

His story sounded like it was right out of Father's classic novels. *Could it get any worse?*

Papa Marco told me that after Hunter's grandson, Stephen, enlisted in the Navy, Stanley Hunter, began his vengeance project.

"First, he made sure the community thought of him as an upstanding citizen. He donated to the poor, joined your young cousin's church, and became a faithful member and volunteer," explained Papa Marco. "That's when I added another man to watch old man Hunter. When your teenage cousin joined Hunter in the church's cemetery to plant flowers, my man was prepared to intervene if she was in danger. I'm troubled that Stanley Hunter's getting too close to your cousin."

Definitely getting worse.

When Papa Marco took a moment to relight his cigar, I checked his glass. Still good.

"Stanley Hunter's trucking company has a clean reputation and is successful, but he's having trouble finding skilled mechanics. And he's getting too old to fix the trucks himself. I think Hunter Trucking is the type of transportation company that might interest you."

Papa Marco was working up to something. It intrigued me how he made his way toward his goal. This man did his research.

"So, Raimondo." He got a kick out of calling me that. "Are you happy running this farm and the vineyard? I'm curious because our country is at war. Money is tight and gasoline rations are a problem for long distance distributions. Your wine deliveries to the El Floridita restaurant have slowed down."

I nodded. He was right.

"If that's happening to all your out-of-state clients, they'll need to purchase their wine from vineyards closer to them to serve their customers."

He was right again. The winery's receivables are reflecting our slower wine deliveries. If this war continues for much longer, my winery could take a financial hit. If I lose those clients, I'd have to support the winery with my personal finances. Which I could do, but did I want to?

I replied, "I can deliver wine to the Washington, D.C., area, but I have strong competition from all the vineyards in this state, and that's a problem. I might have to lower my prices, which lowers my profit. Let's face it. I don't share Father's passion for the wine business."

"Have you thought about selling your vineyard to a competitor before your profit takes a nosedive? You'll want your income numbers to be as high as possible before you go to market."

He advised me to keep the farm. He'd been told José Sr. was an excellent manager. Then he proposed I think about trying something new, like moving south, and getting a job with old man Hunter. I'd be close enough to protect my aunt and cousin and pursue my dream of having my own transportation company.

"Please go on." I was intrigued.

Papa Marco grinned with a twinkle in his eyes. "Well... now... if something happens to old man, Hunter, you'll be in a prominent position to take over his trucking business. I call this strategy—playing the long game. It means to keep a low profile, constantly prepare, and be patient, believing an opportunity will come. If you wait and hope, it pays off."

Papa's long game plan made sense. I could have a different life in Seaport and still keep the farm. I could protect the only family I have left and pursue my own dreams.

He took another sip of whiskey and cleared his voice, "And don't forget you could, discreetly, of course, use Stanley Hunter's trucks to deliver our products."

"Let's say the old man tries to hurt my family and gets whacked," I asked. "Then what?"

"You'll access his company finances and run the business until his grandson sells it to you or makes you a partner."

"And if something happens to the grandson?"

"Well... you're a smart guy, Raimondo. You get the picture. Play the long game and use your management skills. Personally, son, I'm planning on you having a terrific future with us."

Papa Marco sweetened the deal by offering Carmelita and me a bungalow in a wooded area of Seaport that would be under his protection. It sounded tempting.

"Ray, if you decide to take my offer—you need to appear strapped for cash. Which means you need to get a job as a mechanic, buy an older truck, and leave your father's flashy red Packard here."

"The farm's not busy in January. Maybe Carmie and I will go south, enjoy the sunshine, and check it out," I replied.

Papa Marco drained his glass and stood up. "One more thing before we say goodnight. Angelo and Franco told me about your cabin and said it's a healthy walk down the mountain. I'd like to stretch these stiff old legs before the long drive tomorrow."

After breakfast, Papa Marco and his men followed me down the gravel trail to the cabin. It took us two summers to cut back all the heavy branches that crisscrossed and blocked the trail. We had to use a wheelbarrow to bring in the finely chopped rock. The walk was much easier now.

When we entered the yard, we faced the blackened shell of a cabin with only the fireplace jutting upward. He knew my story—no reason to repeat it.

"If you want my advice, Ray, rebuild the cabin around the fireplace and maintain its simplicity. It can provide solitude, or concealment, if you ever require that. You might leave it supplied, so you only need fresh food when you visit. If you begin now, you could finish it before you move south. If you move south, that is."

I took Papa Marco's advice and rebuilt the cabin with its entrance facing the side yard to suppress old memories. As I watched it rise from the ashes, I named it Phoenix.

CHAPTER
TWENTY-SEVEN

One Down, One to Go... Maybe Two
Ray and Stephen
1943

AFTER WORKING FOR HUNTER TRUCKING FOR NINE MONTHS, I was well aware of Stanley Hunter's rigid work habits. He was always punctual and stayed the whole day. That made it difficult for me to dive into his account ledgers, but I found a way.

One day, old man Hunter left the office early, saying he didn't feel good. I chalked it up to the bittersweet high-octane coffee our Cuban driver brewed that morning. After one sip of that disgusting sweet shit, I threw mine down the drain. But Mr. Hunter liked that crap and drank a few cups. I figured it was indigestion.

Complaining about the shitty coffee as soon as I walked in the door that afternoon, Carmelita brewed a half pot of Maxwell House for me. Minutes later, as I headed to the sofa with my long-awaited steaming mug and the newspaper, Junior called.

"Pop said to tell you, old man Hunter stopped by Victor Hellman's place earlier this afternoon. Fortunately, our inside guy overheard him discussing his arrangement to meet your cousin at the picture show later tonight. Then he said he'd bring her to Victor to enjoy first. After that, they'd get rid of her body."

That made me sit up straight. "Aw shit, Junior. Really? Now?"

"Hunter just pulled into the Calusa Heights Hardware Store. It'll be dark soon. If you're going to stop him, you'd better hustle."

I sprinted to the kitchen, plunked my cup in the sink, grabbed the tool I needed, and hauled ass out the door, yelling to Carmelita not to wait up.

Old man Hunter was still inside the hardware store when I arrived. Since he never locked his car, I climbed in and crouched in the back seat. A noisy gunshot would have alerted the shoppers. I learned how messy a knife was when I killed Jack Lee, but an icepick? The perfect weapon—silent and deadly.

After he climbed into the front seat and threw his big bag on the front floorboard, he looked down and began fiddling with his car keys. My icepick entered the base of his skull, puncturing his brain, and killing him instantly. Before he could fall forward onto the car's horn, I pushed his body sideways across the passenger seat, where no one would find him until later. I then took the weapon and the bag with me.

Fifteen minutes later, I pulled up next to Seaport General Hospital's huge trash bin and tossed the bloody icepick and the hardware store bag into it. Stanley Hunter's intentions were disturbing. The bag contained a rope and a tarpaulin.

Since I worked for the old man, my alibi needed to be tight. To make sure everyone in the Old Town Bar remembered me, I staggered in, appearing obnoxiously drunk, and continued slugging whiskey shots for another few hours.

The next morning, I was nursing a killer hangover, when the police arrived at the office asking about Stanley Hunter. I gave them my alibi and assured them I didn't know a single soul who would want to hurt that nice old man.

Stanley Hunter became another of Seaport's unsolved murders.

As I expected, Stephen Hunter, on leave from the Navy, arrived to handle his grandfather's affairs and plan his funeral. He called the office saying he knew about me from his grandfather's letters and would like to set up a meeting after he finished with his grandpa's attorneys. A few hours later, he pulled into the office parking lot. "Ray?" he asked, getting out of his grandpa's pickup truck.

We shook hands and settled in my office, where I explained how I could continue to keep his granddad's business in the black while he was away. He looked confused, so I rephrased it as "keeping it profitable."

I described how I'd increased our productivity and profit by redesigning a large storage space in the building's rear for the drivers who came in late to sleep over, wash up, and leave early the next morning. When Stephen looked at his watch for the fifth time, I thought he was disinterested, so I steered the conversation to his plans after the Navy. As I suspected, he wanted to take over his grandfather's business.

"I'm not interested in being just an employee," I said. "I want ownership or a partnership in the future, so think about that. Also, I'll need authorization to sign checks to take care of everything while you're away."

"Since my granddad trusted you, I will too." He slapped the arms of the chair and stood up. "I'll call my attorneys tomorrow for advice on how to proceed."

He then looked at his watch again. "Meanwhile, I have a hot date with a cute blond chick I just met, so I gotta split."

The blond chick turned out to be my cousin, Grace Martin.

It surprised the hell outta me when he married her two weeks after the Navy discharged him. If I'd known, I would've stopped that damned wedding.

1948

We formalized Hunter & Lewis Trucking after we agreed to a forty percent ownership for me. The deal specified I take all the long hauls across the country since he hated to drive. Funny how that worked out in my favor.

During that time, Stephen's and Grace's relationship deteriorated. Stephen constantly whined that Grace bored him and wasn't good in bed anymore.

Fed up with his bullshit, I exploded, "For God's sake, your wife's lost three babies and her mother just died. Stop bitching and cut her some slack."

"Let's go juking," he pleaded. "I need to get laid."

Sick and tired of his nagging, I relented and took him on my Denver run. After we loaded fresh flowers at the Port of Miami for one of our excellent accounts, we transported them to a wholesaler in Colorado. When we finished our flower delivery in Denver, we headed south to Mexico. Before I introduced him to the seedier elements of Juárez, I dumped a dozen rubbers in his lap and told him, "Always use these, no matter what."

While he got shit-faced drunk on tequila and wore himself out with several whores, our semi-truck was loaded with contraband. Stephen then slept through the border pay-off while I drove into the States on schedule. When he woke up, all he wanted to do was relive his sleazy adventure, oblivious that we were returning to Seaport, hauling millions of dollars' worth of cocaine.

I thought the thrill of Juárez was enough for him, but occasionally, he'd cock an eyebrow and warn he needed "another tune-up."

1958

In January, our partnership hit its ten-year mark and Stephen was acting weird. He couldn't focus, was belligerent with customers and vendors, and would leave the office for hours with no explanation.

Finally, I confronted him. "What's going on with you, Stephen?"

"I'm stressed," he mumbled and gave me the stupidest reason ever. "And I'm pissed off that my leather steering wheel cover for my new Chevy is the wrong damned color."

"Your shitty attitude is chasing away business," I informed him.

Not long after that, I barged into his office and caught him with a straw poked up his nose, snorting a line of cocaine off his desktop.

"What the hell, man! That shit's poison! Where did you get that crap?"

"Fuck off, Ray." He glared at me. "So, what if I dabble a little? It's not like you're lily white." Then he banged the straw down on the desk.

Taken aback, I demanded, "What in the hell do you mean by that asinine statement?"

"Like, how did you know about that Juárez whorehouse?" Stephen returned with a sneer before wiping his nose on his shirtsleeve.

That pissed me off. "Don't mess with me, Stephen, or you'll regret it. Now pull yourself together before you lose the most precious thing you have, which is your wife, in case you're too stupid to realize it." I slammed the door on my way out.

After that, he tried to act normal around me, but the day came when I suspected he needed more drugs. He was nervous and rude as hell, and my gut knew that whatever he was up to would most likely happen that night. And if it did, I intended to see where he was getting his dope.

I parked down the street from his house and waited. Around midnight, he snuck out the front door, holding his shoes. I followed him to The Cat House Saloon in Old Town and watched him greet Rico Catanetti like they were old friends. With his wicked grin, Rico held the front door open and motioned for Stephen to join him upstairs.

Hanging out with Rico was bad news.

Stephen stumbled in late the next morning and left early, muttering something about how hot the June nights were getting, and he wasn't sleeping well.

As soon as he was gone for the day, I rummaged through his desk, searching for his dope. When the lap drawer wouldn't open, I crawled under his desk with a flashlight to see what was blocking it and found a thick envelope filled with photographs of him, Rico, and a bunch of other dirtbags jammed in the rear.

After putting it back, I continued my search. The very slight scent of cat piss led me to his cocaine stashed on the top shelf of his bookcase behind our truck manuals. Unfortunately, that vinegary smell came from a small foil packet of brown heroin. Stephen was spiraling downward.

Playing the long game was almost over. I only needed to wait for the right opportunity.

Unfortunately, I waited too long.

CHAPTER
TWENTY-EIGHT

Lives Changed for Better or Worse
Ray and Carmelita
September 1958

WHEN CARMELITA PRESENTED HER CAREFULLY CRAFTED BUSINESS model to Junior, he hired her to establish an import-export business office in Dallas, complete with discreetly situated warehouses to store the Catanettis' valuable goods. It had taken her less than two years and she was already in the black. Based on her success in Dallas and Junior's blessing, Carmelita was making plans for an additional operation further west.

I knew she was taking a week off so we could celebrate our thirtieth and fortieth birthdays together, so it was a surprise to see her car parked in my driveway a day earlier than I expected. However, as soon as I walked in the front door, the hackles raised on my neck.

Carmelita's suitcase lay on the sofa, the radio was blasting "Jail House Rock," and the refrigerator door stood wide open. She was bound to my bed, gagged, bloody, and unconscious.

"Oh, my fucking God!" I cried over and over as I gently released her arms.

Purple bruises spread across her face; her eyes were almost swollen closed. Angry red welts scrolled up and down her body and thighs. Her red silk dress was ripped apart, laying under her and on the floor in pieces.

With a gentle tug, I freed the gag and whispered, "Carmie, who did this to you?"

Congealed blood made it painful for her to speak through split lips. "Stephen Hunter, followed me here," she murmured.

I lifted her fingers to my mouth and kissed the only part of her that wasn't injured. I hated to leave her, but I needed to gather medical supplies from all over the house. After treating her wounds the best I could, and gathering the bits of information she was able to share, I pieced together what happened and phoned Franco.

My guts were all ripped up and my throat so tight I couldn't talk, which made it necessary to blurt out, "Carmelita's been attacked! I found her raped, beaten, gagged, and tied to my bed—in my own fucking house!"

"Who did it?!" Franco shouted. His chair screeched across the floor as he stood up, yelling and repeating my words to Junior. "Who did it?!" he shouted again.

"Stephen Hunter. He had no idea who she was. They'd never met. Carmelita stopped by my office and ran into him."

"What the fuck happened?"

My voice cracked several times, making it necessary to stop and take deep breaths. "He made a pass at her. When she rejected him... he followed her back here. The selfish prick didn't know it was my house. She was standing in front of the refrigerator when he grabbed her from behind... and said he wanted a big juicy piece of her."

Franco repeated everything to Junior. who yelled, "He's a dead man!"

"Franco, she warned him not to touch her, but he threatened to have her killed by his good friend, Rico, if she didn't shut up. She kept screaming at him so he gagged her, beat her with his belt, snorted a bunch of coke, and raped her multiple times. She's a physical and emotional mess."

When I finished, Franco took a few deep breaths of his own. Through clenched teeth, he said, "You have permission to kill him," before adding angrily, "Or do you want Rico to take that fucking son of a bitch to the Everglades and feed him to the alligators?"

The offer was tempting. "Thanks, but Stephen's wife won't understand if he just disappears. Grace will call the cops and the first person they'll investigate is me, his partner, which will lead them directly to Carmelita, who is incapacitated at the moment. As soon as she is well enough to travel, I'm taking her to the farm to heal. I'll deal with Stephen Hunter when I return."

"Give me a second to fill Junior in," Franco said.

Moments later, he returned. "Understood and agreed. Junior said Carmelita can take as much time as she needs. Tell her not to worry about Dallas, thanks to all the work she's done, it's running smoothly. He said to kill Stephen whenever you're fucking ready. Meanwhile, I'm sending our medical person to your cottage. He should be there within the hour. I hope she doesn't have to go to the hospital."

"I appreciate that, Franco. She's in a lot of pain, but from what I can tell, there are no broken bones. Tell him to bring pain meds and something to help her sleep." Then my anxiety surged. I added, "Could someone monitor Grace? Who knows what Stephen might do next?"

Franco eased my fears before he hung up. "I'll put a guy on her right away and I'll order Rico to stop hanging around Stephen Hunter, or else."

Thanks to the meds, Carmelita was sleeping when I called Stephen at home later that night. I made up a story and explained, as calmly as possible, that a piece of property I owned up north was under contract. It needed quite a few repairs in order for the sale to close.

"I haven't taken a vacation in years, so I won't be back until the deal's done. You'll have to run the business by yourself for a while."

That evil son of a bitch said nothing about Carmelita stopping by our office. Not one damn word. Yup, he's a dead man.

Carmelita and I spent from September of '58 until February of '59 at the farm. After a snowy, peaceful Christmas at the farmhouse, we celebrated New Year's Eve at the Phoenix cabin, making love in front of its blazing fireplace.

Afterwards, I rolled onto one elbow. She looked at me curiously as I cleared my voice several times. "I never stopped searching for your family, Carmie, but until now, I've been unsuccessful. What I've learned in the last week will be painful for you."

She blinked several times.

"You were taken to pay your dad's gambling debt was all I knew at first, so I kept up my investigation. Recently, I discovered..."

Tears pooled in her eyes.

Swallowing a few times, I forced myself to finish, even though I knew it would break her heart as it did mine when I received the startling information.

"When your mother learned it was your father's fault you were kidnapped, she shot and killed him and... she died in prison from pneumonia."

Her voice broke. "Papa and Mama are... dead? What happened to my little... brother and sister?"

That was equally hard to tell her. "The court placed them in foster care. When their foster parents left the state, they disappeared with them. After that, their trail went cold."

As reality sunk in, Carmelita wept. "All the family I have left is you and our baby." She laid her hand on her small baby bump. "Thank you for taking care of me."

I folded her into my arms, and then whispered, "I tried to do my best, Carmie."

We feared it might happen after the rape, so as soon as she felt well enough, she insisted we make love without protection. At least that gave us an equal chance the child could be mine. It also freed her to decide if she wanted to be a mother and keep the child or give it up for adoption. It was her decision.

However, we both knew I needed to deal with Stephen Hunter before the baby came. We decided she would stay at the farm and I would return to Seaport to take care of business. But before I left the farm, I retraced the steps, Maw, and I took down the winding deer path twenty-five years earlier when she taught me how to remove the poison from the castor beans without killing myself.

Maw's words came back to me as if it were yesterday: "Remember, it only takes one or two seeds to kill a man. Within ten hours of swallowing it, they'll throw up, begin bleeding inside, pass out, and death will come soon after. No one will ever suspect it's poison. They'll think it was the flu."

CHAPTER TWENTY-NINE

The Time Has Come
Ray and Stephen
1959

I RETURNED TO WORK IN LATE FEBRUARY AS IF NOTHING EVER HAPPENED. Looking Stephen in the face every day sucked, but I needed time to prepare.

The last week of June, I called in sick with the flu, warning Stephen to be careful, he might catch it. While I was still out, supposedly sick, I went to the office late one night and sprinkled his coke stash with finely ground up castor beans. After that, all I had to do was wait.

A few days later, when I called the office, he didn't answer, so I called his house and spoke to Grace.

"I'm worried, Ray. He came home sick yesterday and vomited all night."

"It's the same darn flu bug I had, Grace. Make sure he stays in bed. Here are the medicines I took that helped me feel better." I rattled off a list of pills I hoped she didn't have.

She said she'd run to the drugstore, which was exactly what I wanted her to do.

As I waited down the street, she got into her piece of crap car and drove off while her husband's brand new '59 Chevy sat parked.

"My dear," I muttered as she drove away, "I'm about to change your life again."

When I entered his bedroom, Stephen was lying in deathlike stillness, waxy and pale, taking shallow breaths. It wouldn't be long now.

"Wake up, Stephen." The mattress squeaked as I sat down next to him.

His eyes fluttered. "Ray," he whispered, trying to focus and too feeble to say more.

"Hey, buddy. I came to tell you some interesting things before you die."

He blinked several times. Puzzled, his eyes darted back and forth.

"Remember that beautiful Hispanic lady wearing the gorgeous red dress you ruined? I could kill you for that alone. I'm sure you recall raping her and almost beating her to death nine months ago. You sick fuck, you probably jerk off every night just thinking about that."

His eyes betrayed him as my startling information sunk in.

"In case you've forgotten, her name's Carmelita, and she's about to have a baby." I paused for effect. "It could be yours."

His mouth moved, but nothing came out. I pressed on because I didn't give a shit what he was trying to say. Since he didn't have much time to live, he was only going to hear me.

"But the baby could be mine, too."

He flinched as I bent over, stopping inches away, my face reeking of the pure hatred I felt for him.

"You are never... going to see that precious child... because I laced your coke with poison before you snorted it up... your... stupid... nose. Yup, you loser, you're a dying man."

When I sat back, his eyes followed me, registering alarm.

"Why would I do such a terrible thing?" I smiled down at him. "Simple, really."

I dug my switchblade out of my left pants pocket, straightened up, and whipped the knife open inches from his face. His eyes widened in fear as he stared at its long blade pointing upward. I used a matter-of-fact tone as I studied my left hand and cleaned dirt from under one of my fingernails. Then I closed it and slid it back into my pocket before looking down at him.

"Revenge for raping and beating Carmelita, you fucking asshole. And for endangering Grace by hanging around with that Mafia shit-for-brains, Rico Catanetti."

I popped him hard on the top of the head with my fist, shocking him.

"The first time you cross Rico, he'll viciously murder you and Grace, and burn down this house and our business, with or without the Mafia's permission. He doesn't give a shit about anything or anyone."

Stephen's eyes closed. I couldn't tell if he was breathing, so I checked his pulse. He felt clammy but, yup, he was still there.

"As for the Mafia, the Catanetti Family sanctioned killing you the night you raped Carmelita. Did you know she's a very important person? She works for an extremely dangerous Mafia Don. They almost fed you to the alligators that night, but I stopped them because, you see, it was my right to kill you. Wanna know how I know so much? Cause the late Don Marco Sr. was my third father long before I started working for your stupid grandpa. I bet you didn't know I haul tons of drugs out of Mexico in our company trucks. Even the night you partied your ass off in Juárez, you and I transported cocaine and heroin back to Seaport together."

His eyes jerked open.

"And just so you know, I have plans for Grace. But first she needs to know you're dead so she can move on with her life."

Stephen's eyes then fluttered, and his breathing became short and shallow.

"Did you know Grace's father caused the accident that killed both your parents? Or that your dear old granddad was going to murder her in cold blood to avenge them?"

Stephen closed his eyes and showed no response.

What? Maybe that fucker already knew. Let's see if this gets a reaction.

"Guess who stuck an ice pick in the back of your granddad's skull?"

Still no reaction.

"I did."

Stephen's eyes flew open, his brows raised. He stared at me, confused at first. His eyes widened as his uncertainty cleared to understanding.

I wanted to fuck with him a little more, so I pretended to hear Grace pull into the driveway. I jumped up and looked out the window, and then laughed, crushing any hope he had of being rescued.

I moved to the end of his bed, facing him. "Remember Barry O'Hara, the guy who used to work for us and was killed in a hunting accident by a kid? The kid didn't do it, I did. He stole a kilo of heroin from one of my deliveries and then tried to blackmail me. That creep took a teenager into the woods and partied until the kid passed out. I shot him in the back with the kid's shotgun. But that wasn't the end of it. Oh, no. I had to pay for that fucking heroin. Then find it and give it back to the Catanettis."

Stephen's breathing was erratic again. His time was almost up. I glanced at my watch. Even if Grace returned, it would seem natural for me to be here, checking on my partner. Besides, he wouldn't tell her anything. He couldn't even talk.

"By the way, did you know Grace is my cousin? Just so you know, if she doesn't sell me the business, I'm planning on marrying her. If Roosevelt and Einstein could marry their cousins, then so can I. She'll trust me when I rescue her from all your poor decisions, shower her with money, and take over the business."

Making a sweeping gesture toward his bedroom walls, "But the first thing I'm gonna do after I move in is paint this drab room a sweet shade of pale blue. And from the way you look, pal, it's gonna be soon. I'm thinking today, July first, is a good day for you to die."

Stephen shot daggers at me as he tried to move his mouth, but nothing came out.

"Don't worry, Grace will have the biggest goddamned diamond ring I can buy and every year, she'll drive a brand-new Mercedes or Cadillac. I'll never complain she's boring in bed because I'll keep her hot and bothered, which you couldn't, you piece of shit. Oh, and don't forget, the gorgeous Carmelita and her baby are mine, too."

A low growl from him prompted me to deliver my final cruel remarks.

"I'm going to paint your grandfather's rat trap house a nice shitty brown. Then maybe I'll burn it down for the insurance money. You're a fool, Stephen. You should've paid attention when I warned you not to mess with me, or you'd regret it."

With his last ounce of life and struggling for breath, the look of hatred in his eyes revealed he wanted to throw himself at me, but he only moved an inch.

"Here, let me help you." I laughed as I grabbed his arm, pulled him off the bed, and dragged him to the bathroom floor. After I kicked him in the stomach a few times and listened to his death rattle, I watched him die. I was stone cold as I walked out of his house. After what he did to Carmelita, I'm sure Grace was next. That evil son of a bitch deserved what he got.

My name was the first word he said to me the day we met, and the last word he said before he died. Go figure. Karma?

As I drove away, watching from my rearview mirror, Grace's rattletrap of a car pulled into the driveway. She stepped out, struggled with a brown paper bag, and pushed the door closed with her hip.

It's too late for medicine now, my dear. Your new life has just begun. Again.

Later that afternoon, I phoned Grace to see how Stephen was feeling. Lo-and-behold, Pastor Mark answered. When he understood who I was, he said Stephen passed away that afternoon.

That's all I'd been waiting for. Now I could pay my respects, like a partner would.

When I got there, Grace was a mess. I knew from personal experience she wouldn't remember anything I said. Fortunately, Pastor Mark did.

"I'm sorry I can't stay for the funeral, Grace. I have some real estate business up north that requires my attention. Our company is closed temporarily, but don't worry, it's in good financial shape, and I'll reopen it when I return."

Pastor Mark nodded when I gave Grace a slip of paper with my northern phone number. Since Stephen spent a lot of money on drugs, I suspected he left nothing in their bank account, but I didn't tell Pastor Mark that. Instead, I told him how much money I was going to deposit in her checking account before I left town the next day.

"I'm sure it will be enough to cover Stephen's funeral expenses and anything else Grace needs for quite a while."

Pastor Mark nodded and thanked me.

The Gulf Coast Independent

St Petersburg, Florida   *Thursday, July 2, 1959*

Local Business Owner Found Dead at 36

Seaport, July 2 - Sheriff Ed Black today said 36-year-old Stephen Hunter of Calusa Heights, Seaport, died at his home, from a virulent strain of the flu on Wednesday, July 1. Mr. Hunter was the senior partner in the Hunter & Lewis Trucking company. Mr. Hunter's wife of 14 years, Grace Elizabeth Martin Hunter, found him collapsed on the bathroom floor when she returned from a trip to the pharmacy.

Navy Serviceman

Sheriff Black said Mr. Hunter, a Navy veteran, served in World War II. Mr. Hunter was predeceased by his parents who perished in a car accident in 1935. Mr. Hunter's grandparents, Stanley and Rachel Hunter, also preceded him in death.

A service will be held at 2 p.m., Saturday, at the St. Peter's Community Church in Calusa Heights. Pastor Mark P. Pruitt will officiate.

My last stop before leaving Seaport was to the local florist. I wrote a generous check and ordered flowers in beautiful vases to be delivered to Grace every week with the same note:

Thinking of you,
Love, Ray

With all my loose ends tied up, and the groundwork laid for my next move, nothing could stop me from being with Carmelita when our baby came.

Playing the long game continued.

CHAPTER THIRTY

A New Life
Ray
July 1959

CARMELITA WAS RESTING IN A ROCKING CHAIR ON THE PORCH when my truck pulled into the farmhouse's grassy yard. She struggled to her feet, her enormous belly poking out so far I was sure she could set a plate on it. Carmelita tried to hug me, but her pregnant belly got in the way.

"It's done," I whispered.

Her dark eyes teared up as she stared at me and nodded. We sat on the porch together, holding hands, and enjoying each other's company while I soaked up the comforting view of the farm. The sunflowers stood high above the rows of vegetables, lifting their faces toward the light, while the cool mountain breezes blew the farm's heady scents all around me. The sounds of a busy farmyard welcomed me back to my favorite place in the entire world.

Ramón Lewis Lopez was born three days later. Carmelita nicknamed him Rayban after me and my aviator sunglasses. She wanted him to have a one-in-a-million nickname.

With the field workers' wives guiding her, she nursed the hungry infant, while I learned to change diapers like a pro. I admit it was sloppy going at first, but I got the hang of it. Laughter and joy filled our lives, and we danced to the tune of a loving couple with a newborn baby, at ease in our relationship. But the world soon intruded.

Grace worried me. Sometimes when I called, she only spoke a word or two. More often, she just listened and hung up. That wasn't a good sign.

Carmelita was also a concern. She wanted a fresh start somewhere else. After the attack, Franco's people packed up her Dallas apartment and stored everything in a warehouse. They were waiting for her to decide where to send her stuff. Without asking my opinion, Carmelita planned her future with our son.

"Denver is where I want to raise Rayban. The bigger mountain range and the Old West aura appeals to me, Ray. Plus, it's a healthy place to raise my child."

"Our child," I reminded her.

"Only if you want to remain active in his life. I love you but... Rayban needs a father. Will you be that person or not?"

"You and the baby can live here, Carmie."

"We could, but we have jobs to do, Ray. The Catanetti family is supportive and has already considered the benefits of my Colorado suggestion. The operation I set up in Dallas will be even bigger in Denver. They've given me plenty of money and time to get established. They count on me just as much as you."

True. I couldn't do my job if she didn't do hers. She knew how much I needed the legitimate guise of Hunter & Lewis Trucking to run narcotics for the Catanettis. And she was well aware that the last thing the Catanettis and I wanted was for Grace to marry someone who could discover my secret life. It would end badly for him if that happened. Rico had suggested many times he could just kill Grace and all this stupid decision-making would end.

Carmie and I discussed it. If Grace wouldn't sell me the business, I only had one choice left. To protect Grace, I had to marry her.

By October it was time to return to Florida, leaving Carmelita and our baby at the farm while she planned the Denver operation for the Catanettis.

By November, Hunter & Lewis Trucking was back in full operation and running smoothly. The trucks were booked out months in advance.

It was time for my next move.

Unannounced, I showed up at Grace's house and rang the doorbell over and over. When she finally opened the door, she looked terrible. Too thin, her hair a grown-out mess, and she had dark circles under her eyes.

Standing on her porch, hat in hand, I offered to inform her about our business, stressing the word "*our.*" As it sank in, she said the magic words and held the door open.

"Come in and tell me about our company."

1960

By January, I was working solo and had simplified the business. An answering service took messages I could retrieve from anywhere on the road and a post office box solved the mail problem. What's more, independent truck drivers eagerly accepted my local deliveries when I was out of town.

Stephen had been dead six months by the time I went through his files, looking for the envelope of incriminating photos and any stash of drugs he may have tucked away. It surprised me when I came across paid invoices for a safe deposit box in an old Seaport bank in the historic downtown area. Knowing I couldn't legally access the box, as soon as the next invoice came, I paid it promptly. If Grace ever learned about that safe deposit box, God only knows what she might find. Those disgusting photographs were hidden somewhere.

Even though I was away from Grace for longer periods, it was worth it not to miss too much of my son growing up. With all its year-round activities, great schools, and killer views of the Rocky Mountains, Denver was the perfect place for Carmelita and Rayban.

Rayban assumed I was his father, but called me Ray. He never questioned my relationship with his mother. We told him it was his mother's cultural tradition for him to use her last name.

He also understood my company was based in Florida and that my job required a lot of traveling, which explained my absences. I called them from my Seaport office in the early morning or late afternoon to avoid Grace learning about them.

During Rayban's summer vacations, he and Carmelita visited the farm, and I joined them as long as I could. José Jr. looked forward to how much Rayban had grown each year and together they marked his height on the barn door. When Rayban began tagging along behind him, José Jr. put him to work. At dinner, our little guy would flex his muscles and brag about how strong he was helping "José Jr. take care of farm *busyness*."

Rosa cooked all his favorite foods, no matter what he asked for. He loved her biscuits and gravy for breakfast and fried chicken for dinner. Don't get me started on her banana pudding.

Becky from Grandma's Diner spoiled him rotten, too. Whenever she baked, she always made an extra pie for him, which Rayban claimed for himself.

He was a good-natured, caring, and handsome boy, full of questions about everything.

When he was nine, I introduced him to the sang hoe and showed him where the ginseng grew. But finding rattlesnakes excited him the most. He made me repeat the story about killing the big rattlesnake to save Uncle Monty from being bitten, especially loving the part when I cut off its rattles and said, "That evil old son of a bitch deserved it." We laughed and laughed. I let him say it with me, but never in front of Carmie. She would be mad if she knew I let him cuss.

Cutting the sunflowers was one of Rayban's favorite things. He arranged them in the big urns his mom kept on the porch. We called him Prince Rayban, Master of Sunflowers and Keeper of Urns.

At ten, he was full of questions about his deceased grandparents and Uncle Monty. I showed him their photographs and told him how wonderful and fun they were. I blamed their deaths on the flu. It's what a little guy would understand.

When he asked where they were buried, we drove out to the cemetery. "Your Grandmother and Grandfather Lewis are next to each other with Uncle Monty on Grandfather Lewis's right," I said as I pointed to each gravestone. "My spot is here—by my mother."

After reading her headstone out loud, "Sleeping with Angels," he turned to me. "Can I be buried here too?"

Why did he think about stuff like that? I don't know, but of course I agreed. "Our family plot is big enough for you and your mom to have the spaces near me," confirming that he would always be with us.

"Can I have 'Sleeping with Angels' on my gravestone too?"

"Of course." I smiled at his serious upturned face. "But you'd better tell your great grandchildren that's what you want because I won't be around then."

PART FOUR

CHAPTER
THIRTY-ONE

The Last Trip to Mexico
Ray
April 12, 1980

Early Saturday morning it was a freezing twenty-eight degrees in El Paso, which is rare for April. It's usually closer to the seventies this time of year.

After I kissed Carmelita goodbye yesterday at the Mountain High Storage, I headed south, away from Colorado Springs. My semi had a full tank of diesel, so I drove through the night, nibbling on junk food. I'm thankful for the winter clothes I left in it because it was colder than a witch's tit the whole way.

While I'm filling my tanks in El Paso with the American fuel I trust, I review the Mexican-American border guards' schedules for the next two days.

Martínez 4136a2p5M, González 4132p10p5M, García 41310p4146a10M,
Bautista 4146a2p5M, Rodríguez 4142p10p5M, Fernández 41410p4156a10M.

Garcia will most likely be the winner tomorrow. He and Fernandez control the cherry time slot—ten at night until six in the morning. They also get paid $10,000, the greedy bastards.

During my forty-two years of making these runs, I've maintained a spotless reputation. My logs say I haul fresh vegetables, flowers, and coffee. That's it. I'm never involved in the handover of cash for drugs, nor am I anywhere near when they load the concealed contraband in my semi. The moment my truck is ready to roll, they send word. I show up and get the hell out of Mexico. Hopefully, this is for the last time.

As big rig slowly inches behind snail-like traffic over the Paso del Norte International Bridge into Ciudad Juárez, every single joint in my body aches from the long drive with no sleep. All I can think about is crawling into my warm hotel bed as soon as possible, then waking up to claim my reward a block away—the delicious margaritas and nachos, smothered in hot cheese and jalapeños, at The Kentucky Club.

A few times in the past, I rewarded myself in other ways. Mexico has some tempting places with some very beautiful women. In my defense, I always generously tipped the ladies, which ended up saving my life twelve years ago. I remember it like it was yesterday.

February 1968

Our government was focused on stopping illegal drugs from entering the States. By shifting its power to Interstate Commerce, they tripled the amount of law enforcement officers on the ground.

Suddenly, the cartel and the Mafia suspected everyone. If you scratched your ass in public, they'd think you were signaling a narcotic agent. It was a nerve-wracking time, to say the least. The Catanettis boosted their efforts to protect their cash until it was exchanged for drugs. The cartel improved hiding their drugs until they could be swapped for cash. Both groups mistrusted each other.

I needed a break. Only one freaking night, for God's sake. Maybe I shouldn't have done it with a loaded truck, but screw it, I convinced myself that taking an extra hour to unwind wouldn't hurt anything. Just this once.

I parked outside one of my usual Juárez brothels and chose the same sweet, brown-skinned girl who always appreciated my large cash tips. As soon as I closed her bedroom door, she whispered, "Un hombre malo estaba aquí."

I stopped in my tracks. "A bad man... here?"

"Si, perguntando por tí y tú camión verde." She sat on the side of the bed, her eyes wide.

I'm not fluent in Spanish, but I know the words for a green truck and a bad hombre looking for me. My stomach churned and my heart beat like a bass drum as I tucked a hundred-dollar bill in her hand and bolted down the hallway, my adrenaline pumping. After pushing through the rear door, I ended up in a foul-smelling alley where waves of horror washed over me, only to be amplified when the door's lock snapped shut behind me.

Between the disgusting odor of rotting garbage overflowing into that filthy alleyway, and the primitive hormones surging throughout my body, I hoped like hell I wouldn't have a heart attack and drop dead right there. Anywhere else, but not in that nightmare of a shit hole.

Even though it was a short distance between the alley's opening and the parking lot where I'd parked my truck, running in a crouched position at fifty years old, strained a whole bunch of past injuries. My hands were shaking as I started my semi.

Four fierce-looking Mexican males, dressed in white tank tops, red bandanas, jeans, and shiny high-top sneakers, jumped from the back of a battered pickup parked across the street and headed straight toward me.

Young and confident, they spread out in a line carrying baseball bats. I didn't wait around to see if they were wooden or metal. After punching on my high beams to blind them, I sped in their direction, trying like hell to run over the arrogant bastards.

I'd spent so much time concentrating on spotting narcotic agents, I'd forgotten about the thugs who kill drivers like me and hijack their trucks. Being arrested by the cops would've been a cakewalk compared to dealing with those evil sons of bitches.

Outside of El Paso, I stopped my rig to puke, determined to never return to that brothel again. Nor any other brothel, for that matter. Those days were over.

Pumped up on tons of coffee, I pushed straight through and pulled into the Catanettis' Seaport warehouse, weary, filthy, and unshaven. My legs were in knots, cramped first from running, then from sitting for long periods. I couldn't walk without stumbling.

Hours later, after switching to my pickup truck, I drove home to witness the most idiotic disaster of my life.

Twin baby girls.

Grace adopted twins while I was dodging murderers. As soon as I stumbled through the front door, she shouted their names with a big smile plastered all over her face. "Ray! You're a father! Come meet your baby girls, Patience and Mercy Hunter Lewis. I'm calling them Patty and Merry!"

I was a grown-ass man, and I wanted to cry.

"Oh, my God! Just frigging shoot me now." I muttered, hobbling into the bathroom, not giving a shit what she named them.

I locked the door and fell apart. She had trapped me with those babies and she was counting on me to be a father to them. How could I leave her now when her dream had finally come true?

And I was a puppet for the guys I thought were my friends—brothers even— but they continued to send me into harm's way. How could I quit the Mafia when I deliver one of their biggest income-producing products? Plus, I was sure they'd kill me before they'd let me leave.

All I dreamed of was divorcing Grace and living peacefully on my farm with the dark-eyed, beautiful girl I fell in love with when I was young and so damned dumb. Back when things were simpler—when I should've made a different decision.

Tromping through the woods, looking for ginseng with my nine-year-old little guy, whom Grace didn't know about, tore at me, breaking my heart.

Facing a life filled with babies I didn't want and more dangerous drug runs to Mexico, it's a wonder I didn't have a heart attack and die among the gigantic bags of diapers and all those stupid baby gadgets that were sitting on the sofa.

But if I did, it sure as hell beat a nasty-ass alley in Juárez, Mexico.

April 12, 1980

Here I am, twelve years later, fingers crossed that I'll leave Juárez alive one more time. I skirt the town, head south, and roll past the airport they've worked on for a long time. Its new colorful Spanish style is a proud accomplishment for these folks. Still, it's okay with me if I never see it again.

My Mexican crew is ready and waiting when I pull into an industrial area about fifteen minutes later. After I back the semi up to the warehouse and remove the loaner pickup keys from my bag, Boss, who's in charge, points across the parking lot. I toss him my semi's keys and ask, "When?" That's all I need to know.

"Mañana," It's all Boss needs to tell me.

As I'm driving into Juárez, headed to the Hotel Del Sol, I'm confident I can leave under tomorrow night's darkest new moon when I remember another new moon night that didn't end so well—at least not for the lady who slipped me her red-lace panties. It was shocking then, but it's funny as hell now.

1979

A year ago in June, Junior insisted I attend a wedding for the daughter of the Mexican cartel's leading family. Much to my annoyance, I was seated next to the bride's flirtatious mother at the reception and cringed every time she winked at me and remarked in her broken English that I looked Mafioso-style handsome in my black suit and aviator sunglasses. I never took them off. Too many photographs were being taken, and I didn't want to be recognized.

When the celebration ended, I tried to excuse myself, but the bride's tipsy parents insisted they give me a ride back to town. Since my hotel was near The Kentucky Club, they begged me to join them for one more margarita. How could I refuse?

After the second margarita, the bride's father excused himself to use the baño when, much to my surprise, the inebriated mother slid her red-lace panties into my lap. Trying to appear sexy, she batted her false eyelashes and grinned. Bright red lipstick smeared both corners of her mouth and all over her perfect, very white, front teeth, giving her a ludicrous, leering clown face.

Taken aback, I tucked the panties into my pants pocket just as her husband returned, ready to call it a night.

Unfortunately, the evening ended rather badly when I helped both of my drunken companions to their car parked in front of the Kentucky Club.

The mother, in heels way too high for her condition, slipped and landed headfirst on the hood of their silver Rolls Royce. When she lifted her head, blood was streaming from her busted lip and nose, and splashed across her low-cut dress.

I'm not sure, but she may have chipped a few of those expensive front teeth. I used one of my handkerchiefs to apply pressure to her face and stop the bleeding.

Their johnny-on-the-spot driver popped the car's trunk, grabbed a small towel, and passed the bloody handkerchief back to me. I crammed it into my pocket next to the red panties I didn't dare return.

How could I ever forget a wedding like that?

April 12, 1980

My room at the Hotel del Sol is ready when I check in. After I install a new padlock on the outside of the door to my room and inside on the closet door, I stow my bag on the closet floor. I only kept a few hundred thousand for border crossing payoffs, fuel, and travel expenses, sending the rest with Carmelita. Even though it's nerve wracking to leave the bag here when I go out, it's plain old stupid to carry it on the streets of Juárez at night.

At last, I crawl into a warm clean bed and sleep like the dead.

It's late, after nine, dark, and cold when I hurry into The Kentucky Club, thankful that their space heaters are on high, warming the main area. The large square room with bright orange, red, yellow, and blue advertising banners and colorful flags hang from the ceiling and plaster the walls. The floor is glazed with both orange and yellow Mexican ceramic tile, which complement the scuffed Formica-topped tables. As always, the place is cozy and welcoming.

It's not busy for a Saturday night, probably because the icy weather has kept most folks home. The bartender greets me when I take a table as far away from the freezing-ass front door as possible. He knows I'll gulp the first margarita, so he sends two as soon as I sit down.

After ordering dinner, I savor the second one, enjoying the relaxing effect of tequila, and think about spending the rest of my life with Carmelita. Our story feels like it happened a million years ago when I rescued her as a little girl. Yet it feels as if it were yesterday that the girl turned into a woman who captured my heart.

"Aquí tiene, señor."

The Kentucky Club server jolts me away from my favorite memory as he places a bowl in front of me piled high with nachos smothered in hot cheese and jalapeños. And a plate of the best chile rellenos I've ever eaten.

"Gracias." I nod and point at my empty margarita glass. "Uno más, por favor."

"Sí." He grabs the glass and heads to the bar, shouting, "Uno más!"

One more delicious margarita for old time's sake.

Who knows, it may be my last.

CHAPTER THIRTY-TWO

She's Her Own Woman
Ray and Carmelita
June 1950

I CURSED THE TRAFFIC GRIDLOCK THAT CRAWLED DOWN MICHIGAN AVENUE, consulted my watch, and cursed again. I thought I could make the long drive from South Florida to Chicago in one sitting. But after the hellacious week I spent crossing the country, I had to pull into a truck stop and allow myself a few hours of sleep. That miscalculation and the tangled Chicago traffic cost so much time, I was too late to see Carmelita walk across the stage and receive her diploma.

Shit, I blew it.

Then I remembered she said not to worry if I was late. We'd get together later tonight, after she finished packing for the trip home.

I pulled my pickup into the Blake Hotel's valet area, checked in, and made dinner reservations for the two of us at eight in The Imperial Room, their four-star restaurant. That gave me time for a haircut, a shower, and a nap. I needed all three. I couldn't wait to see her. Four years was way too long.

When she graduated from high school with honors and left for the University of Chicago, she was eighteen—fresh faced, no makeup, and wore her hair in a single braid. We expected to spend holidays and summers together, but somehow it never happened. Phone calls several times a month and a few snapshots were all we managed to exchange.

My involvement in finalizing the Hunter & Lewis Trucking partnership with Stephen Hunter seemed to drag on forever. Then the long hauls out West, into and out of Mexico, took a tremendous amount of time since all roads ran through the middle of cities and towns with traffic lights slowing me down every damn where.

When I suggested to Don Marco Sr. that a coordinated interstate highway system would increase my turnaround time, the Don relayed those needs to his Washington contacts. After that, Marco Sr. counted on me to give him reliable transportation information and suggestions he could pass along that wouldn't endanger our illegal activities. That was frickin' time consuming.

$$\bullet$$

The Imperial Room buzzed with activity as the sound of tinkling laughter and the popping of champagne corks filled the air, signaling the restaurant was full.

Elegantly dressed ladies, dripping with pearls and mink shoulder wraps, were seated with gentlemen in tailored suits, their custom shirts displaying heirloom cufflinks

Black linen tablecloths draped each table, its centerpiece—two silver candlesticks with tall white candles lit and glowing. A thin crystal vase, cradling a single red rose, was placed at the center of each lady's place setting. The lights were the perfect shade of dim. Just enough to read the menu while creating the ambiance required for fine dining.

I was glad I'd bought a navy-blue suit for this special occasion and thought I held my own among the male dinner guests. I studied the wine list with great interest. The Imperial Room carried my favorite cabernet and chardonnay. I would decide after we chose our main entrée.

"Your guest has arrived, sir," the maître d' announced, as he pulled out the chair for a stunningly beautiful woman I barely recognized.

Carmelita's luminous black eyes crinkled up in joy, her dark red lips curled into a smile, so familiar but also not—my heart skipped a beat. I'd never seen her look like this. Long, thick eyelashes, shadowy as night, were enhanced by a glimmery sheen.

I rose so quickly my chair almost toppled. Frozen in place, feet glued to the floor, my eyes feasted on her. I wasn't the only one staring, either. Every head had swiveled towards us. Murmured questions of, "Who are they?" or "Is that a movie star?" swirled throughout the dining room.

Carmelita's stunning red silk dress encircled her breasts, swept upwards to fasten behind her neck, and clung to every amazing curve of her body. Long glossy black hair spread wide across her lovely bare shoulders, flowing down her back like a midnight bridal veil, and fell alongside her hips, spilling out from both sides. Red nail polish peeked out from her open-toed black satin heels.

"Hi."

That one sound, so sweet and low, assured me this was my darling girl who somehow turned herself into this stunning, elegant woman in four short years—from a duckling to a swan.

She took my breath away. I wasn't prepared.

This was definitely not in my plans.

As I dashed behind her to adjust her chair, glad for a moment to collect myself, her delicate perfume made my knees weak. I'd always been her guardian, her knight in shining armor. Not in my wildest dreams could this happen. Yet, there I was, desiring her.

When our meals came, I moved my food around, taking an occasional bite as I tamped down intense conflicting feelings.

With dinner finished, and the table cleared, the graduation gift I'd sweated bullets choosing took on a whole new meaning.

I pushed a rectangular teal velvet box toward her.

"For you."

Her eyebrows arched with curiosity as she reached for it.

Seeing her eyes widen in surprise when she opened it was worth the thousands of dollars it cost me.

"This is gorgeous, Ray. I never expected something so exquisite. Thank you."

She lifted my sparkling gift from its long, thin case and smiled with delight. Her eyes flitted back and forth between me and the delicate gift she stretched out on the black linen tablecloth between us. Shyly, she offered her left hand.

As I fastened the glimmering diamond bracelet around her slender wrist, the flickering candles intensified her dark eyes.

"I love it... but," her silky voice hesitated. She looked away, swallowing, and tried to speak but could only mumble my name. "Ray, I..."

My stomach dropped. Filled with tremendous dread, I waited as she gathered the courage to tell me something I knew would change my life.

"Ray... I'm... I'm not... confident you'll like what I want... to tell you."

I hung on each word, soaking up every nuance and gesture she made.

She looked down at our fingers lightly touching and the twinkling diamonds encircling her wrist, raised her luminous eyes to mine and whispered, "Ray, I have... always loved you," her voice faltered.

My brain screamed, there's a *but* coming, wait for it.

"Since the day you found me, I've valued our friendship."

Her gaze was constant, unflinching, as she continued to imprison me.

"And your guidance above everyone else's."

My heart thudded; its rushing swish echoed in my ears. The room's hustle and bustle slowed; its sounds muted to a low hum. All I heard were her sweet whispers as she leaned forward, searching my eyes.

"But I've changed. You've changed. We're not the same people we were."

Was I no longer her knight? I quit breathing, waiting for her to say she'd met someone she wanted to be with. It made perfect sense she'd want a normal life with a normal guy. She knew who I was and what I did.

Her eyes were wide, fastened on mine as she delivered my life sentence.

"I am yours. I have always been yours."

She whispered, "I love you."

Carmelita studied my reaction, waiting for my reply.

Astonishment rendered me incapable of speaking. What could I say to this vulnerable, gorgeous creature that wouldn't make me sound like a bumbling twelve-year-old?

Her diamond bracelet sparked around her slim wrist as she tucked her hand inside mine. Its warmth and softness shot straight up my arm.

I glanced away, caught up in the slow-motion fantasy of sweeping everything off the table and taking her right there. But I couldn't move.

When I took too long to answer, her expression changed from nervousness to sadness, her eyes welled, and before tears could escape, she looked away.

"I'm sorry. I shouldn't have told you."

She tried to withdraw her hand from mine, shifting her eyes down as a tear escaped.

"No!" I gripped her wrist, confusing her.

Sounds from the dining room returned with a roar. The clatter of silverware and laughter infused with alcohol rang out louder, along with voices that grew shriller, permeating my brain.

We needed to get out of there. "Carmie, wait, it's not what you think. Give me a second. Trust me, I'll be right back."

My chair screeched against the polished marble floor as I darted from our table, tossed a couple hundred dollars at our waiter, and hustled to the front desk to change her room to the penthouse. I didn't give a shit what it cost.

After returning, I stood behind her chair and spoke softly in her ear.

"My darling, Miss Lopez, would you do me the honor of accompanying me somewhere private so we can continue our conversation?"

Carmelita turned, met my gaze, and offered her hand.

Standing so close I could smell the light floral scent of her perfume, I whispered, "Please follow me."

"Where are we going, Ray?" she asked over her shoulder, her long hair swinging behind her with every graceful step.

"Somewhere much quieter."

With my left hand in the middle of her back, I guided her into the elevator and pushed the PH button with my right.

Her eyes remained focused straight ahead as she stood still, waiting.

The elevator opened at the top floor where the well-crafted doors of the penthouse faced us from the end of the short hallway. I enjoyed Carmelita's look of astonishment as she walked into the extravagant apartment.

"Ray, it's—it's huge."

I laughed. "That it is."

The spacious room was beautifully wallpapered in black and gold brocade. Large glass windows on its left wall revealed a view of the traffic's neon twinkling lights zipping back and forth on Michigan Avenue. An arched opening at the rear of the room exposed an ornate bedroom neither of us acknowledged.

As I led her to the black leather sofa facing a panorama of the city, room service arrived with a chilled bottle of Reisling, my favorite dessert wine, and crystal glasses. After tipping the waiter, I locked the door and poured liberal portions.

We stood in front of a wall of large windows, enjoying the city lights below, filled with the sounds of a far-off train whistle and police sirens. We sipped our sweet wine, glancing at each other as we made small talk about going home, but we both knew it was only filler for the moment that was coming.

I took her glass and set it aside, then pulled her close, searching those uncertain, black eyes that stared up at me.

"Carmie, you said something very important earlier. Now that my heart has calmed down, I'm not sure what I heard. Talk to me."

A somber expression settled on her face as she leaned back, her voice barely above a whisper. "When I was a little girl, you were my protector. My best friend."

She paused, but I wasn't about to let her stop now.

"Go on."

She pulled away, but her eyes held me prisoner.

"These four years we've spent apart... I was always excited to hear your voice and eager for your advice. The boys I dated... were so immature. They couldn't come close to you. I was proud of our relationship and never wanted to lose you. Then..."

She looked away.

"Don't stop now, Carmie."

I drew her chin toward me. "Continue." I said with a wink and smiled at her. "Then?"

"You called me one night mad at Stephen. You told me about taking him to a brothel in Juárez."

A flicker of emotion flashed through her eyes.

Remembering that conversation, I cocked my head, wondering where this was going.

"And?" I asked, drawing her attention back to me.

"I was jealous and upset."

She gave a little laugh at that point, understanding how unclear that statement was.

"I mean, jealous because you knew about those places. You... may have a girlfriend or a woman you make love to. I was upset because... well, you were mine. I didn't want to lose you to anyone else."

"Oh, Carmie." I drew her close.

She briefly rested her head on my chest before stepping away.

I whispered, "But now there's a different you. How did this happen?"

"You taught me to let nothing get in my way when I want something," Carmelita replied.

"But how can I stop being pulled between the young girl I protected and this gorgeous woman who's taken her place?" I asked.

Carmelita took a few more steps backward and pointed at me.

"Look at me, Ray... what do you see?" As she swept her hand through the air and across the front of her body, my eyes followed that movement. "Do you only see the girl who adored you?" she asked as she lifted her chin. "Or... can you see a woman who loves you... and desires you?"

Her captivating beauty and confession of wanting me was intoxicating. Carmelita cast her eyes down, then flashed them back up at me, her voice filled with angst.

"But," she pointed to herself, "if I'm... not what you want... let me go now. It'll break my heart, but I'll live. You've taught me well. I can make a life... without you."

Despite her determined words, her lips trembled uncontrollably.

My head was whirling, fighting for reason and correctness. She pushed me toward a dangerous cliff. One I could jump from or—let her go—forever. The vision of her in someone else's arms sent me spiraling. That's when I knew. She was mine.

I darted forward, seized her in my arms, pinned her breasts tight against my chest, and cradled her head. Her eyes, now deep pools, widened and flickered in surprise at my sudden action.

"Are you sure? If we cross this threshold, there'll be no returning."

"Positiv..."

I crushed her soft, full lips with every ounce of heat flooding my body and forced her mouth wider. My tongue penetrated, invading hers, possessing her, and saturating her with my essence. She went limp against me and a sweet sound escaped as she met each move with equal intensity. We were spinning in the universe. She, restrained in my arms, and I... conquered by her sheer will to mark me as her own. I no longer breathed alone but through her and she through me until we stumbled apart, hearts pounding, struggling for breath. Our eyes locked in a mutual state of amazement.

"Never leave me," I groaned, not recognizing the raspy sound of my voice. "I will die if I lose another soul I love."

Did she understand the gravity of searing her name into my heart—branding me? From this day forward, I couldn't live, think, or move forward without her, and that was a dangerous position to be in. And yet, any other option was unimaginable.

"Carmie, I..."

"Shh." She touched her fingers to my lips and stared up at me, her dark eyes locked on mine. She swept her hands behind my head, pressed against me, and drew me to her, encouraging me to taste her again. A sense of urgency ignited within us the moment my mouth found hers.

As my fingers slid down her silky dress and softly caressed her swollen nipples through the delicate fabric, a deep moan came from the back of her throat. Her leg glided up my thigh, her mound ground tighter against my hardness that strained to be closer to her. With our lips joined, I lifted her up and carried her past the living room and through the arched opening of that enormous, decadent bedroom.

Somewhere along the way, her high heels clattered to the floor. When I set her bare feet on the black marble tile and stepped back to gaze at her, it was as if a spotlight shone on the shimmering deep scarlet of her silk dress, accenting the blacks and golds surrounding us.

Carmelita held my eyes as her hand lifted to the neck of her gorgeous dress and slowly untied it, letting it fall to her waist, freeing her voluptuous breasts. Her swollen brown nipples exposed her burning need.

I instantly knew that I would spend the rest of my life pleasuring this woman.

With a single tug, the dress flowed past her curvy hips to the floor in a puddle of red cream, while she stood naked and silent inside its crimson circle. Waiting.

Within seconds, she was in my arms, laying on the black and gold bed, her glossy hair fanning out across the golden satin pillows like an intricately woven black spiderweb. After kissing and tasting her, I savored each nipple, teasing and nipping until she begged over and over for me to take her.

But she needed one more thing.

"My darling Carmelita Lewis Lopez, I love you with all my heart. I am yours, forever."

A single tear escaped as she closed her eyes and pulled me to her.

I could wait no longer and plunged off that dangerous cliff into her.

CHAPTER THIRTY-THREE

Taking Out the Trash
Ray
April 13, 1980

DESPITE THREE MARGARITAS, I'M UP EARLY SUNDAY MORNING and showered. As I pull the last clean underwear from the bottom of my bag, a small blinking black box spills onto the bed. "What the hell!" And like a punch to the gut, I understand. It's a tracking device. "Fuck!"

I can't waste time. I've got to call Franco and tell him something. But there's no way I'm gonna tell him or any of the Catanettis that someone planted a bug on me in Denver. After I dispose of that damn tracker, I'm getting the hell out of Mexico.

Thankfully, he accepted my collect call right away.

"Franco, something's up. I think I better fly home and come back another time."

"No can do. It's imperative that you make it to the central office. We'll take it from there. Call me later," Franco says.

Shit, he's making me drive to Dallas, anyway. My arrangements had better be ready by the time I arrive.

I can't hold my tongue any longer. "This is a goddamned nightmare. I'm too old for this crap. My bones are getting cranky, and so am I. I'm done. Forever. Hai capito?"

"Understood. Just do your best. I'll get my people ready. Good luck."

Okay, whoever is tracking me knows where I am and, most likely, what I'm driving. I need a fresh set of wheels.

After I push that damn bug under the edge of the mattress, I grab my black bag and head down to the hotel's office, aggravated as shit. A couple hundred dollars gains me use of the hotel manager's piece of junk Chevy for twenty-four hours, but only if he can drive Pedro's pickup truck parked in front of the hotel. Even though I'm smiling, my guts are ripped up as I agree and head to the alley where his Chevy is parked.

As soon as I pull into the warehouse parking lot, Boss signals a thumbs up. The semi is ready. I toss the Chevy keys to Pedro and tell him to wait until tomorrow to switch vehicles with the hotel manager. Frowning and shooting daggers with his eyes, he doesn't say a word, but I can see he's pissed that I traded his pickup truck for the hotel manager's Chevy.

"Here's another five hundred for the extra day's rental, so wipe that fucking look off your face! Tomorrow and not a second sooner." I hand him the cash and stomp across the lot toward my Peterbilt, eager to leave.

A half-hour later, Martínez, $5,000 richer, allows my big-ass truck across the border without even blinking. I follow the Sunday early morning traffic into El Paso and by mid-morning, I'm heading east toward Dallas. Relieved that my tanks are full, I hope like hell no one is following me. I let my guard down back in Denver and I'm kicking my own ass about it.

Abilene, Texas, is where I plan to make a few phone calls and it's at least six hours away. As always, traffic and road construction are the only things that slow me down. But time flies when I drive, and my mind wanders.

I feel my age a lot these days, especially when old injuries flare up. I'm not in tip-top shape anymore either, which is alarming when you know as many dangerous men as I do. I've killed a few of them, but there's always more deranged sociopaths ready to take their place. I have to be watchful if I want to see them coming.

Victor Hellman, the gangster who ordered the hit on my family, should've been a lot more careful. He got comfortable because Marco Sr. let him live. But it gave Marco Sr. pleasure to watch Victor's downward spiral into a sad, disrespected, bankrupt, old alcoholic. Victor foolishly believed he was out of harm's way, and it cost him his life.

I know because I killed him.

1955

Marco Jr. became Don of the Catanetti family when Marco Sr. died unexpectedly. A smug Hellman was sure he could get away with having Junior assassinated as soon as Senior was gone.

He failed.

That's when Junior contacted Paulie Horseface, a well-known hitman for hire from Chicago who resembled a Neanderthal. With a squat, thick, and hairy body and a jutting lower jaw, it was clear how he earned his nickname. Even though Rico Catanetti introduced us years before, it surprised me when Paulie walked into my office at Hunter & Lewis and got right to the point.

"Junior put a contract out on Victor Hellman. He wants to know if you're still holding the revenge card?"

"Ab-so-fucking-lutely. When?" was all I asked.

"Next few weeks," Paulie Horseface confirmed. "A little birdie told us Victor's wife is going out of town. After dark, the old man goes downtown, gets blind drunk, and stumbles home. It'll be fitting for his wife to find him dead when she returns. Be prepared to leave the second I call." With that said, he got up and left.

Almost a month later, Paulie Horseface and I sat in the Old Town Saloon listening to a soused Victor Hellman shouting, "I'm taking my city back! Mark my words, me and my gang are going to wipe all those Catanetti bastards and their snot-nosed goons off the face of this Earth."

His threats fell on the deaf ears of the bar's customers, who either smirked in ridicule or ignored him. However, the owner-bartender, knowing his words were dangerous, signaled a young patron to give Victor a ride home.

We followed the shabbily dressed old man as he shuffled from the bar into the humid South Florida night and stumbled into his young friend's car, pissed drunk again. After the guy dropped him off and drove away, we watched Victor fumble with his front door keys and stagger into his house. We went in behind him.

I waited seventeen years to kill that evil son of a bitch. Even though Papa Marco was dead and buried by then, I fulfilled his wish that Victor's death would be bloody, brutal, and shocking. I've read the newspaper account of his murder so often I can repeat it word for word.

"The body of 75-year-old Victor Hellman, of Old Town, Seaport, was found in his home today, the apparent victim of homicide. He was discovered by his wife, who had just returned from a trip. The retired gangster suffered multiple stab wounds, his throat was slit, and his head flattened by a bloody baseball bat found nearby."

So disgusting. I will never kill like that again. The nightmares aren't worth it. And my accomplice, Paulie Horseface, was a bona fide psychopath with that baseball bat.

Victor Hellman was another piece of trash I took out years ago. When I empty a garbage can or haul it to the curb, it reminds me of the vile scum I've removed from this Earth.

———————◆———————

April 13, 1980

By the time I reach Abilene, Texas, top off my tanks, and call Franco again, he's already booked a flight for me leaving Dallas at ten tonight, arriving in Seaport early Monday morning. He promised my semi would be kept in a safe place until I told him where I wanted it delivered.

Meanwhile, there's one more crucial phone call I have to make.

Before boarding my flight, I call Carmelita to make sure she's arrived home safely and to tell her about my change of plans. I leave out finding the tracking device—no need to worry her.

"I'm leaving the semi in Dallas and flying to Seaport tonight. Tomorrow I'll tell Grace I want a divorce, give her my share of the business, as well as part of the money in the trunk. It's almost over. I should be home in a few days."

When Carmelita asks if I've told Junior or Franco I was retiring, I tell her about my outburst with Franco, but that it was going to be tricky to tell Junior. Then add, "If this situation gets crazy with Junior, we need to be prepared. I already called my attorney. Please make sure my divorce papers and the codicil for my will are on my desk when I get home. My flight's boarding, gotta go."

"See you soon, darling," she replies.

As my jet speeds through the blackest of nights, bringing me closer to Seaport, I know my life's in utter chaos. I have an uncanny sense of a reckoning coming and feel an urgent need to put my affairs in order.

If whoever's tracking me had caught me with the high-grade cocaine I delivered to Dallas, I would die in a prison cell with no way to safeguard Carmelita or Grace and the girls. That terrifies me the most. They need my protection before something terrible happens. I've made so many poor decisions. Asking for forgiveness isn't enough. I have to own my mistakes.

If Grace and her mother had known I was protecting them from Stanley Hunter, maybe Grace wouldn't have married Stephen.

If I hadn't exposed Stephen to the seedy elements in Juárez, it's very possible he wouldn't have met Rico, gotten addicted to drugs, assaulted Carmelita, and I wouldn't have had to kill him.

And then there's Rayban. It's way too painful to think about what our lives could have been like if I had chosen him and his mother over marrying Grace and taking over the business.

Why has it taken me so long to see how the Catanettis have manipulated me? Papa Marco could have had Stanley Hunter killed anytime he wanted, yet he let it fall on me to murder him. It sickens me to know I've been nothing but the Catanettis' hit man—just a killer on their payroll. From the moment I joined them, there have been so many murders and heartbreaking reprisals. Maybe my death is the only way to escape them. If it weren't for protecting Grace, the girls, and Carmelita from them, I wouldn't even care about my life.

I hope it's not too late to ask Grace to forgive me for the empty life I've given her. I wouldn't blame her for hating me.

And if there is a God, I think losing my son is enough punishment for all my sins. He can stop now.

What a fool I've been. I called Stephen a fool, but I'm the biggest fool of all.

If only I could talk to Father. He'd know that I'm shattered on the rocks of my life's storm and understand how important it is to clean up this mess before I die. And he would especially understand that I can't live the rest of my life without Carmelita.

CHAPTER THIRTY-FOUR

Understanding the Clues
John and Tom
April 13, 1980

THE EL PASO LUNCH DINER WAS BUSTLING WITH THE AFTER-CHURCH CROWD when John and Tom, feeling beaten and hungry, took a table. They gave their order to the waitress as soon as she appeared.

"I was almost sure Ray saw us when he slowed down near the Juárez airport," Tom said. "It's a good thing we pulled into the airport parking lot and waited for the Predator's receiver to pick up again. I was starting to doubt Ray was going back into town until that little truck passed us with the predator beeping away." Tom unfolded his paper napkin and put it in his lap.

John added, "And watching him check into the Hotel del Sol on Avenue Benito filled in the missing information from the receipt I found in his jacket pocket."

Tom nodded. "I'm so glad we bought those Mexican blankets at the store next to Ray's hotel. I thought we were going to freeze to death while we waited in the Jeep. I didn't know Mexico could be this cold."

John just laughed. "We needed them at the hotel, too. I wonder how low it got last night. You can keep mine as a memento of this trip." They chuckled and finished their coffee.

Tom waved to the waitress for a refill. She held up the pot and pointed to the kitchen.

"Yeah," John said, "I figured Ray found the Predator when it hadn't moved an inch this morning. Did you see the fear in the hotel manager's eyes when I showed him Ray's photo?"

Tom laughed, "I did. And when you asked him if your friend was still in town, he almost shit his pants."

"Unfortunately, we don't have a clue whether Ray's going back to Seaport or returning to Denver," John mused.

When the waitress returned with a fresh pot of coffee, Tom was studying his notebook again. Within seconds, a big smile lit up his face. "I've got it! Isn't today April 13th?"

Tom pushed the list over to John and pointed to the first name—Martinez4136a2p5M.

"If this guy, Martinez, is a U.S. border guard—today, April 13th—is his shift date, and 6a2p is his shift time. Get it? Six in the morning until two in the afternoon. I bet the number at the end is how much he charges Ray to enter the U.S. without being searched. M is the Roman numeral for a thousand. I think 5M means $5,000."

"Whoa! I think you're right, Tom, but that's peanuts compared to the amount of money we saw in that black bag of his."

They looked at each other. "So, we've hit a wall. What now?" Tom asked.

"My only option is to fly back to Seaport. Grace may need my help, especially if Ray's on his way home. After lunch, let's drive over to the El Paso airport and check the flights. How about you?"

"While we wait for our hamburgers, I'll call my Air Force buddy, who loaned me the Predator. He has the capability of tracking it from now on. I'll also ask him to verify the records of an army soldier named Henry Lee. Anything else you can think of?"

"Let's start there and see what you come up with," John suggested.

John was disappointed the El Paso airport had no available flights until the day after tomorrow. Plus, the closest they flew to Seaport was Atlanta or Miami. He'd have to rent a car and drive for hours. No, he needed to get home faster than that.

Then John had a stellar idea. With all the money Grace had given him, what if he chartered a plane? While John inquired about a private jet, Tom found a phone booth and called his Air Force friend for an update. Missions accomplished, they met in the airport's lounge.

Tom started first. "The Army dog tag information you shared Friday night revealed that Private Henry Lee died on March 11, 1938, in Lewisville, West Virginia, while on leave."

Tom pulled out his little pocket notebook again. "My notes say the young man, Rayban, is going to be buried in Lewisville. There's that town again, John."

"That's interesting. I wonder if I should fly to West Virginia instead."

"There's more." Tom pointed to his notes. "When Henry Lee joined the Army in September 1936, he registered his parents, Sebastian and Marlene Lewis, as his next of kin. Yet a year and a half later, his death certificate listed his brother Raymond Sebastian Martin Lewis as his closest relative. What happened to his mother and father in that short amount of time?

They shared a quizzical look, both wondering who would know?

"Order some beers and let me think for a second, Tom. The family has a cemetery plot in Lewisville. Where's that pay phone? I have an idea I want to check out. I'll be right back."

The operator gave John the phone number for the Lewisville Funeral Home. He was taking a chance to call them on a Sunday, but with a pocket full of change, lucky for him, the funeral director answered.

After explaining that he was a friend of the Lewis family, John asked if there would be a ceremony for Ramón Lewis Lopez. The funeral director said he wouldn't be sure until the boy's mother arrived from Denver with his ashes sometime later that week. Then he mentioned that Ramón's headstone was already there with the inscription, Sleeping with Angels.

He seemed chatty, so John asked if he knew anything about the untimely deaths of the Lewis family. The funeral director said while he was checking out the location of the Lewis plot, he learned the husband, wife, and son had all died on the same date. He didn't know why.

He then questioned John. "Are you from Denver too? Should I inform the boy's mother that another friend has inquired about the graveside services for her son?"

John gave him a false name, thanked him, and hung up.

Well, well, well. Carmelita's heading to Lewisville. I wonder who else is coming from Denver for her son's funeral?

There was a cold beer waiting for John when he rejoined Tom, who had come up with his own plan. "If this private plane thing comes through for you, I'll drive back to Denver and visit Ray's warehouse," Tom said. "If he's storing drugs in it, we'll talk later about what to do next."

"That might work, but for God's sake, don't get caught."

"Not a chance, John. Most of the local cops can't find their ass with both hands."

CHAPTER THIRTY-FIVE

The Puzzle Pieces Start to Fit
Grace
April 13, 1980

GRACE DIDN'T KNOW WHERE YESTERDAY WENT, but it flew past. She couldn't believe how eye-catching her white house looked with the green shutters and rocking chairs. It was a big exclamation point in taking control of her life and painting Ray right out of it.

The painters arrived at daybreak Sunday morning, also known as *on time* in their world. Some men began touching up the outside while others started on the inside, painting everything white. Her baby blue bedroom color had to go. However, the girls' room was off limits.

Grace checked her watch. It was time to leave for church. She stuffed the newspaper articles in her purse and scooted out of the painters' way.

After the service, Grace and Natalie sat in the Memorial Garden while the girls ran to the rectory to collect their things and wait for them. Grace handed Natalie the new key to her house and asked if she knew her ex-husband, Barry O'Hara, had worked for Ray and Stephen back in the day. Natalie didn't.

"I believed he was a freelance delivery driver. My plans were to divorce him as soon as I graduated from nursing school," Natalie said as she looked away. "His death was convenient."

"Another question," Grace said, then asked, "Do you know if there's anyone in the congregation I could talk to about the unsolved murders of Victor Hellman and Tito Zayas—the guys in the old newspaper articles?"

"Maybe." Natalie paused for a moment. "Mark's secretary, Doris, might have some ideas. Her husband, Manny, is a retired local newspaper reporter. Let's call them from Mark's office."

Doris happily invited Grace over to meet Manny.

Since the painters would finish around four, Grace had plenty of time to spare. Natalie and the girls still had a chocolate cake to bake—she could take as much time as she needed.

Since Doris and Manny lived only a few blocks away, Grace rang their doorbell ten minutes later. Manny greeted her with a firm handshake and an enthusiastic welcome. A spry seventy-eight-year-old, he put Grace's notion of the elderly to shame. Slender, with a head full of white hair, Manny was sharp as a tack. He played senior tennis twice a week, puttered in the yard, and Doris bragged he was a gourmet cook. Manny was doing an awesome job. He was tanned as a movie star, their gardens were overflowing with flowers, and Doris was full-figured.

Their chintz-colored sofa, with its down filled cushions, was as attractive as it was comfortable. Doris started a fresh pot of coffee while Manny settled back in his lounge chair to read the newspaper clippings Grace handed him. When he finished, he looked over his reading glasses at Grace. "I worked behind the scenes on the Zayas murder," he explained. "The Seaport Police Department had a tip that Rico Catanetti, the Mafia Don's son, and a known troublemaker, was responsible. The cops only had the ejected shells of a twelve-gauge shotgun—the Mafia's choice of weapon, but they were unable to find the gun."

Manny handed the clippings back to Grace. "And, of course, Rico had an airtight alibi, so the cops couldn't arrest him, which left that case unsolved."

"Anything else happen after that?" Grace inquired.

"Lots. The police found a couple of dead prostitutes known to work in the Catanettis brothel above their Cat House Saloon." Manny ran his hand through his thick, white hair. "I'm sure it wasn't a Mafia hit because if they did it, the girls would simply have disappeared. The rumor is that the Catanettis take their victims to the Everglades and feed them to the alligators. No, someone else tortured those poor working girls to death." He scratched behind his neck and readjusted his chair a little.

"A young man who partied with Rico may have been involved in Tito's murder, but his identity was unknown. There's speculation that the murdered prostitutes might have known something about who he was, which is why they were tortured. I asked around, but I never found out who the mystery guy was."

Doris joined us. "Good grief, Manny! Who would've hurt those poor girls?"

He pointed to the clippings in Grace's lap. "I think Victor Hellman was behind it."

"What do you know about this Victor Hellman person?" Grace gestured to the newspaper article describing his gruesome death and leaned forward, intent on Manny's answer.

Manny didn't hesitate. "What I know is Victor came from a respectable home and his father was mayor of Seaport at one point. But he was a defiant youth and by the time he was a teenager, he had accumulated a gang of homeless young men and had involved them in gambling, prostitution, and running bootleg liquor."

As the delicious aroma of coffee filled the air, Doris excused herself. When she returned with our coffee cups, Manny was describing Seaport's muddy past.

"The whole town knew Victor Hellman to be a spiteful, unpleasant person and that Tito Zayas was his right-hand man and best friend. Even though everyone was sure Rico killed Tito, Rico was Mafia royalty. Victor didn't dare go after the kid." Manny paused. "But if Victor could learn who was with Rico, well... that's who he'd attack. Revenge was the perfect motive."

Manny looked back and forth at Grace and Doris. "This next part is gross. You ladies sure you want to hear it?"

"Yes!" they said loudly.

After he sat his coffee down, he continued. "A week later, the police investigated two shot-up cars parked in the middle of the street outside Victor Hellman's house with four dead guys in each trunk stinking to high heaven. No clue who killed them or how they got there."

Manny lowered his voice and leaned forward. "Here's the terrible part—a severed head," he paused and watched their stunned reaction before he continued, "was lying in Victor's favorite front porch chair."

"Gross!" Doris exclaimed as Grace winced, but Manny went on. "That's not all. Whoever did that also spread the rest of the poor guy's body around Victor's property. They found some hands in his mailbox, holding his mail. Can you imagine? And if I remember correctly, a leg was rotting on his roof."

"Yikes! I bet Victor's neighbors were sick of living next to him," Doris exclaimed.

Okay, I've got to steer this back to the mystery person.

"Manny, are you sure you don't have any ideas about who was with Rico that night?"

He shook his head. "Nothing I could pin down for sure. My sources mentioned a young man who delivered wine twice a month to the El Floridita restaurant. Sometimes he went drinking with the Catanetti boys in their saloon, but my informants didn't know his name. I attempted to gather more information from the restaurant employees, but they were closed-mouthed and cautious."

"Why were they unwilling to talk? I can't imagine not helping solve a crime." Grace said.

"The local Mafia Don and his associates often dined there. The staff had a better chance of staying alive if they kept their mouths shut," Manny assured her.

Grace asked if he knew anything about Victor Hellman's murder back in 1955. Unfortunately, Manny was recovering from an automobile accident and had no inside information.

Manny smiled. "That's all I know. I hope it helps with whatever you're investigating."

Grace thanked them for their hospitality, said goodbye, and headed to Natalie's.

Besides the dead guys dumped on Victor Hellman's street and some murdered prostitutes, Manny's information was a nice history lesson, with not much meat. Most of it, Grace had gathered from the newspaper clippings.

Except, who was that crazy Mafia kid's accomplice? The only lead was pretty weak—possibly a guy who delivered wine to a popular local restaurant. But something about that troubled Grace.

The police never found Tito's murder weapon, a twelve-gauge shotgun. There was one in Ray's trunk, but that meant nothing. Although Ray kept the newspaper clipping about the Zayas murder, was it farfetched to imagine it could be the crime scene's missing gun simply because it was the Mafia's choice of weapon?

What connects Ray to this Mafia kid, Rico?

Grace's mind was whirling with all the unmatched puzzle pieces. Could there be something she had overlooked in Ray's paperwork?

———————◆———————

Fifteen minutes later, Grace pulled into her driveway and waved at the painters. They were taking a break and lounging under a shady tree in the corner of her yard.

Since they had finished painting the dining room walls, Grace removed the plastic sheet covering the table and jumped into Ray's checkbooks and paperwork again. Not even knowing what she was looking for, she found zero new information.

How would John make sense of this? He'd ask if Ray told me anything about his past. Start with what I know. Hmm.

Ray said his family died when he was a young man, and he inherited some businesses. Grace had learned from his checkbooks that Ray owned a farm in Lewisville. There was nothing in his records about a winery.

Are there any wineries in Lewisville?

The painters returned and headed down the hall, chattering amongst themselves. Grace moved into her freshly painted white bedroom with a pad and pencil to use that phone.

The long-distance operator asked, "Information for what city and state, please?"

Grace crossed her fingers and asked, "Are there any vineyards listed in Lewisville, West Virginia?"

"Yes, there's one—the Lewisville Winery and Gift Shop. Would you like the telephone number or address?

"Both, please." Grace's hand was jittery as she wrote the phone number down. Knowing it was Sunday and they most likely weren't open, she called anyway. Maybe they would have an answering machine and would call her back the next day.

A young, high-pitched female answered right away. "Lewisville Gift Shop. How may I help you?"

"Is the winery open today?" Grace asked.

The helpful teenager informed Grace the winery was closed on Sundays, but the gift shop was open until five. She asked if Grace was interested in any of the gift shop's local art—silk scarves, paintings, or handmade pottery.

Saying no to the local art, Grace asked if the teen knew anything about wine and, if so, what was usually recommended if someone liked a light fruity wine—

one that wasn't too sweet. Grace figured she might as well learn something while she played sleuth.

"Easy peasy. The winery's chart on white wines says to try a Pinot Grigio first, and if it's too sweet, sample a Chardonnay. If that's too heavy, give Sauvignon Blanc a taste—it's on the lighter side. If you come to our wine tastings, you'll learn the type of wine you like. Remember, always chill white wines."

The teen seemed chatty enough, so Grace told her she was from out of state, but when she was in Lewisville, she would stop by. Then Grace asked, "How long has the winery been open?" And, of course, Miss Chatty took the bait.

"I'm not sure, but there's a framed picture of the original building hanging on the wall behind the cash register. The photograph looks old. Hold on while I see if there's a date on it."

After the girl placed the phone on the counter, Grace heard a stool, or chair, being dragged across the floor and seconds later, dragged back. The phone clattered as the teenager picked it up again.

"There's a handwritten note on the back of the photograph that says, 'To My Darling Sebastian, from your Loving Wife, Marlene. May this winery fulfill your dreams.' Dated 1914."

Taking a chance, Grace asked, "Is there a sign outside of the building?"

"Yes, Lewis Winery."

Well, how about them apples! His family owned a winery, too. I don't know whether to be freaked out or happy.

"One more question," Grace ventured. "Do you know anything about the Lewis family?"

Grace knew she was pushing it with this question, but most teens were naïve, so she pushed anyway.

"I don't, but my grandma would. She's lived here her whole life and knows everyone. Her stories are amazing. There's one about a big shootout on Main Street when she was my age. She owns a restaurant called Grandma's Diner. Her name's Becky. Call her."

Mental note. Contact Becky when I get a chance.

Grace thanked the young lady, hung up, and checked her watch. It was time to retrieve Patty and Merry.

On her way out, Mr. Morris waved Grace over and confirmed clean-up would start in an hour.

Patty and Merry's bags were sitting by Natalie's front door when Grace arrived, but they weren't ready to leave yet. Patty, who still had chocolate icing on her face, insisted Grace taste their freshly baked chocolate cake.

"You can have more than a taste," Natalie said, "but it's gonna cost you." Laughing, she cut a third of the cake for herself and Mark and sent the rest home with Grace and the girls.

While thanking and hugging Natalie goodbye, Grace promised to call her after the girls were asleep.

The painters were loading the ladders and paint supplies into their trucks when Grace and the girls arrived. As Grace grabbed the rest of the cash and settled with Mr. Morris, the girls ran inside to put their things away. Grace heard them squealing with delight over their newly painted house.

Mr. Morris thanked her for her generosity, adding, "My men said their wives got them up extra early this morning to make sure they weren't late today. This will pay for quite a few of their children's dentist and doctor bills."

"You are more than welcome, Mr. Morris. I have a question, though. Do any of your guys need clothes or bedroom furniture? Everything in the middle bedroom is going to a charity tomorrow except for the trunk—that I'm keeping."

Minutes later, it was all gone.

After dinner, as the three of them polished off the yummy chocolate cake, Merry asked, "Shouldn't we save some for Ray?"

Then Patty asked, "Where's Ray, Mom? Even though we didn't see much of him while he was upset about his friend dying, it was nice to know he was here a lot more than he usually is."

Grace kept it short and sweet. "Ray had a quick trip out of town to save a deal he had been working hard to complete. I don't know when he'll be back. It's time for the two of you to go brush your teeth and then head to bed."

When the girls were asleep, Grace called Natalie and told her about the visit she had with Doris and Manny and what Manny remembered about the murders of Tito Zayas and Victor Hellman from his days as a reporter. Then Grace repeated her conversation with the teenage girl at the winery's gift shop, which Natalie found interesting.

Next Grace added, "Oh, and I'm going to Stephen's bank in the morning to open his safe deposit box."

"Whose bank? Huh? What?" Natalie exclaimed.

Grace had forgotten to tell Natalie about the funny key she found on Stephen's key ring designed to fit a safe deposit box.

"You better call Miss Nosy the minute you're through at that bank." Natalie giggled, and they said goodnight.

Grace's hand was still resting on the cradle when John called collect, upset that he and his friend had lost track of Ray in Juárez. He was chartering a plane in El Paso, Texas, and flying home the next day. Then he said he had to go and hung up.

Grace didn't have a chance to tell him the things she had learned from Manny and the teenage girl at the winery gift shop and realized there was something about John she didn't care for. He was impatient. She didn't like that—at all.

CHAPTER THIRTY-SIX

An Unpleasant Homecoming
Ray
April 14, 1980

I ARRIVE AT SEAPORT'S AIRPORT IN THE WEE HOURS OF MONDAY morning and retrieve my truck from the parking lot. I'm still feeling unsettled and a bit off kilter, so when my gut nudges me to go to the office, I do. I've learned the hard way to pay attention to my feelings.

The first shocker is when my key won't open the front door. Not to be deterred, I used my truck's tire iron to break in through the rear of the building.

Now that I'm on alert, I trot down the hall and find my office ransacked. The file cabinet is missing a lot of files. All my ledgers and checkbooks are gone. That I can deal with. But finding my bookcase pulled away from the wall, and my safe open and empty, is a staggering kick in the stomach. The sudden rush of adrenaline overwhelms me, leaving me feeling dizzy and disoriented. My information book has disappeared and will be extremely dangerous if it falls into the wrong hands.

Who did this? My intuition says it's gotta be Grace. She has no idea what she's done.

If Junior learns what's recorded in that book or it somehow comes to The Committee's attention—it could cause a war between him and the other Mafia families. In that event, the first thing Junior will do is make sure my death is ugly and painful. If he can catch me.

Breathe. Think... I need a weapon.

Despite my bookcase having been moved, two large fake books are still sitting on top of it, undisturbed. There's a loaded handgun in one and ammunition in the other. After placing them on my desk, I glance at my wall clock, surprised to see it's already three in the morning. Most likely Grace has changed the house locks as well, so forget going home now. I close the safe and put my office back together.

Exhausted, I fell asleep on a hard-as-hell cot until one that afternoon. After a few cups of coffee, a quick shave, and a shower in the trucker's bath area, I discover a clean white shirt hanging in a locker. Dressed and ready to face the music, I hastily stow my handgun in my truck's glove compartment and, with a sense of unease, I nervously head home. With the locks changed and my office looted, I'm not sure what else I'm going to find when I get to Grace's.

I'm both surprised and amused to see Grace's house freshly painted in Stanley Hunter Revenge White and trimmed in Stephen Hunter Snotty Green. Boy, I must've really pissed her off. She's been a busy gal.

When I quietly open the front door, Grace is standing in the living room with her shoulders hunched. She's tense and lost in thought as she focuses on something in her right hand, her left hand pressed tightly over her mouth.

Soundlessly moving a few steps closer, I recognize the dreaded objects she's fixated on.

Oh shit!

She's so absorbed she still doesn't know I'm there until I ask, "Where did you find those?"

CHAPTER
THIRTY-SEVEN

Too Much Information
Grace
Earlier that day

SEAPORT'S OLDEST BANK OPENED SHARPLY AT NINE MONDAY MORNING. A minute later, Grace was in the lobby asking for the safe deposit department. The bank manager escorted her to the vault area, where he introduced her to the clerk in charge. Grace handed the older lady the proper paperwork, proving she was Stephen's next of kin, and presented the antique key she'd found on Stephen's key ring.

The clerk updated the records, adding Grace. "The box was rented by Stanley Hunter in 1933, and ownership was later passed down to Stephen Hunter in 1946. Congratulations, it's now yours."

Grace followed the bank clerk beyond the giant steel grated doors into the depths of the vast cold, moldy smelling vault, regretting she didn't bring a sweater with her.

After they inserted their matching keys, the clerk slid the metal box straight out and handed it to Grace. Then she led Grace to a tiny adjoining room with a small gray desk and chair where Grace could view the box's contents in private.

When Grace lifted the long narrow lid, she found several old court documents facing her. Beneath were a few property titles. Underneath all of them was a bulging packet full of photographs. At the bottom, a slim envelope, yellow with age, was addressed to Stephen, from his grandfather.

Where do I start? Maybe not with the legal papers.

Grace set them aside and began with the deed to the building and land that now housed Hunter & Lewis Trucking. It was a lot of property—over a hundred and fifty acres. Mr. Hunter bought it for $6,000 in Stephen's name, as a minor, and his name as Stephen's guardian. It surprised Grace that Stephen had never transferred the deeds into his name.

Next was the deed to Grace's house, which was in Stephen's name, recorded in 1943 while Stephen was still in the Navy.

So why is it locked in a safe deposit box that Stephen never told me about?

After setting them aside, Grace picked up the folded court documents and scanned them. She was stunned and unprepared for what she read. They explained her father's death and a civil suit filed against his estate.

In shock, Grace started over. The legal document began: Stanley Hunter, as Guardian of Stephen Hunter, a minor, Plaintiff, vs. The Estate of Matthew Martin, Defendant. In legalese, it specified the Hunters sued Grace's father's estate for the wrongful deaths of Stephen's mom and dad, citing an automobile accident Grace's father caused by his reckless driving.

The next legal document was a final judgment awarding Stephen as a minor, $100,000, which was a lot of money back in the '30s.

Grace now understood why her mother wouldn't discuss her father. Everything that happened to them after that was her father's fault. It was finally clear why she and her mom had to move from their comfortable home into that tiny apartment. They were destitute.

I wish my mother were still alive. I have so many questions. So many things I'd talk to her about, like Stephen's grandfather knew who I was, yet he befriended me. Why would he do that?

If Mr. Hunter paid $6,000 for the land and building, that left $94,000—somewhere. It wasn't in her and Stephen's bank account. She had constantly scrambled to keep them from being overdrawn.

Stephen must have known about the lawsuit and the judgment. Why didn't he tell me? And where is all that money?

The claustrophobic vault was freezing. Grace couldn't stay one more second. Her teeth were chattering, and her hands wouldn't quit shaking as she shoved the bundle of photographs and the old letter into her purse next to her copy of Ray's book. She'd look at them when she got home.

On a hunch, she pulled the extra copy of the book out and placed it in the box with the legal paperwork. Then she and the clerk returned the safe deposit box to its place in the vault. Now Grace, too, had a secret. Well, other than forging Ray's name on her daughters' adoption papers, that is.

As soon as the bank clerk opened the gate, it took all Grace's willpower not to run out of the building. Thank God, her car was toasty warm from the sun. The next stop was a cold grocery store.

It was one by the time Grace put the groceries away, finished lunch, and settled on her sofa with her feet up on the coffee table. Eager to read the fragile letter from Stephen's grandfather, she slipped it from its yellowed envelope. To her surprise, the handwriting was lovely and old-fashioned.

November 1, 1943

My Dearest Grandson,

If you are reading this letter, then I'm dead or in jail for avenging your parents' deaths. Stephen, you knew your parents died in an automobile accident. What you didn't know is that they were, in fact, murdered. Matthew Martin is the man responsible for their deaths. The Mafia sent Matthew to stop your father from accusing them of burning down your other grandparents' building, which resulted in their deaths as well.

I couldn't take revenge then because your grandmother and I had to care for you, so I took Matthew Martin's estate to court, won, and collected $100,000 on your behalf. I used $6,000 of that money to buy 150 acres of land and the building Hunter Trucking is on, in your name, as a minor, with me as your guardian. You should not have any trouble transferring the title.

That land will grow in value and provide a nice inheritance for your children in the future. I also transferred the deed to my house into your name after you left for the Navy.

Your mother inherited the proceeds from her parents' fire insurance and the sale of their home, which leaves another $100,000, which also passed to you.

I lived through some tough times when a lot of folks lost their hard-earned money in failing banks. I didn't want to risk losing yours, so I hid the cash and instructed my attorney to give you this letter one year after you were married. You might appreciate it the most when you have a family. Enclosed is a map that shows where it's hidden.

Now I'm free to settle the score by killing the families of those people who caused our loss. First will be Matthew Martin's daughter, Grace. I want Matthew's wife to suffer the loss of her child like I have. Then I will kill her. Last, for sending Matthew Martin to kill my son, I will murder the Mafia father's entire family before I put him out of his misery.

So, if I am dead or in jail, you now understand why.

Stephen, even though you have married, I must warn you to guard your money and protect yourself. Trust no one, not even your wife. You are all you have now.

Your Loving Grandfather,
Stanley Hunter

Grace sat back in shock, her hands trembling and her mouth dry. *What in the ever-living hell? But it's in black-and-white.* Proof that Stephen knew about all of this the year after they were married.

What was going through his mind when he read this letter the first time?

Oh, my God! Grace realized she had just repainted her home to honor a monster who had planned to murder her and her mother! And Grace's mother was aware the court had awarded $100,000 of their family's money to Stanley Hunter on Stephen's behalf.

Did my mother believe it was a fitting consolation prize when I married Stephen? Did she want me to reclaim my inheritance? Why didn't she tell me? And where's the damned map? What did Stephen do with it?

Grace remembered asking Stephen how he paid for his new Chevy and that he told her he'd found a little of his grandfather's cash.

What else did Stephen lie about?

Grace also recalled John telling her everyone had secrets. The letter from Stephen's grandfather proved Stephen did. Grace's head was spinning. She rechecked the date on the letter and saw that Mr. Hunter wrote his intentions to murder her the week before he died. Thank God, someone prevented him from carrying out his plan.

But who?

The only person close enough to kill Mr. Hunter was Ray. Could he have known what Stephen's grandfather was up to? It might explain why Mr. Hunter's newspaper article was in Ray's trunk, along with Stephen's and the others.

But why keep Stephen's newspaper article? He died from the flu.

Grace wanted to call Miss Nosy Natalie right away and tell her about Stanley Hunter's letter to Stephen, but figured she'd better look at the photographs first. Miss Nosy would want the entire story, not just bits and pieces. She'd ring Natalie after she viewed them.

Grace settled back on the sofa, prepared to enjoy the snapshots Stephen cherished so much he kept them locked in his safe deposit box. Never in a million years could she have imagined what she saw. Naked young women tied to wooden cross beams, with their arms and legs splayed. Their faces turned to the side and their mouths screaming as someone hit them with a whip. In one photograph, the restrained girl had slumped down, her eyes closed—passed out.

The first half dozen photos were only of nude women. Then the men who beat them showed up in the next shots, looking proud as they held their whips. Grace didn't recognize any of them until she saw Stephen leering into the camera, his hand inside his unzipped pants. Shocked, Grace gasped so hard she choked, leapt to her feet, and started coughing as she tried to catch her breath.

Disgusted, she wanted to throw those sickening photographs in the garbage, but she wasn't going to stop. No, sir, she was determined to look at every stinking one of them. Grace found more photos of Stephen, the man she loved, screwing young women tied to beds, blindfolded, and gagged. In other images, many of them were handcuffed while men raped them. And her husband was among them.

That can't be Stephen! Grace looked closer at another photograph. He was holding a drink in one hand and a whip in the other. Grace swore to God it was the most revolting look she had ever seen on Stephen's face. Shocked, her left hand flew up to cover her mouth. *That disgusting monster!* She had mourned for a man with a demon coiled up inside him.

On top of all that evil, Stephen knew he had inherited Grace's family's money, yet he kept their household budget cut to the bone. *That selfish, conniving, deviant thief!* Grace despised Stephen Hunter and his wicked grandfather with every fiber of her soul. She was glad they were dead because if they were alive, she would kill them herself.

"Where did you find those?" a voice suddenly came from behind her.

Grace shrieked and whirled around, her heart pounding out of control.

"Ray! You scared the bejesus out of me! What are you doing here? I thought you left us."

"I did, Grace, but I wanted to explain and ask your forgiveness," Ray said. "However, when I arrived in the middle of the night and discovered my office ransacked and some valuable information missing, I figured it was you. If that book you took from my safe falls into the wrong hands, it could get me killed. I need it back."

Even though Ray's voice was slow and steady, the look on his face betrayed him.

Grace was so mad she could spit nails. "Yeah? Well, that's too darn bad, Ray. You've got a lot of explaining to do, mister."

"Yes, I do, and I'm sorry I made you angry." Ray smiled wistfully. "So please, let's start over. I'm curious. Where did you find those photographs?"

Ray was trying to be nice and his body language wasn't threatening, so Grace told him about the safe deposit key, which led her to the bank that morning. She left out the part about storing a copy of his address book in the bank's box, though.

Ray said he had seen the photos before but not the letter and asked to read it.

Grace figured why not and handed it to him.

When Ray finished, he gave it back to her, then sat on the sofa, and, patting it, invited her to sit next to him. Grace did, but not too close. Kind of on the edge, facing him.

Ray then looked at her and said point-blank, "That's why I killed Stanley Hunter, Grace." Straightforward and blunt. No emotion at all.

"It was you?" Grace's eyes were wide in disbelief. "Why?"

"He had just left the hardware store after purchasing a rope and a tarpaulin. That evil old son of a bitch was planning to murder you, wrap you up, and throw your dead body into the bay. I killed him before he could harm you.

"Who in the hell are you, Ray?!" Grace shouted.

Finally, Ray showed emotion as he leaned back on the sofa and closed his eyes with a distressed look on his face.

Grace expected Ray to say he was a CIA assassin... she wasn't even close.

Ray's eyes were still shut when he replied, "I'm your protector and first cousin, Grace. My mother's maiden name was Martin."

"What?!" A punch in the gut would've been less shocking.

Ray leaned forward and looked at Grace, searching her eyes. "I'm so sorry. After I lied to you so many times, it was too damned hard to tell you the truth."

"Oh my God!" Grace screamed. Already sick to her stomach from those disgusting photographs, to find out she married and slept with her first cousin was way too much!

When her stomach heaved, Grace sprinted to the bathroom, making it just in time. Ray followed, holding a cold wet rag to her forehead as he kept saying how sorry he was.

Once Ray helped Grace back to the sofa, he asked who should talk first.

Grace didn't know. She couldn't think.

CHAPTER
THIRTY-EIGHT

More Cocaine First
Rico Catanetti
April 14, 1980

RICO SNORTED HIS FIRST LINE OF COKE JUST AFTER TWO, proud of himself for waiting until after lunch. If he snorted too early, he wouldn't eat, and he was getting thinner. That was no good for charming the ladies with promises of fun and all the booze and cocaine they wanted if they visited his Wolf's Den.

Slender was handsome, but skinny was not. Rico, known for his heavily oiled, slicked-back hair and cheeky grin, considered himself to be the best-looking of the Catanetti men, despite what his brothers thought.

He laid out a second thin line of coke with a razor blade when the phone rang, jolting his concentration. His hand slipped, messing up his perfectly straight line.

The operator asked if he would accept a collect call from Juárez, Mexico.

He listened as Boss explained in broken English that Ray left a blinking black box in his hotel room when he checked out.

"What?" Rico shouted into the phone.

Boss stuttered, searching for the right English words to ask Rico if he wanted the black box sent to him.

"Get rid of it!" Rico slammed the phone down. Remembering Ray's brief collect call to Franco yesterday that didn't add up, it sure did now.

Obviously, when Ray found that box, he knew he was being followed, left it behind, and freaked the hell out. Then he called his *mommy*, Franco, wanting to come home. *Oh, boo-hoo.* But Ray didn't have the balls to tell *mommy* about the black box or that he was being trailed. That's the same as lying. No use complaining to Franco about Ray. They were joined at the hip.

And Angelo was no better.

Brother Luca always played for whatever side was the safest.

No, Rico would emphasize his hate for Ray by telling Junior about the black box that Ray neglected to mention to any of them.

Ever since the time he and Stephen partied together, Rico had been blamed for Stephen raping Carmelita. His brothers insisted Stephen learned all his sick sex habits from him.

Angelo, that prick, warned of dire consequences if he failed to cut off his relationship with Stephen. Rico sneered, thinking he'd like to see Angelo, that old fart, try to take him now.

Luca, always an ass-kissing jerk, just smirked and said nothing.

Franco made it even more humiliating by threatening to send him on a sightseeing trip to the Everglades to feed Stephen to the alligators. Rico was glad he didn't have to. He liked Stephen and had a great time partying with him.

He remembered when Stephen hinted he might slip a mickey in his frigid wife's drink, tie her up, and share her. Man, that would've been fun. Actually, it turned Rico on just thinking about it. Maybe, if he got the chance, he'd do it, anyway. He couldn't have cared less that she was Ray's wife now. In fact, that made it even better.

When Franco banned him from all their brothels, insisting injured working ladies don't make money, it didn't stop Rico from having his special brand of fun. He changed his detached garage into a den—and not the type to smoke cigars in after dinner, either. The Wolf's Den had cost him a pretty penny to design and build. He went to some crazy places in New York City to get his dungeon building ideas. His men played for free as long as they shared the gals they brought in and swore they wouldn't utter a single word about it to his jackass brothers.

Rico used a razor blade to cut another line of cocaine and snorted it through a rolled up hundred-dollar bill. While he enjoyed his high, he daydreamed about the damage he wanted to inflict on Ray and couldn't wait to tell Junior what a liar and sneaky bastard Ray was. But he wouldn't ask for Junior's permission to throw Ray a permanent retirement party. Nah. He was just gonna do it and beg for forgiveness afterward.

When he was high enough, Rico sent for his guys, telling them to get ready for a little fun later. "We might set Ray's house on fire this evening. And grab Ray's ice-queen wife and introduce her to the Wolf's Den." Whooping loudly, his crew was all for that.

Rico snorted in laughter. "So load your shotguns and bring a few Molotov cocktails. We're going to party hard tonight."

They all hooted and cheered. Burning anything down was great fun. Maybe they'd even have a go with Ray's blond wife, taking bets on who would successfully snatch her.

That threw Rico into fits of giggles as he chopped extra lines of coke across the glass table, inviting his men to partake, which was unusual. Rico never shared his stash. But tonight, he was feeling generous and opened up another baggie.

His mind was buzzing. Without permission from Junior to attack Ray, he better not make it worse by assaulting the wrong house. Rico remembered picking Stephen up a few times, but always late at night and long ago. He needed to drive by in full daylight to refresh his memory.

Rico glanced at his watch—almost three. Plenty of time to check out where Ray lived.

An hour after Rico returned home, ate a couple of sandwiches, and tossed back a few shots of whiskey, he did a few more lines of coke.

Then surprise, surprise—Junior called with a directive right up Rico's alley. "Capture Ray and bring him to our compound alive. It's permanent retirement time."

Rico pushed it further. "I wanna torch that lying prick's house, too."

"Be my guest."

Rico, smug and vindicated, pictured himself as the Don one day. Boy, would that be spectacular! All that money. All those women at his fingertips to do with as he wished. And all that power... it made him hard just thinking about it.

With Junior's stamp of approval, Rico didn't have to wait until late to visit Ray's house. He could go anytime he damn well pleased. That called for a celebration. "Show time!" he yelled.

But more cocaine first.

CHAPTER THIRTY-NINE

Building New Relationships
Ray
April 14, 1980

IF I'M GOING TO GET MY BOOK BACK, I need to rebuild our relationship on a different level. It's crucial for me to impress upon her the danger we're in right now.

"Grace, if that book falls into the wrong hands, a lot of people will be killed. That includes you and me. What did you do with it? Please say you didn't look at it."

"I flipped through it. People's names, dates, and places were connected to other people who died," Grace explains. "No idea what that means, but I'm sure it's important enough for you to safeguard it. Just like you attempted to secure your room and trunk."

What?

Leaping to my feet, I dash into my bedroom. Empty. My trunk. Open. Empty.

"Oh my God! Grace, what've you done? Where are my things?" I yell, but she's right behind me.

"I hid your stuff somewhere safe and used some of your money to freshen the place up a little. Now that I know about Stephen's grandfather, I should've chosen a different paint color to signify getting rid of you."

I hate it when she turns into Miss Pissy and I try hard not to glare at her. "It doesn't matter how much money you spent. Some of that cash is yours anyway, to help you and the girls start over without me. It's part of the reason I'm here."

Dammit, we don't have time for this. Jesus, the clock is ticking.

I need that book. What's my leverage? She wants to find Stephen's money, and I bet she doesn't have a clue where to look. Impatience is coursing through my veins.

"I have an idea where that map is, but I'm in a hurry. You've gotta tell me where you hid my book."

She just glares at me.

"Come on, Grace. School's almost out. The girls can't be part of this."

At least that registers.

"Hold your britches." She goes to the kitchen and makes a phone call, then comes stomping back.

"Natalie will pick up the girls from school and take them to their Spanish lesson. She has a key to the house, so they'll be fine until we return. If you help me find the map, I'll tell you where I hid your stuff."

It looks like Grace grew a set of balls. Good for her.

"Okay, deal. Grab your keys. We're going to the office. You drive."

As we pull out of the driveway, Rico and his goons cruise past Grace's house in his black sedan. *That's strange. Why is he checking on me?*

I rolled down my window, making sure Grace didn't see me lift my fingers in a small wave. Rico salutes back, and they continue driving.

Since I broke into the back of the Hunter & Lewis building, I make no comment when Grace unlocks the front door with her shiny new keys. She glances at me and says nothing, either.

I suggest we begin in Stephen's office, which is where I think he would keep the map. "I'll take the dusty bookcase. Why don't you check out his desk?" I'm bluffing, but it makes sense to start in these two places.

A few minutes later she says, "There's nothing here," and joins me, hoping the map is tucked inside a manual or book. Again—no result.

Grace then plops down on the edge of the desk and mumbles, "If he already found the money, he wouldn't need the map anymore."

"That's possible. But that much cash would require a sizable storage space. It's gotta be here, somewhere," I reply.

Grace looks around the room, thinking, then turns to me with her eyebrows raised.

"Ray, do you have the building plans for this place?"

"Yes. Top of my bookcase. I'll be right back."

When I return and spread the drawings on Stephen's desk, we flip through each sheet, looking for any nooks or crannies. When we get to the plumbing diagram, I mention that this was the only page Mr. Hunter would let me have when I designed the trucker's overnight area. "I needed to find a water supply for the shower, sink, and toilet."

"Which office was originally Stephen's grandfather's?" she asks.

"This one."

We exchange glances and then look at the oak-paneled walls. Without a word, we split up and begin tapping them, listening for a distinct sound. Nothing.

After we move the bookcase away from the wall, we check behind it. Again, nothing. Grace turns her attention to the ceiling. I know what she's thinking.

I grunt, "Be right back."

Grace is studying the plans when I return with a stepladder. I remove a few ceiling tiles, but all I see are spider webs crisscrossing up to the roof line.

"Nothing but bugs up there," I say, descending the ladder.

"Ray, was this always a small airplane hangar before Stanley bought it?"

She gestures towards the elevation page and a circle beneath this room. "What's this?"

"A well?" I squint at the faded print, then look back at her. "Hey, you're good at this."

"Thanks, butthead. If I'm correct, it's right down there." She indicates the antique Oriental carpet we're standing on, anchored in place by Stephen's desk.

As I push the desk's front legs off the rug, Grace rolls it up and stops in the middle of the floor. "Ray, there's a trapdoor."

"Flashlight!" I rush out again.

When I return, she already has it open and is staring into a black hole. She looks up at me. "Drum roll, please."

It's such an unexpected remark. I laugh out loud, switch the flashlight on, and aim it at the hole. "Okay, Cuz, let's see what's in there."

She shoots me a dirty look, which makes me laugh again. But then there's a sneaky smile on her face. I hope that means she's getting used to the idea of us being cousins.

Two antique suitcases lay a couple feet down, one on top of the other. Beyond that, the hole is filled with concrete. I lay flat on the floor, reach in, snap open the first one and shine my flashlight inside. A piece of paper sits on several stacks of old banded cash.

"It's a receipt for a 1958 Chevrolet costing $2,500.00." I lift it up, offering it to her.

Grace reads it, then frowning, tosses it back into the suitcase. "So that's how he paid for the Chevy. That liar."

Standing up and brushing the dust off my pants and hands, I decide the moment has come to play my card. "Now that you know where the money is, I suggest you move it later. I want us to live a lot longer, so where is my book?"

"Mark has the original. I sent a copy to a friend of mine at the sheriff's office. And another..."

"You did what!" Adrenaline pumps through my system, sending my mind in a million directions at once.

"No, no, no." I drop onto the edge of Stephen's desk.

Holy shit, she doesn't know what she's done. Junior has moles in the sheriff's office. If they intercept that envelope, I'm as good as dead. Crap, crap, crap. Rico drove by my house earlier and saluted me. That shithead knows something. We need to move fast.

"Grace, stay here. I need to make a call!" I yell, bolting out of Stephen's office into mine, frantically dialing Franco's private number. "Hey man, I'm at my office now, but Rico drove past my house a little while ago. What's he up to?"

Franco doesn't know, but he'll find out and call me right back.

A few minutes later, the phone rings. "Our guy at the sheriff's office noticed a package addressed to a detective who's on vacation. He snatched it and delivered it to Junior. It was sent from your wife at your home address. It contained a fascinating copy of an address-sized book filled with information that pissed Junior off. He called Rico with instructions to find you and bring you to the compound with the original, along with any other copies that might exist. Your life is about to get ugly, Ray."

Aw, Jesus. That shithead Rico was checking me out. He's coming back for sure.

"Believe me, Franco. I just learned about this a few minutes ago. I'm working on getting that book right now. The second I have it in my hands, I'll call you. Do everything you can to hold your brothers off. I'm worried that Rico won't honor the rules of conduct. Grace and our daughters are in his line of fire."

Franco reassures me he'll do his best, but I better move fast because Rico's messed up on drugs, is making horrible decisions, and is drawing attention to everyone. Franco pauses, then lowers his voice. "You've got a bunch of explaining to do about the information recorded in that book, Ray."

"I have my reasons. That's all you need to know," I snap and hang up.

Grace dashes into my office, saying she's been trying to call home on the other line, but no one's answering. "It's almost six. Natalie and the girls should be there by now. Something's wrong!"

We expect everything to be fine when we see Natalie's car parked in front of the house. But when we open the front door—a lamp is turned over, a few things are scattered around, and it's quiet—too quiet.

Grace calls out to the girls, then to Natalie. That's when we hear bumping and thumping coming from the kitchen and find Natalie on the floor, gagged, and tied up with the long phone cord someone ripped out of the wall. I've always hated that freaking cord.

The moment she is free, Natalie is madder than a wet hen, stammering and fuming, trying to tell me what happened as I continue to fire questions at her. That's when things start to become even wilder.

The front door opens, and a deep male voice says, "Hello, anyone home?"

I step from the kitchen just as Grace dashes past me and throws herself into some tanned Apollo looking guy's arms.

What in the ever-living hell is going on around here?

"John!" she sobs as he holds her and glares at me over her shoulder. Bawling, she tells him, "Some terrible men kidnapped my girls and tied Natalie up, and Ray helped me find Stephen's money buried in a hole at the office, and now you're here, and I don't know how to get my babies back."

Okay, what am I? Mashed potatoes? I know who took them. And I'm the only one who can bring them back.

While they make nice, I pull Natalie aside. With a look of genuine concern, I say, "I'm glad you're all right, but it's crucial that you call Mark and tell him to bring my book here—immediately. It's the only way to get our girls back. Use the bedroom phone. Go!"

Meanwhile, Grace and Mr. Tan-and-Handsome are still clutching each other.

How would Father handle this awkward situation?

Sighing, I face the obvious. "Please, make yourself at home. I'm Ray and you are?" I hold out my hand, which requires him to unlatch from my cousin/wife to shake it.

Tan-and-Handsome hesitates, then shakes my hand. "Detective John Myers, Seaport Sheriff's Office." He shoots me a confident look that says Grace is going to be just fine. And honestly, it's a relief.

Why am I not surprised?

"How was Denver? Colder than a witch's tit?" I ask because he's wearing a thick black turtleneck sweater. He has to be the one who put that tracking device in my bag. "Sorry to miss our family reunion."

Hah! That was worth the look on his face. However, the last thing I want is a pissing match. I need to concentrate on getting Patty and Merry back, so I slap on my father's charm and use my calm voice.

"Detective Myers, I know who took my daughters and how to find them. You've got to trust me on this."

He nods as I turn my attention to my wife, still glued to his side, wrapped in his left arm.

"Grace, I asked Natalie to call Mark. You said he has my original book. That's our ticket to getting our girls back. Please, go check on her."

She agrees and leaves Tan-and-Handsome with me.

Minutes later, Pastor Mark rushes through the front door, surprised to see Detective Myers and me sitting together on the sofa.

"Mark, your wife's okay. She's in there with Grace." I point to the kitchen. "My book? Please."

He tosses it to me and hustles to where all kinds of loud, distressful conversations are going on.

Just to be a smart-ass, I open the book to Rico Catanetti's name and hand it to Tan-and-Handsome. "Maybe you'd like to peek at this before I use it to buy my daughters' freedom? I need to make a phone call right now."

As soon as Franco picks up, I growl, "Okay, I have the original. You have a copy. Where did Rico take my girls?"

"What are you talking about, Ray?"

Aw crap. He sounds sincere. I hate it, but now I have to play rough with my oldest friend. Starting slow and assertive, "Rico and his goons came to my house. They tied up my wife's best friend and took my twelve-year-old daughters. Do not withhold information from me."

Clenching my teeth to stay calm doesn't work. My voice gets louder and angrier. "This is me being nice, Franco, so tell me where my kids are or I'm going to hurt a bunch of people—Junior included. Now, Franco!"

"Ray, I swear I didn't know Rico took your girls. I need a minute to find out what's happening. You have my word. I'll call you right back."

"I'm at home. You've got seconds." I growl again, slamming the phone down.

Tan-and-Handsome is standing in the bedroom doorway, listening.

"I guess you heard that, huh?" I grumble.

"If you mean, did I hear you threatening Franco Catanetti, the financial wizard of the Mafia superstars? I did, and I want to help. Since I'm officially on vacation, I'm not here."

I think I might like this guy. Or not. The jury's still out.

"So, Rico Catanetti kidnapped your daughters?" He asks and hands my book back.

"Yes, and it worries me because Rico's a sadistic cokehead. Franco's finding out where he took Patty and Merry. Once I know, I have to move fast, but with caution. Everyone in the Catanetti family knows Rico's dangerously insane. I don't get why they've put up with him for so long."

"I'm an excellent shot. Let me go with you."

I stare at him, thinking I can't commit to that right now when the phone rings. I grab the receiver quickly that the base clatters to the floor. Franco gets to the point and hangs up. I lose no time filling Tan-and-Handsome in.

"My daughters are at Rico's house. Franco says to check out his garage first. Also, Rico's planning to set Grace's house on fire. We've got minutes to leave. I need the rest of my weapons, and Grace hasn't told me where she hid them."

"She did what! She didn't tell me she did that. What in the hell was she thinking?"

"Grace!" we shout together, and follow each other into the living room, firing questions at her, one after the other.

"Stop! I took everything from the trunk to Uncle Robert's Storage, ten minutes from here. I have an after-hours key if they're closed."

That means I've got seconds to get this crew organized and out the door.

"Grace, the guys who kidnapped our daughters plan to burn this house down any minute. Ask Natalie to help you pack some bags for you and the girls. Bring warm clothes and heavy coats. It's cold where we're going. You have five minutes. Also, grab all your legal documents, like birth certificates and that kind of stuff. Hurry!"

Grace and Natalie dart to the girls' room.

I then turn to Mark. "Go home and gather warm clothing for both of you. You're coming with us. Since Natalie has seen Rico and his goons, they'll come after her and kill you both. She will join you in a few minutes."

His expression looks like I've just slapped the hell out of him. I don't have time to spare his feelings. He needs to prepare.

"Also, Mark, call someone to replace you at church. I can't tell you when it'll be safe for you to return, either. I need the rest of my weapons, so Grace will follow Detective Myers and me to her storage unit, then she'll join you at the rectory. You only have minutes to do this."

He's a deer in headlights, hanging on every word, nodding, but saying nothing.

"This is very important. I'm counting on you to pack your car and make sure everyone is ready to leave the second Detective Myers and I arrive with the girls. Understand?"

I guess that answers Tan-and-Handsome's request.

As soon as Mark and Natalie are gone, John and I finish loading Grace's suitcases into her Cadillac. "Do you think those guys will torch my house?"

"Yes, I do. You have seconds to grab what you'll be heartbroken to lose."

She returns with Grandmother Martin's antique quilts from the girl's beds, a big photo album, and the girls' baby books.

"Nice choices." I tuck them into her trunk.

She shoots me another of her dirty looks. "I packed all your checkbooks and ledgers in one of my suitcases. I don't think you'll need your old personal files, especially Barry O'Hara's," Miss Pissy says.

"Ouch." I turn away and say under my breath, "Your fantastic new friend and I will follow you in our trucks. Lead the way."

CHAPTER FORTY

The Showdown
John and Ray
April 14, 1980

AFTER JOHN AND RAY FINISHED EMPTYING GRACE'S STORAGE room into the huge trunk of Grace's Cadillac, they loaded the guns into Ray's pickup truck. That's when Grace declared she was going with them.

They both turned and yelled, "No!"

"It's too dangerous," Ray said, lowering his voice. "We need to concentrate on keeping the girls safe. You'll be in the way."

John told her, "Grace, trust us. I promise, we've got this," and opened her driver's door. There was doubt and confusion on her face, but Grace climbed in, started the car, and put it in gear. As soon as she turned the corner at the end of the street, headed toward Natalie's house, John tossed his jacket, turtleneck sweater, and travel bag into the back of Ray's truck.

"Lead the way," Ray said, then mumbled something about trust and making promises.

Ten minutes later, he followed John's truck down a long driveway to a garage apartment at the rear of his landlord's property. Illuminated by Ray's headlights,

John signaled to give him two minutes and rushed upstairs to stuff winter clothes into a garbage bag, grab his gun and ammunition, and lock up. True to his word, within a couple of minutes, John tossed his stuff into the back of Ray's truck.

Ray looked puzzled when John handed him a clean shirt.

"Just in case any blood's involved," John said with a cocky smile.

Ray grunted, which John figured meant thank you. Ray tucked it under the front seat and backed out of the driveway.

"Why don't we call the sheriff's office and get some backup?" John asked as Ray headed to the end of the street and hung a left onto the main highway.

"We do this alone, Detective Myers. No warning, no witnesses," Ray said without taking his eyes off the road.

"It's John."

Ray nodded. He's a man of few words and John wanted to dislike him, but Ray was doing a damn good job of making that impossible.

Ray drove through an upper-class neighborhood lined with two and three-story homes on half-acre lots shielded by high retaining walls or thick hedges for privacy. While searching for a curbside parking place, he pointed out shithead Rico's house on John's right. A tall stone wall surrounded the prick's two-story house with a closed solid-panel driveway gate on its right, making it a goddamned fortress.

They parked on the next block, secured their guns in the back of their pants, and noted that most folks had already turned off their outside lights. It didn't matter. The new moon's dark night concealed them as they followed the sidewalk to Rico's house, only to discover that the frickin' driveway gate was locked. Ray then signaled John to follow him around the block, mumbling that garbage trucks picked up from the alley. John's heart dropped when that entrance was locked, too.

John was thinking about what to do next when he heard a slight metal clanging sound. Ray was standing on the lid of a trash can, boosting himself up to the top of the wall. He motioned for John to do the same before he jumped over the ledge, landing with a thud. Seconds later, they were crouched in Rico's backyard, guns drawn, waiting for their eyes to adjust to the darkness.

Unexpectedly, lights from the kitchen came on, illuminating the two large first-floor windows facing them. Rico grabbed a beer from his refrigerator, pushed through the swinging kitchen door, and returned to the interior of the house, leaving the kitchen well-lit. Thanks to Rico, they could see their surroundings much better now.

A detached garage was on their left, with a clear opening between it, the backyard, and the house. They scrambled across the lawn and crept under the kitchen windows, headed toward the garage. They eased up to the corner of the house and leaned forward a little. The driveway in front of them extended from the garage entrance on their left to the closed gate in front of the house on their right. A car was parked about halfway up the driveway, close to some wooden steps that lead into the house, presumably through a kitchen door they couldn't see. Light shone through another kitchen window that faced the driveway.

They stayed in the shadows, close to the corner, listening for clues, when the rusty hinges of the old-fashioned garage door swung open. One of Rico's men walked out, laughing, and called over his shoulder, "I'll be right back with some food for you hungry ladies. What kind of beer do you like?"

The little girls yelled, "Ew! No yucky beer!"

Great. Now they knew where Patty and Merry were, just not if they were alone. Rico's guy laughed, crossed the driveway, trotted up the steps, and entered the kitchen.

Ray pointed to the partially open garage door. Guns ready, they lined up behind it. As they eased it open a little further, it made a creaking sound. A guy's voice called out, "Hey, man! Forget something?"

John motioned to Ray to go in fast and head left, that he would go right, and then one of them would take the guy out. Ray and John burst through the door so fast the bald guy sitting against the rear wall only caught sight of John. The twins were on the bald guy's right. For John, it was a terrible shot. It angled toward the girls.

Ray's bullet entered the man's right temple, propelling him away from the girls and back against thick black-leather padded walls. The man slid to the floor, still clutching the gun he had no time to use. The girls were unsure what happened until they saw their guard laying on the concrete, missing half his face.

John rushed to their side, blocking their view of the dead guy, whispering loudly, "Don't look at him. Look at your dad."

Their eyes swung to Ray, then rotated back and forth between Ray and John as their hands were untied.

Ray's voice was low and unemotional. "We're getting you out of here. Do exactly what Mr. John and I say."

They stared at Ray as he explained they had to follow him through the backyard and run down the alley to his truck that was parked on the next street. But one girl couldn't control her emotions any longer and broke down sobbing. Ray eased down and pulled her into his arms.

"It's okay, Merry. Mr. John and I have you and Patty now. Mom is waiting for you at Miss Natalie's house."

Ray frowned at John over the top of her head, shaking his head no.

John understood. They needed a quicker exit and whispered, "Okay, the front gate."

Then they heard laughter followed by a male voice calling out as he pushed the squeaky garage door wider to accommodate the tray he was carrying, "Hey! I got you some cold beers to wash down a few pieces of fried chicken."

The second he saw his friend lying near the back wall and all of them staring at him, the food clattered to the ground as he reached for his gun. When John's bullet exploded through the left side of his throat, a bloody spray jetted out, splashing the garage door. The momentum spun him into the driveway.

Patty screamed, and Ray pulled her close with his other arm, telling both girls to listen carefully. "Stay with Mr. John while I make sure that stupid guy in the house doesn't hurt anyone ever again. Take deep breaths, stand up, and stretch your legs to get the wobbles out. I'll be right back, don't you worry."

They nodded and sat up straight, wiping their tears away.

"Hurry, Ray," Patty said, "that skinny man cursed at us when Merry kicked him hard in the *cojones*."

"Be careful, Ray. He's a mean man," Merry says, tearing up again.

"I will. That skinny, mean man will be sorry he ever touched you." Ray kissed the tops of their heads and was gone in seconds.

"Okay, let's do what your father said," John told them. "Take three deep breaths, stand up, and shake those wobbles out. Don't look at that guy lying outside the garage. Just stay close to me, bend down, and move fast. Once we pass the car, we'll head toward the driveway gate. Then I'll find a safe place to hide you until your dad gets back."

Thankfully, they followed John's directions perfectly. At the front of the house, John tucked them into some tall hedges and warned them to stay silent, even if they heard more gunshots.

"I'm a police officer and an old friend of your mom. I need to help your dad in case more bad men are inside this house. Will you be my honorary deputies and follow my orders?"

It surprised them when John told them he was a cop. They immediately agreed to remain silent. "Pinky swear?" John asked. That produced smiles as they hooked their little fingers with John's. He couldn't resist. It was a thing his ex-girlfriend Nora always did, and the girls, with their red curly hair, reminded John so much of her.

He slipped back down the driveway and crouched behind the passenger side of the parked car's hood. With eyes on the kitchen window, John tried to figure out where Ray was inside the house.

Rico bounded into the kitchen, dressed in his robe, with his hair still wet from a shower, yelling, "You guys ready for another couple of snorts before we deal with Ray's fucking little brats?"

When he didn't get a response, he headed to the open kitchen window overlooking the driveway, which gave him a perfect view of his dead guy sprawled out on the concrete with his throat blown out.

John was close enough to see the surprise register on Rico's face as Rico swung his gun up, pointed it toward the kitchen window, and shouted, "It's showtime, Ray! I know you're out there."

"Wrong, asshole." Ray stepped out from behind the kitchen door and shot Rico in the back of the head. John was already standing in the open and shot a hole through Rico's heart before he dropped.

Without warning, John saw one of Rico's bodyguards sneaking up behind Ray, aiming a gun at Ray's back. John hit him dead center, hurling him backward out of the room. Alerted by the unexpected gunshot and a body thumping on the floor behind him, Ray bolted out the kitchen door and slammed into John.

"Damn! That was close." Ray's eyes darted back and forth. "Where's my kids?"

"Follow me, and," John said over his shoulder as they hustled down the driveway to the front yard, "thanks for letting me see your book verifying that Rico killed my detective friend. It gave me great pleasure to shoot that asshole, too." Once again, John interpreted Ray's grunt as "you're welcome."

"Here they are... out of sight... safe and sound." John pulled back the branches and offered them his hand. "Come out, girls, your dad and I are taking you home."

"Ray! You're okay," Patty and Merry squealed and hugged him tightly.

Then John heard the last thing he wanted to hear—sirens way off in the distance. Neither he nor Ray could afford to be found at a murder scene, especially with two little girls.

"Let's go," John whispered harshly, pulling Patty and Merry's shirt collars up around their necks. "Girls, we're going to walk fast—not run—to your dad's truck. Stay tight between your father and me. Keep your heads low and your eyes down. Got it?"

John flipped his shirt collar up and turned to Ray, indicating he should, too. "Ready?"

The girls fell in between Ray and John as they unlocked and pulled the driveway gate open. Then they hustled down the street to Ray's truck. Lights all around the neighborhood were flicking on. John crossed his fingers, hoping the God of luck was still with him. It was a pitch-black night. Because of his experience, John believed it was unlikely anyone could accurately describe them.

Ten minutes later, they drove past the girls' home, now engulfed in flames. Rico had struck again. Neighbors, up and down the street, were standing on their lawns, clad in their pajamas, watching firefighters battle the inferno that had already consumed Grace's house.

Both girls were wailing when they pulled down the rectory's long driveway and parked next to Natalie's station wagon. She and Grace were loading suitcases into its flat trunk space. They surrounded Patty and Merry in seconds, hugging and comforting them, and thanking Ray and John for rescuing them.

The girls were clamoring for attention, trying to tell their story at the same time. "Ray and Mr. John saved us and Ray made sure that skinny, mean man won't do that ever again," Patty said, tears streaming, her face tucked into Grace's chest.

"Mr. John made us honorary deputies and hid us in the bushes." Merry pressed herself underneath Grace's left arm.

Grace was frowning when she glanced at John and Ray. Her eyebrows raised as Patty continued, "Mr. John told us not to look at the two dead guys, so we didn't." Patty then wiped her tears and nose on the handkerchief Ray passed to her.

Grace made soothing sounds while the girls talked over each other, venting their anxiety and displaying their moxie at being involved in such a shocking event.

"Let's go," Ray said, with impatience written all over his face.

Grace led the girls to the back seat of Natalie's station wagon, where their pillows, Lilly dolls, and quilts were waiting to make their trip as comfortable as possible. As soon as they fastened their seat belts, Natalie passed them a lunch bag and a thermos.

Grace gave John her car keys. "I'll stay with my daughters while they eat and talk some more. When we stop for gas, I'll join you."

John leaned in and said goodbye to the girls. "You did such a good job being my honorary deputies tonight. I'm sorry your house burned down. I promise it'll be fun getting a new one and some pretty new clothes, too. Trust me." That brought a smile to their faces.

Ray was shaking his head again when he joined them. "Patty, Merry, you girls were brave tonight. I'm so proud of you." Then, frowning, he waved his hand at Pastor Mark and John, and shouted, "We've gotta roll—now!"

"Where are we going, Ray?" Grace asked as she climbed in next to the girls.

"Home, Grace. We're going home." Ray closed her door and strolled away before she could ask any more questions.

Ray's black pickup truck pulled out first. Natalie's station wagon followed. John was at the rear, driving Grace's baby blue Cadillac—its back seat piled high with clothes, and its trunk filled with $20 million.

CHAPTER FORTY-ONE

Going Home
Ray
April 15, 1980

THE ADULTS TAKE TURNS DRIVING OR SLEEPING, only stopping for gas, fast food, and bathroom breaks.

A few hours away from the farm, Grace joins me, knowing we need to talk. Despite what we've just gone through, we're both feeling awkward, glancing back and forth, waiting for who'll speak first. I guess I'll bite the bullet and start.

"Grace, I'm positive you have questions and you deserve answers. Maybe it'll be easier if I start at the beginning," I say. "Stop me if you need anything clarified."

Thus, I began with the story of Monty and me being switched at birth. When I told her how both my families died, she broke down in tears. At least she understands why God and I are still not speaking.

But certain things I have to leave out—for her protection. Like my involvement with the Mafia, and that I killed Tito Zayas, Victor Hellman, and Barry O'Hara. That's pushing it. It's enough for her to know I killed Jack Lee in self-defense and murdered Stanley Hunter to save her life.

As for Stephen, I swear a rare form of the deadly castor bean flu killed him.

"If there's something on your mind, now's the time to ask," I say when I finish.

Grace doesn't hesitate. "I'm freaked out about some gross stuff that was in your black suit pants pocket, namely the red panties and bloody handkerchief."

"I can imagine how it looks, but there's a story if you'll bear with me. Don't worry, they're not from anyone I've killed."

"Oh my," she says when I finish explaining a simplified version of the bride's-mother-drinking-too-many-margaritas fiasco at the Kentucky Club and how those incriminating items ended up in my possession.

"Remember the time you came home exhausted and could barely walk? It was when I had just adopted the girls, and you were a jerk about it."

Oh boy.

The story of the young Mexicans who tried to attack me with baseball bats needed massaging. The brothel became a restaurant I frequented, and the prostitute who warned me was a friendly server I generously tipped in the past.

Grace nods, looks straight ahead, and asks point-blank, "Did you kill Stephen?"

Avoid and redirect.

"I'm sorry to say that this will be a shocking story you may not be ready to hear, but we both know Stephen wasn't the man you married."

Despite my discomfort and hers as well, I describe how I discovered Stephen's cocaine addiction and disturbing perversions.

"The next part is distressing, but I believe his convenient death from the flu prevented him from hurting you. He was a monster who was escalating." Even though it sickens me, there are some truths she needs to know.

With a heavy heart, I explain how Stephen viciously beat and repeatedly raped Carmelita. Grace's reaction is violent as she gags and starts yelling for me to stop the truck so she can throw up. The other two vehicles quickly pull up behind us. When Natalie and John jump out to check on her, I explain Grace is car sick. She'll be okay. Natalie gives me a worried look and brings Grace a coke from the cooler to sip, which seems to settle her stomach. She assures them both that she feels better.

After we resume our journey, Grace glances at me a few times, looks away, and asks about my son and what happened to him. Just the question itself hits me in the heart. This has been one tough conversation after another and discussing my son with her is a fallout from Carmelita's rape. I push my emotions down, wipe the tears that blur my vision, and keep my eyes on the road, aware she is watching and patiently waiting for my answer.

I cough, clear my throat, and stutter a bit to find the right words and the right place to begin. It's easier for me to start with a happier time—his scholarship to Notre Dame and the accomplishments that got him there. With that said, I progressed to his accident, long coma, and finally his death without breaking down.

"An infection complicating his brain injury killed him two months ago. The longest two fucking months of my life. When he died, part of us died too."

Grace looks away, wipes her tears on her shirtsleeve, and whispers, "I'm so sorry, Ray."

We're silent for a few miles, so I change the subject. "Tell me about painting the house."

It takes a moment for her to wrap her head around it, but slowly Grace recounts how grateful the painters and their wives were for her generosity. But she was sorry my beautiful antique trunk burned up in the fire. She wanted to keep it.

"You know what's strange, Ray? I hate that damned house now. But with the insurance proceeds from the fire and the money we found in Stephen's office, I'm thankfully free to start over. I'm no longer chained to the Hunter family except through our business," she confesses.

"Funny you should say that, Grace, because I plan to give you my 40 percent of the company and a sizable portion of the cash that's in the trunk of your Cadillac. And selling the business, building, and land will make you a very wealthy woman. How does that feel, Cuz?"

Grace looks at me and smiles. "I've never been rich before. I'm hopeful for the future, in a lot of ways."

"You like him, this Detective Myers?" I glance over to see her reaction.

"None of your beeswax, butthead," Grace mutters, and stares out her side window, but not before I glimpse a tiny smile.

"We're almost home. Anything else you want to know before we arrive?"

She says with a deep sigh. "It breaks my heart to ask you this, but was Stephen Rayban's father?"

"Biologically, we don't know, but it makes no difference. He was my son."

"I'm so sorry, Ray. So, so sorry you lost your son."

"Thank you, Grace. It feels good to talk to you about him. I hoped you would meet him someday, but the right time never came. You would've loved him."

As familiar terrain looms, I know that time is running out for me to make amends.

"There's something weighing on me. One of my biggest regrets."

"Go on," Grace says.

"I wish I had told your mom we were family, and that I was protecting you from old man, Hunter. My silence changed all our lives. You may not have married Stephen if she had known."

"You're probably right, Ray, especially now that I know Mr. Hunter planned to kill Mom and me." She frowns and looks down at her lap, picking at her fingernails. "Do you think my father worked for the Mafia-like Mr. Hunter said in his letter to Stephen?"

"Mr. Hunter was a paranoid, vindictive old man. He was mistaken."

That's a touchy subject I need to shy away from.

"Grace..." I have to clear my voice a few times, before I just blurt out, "You're my only living relative. I hope we can remain friends because I care for you and want you to be happy. Please forgive me for stealing your life. You deserve a better man than me." Turning to her, I admit, "I was a shitty husband."

"Yes, you were, and it'll take time to forgive you, Ray. I'm pretty angry about that and how you supported another family with our company's money."

How she figured that out, I won't ask, but at least I can explain.

"I know, Grace, however, I had my reasons. Stephen's vile actions uprooted and drastically changed Carmelita's life. He should pay for what he did. The company he inherited was the only way to seek compensation and justice for Carmelita after he died."

"You love her?" She glances at me with sad, questioning eyes.

It's time to be honest about Carmelita. "Yes, Grace, I do. I rescued her when she was ten years old and raised her as my ward. We didn't become a couple until after she graduated from college at twenty-two. She's always known about you. When we stopped for gas, I called her. She's expecting us."

"Good to know." Grace glances out the window and back at me. "Ray, I want a divorce."

"I know. Our Dissolution of Marriage papers should be on my desk when we arrive."

It's after dark, almost nine, when our caravan turns off Lewisville's Main Street, onto the winding road up to my farm.

The year after I sold the winery, I paved the path to the cabin and the road up the mountain to the farmhouse. Then I installed an iron gate at the upper entrance to the farm, which is now propped open for us. As the last car drives through, José Jr. closes and locks it. Floodlights illuminate the front yard, revealing lots of space for everyone to park.

Carmelita is standing on the porch, her shiny dark hair with streaks of silver at her temples, falls to her waist. Dressed in jeans and black boots, the red silk shawl drapes over her shoulders and ties in front of a thick white turtleneck sweater.

"She's beautiful," Grace mumbles and quickly runs her fingers through her hair, combing it into place.

I can tell Grace is feeling weary and self-conscious. "Come on. Let me introduce you."

As we approach the porch's bottom step, the two women stare at each other.

"Grace, this is Carmelita... my best friend." Yup, this is the most uncomfortable introduction I've ever made.

"Carmie, this is Grace... my soon-to-be ex-wife."

I guess that says it all, huh?

Neither of them moves or smiles.

One is a tall, thin, fine-featured attractive blond whom I do not love as a wife, but married. The other curvy, dark-haired beauty holds my heart. They are well aware of their differences. Yin, meet Yang.

I'm scarcely conscious of our guests exiting their cars because I'm hoping these two ladies won't kill each other.

"Hello," Grace finally says, smiling nervously. She steps up to the porch and offers her hand to Carmelita. "I'm terribly sorry to hear of the loss of your wonderful son. Please accept my deepest condolences."

Carmelita takes Grace by surprise—and me—when she strides forward and embraces her in a powerful hug. She then steps back, still holding both of Grace's shoulders, and looks her in the eyes. "Welcome home, Grace. I hope we'll be great friends."

Grace whispers, "I'd like that."

I almost pee my pants.

Carmie then turns to our guests, urging them to bring their bags inside and warm up. The tantalizing smells of freshly brewed coffee and hot chocolate, roasted meats, and desserts entice the tired, famished travelers toward a buffet in the dining room. Once Carmie shows them where to wash up, she seats our guests and encourages them to help themselves to generous portions of hot food.

José Jr. and I bring the packing boxes from the back of the Cadillac to the far back section of the basement before he moves all the guns and ammunition from my truck into my study. I then ask for everyone's car keys explaining that José Jr. will park their cars down at the barn, but the keys will remain in the ignitions in case we need to move them again.

They don't need to know it's the safest place for their vehicles. I expect the worst once Junior learns I killed Rico and three of his men.

Plus, I still have the original book. No way was I going to drive over to Junior's house and give him that damned book after he sanctioned kidnapping my daughters by that evil son of a bitch, now dead, shithead brother of his. Those jerkoffs also set fire to my house. Well, technically, Grace's house, but what if my family were asleep inside? Or if those assholes left Natalie tied up and then started the fire?

Junior is vengeful, impatient, and sloppy. Everything Papa Marco strongly disapproved of, especially in a Don.

As I join my guests, slipping into a chair next to Carmelita, I whisper, "I have lots to tell you," and squeeze her hand beneath the table.

She smiles and pushes a clean plate over, encouraging me to eat. Her diamond bracelet catches the light from the crackling fireplace, leaping with yellow-orange flames. With a toasty warm atmosphere and full bellies, the sound of laughter soon fills the room.

Carmelita notices the girls yawning and signals that Grace and the girls should follow her upstairs to her old bedroom. When she and Grace return, they report the girls loved the pink room and fell asleep in seconds under their quilts. Carmie shoots me a quick smile that says she and Grace are getting along very well. What a fucking relief.

Twenty minutes later, Franco calls from Crazy Phil's Bar.

"Are you my friend or my enemy?" I ask straight-out.

"My guys and I are here to help you. When Junior learned what happened at Rico's house, he lost his temper big-time and sent Luca and his soldiers after you. He wants the original book, Ray, and will stop at nothing to get it."

"Is Angelo with you?"

"I asked him to stay close to Luca to keep things as calm as possible. They should arrive sometime tomorrow."

"Good to know. Come on up. We'll open the gate and prepare a couple of cabins for you to stay in tonight."

I stick my head into the dining room and tell Carmelita, "Three more for dinner," return to the study, and call José Jr. with instructions to get ready for extra guests.

When Franco and his men arrive, it's awkward introducing them to John. They shake hands and acknowledge each other with alpha-male nods. Franco and I both know I'm not supposed to be hanging out with law enforcement. However, that freak Rico shouldn't have kidnapped my daughters and burned down my house, either. No matter that I already killed him, I'm still royally pissed about that.

Carmelita hugs Franco, who whispers his condolences. She blinks away her tears, then turns to his men, encouraging them to load their plates while the food is still hot.

Grace approaches Franco and offers her hand. "Are you Mr. Franco? It's very nice to meet you. These are my friends, Mark and Natalie."

"It's just Franco. And it's nice to meet all of you." He smiles and shakes their hands.

By midnight, with everyone fed and settled, Carmelita and I amble through the house, turning off lights and locking doors. As we trudge upstairs, it occurs to me that this is the first time my three families are together. I will cherish this for the rest of my life, however long or short it is.

You never know what tomorrow may bring.

CHAPTER
FORTY-TWO

Unexpected Problems
Don Marco Jr.
April 15, 1980

JUNIOR ALMOST SHIT HIS PANTS when he flipped through Ray's record book of murders, finding his name along with Luca's and Rico's, and a whole bevy of his other capos and soldiers. Rico's hit list was huge, no surprise there. Luca's was about half that amount. None for Franco or Angelo—which was a lie. The shithead even left himself out.

Ray detailed names, dates, times, and places of the hits Junior ordered on members of other Mafia families. Junior had always denied any knowledge of their deaths, but if The Commission learned he was responsible, a bloody war would break out and Junior wasn't prepared for that.

He also wasn't prepared to see the names of a few murdered policemen from different parts of Florida, along with the assassination he ordered of one well-known Washington, D.C. politician.

He could dispute the Chicago and Miami businessmen who disappeared on his orders and whose bodies would never be found. But the bottom line was, if

Junior didn't retrieve and destroy the original book before it fell into the hands of The Commission or the police, he was a dead man.

He needed a plan that Franco couldn't know about. One that required someone with a strong edge who knew Ray's strengths and wouldn't underestimate him. When Franco left the compound, Junior made a call, then sat back in his chair and put his feet up. Why did Ray keep those incriminating records? The Catanetti family had given him a prosperous life. Ray knew the rules. Now he would pay for breaking them.

Junior and Ray had spent most of their lives dancing around each other. They met when Ray was nineteen and only a few years younger than Junior. From the very beginning, it was obvious Junior's father, Marco Sr. was impressed that Ray came from such a highly respected, wealthy Italian family.

Marco Sr., always on the lookout for smart young men to join them, told Junior, "Ray's a prize. He's intelligent, humble, and thoughtful. We can groom him over time for a very important role in our organization."

"Why, Pop?" Junior didn't see the potential in the young truck driver.

"The guy's background protects him from being suspected of doing anything illegal. His future inheritance means he can't be bought. We have to earn his loyalty. And he's very smart."

"What's your plan, then?" Junior asked.

"I want him mentored. Who's it gonna be? You or Franco?"

"Let Franco do it. I'm not babysitting mountain boy."

The phone rang, pulling Junior out of his memories.

"What in the hell is going on?" Franco shouted. "Did Rico kidnap Ray's daughters? Why? For that damned book? You could've just asked Ray for it."

"I didn't tell Rico to take Ray's kids. Rico did it on his own accord."

"Where are they, Junior?" Franco demanded.

"At Rico's house. After he tucks the little girls in and reads them a bedtime story, he's sending a few of his men to torch Ray's house. When Ray gives me the original book, Angelo can return the girls to their mother. They'll be okay, don't worry. We'll talk later."

Junior's plan was falling into place. He counted on Franco to tell Ray where his daughters were, so Rico could capture Ray.

If Rico failed, Paulie Horseface wouldn't.

An hour and a half later, Junior learned how badly he'd misjudged Ray. Rico and three of his men were dead and Paulie Horseface hadn't checked in either. Junior was sweating balls. He couldn't ignore those killings or the fact that he still didn't have that goddamned incriminating record book of murders that could get him killed. He was on pins and needles, waiting to hear from Paulie.

Concerned that Ray was getting away, Junior sent his youngest brother, Luca, with seven of their guys and weapons in two cars, to Lewisville. Three hours later, Paulie called him from a gas station across the highway from where Ray and his convoy stopped for food.

"What in the hell happened, Paulie?" Junior snapped.

"When I drove past Rico's house, the driveway gate was wide open. A bad sign. I figured some shitty things had already gone down inside Rico's house because police sirens were getting closer and more neighborhood lights were coming on everywhere. I needed to get out of there as quickly as possible."

"Good thing you did. Ray killed Rico and three of his men. Did you catch up with Ray?"

"I did. I glimpsed his taillights turning the corner several blocks away and followed him. He drove past a burning house and pulled into the driveway of a house behind a church. A couple of minutes later, his truck and two other automobiles left and drove north on I-75. They just crossed over the Georgia state line and stopped for gas."

"Stay on him. He's headed to that farm I told you about in Lewisville, West Virginia, west of Washington, D.C. When he gets to Main Street in Lewisville, he'll turn left and head up a winding mountain road. You take the next left. Ray has a cabin about a mile up on your left with a trail that leads from it to the back of his farmhouse."

Traffic sounds in the background almost blocked out Junior's next instruction, but Paulie understood the undertones.

"If anyone is in the cabin when you get there, get rid of them—quietly."

"What kind of dangerous information am I looking for?" Paulie inquired.

Junior described the book and mentioned that it also contained Paulie's name. "Once you have it, you know what to do."

"You can count on me, Junior. I've never let you down." Paulie crossed his fingers, hoping he never would either.

Despite Junior's threatening tone, Paulie blurted out that his seventeen-year-old nephew, Karl, was with him. "I know Karl hasn't been invited to take the vow yet, but I promise he's an excellent shot, a skillful driver, and he'll do what he's told."

"You're vouching for him, so your ass is on the line. If anything happens, it's on you, Paulie. Make sure he keeps his mouth shut. Hai Caputo?"

Paulie followed Ray's convoy as it drove down Main Street, past Grandma's Diner and Crazy Phil's Bar. When Ray slowed down in front of Buster's General Store and turned left, the next two cars followed him up the mountain.

Junior's directions were perfect. It was pitch black and freezing cold when Paulie left his car parked on the side of the gravel road. He and Karl followed the short driveway and fumbled their way into the unlocked cabin, shivering in their lightweight tropical shirts. After they located the light switch, they found two thick sweaters on the top shelf of the bedroom closet and pulled them on.

"Karl, see if there's a telephone, so I can check in with Junior. Also, find the goddamned control for the heater and turn it on before we freeze our balls off."

Karl looked around the simply furnished cabin and spotted the fireplace, along with the wood stacked near it. "I'll build a fire, Uncle Paulie. We'll be toasty in no time. But I don't see no phone."

Paulie Horseface grabbed a bath towel and wrapped it around his head and neck like a scarf. "I got something to do," he growled. "Check the kitchen for food. I'm hungry as hell."

After finding a flashlight on the kitchen counter, Paulie set out to locate the trail Junior said led to the farmhouse. The exercise of trudging uphill caused Paulie's body to generate heat, warming him up. By the time he reached the top, Paulie was breathing hard. He kicked an old, rotten log that was in his way, and stopped behind the garage, peeking around its corner. Then he slunk across the front of the garage and edged down the side of the house, staying hidden from view. A Mexican man and Ray were unloading boxes from the back of the blue Cadillac he'd tailed from Florida. Then Ray gave the man instructions and his keys before he went inside.

Paulie was satisfied. He knew the lay of the land and, sure nothing would happen until the next day, he returned to the cabin hoping Karl had found something to eat.

CHAPTER
FORTY-THREE

Preparing Everyone
Ray
April 16, 1980

IT'S EARLY, A LITTLE AFTER SEVEN, when my cousin/wife's freshly shaven boyfriend joins me in my study. He places a hot cup of coffee on my desk just as I hang up the phone.

"Carmelita said you like it black."

I look up and fill him in on the call I'd just received from my friend, Becky, who owns Grandma's Diner. "Eight guys are having breakfast at her place and are asking about me. Wanna guess who they might be?"

"No doubt it's Luca and his men. So, what's the plan?"

"I want Franco's bodyguards to take over the windows in the upstairs middle bedroom where the girls slept last night. It has the best view of the entire front yard. I understand they're excellent marksmen, so let's make sure they know to injure—not kill Luca's men."

"Makes sense," John says, sips his coffee and continues to focus on me.

"Tell them not to shoot their cars. I want those guys to leave as soon as possible. I've instructed my employees to stay in their cabins until this is over."

John nods, has another sip, and waits for any other instructions.

I push the letter from Stephen's grandfather and the envelope of disgusting photographs across my desk. "Now that you're Grace's knight in shining armor, look at these later. Grace left them here last night, along with my ledgers and checkbooks."

He nods and shoves them into his jacket pocket.

"Morning, Mark," we both say as Pastor Mark joins us, warming his hands around a cup of coffee. "You're just in time. Will you and John please witness my signature on these legal documents? One is for the dissolution of marriage to Grace. The other document is a codicil to my will."

I hand each one a pen and show them where to sign after they watch me scribble my horrendous signature. "This is just in case today doesn't go quite like I hope it will."

We hear the front door open and the sounds of Franco and his bodyguards stomping off the frosty morning ice from their shoes before they enter. "Morning, everyone," Franco calls out, pushing the front door shut.

"Franco, we're in here," I yell so he can follow my voice into the study, where my phone is ringing again.

Pastor Mark invites Franco's guys to the dining room for coffee, while John and Franco stay to hear my second conversation with Becky.

"So, Luca wants me to know he and his guys are coming here around nine after they pick up some sweatshirts at Buster's. Thanks, Becky, and the next time you bake pies, save one for us, will you?"

As soon as I hang up, the delicious aroma of bacon pours into the study along with Carmelita's voice announcing, "Come and get it while it's hot."

After breakfast, I pull Grace aside for a private conversation in my study and tell her it could get dangerous at the farmhouse today. The brother of the guy who kidnapped our girls had followed us. "I don't want you or the girls anywhere near here when they show up. You'll be safer at my cabin. It's only a mile down the mountain. Use my golf cart parked by the front steps. The paved trail starts behind the garage. I'll show you."

Her confused gray eyes stare at me. "Wait—What? I want to stay and help."

I continue with my instructions and ignore her protest. "Make sure the girls zip up their jackets, even better, wrap them in Grandma Martin's quilts, so they'll stay warm on the ride down the mountain. The cabin's unlocked and stocked with some food supplies, coffee, and hot chocolate for the girls. I've got a thousand things to prepare for. I can't begin until I know you and the girls are safe in the cabin. Your job is to protect them."

She's not thrilled when she learns Natalie is staying, arguing that Natalie has already been attacked and traumatized.

"We need Natalie's nursing skills. There's a medical area already set up in the basement, in case anyone gets hurt. Carmelita and Pastor Mark will help her if she needs it."

As I turn to leave, she reaches for my arm, holding me in place. "Ray, I'm still worried."

"Don't be." I take her hand. "Between Detective Myers and me, plus Franco and his men, believe me, we've got this."

Now is the time to tell her what else I need her to do. "Grace, this morning your friends, Detective Myers and Pastor Mark, witnessed my signature on our divorce papers and the codicil to my will. If anything happens to me, our divorce papers won't be necessary, but promise me you'll make sure the codicil is delivered to my attorney."

She says nothing, but a deep frown reveals how unhappy she is about the situation.

"Promise me, Grace!"

A defiant look comes over her. "Why should I promise you anything, Ray?"

That felt like a slap in the face.

"Because it alters your and the girls' future! If something happens to me, you'll be severely affected if these papers aren't filed. They are your financial protection."

She leans in and points at the study's closed doors. "And what about Carmelita? Is she also protected?"

My heart speeds up. Time is of the essence and I didn't expect this much pushback from Grace. I lean closer, lower my voice, and stare at her while I try to control myself.

"She will be fucked if you don't. All of you... will be fucked if you don't."

She purses her lips. "Not good enough. Explain more than that."

Well, damn. This isn't the time to have a legal discussion, but I gotta do it, anyway.

"I left this farm and my estate in trust for Rayban with Carmelita as his trustee. When he died, I realized I should've included our daughters. My codicil changes the trustees to you and Carmelita for the benefit of Patty and Merry. Okay?"

Her face softens. "Okay, Ray."

"We're going to be fine, Grace. Take the girls and go. Now, for God's sake!"

She still doesn't move. Her gray eyes are quizzical and dart back and forth between mine.

"Out with it!"

"Who are you, Ray?" she blurts out.

That's the last thing I'm going to tell her, especially right now.

I take her by the shoulders and whisper, "Grace, honey. You don't want to know. Now let's get going."

CHAPTER
FORTY-FOUR

Fighting Back
Grace
April 16, 1980

THE GIRLS WERE THRILLED TO RIDE IN A GOLF CART FOR THE FIRST TIME, especially seeing their warm breath turn the chilly air into steamy clouds. They giggled like crazy as soon as the cart started down the winding trail and picked up momentum, shouting for Grace to go faster.

It was almost nine when the golf cart rolled into the cabin's yard and stopped outside an attractive log structure, complete with a front porch and a few charming bird houses hanging from its corners. Supported by log pillars, a couple of steps led up to a sturdy wood door.

The girls, laughing wildly, raced each other up the steps, causing Grace to grin at their typical exuberance. She scooped up her purse and their quilts and stepped out of the cart as Patty and Merry charged through the front door, leaving it wide open. The sound of their blood-curdling shrieks sent a jolt of alarm through her body.

Grace was there in a second.

Two males were sitting at the kitchen table. One was a very unattractive older man with heavy beard stubble who was drinking black coffee. He looked at them but didn't move and seemed unaffected by their arrival. His companion, a skinny, pimple-faced teenager, slurped hot chocolate as he, too, stared at them. A paper plate filled with slices of jellied toast and a handgun sat between them.

The older man scooted his chair back from the table and sneered. "Come in, ladies. The party's about to begin."

"Who are you?" Grace demanded, scowling.

They aren't supposed to be here. Ray would've told me if they were.

"I'm Paulie, the kid's Karl. We're friends of Junior's." Paulie's voice was gruff and rude. "So, shut up and pop a squat on the couch. If you behave yourselves, we won't tie you up."

Who's Junior? Ray's never mentioned him.

When they didn't move fast enough, Paulie abruptly stood up, causing his chair to scrape loudly against the floor. The girls dashed to the sofa as Grace hurriedly draped the quilts over its back and put her purse next to it.

Confident they were no threat, Paulie sat down and spoke quietly with Karl, but his eyes kept darting to his watch. Without warning, he shoved his cup away and moved to the front windows, pushed the red gingham curtain aside, and peered out, listening intently. Karl then put their cups in the sink, smirked at Grace, and proceeded to the bathroom.

Grace dug through her purse, retrieving what she wanted before Karl came back. Suddenly, they heard the faraway sound of loud, rapid bangs.

As Paulie picked up his gun, his gaze locked on Grace. "Get up!" he demanded, before grabbing her arm and yanking her toward the door. He pointed to Karl. "Stay here and watch these brats. It's showtime!"

Grace wasn't taking any of this nasty-tempered brute's orders and shouted into Paulie's ugly donkey-looking face. "You wait one damn second! If that kid touches a hair on my daughters' heads, he's dead. My husband, Ray Lewis, will kill him with his bare hands."

Paulie gave Grace a strange look, then yelled over his shoulder, "Stay away from the little girls," and tried to shove Grace out the door.

But Grace wasn't through, "Girls! Black Belt! If he even looks like he's gonna touch you, you know what you're trained to do, so don't hesitate!"

Nervously, they exchanged nods.

As soon as the door slammed behind them, Paulie forcefully pushed Grace toward the golf cart and commanded her to drive.

The ride up the trail was slower and a little chuggy. The cart gave out just as they reached the top and rolled alongside a decayed log. Unbeknownst to Paulie, Grace quickly slipped on the brass knuckles she had retrieved from her purse and discreetly concealed her fist in her coat pocket.

Paulie then jerked her out of the cart and dragged her to the corner of the garage's rear wall, where he pinned Grace's back to it with the front of his body. They were so close Grace could smell the coffee on his breath, which unfortunately couldn't cover his disgusting armpit odor.

Grace desperately wanted to use her brass knuckles, but her right hand was trapped in her coat pocket, rendering her helpless.

Paulie peeked around the garage corner, concentrating on the gun battle happening in the front yard, while Grace was freaking out about leaving her daughters at the cabin with pimple-faced Karl. A couple more gunshots were followed by angry shouting and three more gunshots. Grace didn't know which was worse—running into Paulie and Karl or being stuck in the madness going on at the farmhouse.

As Grace squirmed, trying to loosen her hand from her pocket, Paulie pushed harder against her. Then over Paulie's shoulder, Grace glimpsed movement coming up the trail. A few seconds later, Patty came into view. Breathing deeply, she tiptoed beyond the log, holding a weapon-sized piece of firewood in her right hand. Paulie didn't hear her approach or see her lift the wooden club high while she signaled to Grace how to thrust her knee into Paulie's crotch.

Grace slowly blinked. Patty blinked back and began a countdown with her left hand.

Three, two, one.

Paulie shrieked and doubled over, holding his crotch with both hands, while his gun skittered away. Remembering Natalie's instructions, Grace swung the brass knuckles as hard as she could, connecting with his left jaw. He fell toward Patty, who wielded her makeshift weapon like a two-handed tennis backswing and slammed it into the right side of his skull, knocking Paulie out cold. He landed face down in the dirt.

Patty was in Grace's arms a second later. They held each other tightly, both asking if the other was okay, with their stressful tears streaming. Grace stepped back, picked up Paulie's gun, and wiped the dirt off on the side of her jeans.

"Where's your sister? How'd you get away?"

"We fooled Dumbo Karl into lighting the fireplace. Then Merry and I hit him with pieces of firewood, and Merry karate kicked him in the head really hard. After that, we tied him up with some birdhouse rope we found in the kitchen pantry. If Karl wakes up, Merry's going to kick him again. Mom, we need Ray and Mr. John to go get Merry now!" Patty cried, visibly shaken.

"First, we have to tie his guy up," Grace replied. "I'll hold the gun on him while you search the garage for something we can use."

Thin wire was all Patty found, so they twisted it around Paulie's hands and feet. Grace's heart was beating out of control as she and Patty dashed to the side of the house, stopping under the kitchen pie window. Grace figured if she could get Patty inside, Patty could get help, while Grace would keep an eye out for anyone coming from the front of the house. She tucked the gun into the back of her jeans, then made a step with her hands and boosted Patty up and over the pie windowsill. She was in!

Patty ran through the kitchen, shouting, "There's a guy outside who attacked Mom! We hit him and tied him up... hurry! Merry's with Dumbo Karl."

CHAPTER
FORTY-FIVE

Unexpected Introductions
Ray
April 16, 1980

LUCA AND ANGELO REMEMBERED THE FATAL MISTAKE Victor Hellman's goons made back in '38 when they pulled their cars side by side and hid in between them. So, when Luca's drivers ease through my gate at nine and park nose to tail, creating a barrier, it shows Luca's mindset. He's ready for trouble. My theory is confirmed when everyone exits on the driver's side and crouches down, using their cars for cover. I hope Luca and Angelo have these guys under control because I recognize some of Rico's men.

Angelo positions himself at the head of the lead car, standing in full view to show he trusts me. Luca steps out on the passenger side, and faces the farmhouse, shouting, "Morning, Ray! Give me what I came for and we'll leave."

I open the front door. "What makes you think I have what you want?"

"Don't play games, Ray. We both know you have it."

I step onto the porch, facing him. "And if I did, how can I be sure you won't try to kill us after I give it to you?"

"You have my word," Luca shouts.

"Franco warned me your word may differ from your brother."

"Junior didn't tell me to hurt you or your people. All he wants is the book, Ray."

While we're arguing, one of Luca's men gestures toward the upstairs windows. "They're gonna shoot us!" he yells and begins firing. I dash back into the house, my heart pounding as I slam the front door.

Within seconds, others join in, scattering glass across the porch roof and inside the upper bedrooms.

A confident fool steps too far from the rear car and screams as one of Franco's men puts a bullet through his lower leg. Surprised, Luca dashes behind his sedan, demanding his guys stop shooting. But those jerks don't listen and continue taking potshots at my house. One more shriek fills the air when another of Luca's dudes is shot in the shoulder.

Franco yells from the front door, "Godammit Luca, control your people!"

Luca screams at his guys, "Get down and stay down or I'll shoot you myself!"

As soon as the firing stops, Luca shouts, "Come outside, Franco! We need to talk," and confidently strides towards my house.

"Be careful, Franco," I say. "Trusting Angelo is one thing, but believing Luca is something else. Get him to come closer to the farmhouse so we can hear him."

Franco nods, hurries down the porch steps, and stops, forcing Luca to step nearer.

Luca tries to keep his voice low as he reasons with his brother. "Look, Franco, if Junior doesn't get the original and any copies they have, he'll kill Ray and Carmelita, plus anyone else who gets in the way."

Franco stiffens. "Don't be part of that, Luca. Ray's our brother, too. He's been with us for over forty years. Pop treated him like a son. We can't turn on him now."

"He killed Rico!"

"Rico deserved it!" Franco barks, poking Luca's chest. "We do not disrespect a man's family. Yet our brother kidnapped Ray's daughters. They're just little girls, for God's sake!"

Everyone could hear how aggravated Franco was as he continued, "Rico tied them up in that foul Wolf's Den of his. Don't say you haven't seen it. What was he thinking, bringing Ray's kids into that disgusting place?"

Luca tries to step back, but Franco, still agitated, closes the gap between them and continues to blast him. "Rico was crazy, always hopped up on drugs. Pop would've stopped him long before now. Come on, Luca. What did you expect Ray to do?" Franco put his hands on his hips. "Walk up to Rico's door, and say, 'Give me my little girls, pretty please?' We take care of our own problems. And that's exactly what Ray did."

"I accept my orders from Junior, not you," Luca snarls.

"You're not Junior's puppet! Think for yourself, man. Junior knew Rico was going to torch Ray's house and didn't stop him. If Ray's wife and daughters had been home, they'd be dead right now. Pop taught us better than that, and you know it!"

"Fuck you, Franco!"

Franco moves close to Luca's face and pokes him in the chest. "If I were in Ray's shoes, I would have done the... exact... same... thing."

Luca looks away. Then, meeting Franco's intense gaze, answers in a hushed tone, "Get the book, Franco, and I promise we'll leave. Two of our guys already need medical care. Let's finish this. Okay?"

Franco nods, relaxes his shoulders, and tells Luca, "I'll be right back."

As Luca stomps across the yard to huddle with Angelo near the hood of the front car, Franco steps inside the house.

I hand him the original and say, "There're no extra copies I know of."

Without a word, he takes it and heads out the front door, across the porch toward the stairs, and holding it high, he waves it at Luca and Angelo.

Unexpectedly, someone yells from behind the front car, "They killed your brother, you fucking traitor!" followed by a gunshot.

Franco's legs buckle. The book flies out of his hands as he grabs his side, tumbles down the steps, and hits the ground.

"Revenge for Rico!" The man screeches, fires at Franco again and misses him by inches as a bullet plows into the dirt near his head.

"Stop! Stop!" Angelo and Luca yell, turning toward the shooter. Luca orders him to "Get over here!" as he and Angelo hurry to Franco's side.

I'm already outside, checking Franco's pulse when they kneel beside me. "How is he?" Luca's eyes are wide, alarmed at how much blood is seeping into the grassy dirt.

"He's terrible. Let's take him inside. We have a nurse who can try to stop the bleeding. Bring your other men too. But tell your guys no more shooting at my house."

Loud grumbling catches my attention as the shooter struts toward Luca. Without warning, three shots jerk his body backward. One from John, who's positioned in the front doorway and two from the upstairs window. One would have done it.

Luca waves at the house. "Thanks, you guys. You saved me a couple of bullets."

Then Luca shouts at his crew. "All of you, put your guns down now!" He points to his closest men. "Place the dead man in the trunk, then take the injured guys inside for medical help."

Angelo picks up the book and, glaring at Luca, thrusts it at him.

Franco's bodyguards rush through the front door and kneel next to Franco, assessing how the three of us are going to move him down to the basement as fast as possible without further injuring him.

Minutes later, Franco is lying on a cot with his shirt cut open. Natalie examines his right side where the blood is pouring out, throws a thick towel over it, and presses down with her knee. A frown creases her forehead, but she remains calm and focused.

"With an injury this severe, he needs to be in a hospital. Time is of the essence."

When Luca's injured men arrive, Natalie instructs Carmelita and Mark how to apply pressure to their wounds, insisting they need hospital care as well.

"I'll get the cars ready to take them to Romney General," I say, hustling up the stairs from the basement. Just as I reach the first-floor landing, out of nowhere, Patty runs from the dining room shouting, "There's a guy outside who attacked Mom! We hit him and tied him up. Hurry! Merry's with Dumbo Karl."

Who in the hell is Dumbo Karl?

I draw my weapon, bolt through the kitchen, and spot Grace through the open pie window. She's standing in the driveway, pointing a gun toward the front of the house. Paulie Horseface is racing up behind her with blood streaming from his nose.

Why am I not surprised that Junior sent this asshole?

He growls like a wild animal when he tackles her. The gun flies out of her hand, and down she goes. He grabs the back of her jacket, yanks her up close to him, then bends to her left, reaching for the weapon.

Time slows to a crawl as my bullet pierces Paulie Horseface's right temple, exiting left, sparing Grace from being spattered with his blood and brains as he falls face down.

"Grace, are you hurt?"

She sees me leaning out the window, stamps her foot, and yells, "You've got to put a door here, Ray!"

Not wasting a second, I leap to the ground and catch Patty as she jumps after me.

"Come on, you and Patty are going to wait at the log while I go get Merry. Where's the golf cart?"

Grace warns, "Sorry but, it's out of gas."

Dammit. Being out of shape is the last thing I need right now, but there's no other option. I have to run. As I dash down the trail, a symphony of sounds swirls past me—rustling leaves, distant chirping of birds—and the echo of my heavy breathing. Ten minutes feels like an eternity when I finally surge into the small front yard of the Phoenix cabin, bend over, grab my knees for support, and gasp for breath.

I'm stunned by the unexpected sight of Junior dressed in a long wool overcoat, sitting in a spot of sunshine on its steps. His two bodyguards are walking around the clearing, slapping their arms, trying to keep warm, no doubt regretting that their jackets are hanging in the back of their closets in Florida.

"Ray! Brother!" Junior jumps up and extends his hand as if nothing negative has occurred between us. That's Junior for you. You never know what to expect. He could just shoot me. Then all this would be over.

"Junior," I'm still breathing hard. "Franco's been shot and needs... to go... to the hospital."

"What happened?" His eyes narrow as he peers over the top of his black-framed glasses.

"One of Rico's men shot Franco when he was bringing the original book to Luca. Are we good now?" I'm finally able to stand up and shake his hand.

"Ray, you killed my brother, and yes, I know Rico kidnapped your daughters, but that was without my permission. You owe me an explanation about the information in that book."

He's trying to provoke me with his intimidating glare and disagreeable frown, but I've seen that expression too many times before to worry about it now. I've got shit to do.

Still a little breathless, I grumble, "Franco's in serious condition... he needs to be in a hospital. Like immediately!"

I nod toward the cabin. "Look, my daughter's inside... with some kid named Karl. I've got to get back to the farmhouse... before more of your people are hurt."

"Be my guest. No funny stuff, though," he scowls.

It's alarming to find Merry sitting next to some wide-eyed young punk who's wearing one of my heavy sweaters, both with their hands tied. While I untie her, I whisper, "Mom and Patty are fine. Everything's going to be okay." As soon as she's free, I kiss the top of her head. "Be right back."

Dumbo Karl watches my every move. *That guy gives me the creeps. He's staying here, nice and tied up.*

Grabbing two more of my sweaters from the bedroom closet, I then scoop the quilts from the sofa, handing one to Merry, who picks up her mother's purse sitting on the floor nearby.

"Ray?" Merry points to Junior standing in the doorway, letting the cold air inside.

Junior's voice is sharp. "Where's the closest hospital?"

"Romney. It's north on Route 220, then east on Route 50. Half an hour if we speed."

Pulling the blanket around Merry's shoulders, I take her hand, lead her past Junior and point at Karl. "That brainless kid stays here."

Junior nods. "No problem. He and his uncle are in big trouble with me."

I don't have the heart to tell him dear old Uncle Paulie Horseface is no longer with us.

When I toss the two thick sweaters to Junior's bodyguards, they look surprised, quickly pull them on, and follow us back to the farm.

It took twenty minutes to complete the uphill trek to the back of the garage. Grace and Patty descend on Merry, hugging her and asking over and over if she's okay.

Unfortunately, it's time for another tough introduction—one I hoped I'd never have to make.

"Grace, this is Franco's brother—Junior." She observes his confident stance, expensive cashmere coat, and the sincere smile she doesn't know is hiding a million evil deeds.

"Junior, this is my wife, Grace Hunter."

He offers his hand with a respectful bow that I've seen his father do countless times in the past.

"Hello." Grace smiles and reaches out.

Junior leans forward, takes her hand, kisses it, then looks up, and says, "Your husband is a fortunate man to be surrounded by so many beautiful ladies."

I see Grace stiffen, but he follows that underhanded compliment by sweeping his arm toward Patty and Merry.

We all know who you're referring to, you subversive asshole.

"Excuse us for a moment, Junior," I say and walk Grace to the back wall of the garage, hoping a little information will ease the situation. But she's on it right away.

"Paulie said Junior was his friend, like he's an important person. Who is he really?"

If I tell her, it'll open a floodgate of questions we don't have time for.

"Let's talk about this later. Meanwhile, the twins need to stay here at the log where no one can see them. They've had way too much trauma already, and it's not over. The upstairs windows are shot out, so there's broken glass everywhere. The girls are safer here."

She doesn't want to leave them, but I insist. "Natalie needs your help. There are three injured men in the basement. By now, there could be more. Throw Grandmother Martin's blankets over their jackets for extra warmth and let's go."

I motion for Patty and Merry to join us. "You've both been very brave, but I want you to stay at the log until we come to get you. Mom's going inside to help Miss Natalie. Got it?"

They blink a few times as they stare at me and whisper, "Yes, Ray."

"Good girls. I'll be back before you know it."

I smile as reassuringly as I can, but Patty steps forward. "Pinky swear?" They both crook their little fingers upward. *Out of the mouths of babes.* With those two innocent words, these spunky little girls destroy my lifelong contract to promise nothing.

"Pinky swear." I shake pinky fingers with them, kiss the tops of their heads, lead them to the log, and signal Junior and his men to follow Grace and me.

As we stroll past the garage, Junior spots Paulie Horseface's body lying face down in the dirt outside the kitchen window. He raises his eyebrows in an unspoken question.

It's all I can do to maintain an unconcerned look. "He stole my favorite sweater. I want it back if there's no blood on it," I say.

Junior shakes his head and tells his bodyguards, "Before we leave, put Paulie in the trunk of one of Luca's cars and return Ray's sweater. For now, the stupid goon stays here."

Tensions are still high in front of the farmhouse. Luca's men are demanding an update on their wounded friends. Angelo yells at them to shut up.

All eyes are on us when Grace and I, followed by Junior and his two bodyguards, walk into the yard and split up. They head toward Luca and Angelo while I guide Grace to the house, telling her, "I don't want you close to any of these people. They're dangerous."

John must've read my mind. He flies outside, nods, wraps his arm around Grace, and escorts her inside.

Angelo is filling Junior in on who's in the basement getting treatment and who's dead and stored in the car's trunk as I join them.

When Junior asks about the original book, Luca hands it to him.

"Any more copies?" He looks at me as he slips it into the deep pocket of his overcoat.

"None," I say.

That I know of.

"Okay, Ray, I understand you and Carmelita want to retire."

You moron. Your brother is bleeding to death in my basement, and you want to talk about my retirement?

"That's right, Junior. I'm getting too old for this business. I've faced younger men carrying baseball bats, guns, and knives, trying to kill me and hijack my semi. It's only a matter of time before I lose. Carmelita and I would like to spend the rest of our lives in peace."

He says nothing and continues to stare at me.

What else does he need to know?

"Junior, Carmie and I care for our Catanetti brothers," I continue. "We wish you prosperity and happiness, along with success, of course."

I then look at my watch, hoping he can feel my urgency. "We need to go."

"Okay, Ray, we're going, but I'd like to talk to Carmelita first."

Christ almighty, now you intend to socialize with Carmie?

John's standing in the farmhouse's open front door with his hands on his hips, listening, so I call out. "Will you ask Carmelita to join us?"

He turns and speaks a few words to the inside of the house. Carmelita emerges with her red silk shawl thrown over her thick white sweater, hustles across the yard, and greets Junior with a hug.

"Thank you for your help through the bad times, Junior. And the good ones as well. I'm grateful to you and your family for saving me as a child and providing for me and my son," Carmelita says.

"You're still one of my favorite people and I'm so sorry your son passed," Junior replies.

The look he gives her is sincere and compassionate, but it changes to stern when he takes her hands, bends a little closer to her face, and warns, "You and Ray must keep the code of silence, so I won't have to break my word to you both."

She puts on her most charming smile, then says, "Of course, Junior, always."

Holding her shoulders, Junior kisses Carmelita on both cheeks.

As Carmelita hurries back to the porch, Junior gestures for everyone to stash their weapons and get in their cars. His bodyguards pop the nearest car trunk and head to the side of the house to retrieve Paulie Horseface's body.

"Ray." Junior turns to me. "I want to see Franco and the injured men before we go to the hospital. Give me a second to work out the details with Luca, so Franco's bodyguards can stay here and drive him home when he's better."

"We need to hurry, Junior." It's hard to suppress my impatience at this point.

As I approach the farmhouse, everyone is watching from the dining-room windows observing Luca's crew climb into their cars and slam the doors. Pleased and confident that the conflict is over, I yell at the house, trying to sound amicable, "Leave your weapons inside, come on out, and wave goodbye to our new best friends!"

One by one, they spread out across the porch. John goes to the left, followed by Grace. Pastor Mark and Carmelita step to the right. Arriving last from the yard, I leap up the two steps and approach John and Grace.

"We seem to make a good team, Detective Myers." I smile and offer my hand.

He grins and shakes it. "John," he says.

I nod and turn to Grace and hug her. "You too, Cuz."

She shoots me one of her wry smiles and mumbles something about me still being a butthead. I walk away laughing.

Mark and I shake hands. "Thanks for keeping the lines of communication open between us lowly beings and the man upstairs, if there is one." He says he does his best.

Carmelita is on Mark's right. I give her a quick kiss and put my arm around her shoulder, pulling her close to me.

Franco's bodyguards arrive from the basement and stand in the open doorway. We grunt and nod toward each other. I'm still not sure what their names are.

While we all watch the body of Paulie Horseface carried to the trunk of the nearest car, I notice he's wearing my sweater. *Shit! He must've bled on it.*

Junior is finishing his conversation with Luca as I glance at my watch. It's twelve-thirty. We've got to wrap this up and get Franco to the hospital. What in the hell is Junior planning over there? A friggin' Christmas party?

Then, out of the blue, the unforeseen happens. One of those when-you-least-expect-it, expect-it moments.

Patty and Merry are screaming at the top of their lungs, "Karl's got a gun! Karl's got a gun!" as they turn the corner of the house, running at full speed towards us. Their red curls are bouncing wildly and their antique quilts are flying out behind them like huge colorful wings. Karl is moving close and fast, holding a gun with both hands. He scans the front porch and rapidly begins firing.

Grace shouts, "Get down! Get down!" just as Karl's initial bullet hits the porch railing near me.

The next two shots strike Pastor Mark in the back of his left shoulder and through his side as he turns to shield Carmelita and me. The fourth bullet catches me mid-chest as I swivel to protect Carmelita. As Mark and I drop to the porch floor in a crumpled, bleeding mess, Franco's bodyguards take Karl out before he can fire his fifth shot.

Carmelita kneels next to me, praying in Spanish for God to spare me, and presses on the hole in my chest with both hands. My blood is all over her jeans and white sweater.

The twins are on the ground in front of the porch beneath my head, shrieking, "Mom, Mom! Karl shot Daddy and Pastor Mark!"

Grace must've thrown herself down the steps because their wailing becomes muffled.

I've been a rotten father, and despite that, they called me Daddy. I don't deserve those wonderful, spunky girls.

Angelo hears Luca's men yelling curses and screams at them, "Watch your language around Ray's daughters! Get that Karl kid outta here. Put him with Paulie."

Natalie appears, gently telling Carmelita she'll take over. The pressure on my chest increases, making it easier to breathe. She takes her eyes off me for just a second and instructs John to use his knee to apply force to the wound on Mark's side. When Luca asks what he can do, she tells him to press the heel of his hand to Mark's shoulder to stop the bleeding.

Carmelita hovers over me, sobbing, begging me not to die. I try to tell her I love her, but I can't move my lips.

My world grows dim. Sounds diminish. Breathing is difficult again. Natalie's voice fades. Everything recedes from gray into pinpoints of black.

Darkness descends.

CHAPTER
FORTY-SIX

All You Can Do is Pray
John
April 16, 1980

NATALIE WAS YELLING FOR SOMETHING SMALL, like a credit card, to cover the hole in Ray's chest. The urgency in her voice sent shivers down John's spine as he ripped his wallet open and passed her his American Express card. As soon as Natalie pressed it against Ray's wound, he stopped struggling for air.

As long as John held his knee tightly to Mark's side, the blood seemed to have halted, but Natalie's eyes darted back and forth between Ray and Mark. Her knitted brows and frown conveyed it was a life-or-death situation for both of them. They remained unconscious but alive, and everyone was helpless to do anything other than rely on Natalie's expertise to keep them that way.

Luca seemed composed as he monitored Ray and maintained pressure on Mark's shoulder. His eyes darted everywhere as he took in everything.

Meanwhile, that damn Mafia Don, Marco Catanetti Jr., loomed over everyone, asking how to help, but John knew only Natalie could answer that question.

Her voice trembled with a hint of desperation. "Franco's injury is grave. The bullet may have nicked his liver. I've taped his wound to stop the severe bleeding, but if he doesn't get to the hospital soon, he could bleed to death. Now my husband and Ray need emergency surgery, or they'll die."

"Bring the cars!" Junior turned and yelled to his bodyguards.

It's about damn time, you Mafia shithead! But John didn't say that. Instead, he shouted louder than Junior.

"Get Ray's truck! You!" John waved at Luca's guys standing in the grassy yard nearby and pointed to the barn where their vehicles were parked. "Get the station wagon, too. Keys are in 'em!"

Pointing to Franco's bodyguards lingering in the doorway watching everything, he shouted, "Go upstairs and pull the mattresses off the beds. Bring pillows, bedding, and blankets too. Build beds in the truck and station wagon."

Filled with urgency, Angelo sprinted upstairs to help them.

Grace alerted the Romney Hospital to prepare for five injured men, three of which were severely wounded.

At one thirty, several cars roared into the emergency room's entrance and were met by a prepared medical staff who rushed the critically injured into surgery. Everyone else was directed to a brightly lit, cold waiting room to do exactly that—wait.

A huge industrial clock hung on the center wall of that antiseptic white space. The room was filled with uncomfortable teal chairs attached in groups of four to form couches. Large square gray melamine coffee tables were covered in sloppy piles of torn magazines that dated back five years.

That clock became the lifeline and focus of everyone's attention. Some looked at it occasionally, while others constantly glanced at it. It was the epicenter, determining how long they had waited or how long they might still have to wait. It offered hope and tugged at the hearts of each person who sat in that freezing ass, ugly, uncomfortable, boring-as-hell space, praying for a positive outcome for their loved one.

The emergency room nurses patched up Luca's men in two hours. They were fortunate, thanks to the exceptional shooting skills of Franco's bodyguards. Both high on painkillers, one man hobbled on crutches, and the other, with his arm in a sling, wandered into the waiting room, grunting and groaning. Junior and Luca huddled in a tense conversation against the furthest wall, saw them, and pointed to nearby chairs where their other men sat.

In strained silence, Angelo and Franco's bodyguards stood apart from them with their arms crossed, glaring and frowning. In unison, they shifted their stance, then consulted their wristwatches and looked up, comparing their time to the big clock. It was after five, when Franco's surgeon appeared, his blue scrubs wrinkled and worn. To hear better, Angelo's group stepped closer to Junior and Luca, so Natalie, Carmelita, and John also moved nearer.

"The bullet sliced through Mr. Catanetti's liver, which caused a great deal of blood loss. After multiple transfusions and a successful repair, he's now in stable condition. As soon as he regains consciousness, we'll move him into a private room. You're allowed to see him for a few minutes, but don't stay long."

The Catanetti guys hung around until Junior and Luca had finished their visit with Franco, and then they all slithered out the door without so much as a backward glance.

Angelo and Franco's bodyguards visited Franco briefly, then stopped to check on Carmelita, Natalie, and John, saying they were going to a hotel and would see them the next day.

The huge white clock showed it was after eight when Pastor Mark's surgeon shuffled into the waiting room. His wrinkled blue scrubs with big armpit stains accentuated his slumped shoulders. His body screamed with fatigue. Natalie, John, and Carmelita stood to greet him, braced for troubling news.

"Mrs. Pruitt, your husband is in poor condition due to severe blood loss. He needed multiple transfusions before we could repair a section of his bowel. I'm afraid that injury requires extensive recovery time. He can expect to live a normal life after his gut heals. Also, his shoulder wound was straight through and only required stitches, but he will need physical therapy to regain full range of motion."

"That's good news," Natalie said stoically. "Under the circumstances, he could've died. I'm very grateful you saved his life. Thank you."

"You can see your husband for a short time. When he's conscious and comfortable, we'll send a nurse to get you. If he shows a significant improvement by tomorrow, he'll be moved to a private room."

As soon as the doctor was gone, Natalie and Carmelita sat in silence for a few minutes. The one with the answers watched the clock, estimating how long before she saw her husband. The one with no answers studied her hands and picked at her nail polish.

Natalie asked John if he had talked to Grace yet.

"I should call her," John said.

"I'm glad they stayed at the farm," Carmelita said. "This is not a good place for the girls." She pointed to the pay phone in the waiting room's corner. "Tell them the successful news about Franco and Mark. You can call again after Ray's out of surgery."

John nodded. "You're right. Be right back."

Natalie was already with Mark when the big white wall clock, their ruthless prison guard, said it was way after ten.

Ray's surgeons appeared, looking like zombies in their sagging, stained, sweaty blue scrubs. Exhaustion was visible in their carriage, and their frowns showed the weight of the information they were about to share. It didn't look good.

Carmelita and John rose, bracing themselves for the worst.

"Mrs. Lewis." The first surgeon assumed Carmelita was Ray's wife. "Your husband's surgery was extensive and complicated. His blood pressure dropped dangerously low for way too long, which caused acute respiratory distress or what we call shock lung. He'll remain in the ICU, sedated, and on a ventilator."

Carmelita's face paled as her knees buckled. John grabbed her waist and helped her sit before she heard the rest. The second doctor stepped closer, his voice halting, uncertain if he should continue.

"We can't predict if... or when... your husband will wake up. Keeping him in a coma for too long... uh... also lessens his survival chances."

Carmelita's composure crumbled. She buried her face in her hands and sobbed.

The second doctor then leaned down and tenderly touched her shoulder. "I'm sorry, Mrs. Lewis. We've done everything possible. Your husband is in critical condition. All you can do is pray."

CHAPTER FORTY-SEVEN

An Uninvited Visitor
John
April 19, 1980

CARMELITA, NATALIE, AND ANGELO WERE CONSTANTLY AT THE HOSPITAL, keeping vigilance over Ray, Pastor Mark, and Franco while José Jr., John, and Franco's bodyguards spent their days repairing the upper floors and windows of the farmhouse.

Grace and the girls removed all the broken glass, shopped for and replaced the mattresses and bedding, and put the house back together.

At the end of each day, everyone was exhausted and fell into bed early every night. With the girls always around, it was difficult for John to go into detail with Grace about Ray.

Saturday afternoon, they finally grabbed a few minutes of privacy in Ray's study. John knew it wouldn't be easy to tell Grace everything he'd learned, and he was right. It was gut-wrenching to watch the horror on Grace's face as he explained Ray's involvement with the Catanetti Mafia family.

"And that book they were all fighting over?" Grace snapped with tears in her eyes.

"It was a list of the murders Junior ordered his men to commit over a long period. Some of the deceased were politicians and policemen, which was bad enough. Some were other Mafia family members, which put Junior in a very precarious position if they found out. His life was on the line."

Even though Grace understood it was Ray's insurance policy so he could break away from Junior, she was still furious he endangered their daughters. They sat in silence while she sorted out a lot of unexpected, crazy information.

Tearfully, she asked, "Why did he marry me then?"

"Near as I can tell, to save your life. If you were only Ray's business partner, Junior could have had you murdered, so Ray could take over the company. Or if you remarried and your husband discovered Ray's secret activities, you both would have to be silenced. Ray gave up marrying the woman he loved to protect you, his only living relative, from Junior and Rico."

"Rico is the skinny, mean man who kidnapped my daughters? My friend, Manny, thinks he shot that guy, Tito Zayas, a long time ago. You and Ray killed him?"

"Yes, we did," John confirmed. "He's also the cold-blooded killer who murdered my detective friend. I don't regret pulling the trigger one bit."

Her eyes flashed. "Who is Junior? Why is everyone so afraid of him?" Grace blurted out.

John leaned in, took her hand, and lowered his voice. "Grace, honey, did you see the movie *The Godfather?* Junior is the Don—the leader of the Catanetti Mafia family. Everyone takes their orders from him, including Ray."

John was patient as Grace processed that information. She swiped her hair behind her ears and squared her shoulders, sitting taller. "Is that why Paulie was hiding and waiting in the cabin? Did Junior order Paulie to kill Ray? Grace searched John's face, expecting an answer.

When John nodded, her eyes widened. "Ray's in danger! Junior could send someone else to murder him. We have to do something!"

"I'm already working on that," John said. "As soon as the ICU takes Ray off the respirator, he'll be moved to a private corner room away from all the hustle and bustle of the hospital. The administrator will allow security guards to sit outside Ray's door around the clock, as long as they are the only one with firearms. I've reached out to several local cops who have agreed to work a shift in their off-duty time.

Three weeks later, John was finishing breakfast at the farmhouse when Ray's security guard called from the hospital saying he had forgotten about his son's dentist appointment that day and had to leave early.

"No problem," John said. "Go take care of your kid." John figured he would manage the rest of the shift himself.

On his way out, John spotted Grace's purse by the front door. Not feeling the least bit embarrassed, he dug through it, found the second set of Ray's weapons, and shoved them in his jeans pocket. *What good is a security person without weapons?*

As John expected, the guard's chair was vacant when he strolled past it and into Ray's stark white hospital room. It was a few minutes after eleven and Carmelita was in her usual place, close to Ray's bed, reading a magazine she must've read a hundred times. Her manicure kit was on the table next to an empty coffee cup.

"Hey, John. What're you doing here?" Carmelita smiled, but the dark circles under her eyes revealed the sleepless nights she had spent this last month worrying about Ray.

"The guard had to leave early, so I'm finishing his watch. Why don't you take a break? Go buy some magazines or stretch your legs. I hear the hospital's meditation garden is lovely."

Carmelita glanced at Ray, who'd been off the respirator for a week. He was still unresponsive, but at least Ray was breathing on his own. Reluctantly, she picked up her purse and frowned. "Promise you'll stay until I get back."

John put his arm around her shoulder and guided her to the door. "I'll be right here, I swear. Some fresh air will do you good."

Carmelita still hesitated, but then remembered something that brightened her eyes. "I might visit the newborns. Those sweet little angels always lift my spirits."

"Take your time, Carmie. Ray's safe with me."

As the door closed behind her, John settled into her chair, fidgeted around, and picked up the magazine Carmelita had been reading. It was all lady stuff, so

John tossed it back on the table and hoped like hell she would buy something he was interested in. A sports magazine, or even a newspaper, would be nice.

The gray beard thing Ray has going on looks pretty good the way Carmelita trimmed it off his neck. And his color is much better. He's not so ghostly white now.

Ray's hands, stretched out across his chest, were manicured. John was pleased that ladies thought about that kind of stuff.

The nurses had told them that Ray was not brain dead, so they should talk to him as if he could hear them, but to keep their conversations light. With nothing good to read and bored as hell, he thought he might as well try.

"Morning, Ray. Your color's better. And the beard makes you look more like a professor than a tough guy." John laughed. "Oh, and about the tape across your nose? You broke it again when you fell on the porch. The doctors fixed it up as best as they could, but said plastic surgery would do wonders these days. Of course, you'd have to choose between looking dangerous or handsome. Maybe handsome is pushing it a bit too far. How about not dangerous?"

John updated him on the girls and how they were back in Seaport, living with Mark and Natalie while they finished school. "Patty and Merry call every day, asking about you. Oh, and Mark's doing well, but it'll be some time before he preaches again."

What would Ray be eager to learn?

"Grace delivered the codicil to your attorney but hasn't filed the divorce papers yet, just in case she becomes your widow. Smart woman, huh? However, if you live, I want them filed as quickly as you do so I can ask Grace to marry me if she'll have me. Don't get me wrong. I'm not asking your permission. I'm just trying to light a fire under your comatose butt. So, get well or kick the bucket."

Let's see, who else?

John mentioned Luca was still in town and pissed off that they had left him off the visitor's list, which was too damned bad. John chuckled, "I'm making sure Junior's minions aren't getting anywhere near you."

Hmm, keep it light.

"Becky from Grandma's Diner stopped by the farm with a few freshly baked pies. They were delicious! We froze one for you. Becky wants to know if you'll rent your cabin to her new waitress and her two-year-old son. Can you believe it? They're from Denver. I told Becky you'd call her when you're feeling better. She sends her love."

Okay, maybe I should prepare him for the changes we made at the farm.

"By the way, Grace had a telephone installed at the cabin and directed Jose Jr. and me to convert the pie window to a door with a landing and steps. Don't worry about the broken windows, they're all fixed too."

In case he wondering what I'm still doing here.

"I took a leave of absence from work to rethink my life. When I learned that dirtbag Junior had people planted in the sheriff's office feeding him information, I was furious. That's probably how my detective friend's murder was covered up. Plus, someone needs to be here to protect your sorry ass."

John glanced at his watch and squirmed, trying to get comfortable in the rock-hard chair.

When was the last time a nurse checked on him? We've all got questions about home care when he finally gets out of here.

Ray lay vulnerable and still, quietly breathing on his own as John inwardly cursed the Catanetti family. In John's estimation, Ray would have made a great undercover cop. When Grace explained Ray's life story, it sounded like a freaking Thomas Hardy novel.

If Ray lived, John was chomping at the bit to ask him a whole shitload of off-the-record questions, like why Ray kept the news articles for Tito Zayas, Victor Hellman, and Barry O'Hara?

John wasn't even considering questioning Ray if he killed Stephen. Once John saw those disgusting photographs and learned Stephen had viciously assaulted and raped Carmelita—he realized Grace was next. It was only a question of time. So, really, it didn't matter if Ray killed Stephen—John might've killed Stephen, too—knowing what he knew now.

It was a shitty thing for Ray to be stuck in this boring white room with only a thin blue privacy curtain pulled to the head of his hospital bed. *Privacy, my ass.* Nothing could conceal the plastic bags hanging down the side of his bed, with tubes that plugged into Ray's body. One tube, inserted into his left arm, kept him fed, medicated, and hydrated. The other drained whatever needed draining.

Gotta appreciate the bags.

"So, Ray, it's an enormous relief to learn you're not a psychopathic killer—just a garden variety rescuer and vigilante. Much as I hate to admit it, at least we have that in common."

Moving on, nature calls.

John stood up, stretched and left the bathroom door cracked a little in case a nurse came in to check on Ray. Once John's questions were answered, he could make security arrangements for Ray's protection during his home recovery. Also, build ramps or whatever else needed to be done to accommodate his recuperation needs.

Just as John zipped up, he heard the door to Ray's room open, then close, and a male voice said, "You look like shit, pal. I brought you a little something to put you out of your fucking misery."

What the hell?

Through the slightly ajar bathroom door, John saw Luca standing on the left side of Ray's bed, with his back to John. Luca's head was tipped, looking down as he studied Ray's IV bag. Luca then followed it with his fingers to where the needle was inserted into Ray's arm.

John slipped on the brass knuckles and waited to see what Luca was planning.

Luca bent closer, muttering, "Seems a few hundred bucks helped your dumbshit guard remember his kid's dentist appointment."

John couldn't see what Luca was doing, but he thought the asshole was pinching Ray's feeding tube.

"There're some things you don't have a fucking clue about," Luca said, and John heard Luca's jacket unzipping. Luca's right elbow moved up and out of sight.

That turd is getting something out of his jacket and I bet it ain't a get-well card.

Luca continued, "Franco didn't know Pop wanted you promoted to Underboss when he died, but Junior knew and wouldn't do it. He was sure if you were second in command, you'd whack him and take over the organization. That's why Junior always gave you the most dangerous runs—hoping you'd get killed. He even tried to set you up a few times, too."

Man, this blabbermouth is enjoying the hell out of telling his asshole brother's secrets.

"Remember the wedding Junior insisted you go to in Juárez last year? Boy, it pissed him off big time when you didn't fuck that cartel leader's wife. Junior and he hatched a plan to catch you screwing the gal so her husband could kill you."

I'll be damned. So that's why the red panty thing went down. Ray didn't know he was being set up to be murdered.

"That cartel guy said you were a perfect gentleman and called him 'loco en la cabeza.' Junior was so angry at being described as crazy in the head he almost had a stroke. Now look at you, a lifeless nobody thanks to that nitwit Karl, who followed Junior's directions perfectly."

Whoa! That sneaky fucker.

"Betcha didn't expect I'd be the one finishing the job. Time to join your dead kid. Yeah, sorry about that mistake."

You cruel asshole, Luca.

"By the way, Junior says thank you for getting rid of Rico. He knew our brother was insane and creating a lot of trouble. You did us all a favor."

Luca turned sideways, lifted the syringe to the light, tapped it a few times and squirted the excess air out. "Congratulations, you now have the Don's permission to retire. Permanently."

Jesus Christ! He's going to inject...

John's heart was racing as he launched himself onto Luca's back, wrapped his left arm around the prick's neck, and pounded Luca's skull as hard as he could. Startled, Luca spun in circles, colliding with the bed, while John kept hammering away. The bed screeched against the tile floor, rolling the IV poles with it as it was pushed three feet to the right. Luca then reached across the sheets and stabbed the needle into Ray's thigh.

John clung to Luca like wet toilet paper, strengthening his grip on Luca's neck, choking him. Luca backed up and slammed John into the wall by the bathroom door. When John's head crashed into the hard plaster, it knocked his breath out, stunning him. John slid down the wall, dizzy as hell and nauseated. He now saw two Lucas and two right-handed fists aiming for his face. Pushing through the double vision, John rolled to his left in the nick of time. Luca punched the wall behind John's head full force and howled, shaking his hand.

The distorted vision disappeared just in time for John to recognize the prick was open for a perfect body shot, so John kicked the shit out of Luca's left knee. John was puking up his breakfast as Luca stumbled backward, lost his balance, and fell on his ass. It was obvious to John that he had damaged Luca's left leg when Luca used the power of his right leg to hop up and come at John again.

Still on the floor, wiping the puke off his chin, John kicked Luca's left knee once more as hard as he could. Luca screamed and cursed, threatening to kill John before he killed Ray, and limped backward toward the bed where Ray was stretched out with that goddamned needle still sticking out of his right thigh.

Sliding upward against the wall to steady himself, John dropped the brass knuckles and snarled, "You're going down, you Mafia scumbag!" and charged straight into Luca's chest, head-butting him in the solar plexus. The impact hurled Luca backwards and across Ray's ankles, landing face up. The power of the collision pushed John in reverse a few steps, where he struggled to keep his balance and focus on Luca as the dizziness slipped in and out. Luca glanced over at Ray's thigh and rolled toward it.

Oh shit! Luca's going for the syringe.

Lunging, John grabbed Luca's right arm and heaved him face-first into the entryway's closed door.

Luca spun around, growled, and launched himself at John just as John flipped Grace's switchblade open and punched it through Luca's shirt into whatever organ was in its way. John had one goal: Stop this guy.

Rapidly twisting the knife back and forth several times, John switched to short, little jabs in and out. Shocked, Luca stumbled backward, dislodging the knife. They looked down as bright red blood pumped from the center of Luca's body. Seriously—squirting out. John knew he had hit something Luca could never recover from. Shuffling in a circle, Luca floundered, and dropped to his knees.

The brass knuckles were inches away from John's foot. He slipped them on, and cold-cocked the top of Luca's head, sending him face down on the vinyl tiles, blood pooling around his body.

John's beige sweater and blue jeans now looked like a goddamned Jackson Pollock painting—spattered and spray-painted deep red, as were the walls and once shiny floor.

As John dislodged the syringe from Ray's thigh and slung it toward the trash can, Angelo and Franco burst through the door.

John smirked. "Better late than never, huh, guys?"

They surveyed the room.

"You look like shit," Angelo said, stooped, checked Luca's pulse, and shook his head.

Franco fished through his brother's jacket, found Luca's car keys and wallet, and shoved them into his own coat pocket, mumbling, "Makes it difficult for the cops to identify him."

Police can't question the dead. I should know, John thought.

"Here's your story." Angelo glared at John and pointed to Luca. "This man tried to attack Ray, but John, you stopped him. Say you've never seen him before. Keep it simple, stick to it, and manage the details."

Then John heard a strange raspy voice and looked up.

Ray's eyes were open. "You saved my life," he croaked, sounding like an old bullfrog.

"Yeah, it seems to be a common practice these days. Tag, you're it."

CHAPTER FORTY-EIGHT

Heaven or Hell
Ray
May 12, 1980

FOR WEEKS, I WAS CAUGHT IN THE SURREAL LIMBO OF ANOTHER WORLD, enjoying a bittersweet reunion with my family. Rosa and I sit on the front porch of the farmhouse listening to Monty's incredible stories about the future—powerful computers so small they can fit into a coat pocket and, after the turn of the century, America would elect their first black President.

Father and Mother laugh and point to the sunflowers in full bloom, swaying in the light afternoon breeze. They wave at José Sr. and Rayban, who are in the field cutting stalks, their arms filled with dozens of the bright yellow giants.

I must be in heaven, because I can't imagine anything better. Even though I miss Carmelita terribly, I try hard to ignore her loving voice beckoning me from far away. Sometimes I feel her warm hands massaging my arms and legs, or caressing my face, and kissing me. I am torn between returning or staying.

Suddenly there is a bumping, spinning, disorienting movement.

Rayban appears next to me, his tone urgent. "Dad! Go quickly! They need you."

Then everything around me whirls, turns gray, and recedes into a long black hall with a speck of brightness at the far end. I run toward it until I can no longer move my arms or legs, or even my head. Just my eyes, opening and closing against a brilliant blinding white light.

Where am I? Is this hell?

Blinking rapidly, I struggle to make out the fast-moving blurry images, but only my ears can tune into the frenzied grunts and growls of violence.

What's happening?

I strain to see across the top of my feet as something falls on my lower legs. I recognize Luca when John grabs him and hurtles him against the door.

Why are John and Luca fighting?

Then John stabs him, over and over—blood is squirting everywhere as Luca sinks from my sight. Afterward, John pulls an object out of my thigh just as Franco and Angelo rush into the room.

Events are a little wonky after that as I fall in and out of consciousness. People are entering and exiting the room, talking excitedly. Then the odor of disinfectant hits me, along with the sounds of scrubbing. Franco talks to a guy in a suit who agrees to wait an hour before he calls the cops in exchange for a generous donation to the hospital fund.

Nurses are all over me, taking my vitals, putting ice chips into my mouth, removing tubes, bags, and equipment until Franco demands, "Everybody, out!"

He locks my hospital door and checks his watch. "Let's get down to business."

Franco, Angelo, and John stand at the end of my bed so I can see them. John is near my left foot, Franco in the center, and Angelo on my right. Franco, still pale and thin from his injuries, looks downcast, clears his voice and swears on his mother's grave, if he'd known, he never would've gone back to Seaport.

Known what?

"But I better start at the beginning," he says, holding onto my bed's foot railing. "When Angelo and I learned from John that you'd been moved to a private hospital room with security around the clock, we were relieved. Yesterday, I overheard some of Junior's phone conversation with Luca about a contract being taken out on you. I immediately contacted The Commission to verify if they had sanctioned a hit on you because of the information recorded in your book."

Franco sways a little, then steadies himself while Angelo slides a chair over and motions for him to sit down. John stands, listening with a neutral expression on his face as Franco continues.

"The Commission knew nothing about your book. When I told them you had documented Junior ordering the deaths of a Washington politician and businessmen in Miami and Chicago, many of whom they had lucrative and imminent deals with, they were very upset. Those killings nearly sparked a war between a few of the Mafia families who accused each other of them. Plus, when they learned it was Junior's soldiers who whacked some of their men, then stole their product and money, they were furious with Junior, not you. They already had a history of dissatisfaction with him when he disrespected Pop's last wishes."

Breathing heavily, Franco continued, "I didn't know this, but Pop told them long ago that when he passed, I would be Consigliere, but he had groomed you to be Junior's Underboss, not me. They knew how much Pop respected you."

Oh my God, guys, slow down—my ears can't listen this fast.

"Where is Junior now?" John asks, frowning.

Angelo answers that Junior and his wife hopped a private plane to Panama early that morning and that The Commission had vowed Junior was a dead man if he ever steps foot back in the States.

"And where are Junior's bodyguards?" John quizzes Angelo, but Franco butts in, "They refused to follow Junior, saying Ray cared more about them than Junior did. They wanted to stay and work for Ray, if they are allowed."

"How'd you get here so fast?" John asks.

Franco is a little breathless. He sits back against the chair and glances at Angelo, who answers. "After we spoke to The Commission about Junior leaving for Panama, we chartered a plane to fly us straight to the Romney airport. A car was waiting to bring us to the hospital."

John's worried look is reflected by his question. "What actions will The Commission take against Ray since they now know about his book?"

Angelo turns to me and answers John's query. "Ray—New York, New Jersey, Chicago, New Orleans, Kansas City, Las Vegas, and all the rest of them—have agreed to honor Marco Catanetti Sr.'s last wishes. And with Junior no longer here?"

Good God, man, what? Get on with it.

Angelo walks to the side of my bed, glances at John, who is silent, and Franco, who swipes his hand toward me, encouraging Angelo to continue. Angelo picks up my right hand and looks me straight in the eyes.

"Raimondo Sabatini Martinelli Luigi, with the blessing of The Commission and Franco Catanetti, you are the new Don of the Catanetti organization. The

Commission wants to meet with you as soon as you are well enough. We're here to serve and protect you. What are your orders?"

Holy fucking hell. I didn't see this coming. When you least expect it...

John joins Franco and Angelo at my side. They all wait, stony faced, for my response.

My voice comes out low and gritty. "Franco, what are our assets and... liabilities?" I take a deep breath, cough, and focus on his words.

"Junior took $100 million from the Cayman account yesterday before I locked down all our other accounts. Our remaining assets are close to $900 million. More than half of that's in real estate holdings. The rest is in cash, stocks, and bonds. Our liabilities are between $10 and $30 million, depending on purchases, payoffs, and mortgages."

Since my head hasn't quite caught up with my eyes, I blink instead of nodding. "Then we're going... legit. No more... illegal drugs or prostitutes." I inhale, cough, take a deep breath, swallow, and cough again. "Build hotels, resorts, casinos... hospitals and schools."

I draw in another deep breath. "Invest in sports teams, new companies... ones that help people and... supports medical discoveries. Find out if there's... a computer company named after some... kinda fruit."

That's it for me. I'm struggling to form words and my throat is raw and painful.

"Find Carmelita. Then get out and let me sleep. This Mafia business... is exhausting."

CHAPTER FORTY-NINE

New Beginnings
Ray
June 4, 1980

During my hospital recovery, I thought about my life. I was a twenty-year-old kid when I resolved to trust no one. But it wasn't true. I had trusted my families and my farm employees. I trusted Franco and Angelo. Even John has joined that list.

I refused to make promises, but my darling daughters and a small pinky swear showed me how wrong I was. After failing to save my little sisters from Jack Lee, I spent my life subconsciously promising to protect my family. Although I'll never forget my sisters' deaths, first saving Carmelita, then saving Grace, and now saving Patty and Merry from harm has helped heal some of that guilt.

I've truly experienced what it's like to bask in life's sunlight one moment and be shattered on its rocks the next. I hope the man I've become would've made Mother and Father proud. It seems my moral compass gained the respect of many powerful people, despite how flawed I am.

Carmelita takes it easy, driving up the winding road to the farmhouse and parks her red Mercedes in the grassy front yard. As she helps me struggle out of the passenger seat, John and Grace warmly welcome me home from the porch where they've pulled the four rocking chairs together, gesturing for us to join them.

A sense of peace washes over me as I take in my surroundings. While I steady myself against the door of the Mercedes, a cheerful rooster greets me. Above, the light blue sky with wispy white clouds looks like a Monet landscape. There's a chill in the air, but my navy-blue cashmere sweater Grace returned is keeping me warm enough.

Funny how my first view of this place as a young man riding in a wagon filled with farm supplies pulled by an old mare was a fantasy that consumed me with a deep longing to live here with a loving family. The universe had to put in a whole shitload of energy to make that boy's dream come true.

I've missed these everyday farmyard sounds and the earthy musk of soil and animals. The fields beyond the barn are silent and empty. It's good to have this quiet time while I regain my strength. When the migrant workers arrive from Mexico, the farm will become a beehive of noisy activity again.

Carmie has her arm around my waist and guides me up the porch stairs. She wants me to go straight to bed, but I'm determined to stay and breathe the fresh mountain air I've been longing for. Besides, I have important questions that need answers.

"Grace, how's Patty and Merry?" Holding onto the arms of the rocking chair, I ease into it, lean back, and take a moment to catch my breath.

"They're great. They've caught up on all their missed schoolwork, and they're looking forward to joining us when school's out in a few weeks. Both of them can't wait to see you."

I'd forgotten how her gray eyes twinkle when she's relaxed and happy. "I'll call them this evening. Hopefully catch up with Mark and Natalie, too."

Turning my attention to John, I ask how his search for my bodyguard is progressing.

"Damn good. Tom Fisher arrives at Dulles International Airport on Friday. Franco and Angelo are flying in from Seaport at the same time to meet him. I'm picking all of them up around noon, so if we beat the weekend D.C. traffic, we should be here by dinnertime. If you guys come to an arrangement, Tom's ready to start in two weeks. Just so you know, Franco has men he trusts guarding the girls, Mark, and Natalie, nonstop."

It's a relief to see John's already on the job. Squinting against the midmorning light, I mumble, "Looking forward to meeting the guy who put that damned tracker in my bag."

Turning toward Carmie, I close my eyes for a moment as a wave of exhaustion rushes over me. "Okay, you win. I need to rest," I murmur.

But John interrupts. "Wait, guys, stay a few more minutes if you can. I haven't said anything before because I didn't have all the facts. I do now. Forgive me for being slow to divulge this information." He looks back and forth between all of us, waiting.

The Don in me emerges as I impatiently frown at him. "Out with it."

John takes a deep breath. It's his tell when he's anxious. "Don't shoot me, Ray."

I try to lean forward but can only move my shoulders. "Since I don't have a gun, you'd better get on with it."

He nods. "Twelve years ago, my girlfriend, Nora, a wealthy gal who lived in Palm Beach, broke up with me. Said she was going to Europe indefinitely. It surprised me, as our relationship was progressing nicely."

He looks over at Grace, but her face is expressionless.

That may be a good sign. Or not.

John continues, "Nora said her lifestyle was too sophisticated for a cop like me to accept and left Palm Beach soon after. I ran into her three years later at the Taboo Club on Worth Avenue with her new husband. He looked wealthier than God and was at least twenty years older. I congratulated them and wished her the best."

Relaxed against the back of my chair, I close my eyes and wave my hand, hoping John's old love life is going to get more interesting. "Continue."

"When Grace showed me a photograph of Patty and Merry. Their curly red hair and freckles reminded me of Nora. When she pointed out their dolls dressed in Lilly fabric, I recognized the pattern. It's from clothing Nora often wore."

I take a quick peek to see how Grace is receiving this news.

She's frowning. It ain't looking good.

"Keep going, John." I say, closing my eyes again. "Don't make me get my gun."

"Some individuals I know are clever at tracking people's lives and getting into sealed information. They discovered Nora didn't go to Europe. She went across the state to Seaport. She probably assumed she wouldn't run into any of her rich Palm Beach friends over there."

John swallows and takes another deep breath.

"Come on, John! And?" I ask impatiently.

"She gave birth to a set of twin girls she put up for adoption."

My eyes fly open. The stricken look on Grace's face tells me John's in so much trouble. She attempts to compose herself by swiping her hair behind her ear.

Hold on to your panties and get ready, John. Miss Pissy is on her way.

"So, you lied?" Grace spat out. "Or just kept secrets from me, like my mother, Stephen, and his damned old grandfather? Or my soon to be cousin-ex-husband King Raimondo, something or other? What are you trying to say, John? Please. Go on."

Too late, Miss Pissy has arrived.

He glances at her and looks away with a worried expression.

"John." My raspy voice warms up. "You're driving everyone crazy with the drama. Just spit it out."

His eyes dart among the three of us.

"There's a strong possibility Patty and Merry are my biological children with Nora."

Stammering, he adds, "But it's... it's impossible to prove. I checked into it. There is no way to be 100% certain. So far, the only testing available is inconclusive. Maybe in the future, though..."

He shakes his head. "I promise, I knew nothing about them. My investigator friends gained access to the original birth certificate. Nora didn't name their father."

Grace stares at him, speechless.

I don't know what's gotten into him, but he's inspired and adds, "That brings me to the next thing, so let me say it before I have a heart attack and drop dead on Ray's front porch. And, Grace, before you ask... I'm positive."

She's still digesting that last tidbit of info. How can he top that mind-blowing epistle?

"I love you and those crazy red-headed girls I've gotten to know. Life's too short to waste one more minute. Will you marry me?"

Holey-moley, work on your timing and delivery lines, man. No ring? No bended knee? No champagne? No frickin' privacy?

Grace gazes off into the distance, pushes both sides of her hair behind her ears, licks her lips, and turns to look straight at him.

After a few God-awful long seconds of dead silence, I say, "Drum roll, please."

Grace shoots him a wry smile. "I have two stipulations," she begins. "First, it's important to get to know you better before I agree to marry you. I've already made a couple of mistakes. Sorry, Ray, no offense."

That makes me grin. "None taken. I was a shitty husband."

"What else?" John asks.

"I'm in charge of myself and intend to make my own decisions from now on."

I need to handle this quickly.

"Grace, before you continue to bust his chops, Detective Myers is my new chief of security. It's his job to keep you informed of our plans to protect you and our daughters from this point on. Sorry, Cuz, but you should prepare yourself. I'm about to change your life again. Get used to it."

I scoot forward and nod toward Carmelita. "We have some things to discuss in private. Right, Carmie?"

She laughs. "Yes, we do. Lots of shiny things." Her diamond bracelet glitters in the sunlight as she flashes her empty ring finger. She helps me stand and puts her arm around my waist while I gain my balance.

"Folks, I hate to leave this party, but I've got to lie down."

As Carmelita directs me toward the front door, I stop and gaze down at her concerned face. "My darling Miss Lopez, will you do me the honor of accompanying me upstairs so we can continue our conversation in private? Your life is also about to change."

Her lovely eyes are merry as she recalls my invitation the night we made love for the first time. "Of course, Don Raimondo Sabatini Martinelli Luigi, I am yours, forever."

The End

ACKNOWLEDGEMENTS

I couldn't have written this book without the encouragement of my friends and family, who gave me their positive feedback and constructive criticism.

There have been a few editors along the way who guided me through the early drafts and helped me push through some tough sections. Thank you to Lou, Mary, Lorin, Brenda, Celina, Neil, and Martha. Also, my publisher, Charlie Levin of Munn Avenue Press, whose kindness and enthusiasm quelled my jitters and self-doubt.

A special thanks to Mark Malatesta, who schooled me on the many aspects of presenting my manuscript to agents, held my hand through all the rejects and consistently encouraged me to keep trying. To Scott Deitche, author of seven non-fiction mafia books and a top mafia expert who read my manuscript and gave me a fabulous review. And Denise Meyers, a Cannes Film Festival Screenwriter, who enthusiastically encouraged me right from the beginning. To Linda Maran, a retired Detective Sergeant who guided me through all the do's and don'ts of police procedure and mafia interactions. Last but not least, my friend, author Rick Pullen, who was the first person to read my initial thirty pages and say, "you can write, now go learn your craft." I hope I made you all proud.

ABOUT THE AUTHOR

Ginger Wakem is a fourth-generation Floridian from South Florida, a region known for its intense hurricanes, incessant mosquitoes, and dramatic sunsets. From a young age, Ginger was enchanted by books, developing a passion for mystery novels and, later, historical romance and spy novels.

Her storytelling evolved from weaving tales for her young children, featuring adventurous, red-headed twins, to a diverse writing career. She has contributed to a BBC documentary on Tourette's Syndrome, appeared in the movie "Marcus" (2020), and written across various mediums, including product descriptions, web content, and magazine articles. Her nonfiction book, "The Water Treatment Buyer's Guide," has reached its third printing in both English and Spanish.

In addition, Ginger's love for capturing the world and telling its story through photography has culminated in a portfolio displayed on her website at ggwakem.com. Her coffee table photo book of Conch Key hosts over twenty years of photographs depicting the sixteen-acre key nestled between Islamorada and Marathon. Individual photographs can be found on her website at ginger-wakem.pixels.com.

To contact the author or learn more, visit ggwakem.com.

Made in United States
Orlando, FL
02 February 2025

58106028R00192